John Ramster is an opera and theatre director based in Brighton. This is his first novel

Praise for *Ladies' Man*

'Goes straight to the parts that many of the current spate of stories about love in the Nineties have failed to reach'
Observer

'This delightful comedy has some excellent twists and astute observations'
Bookseller

'Old Compton Street will never look the same again'
Time Out

A thirtysomething novel that changes the rules – scattered with comic set-pieces'
The Times

'Delightful – a comic novel which also explains a lot about sexuality and how men love'
Daily Express

'*Ladies' Man* is a "my dating hell" novel with a difference – and the speed of light wit will have you in stitches'
Company

'A welcome through-blast of political incorrectness'
Evening Standard

'Simon Lyndon takes us through the inevitably messy consequences of his unexpected passion and reveals a great deal about how men, in particular, love'
Harpers & Queen

'More broadminded than most commercial thirtysomething fiction, and all the better for it'
Daily Mirror

'This is one novel which never fails to keep its lightly humorous touch, even when dealing with the normally angst-inducing complexities of human sexuality. The result is a very funny, affectionate and very wry look at male/female relationships at this sexually confused end of the 20th century'
Irish News

'This is a wonderful debut novel that tackles a crisis of sexuality in a completely unique, comical and sometimes moving way'
Books Magazine

Ladies' Man

JOHN RAMSTER

WARNER BOOKS

A *Warner* Book

First published in Great Britain in 1999
by Little, Brown and Company
This edition published by Warner Books in 2000

Copyright © John Ramster 1999

The moral right of the author has been asserted.

The author gratefully acknowledges permission to reprint copyright
material from *Darlinghissima: Letters to a Friend*
by Janet Flanner, © 1985 by Natalia Danesi Murray,
Rivers Oram/Pandora Press.

Anything Goes Words and Music by Cole Porter © 1933 Harms Inc.
Warner/Chappell Music Publishing Ltd. London W6 8BS
Reproduced by permission of International Music
Publications Limited

You Make Me Feel So Young Words and Music by Josef Joe Myrow
and Mack Gordon © 1946 (Renewed 1975) Twentieth Century
Music Corp and Bergman-Vocco-Conn Inc. Warner/Chappell Music
Publishing Ltd. London W6 8BS Reproduced by permission of
International Music Publications Limited

A CIP catalogue record for this book
is available from the British Library.

ISBN 0 7515 2903 6

Typeset in Berkeley by M Rules
Printed and bound in Great Britain by Clays Ltd, St Ives plc

Warner Books
A Division of
Little, Brown and Company (UK)
Brettenham House
Lancaster Place
London WC2E 7EN

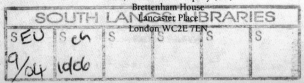

For R and S

watching a baseball game. Have you ever *seen* a baseball game? The difference between Europe and the USA in one completely pointless non-sport. It is marginally less odd than changing one's sexual orientation but not by much. What happens is that a man runs in what is fundamentally a big circle and if he manages to end up back where he started he waves his arms in something approaching relief and celebration. Baseball is strange as well.

Until that point, I never expected to reach the end of my twenties and be in a stable relationship. I knew it could never happen because the job description for being my lifelong companion was far too detailed and specific.

I spent those prime real-estate years of my twenties waiting, wishing and hoping for a best friend to fall in love with me. Soulmates who then become even closer, that was what I thought I wanted. In my wilder, more utopian moments two or even three of my closest friends would declare their passion simultaneously and we would all live together in a big house. I could go around saying, 'Hello, I'm Simon Lyndon, pleased to meet you. Do you know all my husbands?'

I loved my friends so much I was *in* love with them, had fantasies about them, wanted them to be in love with me. But since Life isn't like that, this completely shafted any chance of a significant relationship for longer than I dare think about.

And I *did* have my chances, I coulda bin a contendah, he said with a defiant tilt of his chin – I'm not completely unpresentable. I *know* I have great eyes, which are my mother's finest contribution to the Lyndon gene pool, and I always wear a lot of blue to bring them out. I *know* my chest hair is in a great 'T' shape (my dad was the same) and I *know* that in a certain light, if you squint and look at

Chapter 1

'If the Sun & Moon should Doubt
They'd immediately Go out'
William Blake

It is a fact that I never had a profound post-coital conversation with anyone until I went straight.

The look on a close friend's face, as I confided in him that I never *really* talked with any of the men with whom I went to bed, remains one of the low points of my life. Astonishment, pity and a trace of contempt all mixed up. I was younger then and subsequently discussed literature, politics and high art with the occasional bemused bedfellow, but that total concept of 'let's get completely naked, make love like sewing-machines then confide in each other and tell innermost feelings until dawn' continued to elude me.

Until I found myself doing just that. With a woman. And the world changed.

Americans call it a curveball, a baseball term. I just call it fucking *weird* that life can suddenly make something like that happen. Much more odd than the experience of

I would like to thank for their help and encouragement Imogen Taylor and all at Little, Brown; Judith Murray and all at Greene & Heaton; also, Rachel Dominy, Mark Down, Robert Douglas-Fairhurst, Jake Lushington, Rob Mills, Sarah Plummer, Dominic Rowan, Clare Venables, Ingrid Wassenaar and Jane Green.

me full on (slight bump on the bridge of my nose so steer clear of either profile), I'm boyishly handsome and look younger than my thirty, count 'em, thirty years. I'm not thinning on top, thank God. I have exactly seventeen grey hairs on either chestnut temple, not that I have counted. I dress pretty well, more smart than casual and am adept at covering up my Achilles' big butt (my dad was the same).

I've always made the most of what I've got (that cheap trick with the loaves and fishes has *nothing* on me) but I might as well have covered myself in ashes and hibernated through my twenties because I never wanted the men who wanted me.

Because, to be more specific, I only ever wanted my straight friends. The ones I couldn't have. The ones who outnumbered the possibly available gay ones two to one. And the awful thing is, I knew this even as it was happening. I am an emotional cripple and I am at my peak, fuck it, I used to think to myself. Then my peak came and went and I tried *not* to think about it.

I have no idea if any of this is normal.

Evidence that it might be vaguely usual for people to have this type of futile sexual fantasy is that many of my straight male friends have taken me to one side and have gruffly told me. 'If I was gay . . .' and then they talk *very* fast, '. . . and-I'm-not-but-if-I-was, I want you to know that you would be the one for me.'

They are invariably intoxicated when they do this. They look at you like they've just given you a Mercedes for your birthday, they smile at you like Daddy Walton used to smile at John Boy. You want to hurt them so bad you can taste it. They tell you in so many words that a miss is as good as a mile and expect you to admire them for their honesty. Men can be such bastards.

One time, to my very drunk and very best friend Callum, I asked if this protestation of affection meant that I could go down on him from time to time, since he felt this way and a BJ's a BJ whoever is giving it to you. He laughed and gave me a big *hug*: my life as a sexual mascot. There was not one of my straight male inner-circle über-friends I would not have died for or alternatively lived for ever with. Not one.

The huge problem that flowed directly from this bottomless reservoir of love is that anyone new and interested whom I met could not ever hope to measure up. They would never be clever, witty, sexy, wise enough and they didn't know me *at all*, if only because they had not had my devoted attention for the best part of a decade. The future didn't stand a chance because I was still gagging to go down on the past.

This is known in the trade as painting oneself into a corner. It also downgrades sex to a purely physical act. Nothing wrong with that, you might think, but I did hanker for a better class of pillowtalk. Something with a touch more . . . you know, *something*. A third dimension. Meaning.

What that might feel like was one of Life's great mysteries to me until I heard myself saying in the darkness of a hotel room in the early hours of the morning:

'I'm here with you because I want to be with you and no one else'

and I said this to a woman who the previous day had thought I was her gay best friend. Being together made us more than the friends we had been but it was the quality not the quantity of the love that changed: there are no closer friendships than those between straight women and gay men. For me, they were relationship substitutes.

In fact, it is no exaggeration to state that my closest relationships in my twenties were as Gay Best Friend to a stunning array of babes. A non-misogynist single gay man with an IQ over 95 spends the majority of his waking hours with straight women and I was no exception because, boy, was I single. There's no judgement to make about this fact of life, it's just a truth. The common ground is so huge between gay men and straight women that the conversational possibilities are endless. Behind every good woman is a man with irony and a damp shoulder making the salad dressing.

The secret of being a really good Gay Best Friend is to ensure that the conversation is like keeping a meringue in the air with a tennis racquet: keep it light, keep it airy, not too hard. If the relationship has this bedrock of light comedy then one is allowed a thin topsoil of profundity at some point in the proceedings. That way, the GBF's best friend can hug him at the end of an evening and she can say, 'You really cheered me up. Sorry I got a bit weepy.' A perfect evening's entertainment: we laughed, we cried and then we laughed through our tears. *Stonking*, we must be so *deep*.

However, the golden rule I always kept to conversation-wise was that you must never bring up what gay men actually *do* with, to and for each other (and after I started sleeping with a woman, that rule went platinum). Having said that, dirty talk was far from off the agenda (oral sex was a big topic) but what cannot be spoken about in the position of Gay Best Friend to a straight woman is gay sex. That is not what the relationship is for.

I was a eunuch with humour and panache, an emasculated escort who knew only too well that 'men can be such bastards'.

I miss those conversations. Back then, I was like a magician who should be expelled from the Magic Circle for divulging trade secrets. A few examples:

i)   The rabbit is in a secret compartment under the table and there is a hole in the top hat.

ii) Men are afraid of displaying emotion because it will make them vulnerable. Obvious but often forgotten in the heat of the moment.

iii) There is more than one ace of spades in the deck.

iv) Leave a man alone for about ten seconds after he has come because he *hates* you and does not want you near him; after that he'll be fine.

v)   The little red spongy balls squish up really small.

vi) If you suddenly cannot tell what a man is thinking, you seriously do not want to know and pray he never tells you.

Last, but by no means least,

vii) Straight men are far more obsessed with anal sex than gay men. It's the El Dorado of male heterosexuality. For women, commitment means fidelity and children. For straight men, the ultimate commitment is fidelity and anal sex: '*Come on, honey, let's just try it out, I'll go reeelly slow and if you reeelly hate it I'll take it out straightaway, I love you so much, baby, please do this for me, I promise I'll be gentle, I love you so much, I reeelly mean it.'* For a straight man, if a woman takes him up the scullery, she must love him *very much.* An eternal truth for the *Loaded* generation.

I used to be very clear about what I saw as ultimate commitment and it didn't have to include scullery sex. Great if it did, but not strictly necessary. For me, commitment was being faithful to someone I had adored for years, whom I missed a lot because he was always away doing something marvellous and exciting. We got together at regular intervals for good times and holidays. Tragic to report, *I would rather have missed someone than been with someone.* The upside of this fantasy is that there would be only distilled relationships. Fidelity is hard enough without the awfulness of domesticity getting in the way as well. 'I love you and have you put the Wheeliebin at the end of the drive?' has never cut the mustard for me as an adequate overture for meaningful sexual intercourse. It still doesn't.

Most people kid themselves they are playing Fidelity when really they are playing Serial Monogamy, the draughts to Fidelity's chess. You use the same board but one game is much harder than the other. More rules, for one thing. Serial Monogamy is a very easy game where you sleep with as many people as you want but with three important conditions:

a) You sleep with them *one at a time.*
b) You delude yourself that you are in *love.*
c) You are convinced you want to be with them for *ever.*

I played occasionally but I could never kid myself that much. I didn't want people I could *have* – where's the point in that? And there was always a third game to play: Occasional Promiscuity, the bar-room brawl to Fidelity's chess. No board, usually no bed, no rules, anyone can join in.

Anyway, back in my gay but not very roaring twenties. I knew that Fidelity was the only real game in town. I just could not persuade any of my perfect best friends to play it with me. Undiscerning bastards. But as I turned the corner into the big three-oh, voices in my head started telling me I should perhaps look beyond what I couldn't have to what I could. I sound like Joan of Arc. Now *she* had sexual hang-ups too, I bet. My mistake lay in thinking that the ideal person for me would have a large penis, a full head of hair and preferably be uncircumcised. But two out of three isn't bad . . .

Chapter 2

*'What on earth deserves our trust? Youth and beauty
are but dust'*

Katherine Philips

'Oh, fresh *air*, thank God for that,' I spluttered, taking in
big gulps to try to clear the cigarette smoke out of my
lungs. The bouncer of the club, a sweet guy called Rick
with biceps the diameter of hubcaps, looked at me sym-
pathetically.

'Bit hot in there, is it?' he asked.

'Too hot. I'm going home.'

'Afraid you'll turn into a pumpkin?'

'Afraid I *have* turned into one, more like.'

'What?'

'Never mind. I'm a bit pissed.'

'You'll miss the stripper,' Rick pointed out.

'Who is it?'

'Silverboy,' Rick said with relish. 'Cock like a tube of
Pringles.'

'Him? I've seen him twice before,' I said cheerily. 'Tired
old tits and tackle. Goodnight.'

'Mind how you go, love,' called out Rick.

I wove my way down to the Palace Pier, all lit up and

still doing a roaring trade. I bought some chips and wandered home along the front. Why had I left so early? I usually quite enjoyed myself. My friend Truman the policeman had been surprised.

'Haven't you seen anything you like?' he had shouted in my ear, waving at a crop-haired, bare-chested dinky toy across the other side of the dance floor.

'Plenty,' I had shouted back. 'Nothing that likes me, though.'

'Simon, you're not even trying any more. Stay a bit longer, come and dance.'

'I'm a bit bored. I can't dance to this stuff.'

'What do you think about the one I waved at?' Truman had asked.

'He shaves his chest. I hate that.'

'Of course he does. He's quite cute.'

'I'm off.' Life is too short to shave your chest.

'Give me a ring in the week, yeah?'

Truman had sauntered casually on to the dance floor, twenty-six and lord of all he surveyed. The other guy would run a mile when he found out Truman was a copper. Truman always told them up front. Insane.

I stood and looked out to sea, exactly mid-point between the two piers, one so garish and brilliant, the other almost invisible in the dark, its half-ruined buildings ghostly pale. I knew which one I felt like. I had been *sexually invisible* in that club. Not like me. Or was I just low because I had turned thirty? The terrible option that *both* might be true occurred to me. Yuk.

Scarfing back potato deep-fried in lard did not help, of course. 'Fat Fuckers Fail to Fellate,' I enunciated carefully to myself, threw the offending chips away half-eaten, and went down and sat on the stones to commune with

Nature for five minutes. The sea in the moonlight looked too still and perfect not to be a fake: it could have been a studio tank for some blockbuster movie. The murmurs of a group of teenagers over the other side of the beach travelled across the stones. I played with the pebbles, glad as always that Brighton beach isn't sandy. I loved the crunch underfoot, the way the sound anchored me to the ground.

I let out a frustrated sigh and lay back. Truman had been right, I hadn't been trying back in the club. Maybe it was just an off-night. I was going out again at the weekend. God knew there had been some beautiful men in the club tonight but the ones I wanted were too interested in each other for me to cut in like a Ladies' Excuse Me. But as I looked at them, their bodies gleaming and lean, I had had this hunch none of them had opinions about . . . about, well, *anything* apart from how scandalously expensive the best gyms were these days or if Donatella is truly filling her brother's shoes at Versace. I'm sure they do have opinions about constitutional reform but they don't look like they do. I couldn't get near to talking to them.

I'm very bad at talking to gay men I don't know. Always have been. I have this overwhelming desire to call them 'mate'. And at the first trace of camp on their part, any desire I'm feeling in my part evaporates. I like men *manly*, call me old-fashioned. It was good to see Truman but he had been angling for bigger fish and hadn't really been in the mood for talking. I wondered who was going to be the proud holder of Truman's buff little body tonight. He'd really blossomed since we stopped going out with each other. Seemed happier, anyway.

Ah, the effect I have on men, I thought, and threw stones at an empty plastic beer glass left on the beach. Truman was a lovely guy and a real pal but it would never have worked. I knew this from one very specific occasion: we had gone to see *Pulp Fiction* during the seventeen or so minutes we were going out and I had left the cinema thinking it had been rather good (not as good as *True Romance*, as I think Quentin's true vocation is as a writer, but let it stand that I thought *Pulp* was good), while Truman came out saying it had been dull and slow.

'But didn't you like all the flashbacks and flash-forwards?' I had asked.

'What flashbacks?' Truman had replied.

What flashbacks . . .

Of course, he had to go. But what was I expecting? He was a police constable, not Barry Norman. *Not that I'd shag Barry Norman.* I had let it all slowly fizzle out but we had stayed good friends and occasional lovers, just fumbles and fiddlesticks usually. I think it suited us both. Well, it suited me.

It was so quiet down on the beach. I loved the beach being just two minutes away whenever I needed it. I loved Brighton, still do. I moved there when I was about twenty-three and had set up my own business, a travel agency. I slowly built up to three branches, two quite tiny, all on the south coast, six staff in total plus me. I had inherited a small firm from my father just after my graduation and had decided to stick at it, rather than cashing it in. Looking back, I could have done anything but I had also inherited Dad's lack of ambition. I quite liked both his legacies, truth be told. I did have the gumption to move the business along the coast from Hastings to Brighton, though, and started afresh from there. Brighton's funkier than anywhere else on the south coast and it's not London. Funkier than Hastings, not so funky as London. Perfect for me.

I had arrived in Brighton, a young fogey twenty-three going on forty-three, expecting the streets to be paved in lamé and a niche to be waiting with my name on it. I expected to fit in. But I found that unless you are a very young disco-bunny type with pecs you can knock on, or a middle-aged queen with a pink pound oozing from every pore, Brighton isn't quite what you expect.

However, there is a *lot* of sex in Brighton. You can even leave messages for the milkman: 'Two pints of semi-skimmed and a hand-job on Thursday, please', but only if you are with the gay dairy where all the cows are lesbian. And if you have a fetish for BA air-stewards then Brighton is the town for you (handy for Gatwick), but bleach gives me hives so no highlighted trolley-dolly ever woke up to my sea view, alas.

Basically, there's always someone to scratch your itch, if you feel so inclined and you're not too picky. But I was wanting and getting my itches scratched less and less lately. It couldn't be down to something as simple as that I was getting older and wasn't so attractive any more, surely? Surely not. I was only thirty, for crying out loud. A whipper-snapper. On a good night with a following wind, I could hold my own with all comers.

That was enough sodding beach-introspection. Those chips and the booze were making me feel a bit sick. Nightclubs on a weekday night, what an *error*. I got to my feet, a bit wobbly on the pebbles. If I hurried, I'd be in time for a late-night *Jerry Springer*. That would cheer me up; tonight it was 'I Raped My Uncle and Now He's Having A Sex Change', with some redneck white-trash family from Alabama. Fabulous.

I got back to my flat like my life depended on it, flipped on the TV with time to spare, and icing-on-the-cake moment or what – I had voice-mail. Top. *Somebody* loved me enough to ring outside of office hours. In fact three people did. I hit 'Play'.

'Simon your machine still makes the most awful farting noise, please do something about it . . .'

It was Toril. She's *Norwegian*. I know lots of people, me.

'. . . It's Toril at about nine o'clock. Are you going to the surprise party Helen's giving for Nick? I'll go if you go. Call me, lots of love.'

Party? What party? There was a party for my adored straight best friend Nick and I was Not Fucking Invited? I went on to an NFI Paranoia Alert. The second message beeped in.

'Simon, your machine always makes me laugh . . .'

It was Helen. I was loved after all. Alert over.

'Helen here. It's 9.45 p.m. Tuesday the tenth of August . . .'

What can I say? She's always been a stickler for detail.

'It's Nick's thirty-first next month, as you know, and I'm throwing a surprise party for him. Not a big do, just the gang really. Not a *word* if you speak to him. Clear your diary for the 13th, that's an order. I'm giving you lots of notice so no excuses. Call me at work to RSVP. Bye.'

The third message was from Ruth. All my gels ringing me up at once: I felt like Jean Brodie.

'Si, it's me. I might be a teensy bit late in to work tomorrow morning because I've got to do the school run because one of the other mothers has done her back in . . . but you don't need to know that, do you? I'll be late, sorry. We're still on for *ER* tomorrow night, aren't we? Last of the series, ooh-er. Bye.'

Of course she could be late. Ruth was deputy manager

of my main shop and had been my Brighton best friend (as opposed to my London friends, mostly old university cronies like Helen and Toril) for three years now. Ruth could do no wrong in my eyes. What bound Ruth and me together was that neither of us had ever really thought we'd end up being mundane old travel agents. I was in it because it had been handed to me on a plate and I had had no life-plan, and she was there because she had two daughters to support. Both of us had friends doing phenomenal things in business, lots of them working abroad; Ruth and I *sent* people abroad to do incredible things. Spot the difference.

It wasn't that we thought we were somehow above what we did . . . OK, maybe we did. I don't know. What we did know almost from the outset, three years ago, was that we were kindred spirits. She had been down in Brighton for a weekend staying with an old school friend and she saw the advert for deputy manager I had placed in the local paper. She came in to the shop, walked up to me and asked to see Simon Lyndon.

'Hi, that's me,' I answered. 'What can I do for you?'

'I don't know,' she said with a big, open smile. 'Lots, I hope. I've come about the deputy manager's job. Ruth Whittaker, hello.'

And we shook hands. Start of an era.

She had a much broader Mancunian accent back then. It gradually softened as the three years went by but she always retained those trademark vowels. I liked her immediately: you looked at Ruth for two seconds and you just knew she was a real person. Her chief glory was a mane of curly auburn hair that she mostly wore down but sometimes piled on the top of her head, securing it by jamming in pencils or chopsticky things she bought especially. She had it piled up on the day we first met and, being a queen, I loved that look.

We went through to my office and sat down. She handed me a CV. I scanned it quickly. She had no travel business experience at all, mostly office work and temping by the look of it. But under her interests it said 'Classic Cinema'.

'What sort of classic cinema?' I said, looking up at her.

'Thirties to fifties Hollywood. Golden Age stuff mostly,' she replied, her face crinkling in amused curiosity. It was not the first question she'd been expecting.

'Favourite movie?'

'*The Philadelphia Story*, of course,' Ruth said immediately.

'Good choice. That scene with Jimmy Stewart pissed in the bathchair thing – just the best. And the other woman in it is fantastic, the reporter, not Katharine Hepburn . . .'

'Ruth Hussey. Easy to remember for me,' said Ruth authoritatively.

'Why is it easy? Are you a hussy?'

'No. I'm called Ruth.'

'I know. I'm just teasing.'

'I know,' she replied coolly, with a lift of an eyebrow. What a woman. Then in an endearingly trainspottery tone she told me far more than I needed to know about the making of *The Philadelphia Story*. We discussed our favourite movie-star biographies and discovered a shared passion for Montgomery Clift.

'God, but he was lovely,' I groaned and caught Ruth looking at me strangely. 'What? He *was* lovely.'

Ruth beckoned to me and leaned conspiratorially across the desk, brushing a long tendril of hair out of her eyes. I craned forward to catch what she was whispering.

'This is a very strange job interview, Mr Lyndon.'

'I know, Ms Whittaker,' I whispered back. 'Fun, isn't it?'

'Yes.'

'Do you know anything about the travel business?'

'No.'

'There you go then.' We both straightened up and resumed our normal speaking voices. I said, 'Shame about Henry Fonda.'

'What?'

'He's dead.'

'Oh.'

I really liked her. She came across as so honest and friendly, I knew she would be great with the customers. And I found her beautiful. I've always known when a woman is beautiful, doesn't at all mean to say I've always fancied women, but I always knew Ruth isn't beautiful in a launch-a-thousand-ships way but she is *memorable*. When you leave her company for the first time you remember the way her laugh lights up her face, and how her brown eyes glint when she cracks jokes. She has a great jaw, really strong. I like being with beautiful, clever, funny people (controversial, steady Simon) and Ruth had all those qualities in spades. I knew a possible friend when I met one.

I looked at her CV again. She had a Manchester home address.

'So when are you moving to Brighton?'

'When I get a job to move for,' Ruth replied, snapping back into a more formal mode.

'Why Brighton? A hankering for the sea?'

'Honestly?'

'If you want.'

She took a big breath. 'OK, my life in under ten seconds.

Don't get bored. My marriage folded eighteen months ago, I've two daughters both under eight, I live with my mother in the house I was born in, my decree absolute came through last week and I need to get away from Manchester before I go crazy.'

I whistled. Two kids under eight? She didn't look old enough.

'Why Brighton?'

'It's as far as you can run without getting wet.'

'And you're how old?'

'Twenty-five.'

'You've packed a lot in, haven't you?'

Amazingly, she smiled. Not a trace of self-pity. What a spunky woman. I liked her even more.

'I'll be a *great* deputy manager for you, Mr Lyndon—' she said, tapping my desk to emphasise her point.

'Call me Simon,' I interrupted.

'OK, I'll deputy manage for you brilliantly, *Simon*, and I'll learn about travel agenting faster than you can name Montgomery Clift's debut feature—'

'*Red River*, 1948,' I said instantly.

'I'll learn quicker than that, much quicker. No probs.'

She could stop pitching for the job, I loved her already. But she was still talking.

'. . . And before you ask, I'll make it work having a full-time job and kids. It's not a problem from your end of things.'

For the first time, I saw a flicker of anxiety on her face.

'And with a bit of flexibility, it'll be even easier,' I stated. She nodded. I was nothing if not flexible. I wanted this woman to be my friend so she wasn't getting away now. Her shriek as I offered her the job stopped traffic.

We were close from that moment. Ruth took a long

time to heal the wounds from her divorce and I knew it made a material difference that her boss and new best friend was gay. It de-sexualised her life, let her step back from all the crap she had left behind in Manchester. She could lark around with me and knew it would not have undertones and subtexts. If we wanted to curl up together on a sofa and watch *ER*, we did. And I got a big kick out of watching her kids, Sarah and Hannah, grow up. I was an honorary godfather and I loved that, not having nieces and nephews to spoil.

But for all her confident exterior, Ruth saw herself as damaged goods. I wasn't much better, living for the odd unrequited evening in London with my straight best friends or half-heartedly seeing people like Truman down in Brighton. From day to day, Ruth and I lived in each other's pockets without a cross word. We were too precious to each other to have arguments and under the cover of oh-so-camp-and-ironic banter, we kept each other going.

I'd learned to be very flexible over the years as Ruth coped with the impossibility of being single and having a job and two daughters. You could set your watch by her ringing up, like she just had, saying she might be a 'teensy bit late'. But how busy could a Wednesday morning be? It'd be fine. I got a Diet Coke out of the fridge and flopped in front of the *Jerry Springer Show*. What a stormer. The hopeful-transsexual uncle who'd been raped by his nephew was the least appropriate candidate for a sex change I had ever seen. The electrolysis bill for his back alone would be vast.

The phone rang. It was Ruth, just as agog as I was. We often watched late-night TV together over the phone.

'Simon, are you watching this?'

'*Oh* yes. Vintage Jerry.'

'Why are you back from the club so soon? I didn't expect you to be back.'

'So now you're my mother?'

'No, it just means you haven't got laid *again*.'

'So now you're my pimp?'

'Why are you back so soon?' Ruth said patiently.

'Where are all the clever men, Ruth?' I wailed.

'They're avoiding you, Simon. That's how you can tell men are clever. Bit of a catch-22, sorry,' Ruth said levelly. 'Oh, I've just seen the man for you. Look at the state of him.'

Bubba the Uncle-Rapist from Sonofabitch, Alabama, was indeed one of the sorriest, ugliest, most inbred unfortunates I'd ever seen.

'I tell you, if I'd stayed at that club a minute more, even he would have started looking good.'

'Oh, come one, it can't have been that bad.' Ruth was on automatic pilot now. We'd had this conversation a *lot*.

'I'm starting to see the attractions of rent boys. I've got credit cards. Maybe I'll dial one up.'

'Rent boys take credit cards?'

'They swipe them through their buttocks, they have a gadget.'

We watched the uncle try to hit Bubba with his handbag. They had to be split up. Ruth said slowly, obviously distracted by the freak show, 'Maybe clever men don't *go* to that club, Simon. Have you thought about that?'

'Obviously, they don't. But loitering in bookshops by the Gay Interest shelf is so dull.'

'You loiter in bookshops waiting to meet clever, gay men?'

'No.'

'You *loiter* in *bookshops*?'

'*No.*'

It was specialist classical music shops, actually, but I wasn't telling her that.

'Who did you go to the club with?'

'Flashback Boy.'

'Truman? You still see *him*? Hopeless. When was the last time you scored?'

'Horrible eighties slang. Why do I like you?'

'When was it?'

'Cabinet reshuffle.'

'How *loyal*.'

'New Labour, New Shag. What about you?'

A bit of a low blow. Ruth hadn't been to bed with anyone for ages, to my certain knowledge.

'I get confused. I think Grenada had just been invaded. Oh, sweet Jesus, look at that.'

I focused on the TV again. Jerry had just introduced a woman the size of a Luton van who had to be wheeled on. It was Bubba's mom.

'And I thought I had a problem with water retention,' said Ruth in an awed tone. 'What a terrible programme.'

'Isn't it awful,' I tutted.

'I love it.'

'But I love *ER* more.'

'Of course. Oh, while I remember, I can't come to yours tomorrow night, my babysitter's cancelled on me.'

'You just can't get the staff, can you?'

'Is that a dig?' sniffed my deputy manager. 'Come round to me, the girls haven't seen you for ages. I'll make something quick and easy for us all and I'll try to get them both in bed before *ER* starts.'

'Yeah, *right*.'

'I can always tape *ER*, they're repeats anyway.'

'But we have to watch. I love Dr Greene.'

'*I* love Dr Carter,' intoned Ruth.

'Cradle-snatcher.'

'And proud. I'll see you a bit late tomorrow morning, yeah?'

'Yep.'

There was a pause.

'. . . I *may* have some news tomorrow.'

'Oh yes? What's that then?'

'Top secret for now. But it's big and it's exciting.'

'Is it as big as a tube of Pringles?'

'*Bigger*. Don't ask me to tell you, I'll tell you tomorrow. Maybe. If I hear. G'night.'

What was that about? I vegged out in front of the rest of *Jerry* and did not even blink when the raped trans-sexual uncle turned out to be Bubba's father. Of course he was. Who else was he going to be? The movie of Bubba's story was going to be called *Oedipussy* apparently.

But they all had sex lives: convoluted, involving surgery and not necessarily consensual, but *sex lives*.

I decided it was going to be less fun being a youngish man in a young man's town. A different kind of fun, perhaps. So what did I have to do to get laid by someone I instinctively knew read non-Murdoch broadsheets? Or even someone I instinctively knew could read? Where did people like that hang out? I fell asleep in the chair, the TV still on, adverts made on a budget of tuppence blaring out chatline numbers.

Chapter 3

'But I do not know how one can ever change one's heart in a single day'

Lorenzo da Ponte

Ruth didn't turn up for work at all the next morning. I was just about to send up flares when she burst through the door of the shop looking like she'd just won Olympic gold. She waited for me to finish with my only customer, all of the time bouncing up and down, mouthing, 'I have news, I have news.'

The rather pretty Aer Lingus return flight to Cork left, Ruth opening the door politely for her. She closed it tight, locked up, changed the shop sign to 'Closed' and scooted forward and sat in the recently vacated chair. She leaned across the desk, took me by the face and gave me a big kiss. Very masterful, I can remember thinking. She relaxed back in her chair, slapped her thigh and said, 'Why, *lawdy*, Miss Simone, you're one hell of a gal, give me a sarsparilla.'

'You're very late. We haven't been busy. You have no foundation garment on,' I said, pretending to be annoyed. I had actually been quite rushed on my own but I didn't want to break Ruth's mood. She looked very excited.

'I am *au natural*, quite correct.' She pulled up her top and flashed her tits at me and laughed at my expression. Ruth had very lovely breasts, I noted.

'Good news?' I hazarded.

'You've got lippy all over you. What will your men-friends say?'

'"Good shade for you" probably,' I said. She wiped at my mouth with her thumb. 'I can tell you've got kids. Do mums really *still* do that?'

Ruth sat back again, the cat who got the dairy. She looked very smug. She looked slowly round the four walls of the shop with a strange expression.

'Well?' I said eventually.

'No, come around tonight, I'll tell you then.' She looked at her watch theatrically. 'Must dash. I'm *so* sorry about today.'

A customer knocked to get our attention, peering in at us talking. I got up and went to unlock the door, protesting. 'You're *going* again? You're joking.'

'People to talk to, phone calls to make. It's enormous,' said Ruth. 'See you tonight.'

The customer came in and headed for the brochure rack.

'All right,' I said reluctantly and gave her a kiss good-bye. 'Hang on, I've got a good one for you.'

Ruth turned in the doorway. 'Go on, then.'

'Connect the blondes. Marilyn Monroe to Sharon Stone.'

This was our unashamedly anorakish cinema game. Ruth had read about it in *Empire* yonks ago and we'd played it ever since. It's easy if you have an encyclopaedic brain for movie trivia. You have to connect unlikely pairs of movie stars via other stars with whom they have been in films. It had helped to pass a lot of slow afternoons. Say, for example, you have to connect James Dean to River Phoenix, you go via Dennis Hopper who had a tiny role in *Rebel Without a Cause* with Jimmy and was also in *Speed* with Keanu who was in *My Own Private Idaho* with River. Very nerdy.

'Mazza to Shazza, huh? Leave it with me. You bring the dessert tonight?'

'Low fat and healthy?'

'Fruit and Greek yogurt, I hope?' said Ruth, looking very Calvinist suddenly.

'Of course,' I replied. The customer coughed and I had to attend to him. A long weekend in Bruges. I watched Ruth walk down the street, looking triumphant. Maybe she was in love all of a sudden. Maybe she'd been having phenomenal sex all morning and now was going back for another session. I hadn't made love in the afternoon in ages. Ruth didn't look sated though, she looked more stimulated and perky. The afternoon on my own in the shop was a fucking nightmare and I staggered home and dived into the shower.

Still reeling from the day but spruced, I turned up at Ruth's flat right on time. She lived in a rather nice rented place above a greengrocer's. It was a bit tatty to tell the truth, but on the money I paid her, it was a palace. Ruth's eight-year-old, Hannah, opened the door to me in her pyjamas, turning round and running back up the stairs as soon as she saw it was me.

'Mummy, Simon's here,' she shouted. 'I've got to run, Simon, because we just got into trouble with a dinosaur.'

'You've got to be careful, Hannah,' I said, following her up the stairs.

'It's great, come and look. We can't let you have a go, though, because you might get us killed.'

'All my life, women have protected me, Han. Perhaps I should stand on my own two feet and have a go. I got a pecan pie.'

Hannah turned at the top of the stairs and looked at me quizzically. She's got a great shock of dark unruly curls, a real moptop and she toyed with a curl of it as she said, 'You're funny.' I sensed she did not mean funny-ha-ha. 'What sort of ice cream?'

'Toffee.'

Hannah's brown eyes flashed approval and she pointed at me like a superheroine, legs astride, puffing out her little chest. 'Good choice, Simon the Pieman.' I had done something right. How gratifying. Hannah disappeared into the living room shouting, 'Toffee ice cream and pecan pie' to her dressing-gowned sister, who was sitting in front of the television being ripped apart by a T-Rex. I leaned on the doorjam and watched a voluptuous woman with a big gun be devoured and collapse to the floor in a pool of blood. Hannah wailed.

'Sarah, we've got to go back to the start now.'

'You left! You know you're better at fighting than I am. I do all the brainy bits and the swimming.'

Ruth came out of the kitchen, wiping her hands on a cloth. She gave me a big hug.

'I am so sorry about today,' she said, trying to mean it. 'Was it OK?'

'It was hell for about fifteen minutes,' I lied with a reassuring smile. 'I hope your news is worth it. Tell me, tell me.'

'Ssshh. The girls don't know either.'

'Don't know what?' Sarah called out from in front of the TV, her ears flapping.

Ruth looked in on the girls. Sarah, the ten-year-old,

had relinquished the control to her sister, who was now trying to jump across a river. Sarah's serious face was looking up at us expectantly. She waved at me as she saw me for the first time.

'You know what curiosity did to the cat, don't you?' I asked.

'No,' responded Sarah. 'What don't we know?'

'Who played Melanie in *Gone With the Wind*? You don't know that, I bet,' said Ruth.

'Olivia de Heffalump or something,' said Hannah and promptly fell in the river. 'Mummy, you put me off.'

'Have you ever played one of these?' Ruth asked me.

'They look like the death of reading and the devil's work,' I said only half jokingly as the Amazon on the screen picked herself out of the water and started her trudge through a network of caves all over again.

'Bollocks. We read all the time. No, Hannah love, you've not quite got the hang of that move.' Ruth demonstrated something with the control and handed it back.

'So this is how you spend your evenings,' I deadpanned.

'You'd be surprised,' said Ruth, looking at the screen like a seasoned professional. Her brow furrowed a little and she called out to her daughters, 'This game's a bit old for you two. I shouldn't really let you play it.'

'So don't,' said Hannah.

'I really shouldn't. It says fifteen and over, I think.'

'Maybe you should,' said Sarah in a movie-trailer-deep voice. 'We're learning to be strong and powerful women.' She batted her big green eyes at her mother. Ruth knew when she was beaten.

'My daughter the ten-year-old feminist.'

'What's a feminist?' asked Hannah, watching her sister manipulate the curvy heroine to pick up a shotgun.

'Duh. Mummy told us and you always forget. They were women who fell under all the king's horses trying to vote.' Hannah seemed satisfied with this.

Ruth and I retreated giggling to the kitchen. Ruth got on with chopping vegetables and I put the ice cream in the freezer and a bottle of wine in the fridge to chill. As I closed the fridge door, I looked expectantly at Ruth. She feigned exasperation.

'I'll tell you later.' she said. 'I can't have the girls finding out by accident. Enough to say, I am turning into Lara.'

'Lara?'

'The girl in the game. It's her name. Perhaps you can't get that game for your ZX81.'

'Ha bloody ha.'

Ruth chopped busily through a list of Lara's virtues. 'She swims, fights, works out problems and puzzles, jumps somersaults. She's like Indiana Jones but with a really good bra.'

'The one thing Harrison lacked, I always thought.'

She paused to dump the veg into a saucepan. The sound of rapid gunfire and shrieks of victory came out of the living room.

Ruth continued, 'Lara's an icon of modern womanhood and, oh yes, now so am I. I am so proud of myself.'

This *was* news.

'Woah. Hold the front page.'

'Oh yes, I've finally done something right.'

'So it's *not* a guy,' I said.

Ruth stirred the saucepan with nonchalant vigour. 'Not a sniff of a cheesy dick in months. This is *better* than sex. I did that Marilyn to Sharon thing, by the way.'

'Tell me, tell me,' I said, putting my nerd cap on (backwards, of course).

'Well, Marilyn was in *Some Like It Hot* with Tony Curtis who was in *Spartacus* with Kirk Douglas.'

'"Some people like oysters, some people like snails. Why can't people like both oysters *and* snails",' I quoted.

'Hugh? Well, you go via Burt Lancaster with Kirk in *Tough Guys* to Burt in *Atlantic City* with Susan Sarandon . . .'

Ruth threw down the wooden spoon and had a moment of decision and victory. I could see it happening. She turned to me looking like Scarlett O'Hara vowing her family will never be hungry again.

'I'm not going to finish that game. I'm never going to play it again. Anyway, that one was easy—'

'Sarandon to Sean Penn to Michael Douglas to Sharon,' I said to appease the completist in me.

'Of course. But I am not going to be just a spectator any more. I'm sick of watching. I'm a *do-er* from now on.'

'Get you,' I said as the kitchen door suddenly swung open and Sarah and Hannah burst in, shouting that they had discovered a secret cave under a waterfall.

'We died again though. But we got a rifle and ammo this time.'

They chattered away for a while then ran back to play their game while Ruth and I got the dinner together. The big topic was on hold until after bedtime now. I guessed we'd tape *ER* because we were do-ers now after all, not *watchers*. We took the food through on trays to Hannah and Sarah, who freeze-framed Lara just as she was about to jump a broken rope bridge. It was all go in Lara-land.

'Simon, how's the business going?' Sarah asked formally, trying to make adult conversation.

'It's going very well, thank you for asking. We're working very hard.' Sarah inclined her head at me, looking like a midget dowager duchess, indicating I should continue and that she was very interested in what I had to say. I went on, 'Actually I'm not working hard at all. I just make coffee for your mum.' Hannah pondered management structure briefly then brightened.

'So you do nothing but make coffee all day *because* you are in charge.'

'That's totally correct.'

'I want to be in charge,' said Hannah. 'It sounds fun.'

After we had Häagen-Dazs'd ourselves an inch nearer to a coronary, we all played the adventure game again. I was spectacularly bad at it but I shot a couple of small dinosaurs (they were thin but they were wiry), which was exciting to the max, as I believe the young people now say.

'I feel like a stone-age hunter-gatherer,' I boasted, puffing out my chest.

'Anyone we know?' quipped Ruth. 'Has he got a friend?'

'What did you say? Have you got a new boyfriend, Simon?' said Hannah, not taking her eyes off the TV screen. I quickly looked at Ruth, who looked as startled as I did. These two did not miss *anything*. Ruth quickly dinked her head towards Hannah as if to say, 'Answer her, you dork.'

'Not at the moment, Hannah. I haven't met anyone nice enough.'

'But Mummy just said you had.'

'I was making a joke,' said Ruth, grinning broadly at this late twentieth-century vista before her. An eight-year-old girl trying to shoot a dinosaur on a video game while talking to her single mother's best friend as to whether or not he had a new male lover. Virtual or *what*.

'Well, your joke wasn't very funny, Mummy,' Sarah said carefully. She's a grave child. 'Simon might be very upset he's not in love. Lots of people on telly are upset about things like that.' Then we all went ballistic as some wild gorillas swung into view and tried to tear us apart again. Hannah despatched them with the bravado, grit and tenacity we had come to expect from her.

'Anyway, where were we? Are you upset you're not in love?' said Sarah, after we had applauded Hannah's lap of honour round the room. I blinked.

'Sometimes a little. But not often and certainly not at the moment.'

Ruth seized her opportunity to start the lengthy process of getting them to bed as they paused briefly to contemplate the single gay life. The bait was me reading them a bedtime story and there was sufficient novelty in the prospect for the offer to succeed. I sat on the floor between the girls' beds and read them a story from *Funky Fairy Tales*. Hannah had her thumb in her mouth as she listened intently, her sister meanwhile dropping off almost at once.

In the funky fairy tale, the princess was a car mechanic in her spare time, the dragon turned out to be quite sweet, with an interest in the environment, and the handsome prince's big, red sports car wouldn't go. The dragon persuaded the prince to convert to unleaded fuel, the princess fixed the big red car and they all lived happily ever after. As I was about to turn out the light, Hannah asked me if I knew how to repair cars. I said that I was not very good at stuff like that.

'But you'll never find your handsome prince then,' said Hannah, thoroughly alarmed. I told her I did not want to fall in love with anyone if their car didn't go.

'Fair enough,' she said, kissing me goodnight and snuggling under her Princess Leia duvet. I left the door open an inch so a crack of light from the hall spilled into the bedroom.

In the kitchen. Ruth had just finished washing up and was preparing two packed lunches for the next day. While she washed up, she'd put her hair up out of the way with pencils. I jiggled the pencils to tell her I was back from story-duty. She looked round.

'Thanks for that. They like you coming round,' she said, putting little plastic bags of sandwiches and cartons of orange juice into colourful lunch-boxes. 'Crack open that wine you brought, I think I need a drink after all that killing dinosaurs.'

'Thirsty work. Corkscrew?'

'Second drawer.'

'. . . Got it. Good story book by the way. The princess was a greasemonkey and the prince was metaphorically impotent until she fixed him up.'

'I love that book. They both think all princesses repair cars.'

'And that men are all metaphorically impotent?'

'A valuable lesson can never be learned too early, Simon, I don't mean you, of course. If it helps them avoid all the mistakes I've made, I'll read that story to them every night.'

This point in any similar conversation is the part of a roller-coaster ride where you've cranked up the slope and you're rounding the bend just before the first big descent. I wondered where this conversation was going as we wandered through to the living room. I turned off the main light, leaving some smaller lamps on. Grown-up serious talk needs obscurity. I sat in an armchair. The doctor was in.

'But you love your two little mistakes, Ruth. You can't beat yourself up over them.' She stretched out on the sofa with a sigh of relief and arched her back to get a kink out of it. *Ooh la la*. I felt that startled, shooting, waking-up sensation you get when something happens to make your dick twitch into life.

Strangely nervous and excited, Ruth replied, 'Of course I love *them*. All the mistakes *connected* with them are the ones they can't repeat – falling for their father, being separated with two children under six before I was twenty-three. Because I would have loved them just as much if they had been born five or seven or ten years later.'

While saying this, she reached up and pulled the pencils out of her hair, and as it fell around her shoulders, she flicked it back over the arm of the sofa. It didn't need much expertise to know that she still wasn't wearing anything under her top. As she lay back, her breasts moved slightly to either side, just enough to let you know they were one hundred per cent real, thus creating a convenient place for Ruth to rest her wine glass.

'But they weren't born later,' I said as gently as I could. This was old territory for Ruth and me.

'But that doesn't mean I can settle for less than I'm worth any more just because I fucked up when I was seventeen. It's taken five years for me to get my head together. I had to maroon myself here to do it . . .'

Marooned – was that what I was? I had not been going anywhere for a while . . .

As she spoke, she did that awkward movement you make when trying to drink lying down; she slightly tipped the glass but it was too full to tip all the way so she had to bring her head up to the glass to get some wine anywhere near her mouth. The end result always looks like Christopher Reeve trying to do a sit-up. She spilled some wine on herself of course, which settled into that *English Patient* crevice at the base of the throat.

I watched her absentmindedly rub the wine into her skin and then for an eternity we both contemplated a drop of wine on the end of her finger.

'So you're going to . . .' I trailed off as she caught the drop on her tongue.

As she did this, the strangest thing happened: by the end of the conversation, during which I was meant to be a sounding-board and confidant, I had an erection. I can remember analysing this hard-on as just one of sexual aesthetics: a good body with good skin having wine rubbed into it, then a jewel-like droplet catching the light before being licked up, what's not to get turned on by? I sometimes thought I'd fuck a hole in a garden fence if the lighting was right. But it rattled me. This was an instinctive reaction, taking me by surprise.

Looking at Ruth, I tried to censor my thoughts as she spoke, telling me how she was going to completely change her and her children's lives. I felt perverted. Just call me Mr President: here I was leching after this beautiful woman whom I valued as a friend and employee, as she entrusted me with her deepest ambitions and thoughts. Some Gay Best Friend I was turning out to be.

I was fascinated by the unconscious sensuality of the action and it aroused me more. A picture of her naked popped unbidden into my mind: I wanted to ease her out of her jeans, to touch her between her legs. Jesus, she was practically my sister, what was I thinking? The secrecy of my arousal felt exactly the same as when I was in the school changing rooms or at swimming lessons. I had always been terrified of getting hard in front of the other boys, some of whom I remember worshipping and looking forward to seeing naked. The captain of the football team (I kid you not, the captain of the school football team) had fantastic hair on the inside of his thighs that promised so much. I remember him coming into the VI Form tuckshop fresh from games (this erotic anecdote is getting more twee as the years go by) and being made dizzy by the sheer masculinity of his smell and his body.

This time Ruth's tongue, her long hair burning russet in the lamplight, the angle of her body, the soft strength of her breasts made the words catch in my throat. '*So you're going to . . .*' It seemed that she thought I was leaving the words hanging in the air deliberately.

She suddenly sat up and looked at me. *Oh, don't change position, you looked fantastic*. She was tense. That made two of us. I was rigid.

'You know I've been back to Manchester a lot lately?'

I had to change position so she would not be wise to the rise in my Levi's. I think Rizzo says this in *Grease*. I can remember being thrilled by the phrase when I was ten. I wasn't actually wearing Levi's but 'she knows something grows in my chinos' isn't quite so snappy.

'Manchester?' I wheezed. It really was very uncomfortable.

'Well, I've been going up for open days and interviews.'

'Open days.'

Even through my testosterone haze, I could see where this was going but wine was still glistening on her skin and all my Type 'O' was heading Mexico way. Ruth was bright-eyed now, her face shining with anticipation in a way I had not seen for years as she said: 'I'm giving you a month's notice and I'm going to Manchester University in the autumn to do what I should have done ten years ago.'

Fuck, she was resigning. She practically ran the business. I was not really kidding at all when I said I made the coffee. I was half-crouching over my hard-on now. Not since Nixon has a resignation been more rapturously received. I think Ruth thought I was upset. She waited for me to say something. I physically couldn't.

'I know it's a shock,' she said, a little nonplussed. 'But it's something I've really got to do . . . Simon, did you hear what I said?'

'I heard you. Wow . . . what a big decision. Congratulations.'

And then the roller-coaster was off and away. Ruth let it all tumble out in a rush (I wished I knew how she felt).

'I couldn't tell you before because I didn't know I had a place until today . . .'

'When are you going to tell the girls?'

Ruth grimaced. 'That's going to be the most difficult part. They've only ever known Brighton. Hannah was only four when I came here.'

She switched back to talking about the ins and outs of the English course at Manchester and showed me some reading lists she had been sent. She was so excited about regaining (and perhaps even finishing) her paradise lost, but I was thinking too fast to properly listen.

Why was she giving me a hard-on? What was happening? I had been gay for a *decade*.

'. . . So then when my grandmother died and left me that money, do you remember, I suddenly realised this was what I had to do. Mum's got loads of room now that Gran's gone and she always wanted me to go to uni. I just couldn't make it work when the girls were babies . . . Simon, are you crying?'

I wasn't *crying* crying. One tear was making a bid for freedom, out of confusion more than anything else.

'Something in my eye,' I said. 'I'll miss you, you know.'

I think Ruth assumed I had been crying over her going but that, being a man, I couldn't admit it. It's handy being part of the emotionally constipated half of the population every now and again. But I wasn't lying. I would miss her like hell.

'Oh, I'll miss you too, Simon. I wanted to tell you ages ago but I thought I wouldn't get a place. There was no point in saying anything until today.'

If she'd been a man, I would have made a pass at her. If she'd been a man, I would have done everything to seduce her. I thought about curling, show-jumping, test matches, macramé and needlepoint until I calmed down. We talked some more and one of the few things I registered Ruth saying stayed with me. 'I want to fall in love again, Simon. It won't happen here because I'm not happy enough. I'll only fall in love if I'm happy. Or happier, at any rate.'

My head could not get round it. Happy Gets You Love or Love Gets You Happy? I kept returning to it in the days following Ruth, Sarah and Hannah packing up and moving to Manchester. Whichever was true, I realised I was still gay, I just needed to fall in love again. That was what my body was telling me, perhaps. Yes, that was it.

Chapter 4

'Debauchery is an act of despair in the face of infinity'
Goncourt Brothers

Ruth had been gone two and a bit weeks. The business had tottered but we were still standing. Ruth's replacement was efficient but *sooo* dull. She made her own coffee, if you get my drift. While she was settling in, I was doing much more routine admin than usual so it was a wrench to leave work early and head for the station in order to attend that surprise birthday party for my old friend Nick Robinson. But if I were not here, lots of people I loved would *understand* and *forgive* me: a fate worse than death.

However, getting up to London on a weekday night with work the next day was not my idea of a great time, so as I hit the Piccadilly Line, I vowed to make a quickish getaway and try to be back home before pumpkin time. Grimly clutching a gift-wrapped book Nick either already had or would never dream of reading, I pondered my fellow human beings in the carriage. A sorry lot, but I knew I looked just as bad. At 6 p.m. on the tube, nobody can be at their best. Bachelor City boys are deciding that today's shirt will make it another day while shopgirls from Harrods just *know* their tights can't.

I knew exactly who would be at the party. The guest-list for these evenings had not changed in a while. The host and chief conspirator tonight was Helen, who'd been with Nick mostly on but sometimes off for years. Nick had had to move up north for his job but they were the likeliest candidates of all of us for a wedding. My best friend Callum would be there too and I always needed to see him. It was a friendship now conducted mainly on the phone very late at night. If the phone rang at two thirty in the morning, it was always Callum chirping, 'I knew you'd still be up.' He is a one hundred per cent, down-the-line, completely straight version of me, notwithstanding his declaration of passion I told you about before. I adore him without reservation in the full knowledge that all his faults are ones I share. You're probably picking up on most of them already. When Callum and I kick into our stride, we are unbearable together.

The main difference between Callum and me is the sheer magnitude of his sex life. The volume of women through his flat is an awesome spectacle not unlike the entrance of Cleopatra into Rome. He keeps the 73 bus route in business most weeks. Sometimes I adopt a disapproving tone but I am always keen for the prurient detail, which Callum is invariably willing to provide. Imagine a small child firing a water pistol then visualise Niagara Falls: my sex life, Callum's sex life. I could be pretty rancid when I wanted but he could always outdo me. Not that I was ever jealous, oh no.

I got out at Turnpike Lane and crossed the congested traffic system to get to an off-licence. I asked for the usual oaky, Australian Chardonnay (I was just beginning to be sick of it) and handed my money through the grille to the nice lady sitting behind three inches of Plexiglas, with the baseball bat under the counter. I decided that civilisation would crumble only if Mothercare had to be built like this one day. Juggling the bottle, the book and my *A–Z*, I walked to Helen's flat and tried to find some energy from somewhere. It would not be a 'party' party, more of a get-together, but there would be a lot of banter, so I had to have my wits about me.

Passing some tennis courts, I stopped to watch two men playing in the twilight. They would have to stop soon. The Italian-looking server was wearing very short shorts, showing off muscular and hairy legs. I have a thing for male body hair, not quite a fetish, not quite not.

So I pretended an interest in tennis. In the gloom, you could hardly see the skin on his legs for dark, curling hair, apart from a bare circle on the back of each calf where his trousers rubbed. He looked at me as he walked back to the baseline, thinking about his tactics. I could see that he dressed to the left like most men (because most men are right-handed). I mention him, let's call him Luigi, for two reasons. Firstly that I did and do this sort of thing all the time. I stop and look at attractive people and remember details about them. I think it is a quality I inherited from my grandmother; she thinks nothing of travelling across town to save six pence on a packet of biscuits and I'll walk across hot coals with ten full Sainsbury's bags to gawp at a well-formed backside disappearing round a corner. I can remember the salient attractive features of complete strangers I saw on buses five years ago. It's the kind of brain that proved useful in O Level History. I should also mention it to emphasise the complete sexual meltdown that happened to me later that night at Nick's party. It would be a long while before I saw things this simply again.

'Good shot,' I called out as he glanced my way.

He grinned, 'Thanks, mate.' Great teeth, really sweet smile.

I walked on, cheering myself up with thoughts of Luigi Hairylegs bending Nick over the net and fucking him stupid, Luigi's dark, strong body contrasting with Nick's lean, English-rose looks. *Happy Birthday to you, Happy Birthday to you . . .*

I have no idea if these kinds of fantasies about one's friends are normal but I've a hunch they are not completely abnormal. My pace increased and I arrived at Helen's right on time. Seven-thirty for eight, so that we were all ready in place with party poppers for the birthday boy. I looked round as I waited for someone to answer the door and saw Toril drawing up in a new car. I waved like a loon but she didn't see me. A Norwegian of enormous cheekboneness and blondness, I first got to know her properly when she went out with Callum in the late eighties for about five minutes. Now she was like the glue that held a lot of us together, being great at keeping in touch and being a pal in times of crisis. Toril was still inexplicably single and we had been having the same 'Does Mr Right exist?' conversation for nearly a decade.

Nobody was answering this bloody door. I couldn't have got the wrong day because Toril was here too. I sat on the stoop and watched as she laboriously attached three enormous locks to her driving wheel. I guess the crime rate was lower in Tromso or wherever it was she grew up. She finally got out of the car, straightening her suit. She looked great, a tall, slim vision in cream.

'Keep the creases, Toril – it's linen, it's chic to have creases,' I called out.

She looked up, spotted me and waved. 'Simon! You look like a tramp in a doorway.'

'And you look very foxy with your new outfit and your new car. Do you think it will be safe? Just one more lock, perhaps?'

'You never know. London is a city of sin,' she called back solemnly. She ran up the path and squinted at the door. 'Have you rung? Are we late? What if Nick is already here?'

'No answer. Perhaps they're all in the back garden.'

Toril pushed at the door and it slowly opened.

'Oh,' I said.

Toril gave a delighted laugh. 'That Outward Bound course really paid off, Simon.'

'Sod off, you Scandinavian tart.'

'Lovely to see you,' she said and kissed me on both cheeks.

'Lovely to see you too.'

Helen met us in the hallway and yelped with hostly delight. 'There you are! Double trouble! Toril, you look gorgeous, you cow. Put your coats in there. Are those bottles for now? Nick's just rung in and he's on his way over from Euston. He doesn't suspect a *thing*. Everyone's through in the garden. *Great* to see you both.'

Not only were Toril and I exactly to time, we were the last to arrive: a really nasty combination of the effort of punctuality with the aftertaste of being late. If I had been a superstitious man, and touch wood I'm not, I would have regarded this as an inauspicious beginning to the evening. I really should have left there and then, as it turned out.

As Toril and I walked into Helen and Nick's bedroom to put our coats away, I asked her how she was and was rewarded with a 'so-so' sort of noise.

'What's up?'

'Oh, I don't now,' Toril said, trying to make light of whatever was bugging her. 'It's these evenings. I almost dread them, you know?'

'You don't have to come,' I replied a little stiffly. I loved these evenings and I had assumed she did too. 'Don't you like seeing everyone once in a while?'

Toril looked like she regretted saying anything. 'Of course I do,' she said, patting my arm and trying to placate me. 'It's just that . . .'

'What?'

'We're better in twos and threes now, not this big group. You can't talk at these things, you just get reminded of chances you missed years ago. I couldn't talk to anyone tonight if I was unhappy or something.'

'Since when do you talk to anyone if you're unhappy, Miss In-Control?'

'Pot calling the kettle black.' Toril laboriously worked her way through the English proverb with a smile and we went back into the hall.

'Are you unhappy then?' I asked her.

'Hang on, I'll just freshen up,' she said and dived into the bathroom. I hung around outside and watched her run a brush through her hair, checking herself out in the mirror. She quickly repaired her make-up. I love watching women get made-up, always have. I don't have a problem with them taking ages. All those little *brushes* and *things*.

Toril had always prized her sophisticated appearance and, to some extent, hid herself behind it, sometimes appearing distant. I knew different, but that was after years of knowing her. She has the most incredible sense of humour but most people don't get to see it. Glimpses of the real Toril were rarer than Yeti sightings, but occasionally something would get through and there was never a face on which feelings could be more plainly etched. All sophistication fell away.

'Are you unhappy then?' I repeated. If she'd mentioned it, that was revealing in itself. Toril looked at me, mascara brush in hand, not giving anything away.

'Hey, how could I be, I've just got a new car.'

'You could talk to me tonight if you're not happy about something.'

'I know that, Simon. Thank you. I'm talking rubbish as usual.' She finished primping and turned to me. 'Well, that's as good as it gets tonight, I'm afraid.'

'You look fantastic,' I said truthfully.

'What do you Brits say, good enough to eat?' she asked flirtatiously, putting all her make-up away.

'Say "good enough to fuck". It's more direct.'

'Not at *this* party. Either I've been there and done it or it's not on the cards.' And she tapped me on the shoulder with a smile.

'You never know,' I said roguishly, as we walked through the kitchen to the garden.

Mmm, *pretending* to have a heterosexual urge now, Simon. But she did look good enough to sleep with. *Toril*. First Ruth, now Toril. I had thought I was gay but it turned out I was a straight-sex addict. Not.

We stood in the back doorway, looking at the very familiar huddle of people preparing for the party.

'Well, the gang's certainly all here,' I said, giving Toril's hand a squeeze.

'I can feel my horizons broadening even as you speak,' she said drily.

'It's the effect I have on women.'

'Is it now?' Toril said with a doubtful look.

Callum spotted us from the other end of the garden and ran over. 'You're *late*. Not like either of you. Toril, Toril, *Toril*, you look a million kröne.'

'Is that a lot?' I asked her.

'Not enough by half,' Toril laughed, kissing Callum hello.

'And how do *I* look?' Callum enquired, striking a Grattan-catalogue pose. 'New jumper – Ted Baker – cost a bloody fortune.'

'God, you look *brilliant*, Callum,' puffed Helen, appearing behind us with an enormous box of Christmas decorations. 'Make yourself useful, you vain child. Help me put up some fairy-lights, would you?'

'No tinsel: it's unlucky if it's not Christmas,' Callum declared authoritatively.

'Rubbish,' said Helen, handing one end of the lights to Callum and the other to me.

'You've never liked me, have you, Helen?' said Callum, looking for a chair to stand on.

'People who have known each other for a long time don't *have* to like each other,' Helen stated firmly. 'It's a known fact.'

'Quite right,' Toril confirmed. 'I've never liked you, Callum, and as for Helen and me, we've always loathed each other. Isn't that right?'

'Oh, God, yes,' Helen said feelingly, rooting around for more lights.

'Anything else I could do? Anything else in the box?' asked Toril.

'"*What's in the box, what's in the bo-o-x?*"' wailed Callum, doing his best Brad Pitt impersonation.

Helen stepped back, shaking her head at Toril. 'No, there's just the one set, I think. Let's leave these strapping lads to it, why don't we?'

Both women looked at Callum and me teetering uneasily on garden furniture while attempting to wrap the lights around the washing line. Strapping lads we weren't. Shaking their heads and laughing, they went inside to get a drink.

'Don't we have to test them individually or something?' mused Callum, fingering a fairy-light. 'Or did our fathers make that up as well?'

'They almost certainly lied,' I said, returning safely to *terra firma*. 'These'll be fine. Plug 'em in.'

Callum plugged them into an extension lead and switched them on. People who should have known better went *Ooooh* behind us. Callum and I looked at each other, then hugged.

'Good to see you, Cal. You all right?'

'Really good, actually. Cream-crackered, though. I was shagging until five with my downstairs neighbour's best friend. Legs like a giraffe.'

'Five this morning?'

'This *afternoon*, love. Fucking brilliant. I was working from home today and she rang the wrong doorbell.'

He wasn't even having to leave his flat to get sex now. Bastard.

'Did she bring a pizza around with her as well?'

'Nah, life's never *that* good,' Callum said with a grin.

'Is she here tonight? I always like to meet them once,' I quipped, looking around for a tired but flushed giraffe.

'Here? With you lot? I don't think so.'

'What's the matter with us lot?' I complained. First Toril, now Callum.

'You'd all eat her alive.' He sniffed and more out of politeness than anything else, asked about my love life.

'Slim volume, mate, slim volume,' I replied, putting a

clear full stop on that line of conversation. Callum nodded and grunted.

'Nuf said. I was on the point of telling Callum about nearly making a pass at Ruth when I caught sight of Toril standing in the doorway, tapping her long fingernails against her wine glass and staring at us both. She looked incredible and what was she now? Thirty? Looking her absolute best. In some alternate universe, we were sleeping together tonight. She smiled as I caught her eye.

'You thinking what I'm thinking, Toril?'

Why did I say that?

'Now why should you suddenly be able to tell what I'm thinking, Simon? I know for a fact you've never been able to before,' she answered with an enigmatic look. What an international woman of mystery she was trying to be tonight. She changed the subject. '*Lovely* fairy-lights. Well done, boys.'

Toril was about to say something else when Helen ran into the garden, hissing that Nick had just drawn up in a cab. She then disappeared swiftly back into the hallway to greet him. We lined up in the garden, a phalanx of frivolity armed with champagne and presents, trying not to knock anything over or laugh too loudly.

Nick came into the kitchen saying something about what a bloody awful trip he'd had and looking shattered. He looked more in the mood for an evening in front of mindless TV than a party. He headed straight for the kettle and while filling it up at the sink, looked out and saw us all. Classic. Corks popped and fanfares fanfared.

He came out into the garden, looking very shocked and still holding the kettle, Helen beside him, glowing with the success of her plan.

'Cup of tea, anyone?' he said, starting to laugh. He

coped much better than a relative of mine who barricaded herself in a bathroom, saying 'Why are you here? Why are you here?' because her hair was not done. There was no such problem with Nick, as he is very vain about his strawberry-blond locks and he looked just fine even after his train journey from the frozen north. Handing the kettle to Helen and circulating amongst us like the Queen on a walkabout, he seemed genuinely touched. He opened my present.

'Simon, it's perfect! I nearly bought it last week. Oh, wow, Helen! Helen, look,' and he brandished the book at her. She nodded, made an 'ooh, fab' face and went back into the kitchen with the kettle.

As Nick moved on, I whispered to Toril and Callum. 'Don't you just adore men who lie well?'

'Absolutely,' breathed Toril. 'Helen should pin him down and not let him go. Lucky cow.'

'*I* lie well and you let *me* go,' Callum said to Toril, his face all fake innocence.

'Nick lies well about nice things, Callum, like presents being perfect,' retorted Toril. 'You lied badly about not sleeping with Lucy Murray, if you recall.'

Callum burst out laughing. 'God, that's *right*. Lucy Murray, whatever happened to her? More fizz anyone?'

Toril stuck out her glass and Callum refilled it as they resumed their good-natured bickering. I'd always thought they made a good couple during their dangerous and brief liaison way back when and I harboured a secret hope they might get it together again, Toril's innate good taste and sense complementing and counterbalancing Callum's more repulsive proclivities. Callum had to settle down at some point, God knew Toril wanted to and I really didn't want to see Cal turn into an oldest-swinger-in-town type:

so why not Callum with Toril? She'd loosen up, he'd calm down, I'd turn into Gwyneth Paltrow and marry Mr Knightley. Stranger things could happen.

I took a step away and surveyed the scene, Nick greeting his guests, turning on all that charm even though he was plainly exhausted. Time slipped away and it did not matter that I had not spoken to some of these people in months. In those days, I was at my happiest with them. How could anyone have hoped to compete? The party glowed and shimmered, the fairy-lights and garden flares smoothing our faces and making time slip a little more. It was all very familiar. That was why I liked it.

A scream of welcome from the kitchen (it sounded like Helen's voice) meant that a latecomer had just made their entrance. I scanned the garden and could not figure out who it could be. For some reason I hung back as everyone crowded back into the house. Nick was whooping now, his arms around someone. I caught sight of Toril's face shining, her not wanting to miss a thing. My stomach flip-flopped as I realised who it was. Callum appeared at the kitchen window and knocked to get my attention. 'It's Patrick,' he shouted through the glass. 'He's just got back.'

Patrick.

I walked into the now crowded kitchen and there stood the great unrequited love of my life, fresh off a plane from Hong Kong. This was turning into some surprise party. Patrick had been away for nearly eighteen months and, since he was a notoriously bad keeper-in-touch, contact with any of us had been sporadic at best. Resolutely straight, he was nearly four years younger than me and had looked upon me as some sort of mentor, silly bugger. I had never applied for the position but it was the best one available since 'boyfriend' was never going to be an option. I had tried to look after him. He was my brooding, morose, funny, darkly handsome Patrick and he had the most beautiful legs in the galaxy. Luigi at the tennis court was Quasimodo by comparison.

Looking at Patrick now, I was shocked by how much he had changed. A chunky and powerful build had been replaced by something much more rangy and boyish. He still looked great in his Daniel Day-Lewis way but there was a wildness I had not seen before. What many people had mistakenly perceived as arrogance was now plainly closer to insecurity.

Callum slipped into place beside me and whispered in my ear. 'He's been through a ton of coke or I'm a Dutchman.'

'Do you think so?'

'No doubts. He's got the look. He's on it now.'

'He's so thin, Callum, it changes him so much.'

'You always liked him with a meat-suit on him, didn't you?'

'Rack off, here he comes.'

Toril was pointing in my direction as Patrick called out my name. She watched with delight and concern as he enveloped me in a bearhug. She had noticed something was wrong too.

'It's so good to see you, Simon, it's so good to see you. I've missed you so much.'

'Not enough to send a letter,' Callum interjected and received a bearhug of his own, although Patrick looked peevish.

'You know what it's like, it's difficult,' Patrick said, pulling the corners of his mouth down. 'I'm crap, I admit it.'

He told us all about Hong Kong, about a girl he had met (at which Toril glanced at me and withdrew slightly) about the firm he had been working for. Everything except how *he* was. He did not touch a drop of alcohol but as the evening went on Patrick became more and more hyper, seizing an opportunity to get me on my own as food was served up in the living room. As he spoke, he almost pinned me against the wall.

'Why didn't you keep *trying* to get in touch with me, Simon? I missed you all so much out there, and there were times I needed you most of all and you weren't there to help me. I can't believe I'm with you now. I needed you and you weren't there.'

He ran his hands through my hair (not too much product in it that night, thank God) and kissed me on the forehead repeatedly. Oh my God. Helen sailed past carrying some plates, mouthing 'Are you all right?' at me. Ohyesohyesohyes. As Patrick drew back I looked at him with big question marks in my eyes. He said, 'I thought you didn't love me anymore, that you'd forgotten me.'

I was astounded. Patrick never talked like this.

'That's not the way it works, Pat,' I finally managed to get out. 'You are thousands of miles away and you never replied to my letters. I thought you were just getting on with life. If you needed me so much I was always here, all of us were. You know I love you.'

'I didn't know, I wasn't sure. I thought—'

'Don't think. It crucifies us all in the end. Just know that I couldn't love you more, you stupid paranoid twat.'

'Don't call me stupid.' He raised his voice and that wild look intensified. He wasn't arguing about 'paranoid twat'. He put his hands against the wall on either side of my head, just like in the movies. *Yes.* Now *this* was exciting.

'Of course you're not stupid. But you know I love you, yeah?'

'Unconditionally?'

Well, *he* wasn't asking for much. Luckily, the answer was easy.

'Of course unconditionally, Patrick, as much as I love Callum and Toril and the rest of th—'

'No, *no*, no,' he interrupted, spinning away, his face in his hands. *Oh come back, it was great.* 'Not like them, I want to be . . . I want to be . . .'

'. . . special,' I completed his sentence for him. It was like I was talking to myself .

'Special to you, Si. I want to know you for the rest of my life, I want you to be there for me. Always.'

Not long enough for what I felt about Patrick. I was nearly crying, he was nearly crying, we were having ourselves quite a little moment and for the life of me I didn't know why. What was Pat trying to tell me? He rushed at me and hugged me like his life depended on it, kissing my eyes, my forehead, my temples.

My temples? With a familiar sinking feeling I realised these were not sexy kisses, these were *guru* kisses. What a bore. I tried to lift my mouth to his but Patrick was too busy kissing between my eyes. *Not between my eyes, you bastard.*

Callum walked in.

'Oh, sorry you two,' he said disingenuously.

Patrick stopped kissing me and hugged me so tight I couldn't move, me looking over his shoulder at Callum, who was beside himself. He stopped himself laughing, spotted a pen by a phone and wrote something on a napkin. Turning back he held it up. WHAT THE FUCK IS GOING ON?!!!

'I-don't-know,' I mouthed back. 'Piss off.'

He did, nearly sprinting back to the party to fill them in. Patrick raised his head blearily. A big change of mood had come over him. Mr Hyde was obviously in and receiving visitors.

'I love you and you let me down. You should have been in HK.'

'Aitchkay?'

'Hong Kong. Now who's stupid?' Patrick smirked.

'Oh. Well, I wasn't. I was running my business.'

'Your fucking stupid *business*. Tinpot piece of shit. You should get out into the fucking *world*, Simon.' He moved off again, leaning against the kitchen table, leering up at me from under hooded eyes, repeating, 'Get into the fucking *world*.'

'Like you, you mean?' I said, my patience beginning to chafe me.

'No . . . *yeah*, yeah, like me, why not? I'm no more of a fucking fuck-up than you are . . .'

'Can I quote you on that, when you're in a better mood?' It was official, he was getting on my tits.

'Huh?'

'So, you think I'm a fuck-up? Two seconds ago I was the answer to your prayers,' I said testily. I do like having a hold over someone – is that bad? I pressed the button, Mr Hyde disappeared and Patrick was back.

'Simon, no, no, I'm sorry I said it. I'm sorry. Oh my God I wouldn't ever want to hurt *you*, you have to know that . . .'

That was enough. I held out my arms to him. He could come and do that kissing my eyebrows thing again. It wasn't much but it was better than him burbling crap. I hugged him as he apologised over and over again. I stroked his hair and whispered that I loved him. I won't deny it was a turn-on. Big time.

'Promise me you'll keep in touch now,' Patrick said.

'Of course I promise. That's all part of the unconditional love thing,' I found myself saying, 'but you have to be there for me too. I needed you in the last eighteen months and you weren't there either. I can't be strong for people without something coming back.'

Patrick looked astounded. *I* was asking *him* for help?

'Of course, whatever, whatever, you *know* that,' and he held me again. I hugged him back this time. He was so lovely. What drug was this? I had to get him some more.

'Can we talk later?' I said after some more of that kissing of obscure parts of my face had happened. 'This is Nick's night and we should at least see him.'

'Yeah, yeah. Nicky Birthday Boy,' and Patrick whirled away down the hall, hitting the lounge at maximum velocity. I followed, widening my eyes as I went in at Callum, who laughed like a drain. He knew how I felt about Patrick and also knew Patrick's substance-aided, clingy mood would not have been entirely unwelcome to me. I sat on the arm of Toril's chair and exhaled meaningfully.

We watched Patrick mime an anecdote about rickshaw drivers for Nick's obvious delight. When in doubt, entertain the room. I had seen Patrick do it a thousand times.

'How is he?' Toril asked quietly.

'Mad as a balloon, darling, mad as a balloon. Red alert, all hands on deck.'

'You don't have to look after him, Simon. That might be a part of his problem, you know?'

'So, *he* thinks I let him down because I didn't look after him. *You* think I've fucked him up because I *tried* to for all that time. Good one, Toril, that makes me feel so much better.'

She looked quickly at her hands. I could not tell if she was upset or furious. Probably both: not that I gave a monkey's at that moment. I reached for a bottle of gin and poured myself a large one as Patrick switched on his Life 'n' Soul function and did his floor show. I pressed the mute button in my brain and took the opportunity to observe Patrick at close quarters. He was not doing any of that wiping-his-nose-and-sniffing acting that always means cocaine in the movies. I know nothing about drugs so I only have Tarantino as my guide on such things. One time, a house I lived in at college with lots of potheads was subjected to an LA dawn raid by the drugs squad and the police snorted in disbelief when I said I did not know the difference between hash and grass. I still don't. Anyway, something had certainly happened out in Hong Kong or Patrick was taking something that was making him come out with an almighty crock of shit.

The evening wore on. Of course, I stayed far too late, got horribly pissed and missed all my trains. I would have to get up at the sparrowfart to get back to work on time. The party broke up at about two. I was going to suffer the next day, no doubts. Helen dug out lots of bedding and threw it into the centre of the living room.

'You'll have to fight for the duvet and the airbed, you lucky people,' she said to the three of us crashing. Patrick and I were out-of-towners and Toril had said she was in no condition to drive. Helen added, 'It's a big moment for me – you're christening my new futon.'

'I'll take it,' said Patrick, throwing himself on to it.

Helen then joined the snoring Nick in her room. He had bottled on the party very early on, being a tired commuter. I knew how he felt. Toril laboriously blew up the comedy airbed and gave herself neuralgia. I eyed the sofa suspiciously as it seemed the only space available but it looked very uncomfortable. I lay on it to try it out. Toril took off her earrings with a grimace and placed them carefully on a wooden coffee table. She touched the table top.

'Have Helen and Nick just bought this? It looks like real monogamy,' she said and laughed uproariously at her own joke, throwing back her head like Snoopy.

'Belt up, Toril,' said Patrick. 'It's a bit late for gags like that.'

I did not even get it at first. Scandinavians love puns and never understand why we hate them. My Norwegian does not quite run to humorous double meaning, being of Oslo a quality as you could conceive.

Toril blew a raspberry and headed for the bathroom, toothbrush in hand. I sat up like a mummy rising from the dead and stuck out my lower lip.

'Doh. Iz Patwick feeling a lickle fwagile? Poor jet-lag Patwick.'

'Hardly. I've been back a month,' which stopped both Toril and me in our tracks. Patrick stared at us with empty, tired eyes.

'And you didn't ring any of us?' said Toril, looking hurt. 'Are you OK, Patrick? Are you in trouble?'

'I wanted to call all of you but I had to sort out . . .' he hesitated '. . . a lot of stuff and the time went by before I knew it. I've not been fired or anything but I've transferred back here to be nearer my mother. Mum's not well, you see. She needs me,' he said quietly, looking at me properly for the first time. No wonder he was taking something: he was at his wit's end.

'Why didn't you tell us before?' I asked, feeling like a complete heel for being so short with him earlier.

'You didn't ask.'

'That's because we thought you'd only just got back. You said you had,' said Toril. She went over and put her arm around Patrick's shoulders. Patrick lowered his head and I thought he was going to cry.

'Can we go to sleep, please,' Patrick said in an older, more serious voice, which I had never heard before. 'I feel dreadful.'

We all quickly did bathroomy things. Pat first, then me, then Toril. She had the full routine of make-up removal and contact lenses to do. I assumed we'd see her sometime next year. Patrick watched me arranging blankets on the sofa.

He said, 'Don't sleep there. We can share, we've done it before.'

Only the most frustrating night of my life. I thought. Toril walked back in at that second, arching an eyebrow.

'Now there's an offer you've been waiting for, Simon,' she remarked.

'That was fast,' Patrick said, trying to lighten the mood, 'for a *girl*.'

'I can be when necessary. That sofa looks great, Simon. You'll be fine.'

'I have back trouble, Toril, it's terrible,' I replied primly and slipped into bed beside the man I loved most in the world. The evening drew to a close as Toril switched off the light.

Or so I thought.

In the darkness, I could sense Pat's restlessness but I tried to fall asleep. I had to be up in three minutes' time or something silly like that. Why hadn't I just left when I had promised myself I would? I almost succeeded in dropping off.

Suddenly Patrick sat up, the futon creaking noisily, and took off his T-shirt. I saw him silhouetted against the window, so much thinner now. Then, incredibly, he shifted again and slipped off his boxers. What was he doing? He lay back for a second and I could hear him breathing.

Let's see how far he wants this to go, I thought, and slipped off my boxers. We were both naked now.

I turned towards him carefully, reached out and touched his hair. He edged over to me and put his head on my chest. I could feel him against my thigh. *Oh my God.*

This was my dream coming true. A man I adored as a best friend was letting me make a move on him. That was the way round it was, for all that he precipitated it. He was trembling. I wrapped the duvet around us and eased myself down so that our faces were level. I can remember thinking, *Is this what it's like at public school?*

I put a decade's friendship on the line and decided to go for it. 'Carpe diem, boys.'

I touched Patrick's chest, a moment I had dreamed about, brushing the hair back and forth. I touched his nipples, trying to find out what he liked. I kissed him. He responded tentatively at first, then matched me step for step, enormous error for enormous error, his tongue deep in my mouth. It was incredible: all thoughts of hetero-sexuality were gone, any doubts about being gay were banished. I was good at this, I could show Patrick the ropes. It was just the logical extension of our relationship. Unconditional love, just like he said. He kissed me again, his hands on himself now, trying to get himself erect. No problem for me, I was ready to roll. I touched his cock, still limp.

'Ssshh,' he whispered. 'Just lie back.'

He spoke so softly, it was almost telepathic. However, any shift of weight from either of us was accompanied by a huge creak from Helen's much-prized new futon. Somewhere in my head, I knew that Toril had to be listening to this. I didn't care.

I lay back. Was this Love? I wanted it to be. I prayed to a God I didn't believe in. He seemed to be paying me some attention for the first time in a while. Please God, let this be Love. Patrick lay by me, still kissing me. *Patrick was jerking me off.* Jesus.

His tongue was in my ear now, driving me crazy. He started whispering again.

'Do you love me, Simon? Please say you love me.'

'Yes I do, I always have,' I whispered back.

Then he went down on me. *Patrick went down on me.* I arched my back, trying to get all of myself into his mouth. He reached through my legs. Had he done this before? He stopped suddenly and he moved back so that his face was level with mine again. His breathing was ragged. I reached down. He was hard as well now. I kissed him but found his face was wet. His body was locked with tension.

'What's the matter?' I asked. What a dork of a question.

'Just do it, *just do it.* If you want to,' Patrick said in a dead voice, far too loudly. Toril must have been riveted.

I froze. Patrick was doing me a favour. A charity-fuck so I would love him.

There was a little pause as all three of us held our breaths. Insanely, I touched him again, he was not so hard now. Patrick pushed my hand away.

'Just forget it,' he hissed. '*Forget it.*'

How could I? It's a terrible thing when your dreams come true. They can never survive the build-up and the anticipation. They need the rarefied air of the imagination, not scuzzy old reality. This was a disaster. As my illusions disintegrated around me, my brain started the post-coital analysis. He had been willing to do something he did not want to do because he wanted me to love him. He wanted to be special. I must be such a bad friend. Hell, such a bad person.

I was not an answer to Patrick's problems. And if not for him, the man I loved most of all, then who? I had hit a brick wall. Nowhere to go.

I heard him crying again and tried to make out his face in the shadows; his breathing gradually evened out and he slept. From Patrick taking off his clothes to him pushing me away was only about ten minutes but it was ten minutes that changed everything. I did not know it at the time but my old life was over. I tried to sleep but could not, my erection all dressed up and nowhere to go so I had to jerk off as quietly as I could on the noisiest futon in the EC. Thinking about it, I could have got up and gone to the loo but it didn't occur to me. Trappist monks masturbate more noisily than I did that night, but Toril told me much later that she heard me all the same.

As it was, I slept badly. Patrick slept like a dead man. What a catastrophe.

Chapter 5

'There is no spectacle more enjoyable than watching an old friend fall from a roof'

Confucius

It is possible to avoid a nervous breakdown. After the disaster of my and Patrick's midnight munchies, I went into a spiritual tailspin; if the best friends I adored and wanted as lovers turned out to be as psycho as the rest of the planet, perhaps my life was going to be endless gourmet meals-for-one in front of crappy television. As a lip-smacking alternative, life could become an endless seek-and-ye-shall-find of casual sex: there are always people to cling on to for ten minutes before they drag you down with them. Neither of these options made my heart leap and I had a go at both of them in the weeks following Patrick's pass. Somehow my twin destiny of microwaved celibacy and pointless promiscuity (the combination sounds impossible but it isn't) had to be dodged, but they were like the ground rushing up to meet a freefalling plane: I could not see how they could be avoided.

I needed something to take my mind off my problems, a displacement activity that combined all the pleasures of eating, fornication, excreting, idleness and exercise in one neat package. Then it came to me in a near-sexual revelation that several buffoon companies had deemed me credit worthy. I grabbed my plastic, adopted St Michael as my patron saint *du jour* and I shopped for my country and my sanity. The small increase in consumer spending reported that month was due to me alone, I believe. I wish I could tell you that I sought counselling, found solace in poetry, learned a language or helped those less fortunate than myself, but I did none of these things. I did, however, kneel by the homeless and tell them of my overdraft to help them get their problems into perspective. If they'd had muscular dystrophy as well, I could have been the Duchess of York.

Should there exist a thrill comparable to making a major unnecessary purchase, I want it now. At the same time as you spend, you acquire. The male orgasm has no such exchange, it's just spend, spend, spend. Post-purchase, there is something physical in your hand rather than in a condom, on your stomach or, if the gods have been with you, over your head. Even guilt is involved. Cracking fun. Sometimes I would wake up in a store as if from a deep sleep, like a long-distance lorry driver on a motorway: I had been buying on cruise control, following the rituals of credit like the consumer ideal I had become. I would look at the shop assistant for the first time and wonder what I had just bought.

Looking back, I was living on Planet Janet, completely out of control. But it did stop me thinking about the fact that the men I loved were *never* going to love me in a month of surprise parties. Patrick had rubbed my nose in that. Well, he hadn't actually rubbed my nose in it . . . that might have been quite nice.

At the same time, I buried myself in work, got little-men-who-do into my flat to decorate (one of them even turned out to be a man-who-*definitely*-did) and put in a shiny white bathroom. By the time they had finished my home looked, felt and smelled like a hotel. I walked around it a stranger. I now lived in a transit lounge of comfort, living for design. Possessions I barely remembered buying took pride of place alongside books I would never read, which sat on shelves only recently put up. I had turned my home into a one-night-stand who refused to leave. But my breakdown was avoided as opposed to merely postponed: time was passed.

Toril looked after me a lot in those two weeks or so that I spent as a professional depressive consumer. I couldn't tell Callum what had gone on with Patrick but Toril had actually been in the room. I break out in a sweat when I think of it. How awful. The morning after Nick's party, she had driven me to Victoria and watched me as I spluttered, wept and coughed my way through a tea and croissant £1.49 bargain offer (my appetite is always unfazed by trauma), trying to explain to her why I was so upset, why this wasn't something I could laugh away.

'Patrick's always been the one for you, hasn't he? Your . . . what's it called . . . Holy Grail,' she had said, regarding me intently. Both of us were looking ragged; she hadn't got much sleep either. I'd never known her appear in public looking *quite* such a heap. I was grateful she was there.

'It nearly happened, Toril, I nearly had Patrick. For a split second, it was real . . .'

'A miss is as good as a mile.'

'It's much worse.'

'Not that I have any personal experience of just missing.

I've only ever missed by a mile, haven't I?' Toril had remarked airily, reaching over and brushing a crumb of croissant from my cheek. *She is so like me*, I remember thinking: say what is central to you but as a throwaway remark.

I had wiped at my mouth with a serviette. 'Have I got jam on me?' I asked, but there was nothing on my face except tears and a lot of proverbial egg.

She kept in close touch by phone in those days after Nick's party, sometimes ringing two or three times a day. I was in my retail chrysalis, trying to turn into a human being again and she was the only person to whom I could talk. I saw her twice up in London, then just as my spending jag was burning itself out, she came down to see me and was staggered by my sudden lack of a third dimension. Picking up a cut-crystal bowl filled with orange-blossom pot-pourri, she looked at me quizzically.

'Don't ask, Toril. It looked nice in the shop. It *did*. Don't look at me like that.'

'Ah, the national debt of Guatemala,' Toril said, peering at the underside of the bowl. 'Do you want the price tag still on it?'

'You can have it, if you like.'

'Well, if it makes my life as complete as yours, I'll take it.'

'Don't be horrible. Just put it down carefully, it's not paid for yet. Several dozen more people have to book safaris in the Serengeti before it is.'

She sifted the pot-pourri between her fingers. Why had I bought pot-frigging-pourri?

'The orange blossom isn't as good as vanilla,' she said. 'Get some vanilla.'

'Vanilla?'

'Vanilla. I have loads at home, you know that.' Toril blinked, was silent for a second, then continued drily, 'Then your life could be as complete as mine.' She replaced the bowl carefully. 'God, *Simon*, the table's new as well, isn't it?' I gave her a weak grin. She settled back on my sofa, crossed her legs (great legs – all that skiing as a child, I guess), her arms spread out expansively on either side. She looked confident, she looked like she had a complete life. But I knew different. Pound for pound, she'd had as many mishaps of the heart as I had, but her façade, which she relied on to get her through from minute to minute more than I did, was flawless as ever, lucky cow. Mine was in smithereens.

Toril stayed for some take-out, then we curled up together with a drink while some music played in the background. She had work in the morning so she had to go soon. I lay with my head in her lap, trying to relax, trying to rediscover Simple and Certain Simon. But he had gone and it was taking several thousand pounds and the stretching of my bank manager's patience for me to claw back an equilibrium. Toril sipped at her apple juice (she was driving), looking not just confident but rather contented and happy. I told her so.

'I am content, at the present moment,' she said softly. *There must be a fellah*. She was running her hands through my hair.

'That's so nice,' I said. 'My mum used to do that to me.'

'I'm a mother substitute now, am I?' Toril said, pretending to be dismayed. She slapped my forehead.

'Ow. My mother used to do *that* as well. Start breast-feeding me and you've got the job.'

'So if I'm your mother, does that make Callum your father?' Toril wondered aloud. I snorted with derision and shifted suddenly, causing Toril to spill a little of her drink. It wouldn't stain: we settled down again.

'Callum is *not* my father. He is *maybe* my evil twin.'

'Separated at birth but brought together by fate,' Toril declaimed with a smile.

'You haven't told Cal about what happened with Patrick, have you? He mustn't know,' I said seriously, looking up at her. I knew how fast the jungle drums could operate around our little group.

'Oh God, but I just faxed him, now what can I *do*?' said Toril in a dumb-blonde voice. She's anything but a dumb blonde. 'Of course I won't tell him. All families should have a few secrets.'

A drop of apple juice was hanging off the bottom of Toril's glass, burning gold in the light from a new lamp. I looked at the jewel-like droplet, reminded of the night Ruth had resigned. Just looking at its brilliance against the dark of the rest of the room made me remember the lines of her body that night, her hair, her excitement at not being stranded any more in a life she had grown, if not to hate, to dislike. She had been gone over a month and my life was certainly darker without her. Without Ruth, I was even more marooned. I had to bend my knees up so that there was a bit more material covering my crotch. What was the matter with me? I was getting turned on by a urine-coloured drop of apple juice. Being aroused by wee-wee, now *there's* something I've never been able to understand.

I wondered how Ruth was getting on. I'd had one postcard soon after she arrived but that had been it. I envied her her new start so much. I would have given anything to start over with a clean sheet. It wasn't that if I had my twenties over again, I'd do it all differently, it was that I'd do *something* with them this time. I had to start again like Ruth and go back to square one, sliding down all those snakes. God knew there had been quite a few.

Toril was blathering on about something. I hadn't really been listening, thinking about Ruth's hair, new beginning and her backside. I *love* a nice bum, don't you? I remembered Toril walking away from me at Victoria, her behind like baby whippets jockeying for position. Patrick's butt is quite wide because he's got strapping legs but he'd lost a lot of his bulk now. His legs just kept going in that young man way, the bum all the more attractive for being incidental. Ruth's is more rich and luxuriant because she's had kids. Patrick was never going to have child-bearing hips. I indulged myself with thoughts of the children I could have with Patrick.

The drop of apple juice fell on to my T-shirt. I watched it glisten and soak into the cotton.

'Have you rung Patrick? You should, you know,' instructed Toril, reading my mind. Sometimes her Norwegian accent, slight as it is, makes her sound just a little schoolmarmish.

'No, miss, but I have left a message,' I said. 'Is that all right?'

'Yes, it is,' she said, going honk on my nose and putting down her glass. 'I've got to go. I'll call you.'

'Fankoo for coming to see me, Mummy.'

'Simon, don't call me that,' Toril said with just a trace of reality and kissed me goodbye. She smelled great as ever: Issey Miyake, if I wasn't mistaken.

'You look wonderful,' I said as she put on her coat. Very swish.

'You can't get round me *now*, Simon. You should say

that when we meet, not as I'm leaving. Don't you know anything about female psychology?'

I thought I did but I played the game. 'Not a jot or tittle.'

'Tittle?' said Toril, frowning at a new word.

'It's a little thing.'

'I wouldn't say that, Simon, it looked like it was getting quite large a moment ago while you were completely ignoring what I was saying.'

How *grim* for her, she'd noticed me get an erection. I bundled her out the door, telling her I was insane, thanks for looking after me, ignore my crotch, nothing to do with me, mind of its own, bye. I waved her off out of the window and then went and sat down, deep in thought. I'd reached a dead-end with men. I was going nowhere but only because I was being pulled with equal force in two directions. Perhaps. Another law of physics seemed to be coming into play: for every action there is an equal and opposite reaction. Put simply, I'm one of Nature's rebounders.

I was rebounding from men, from Patrick to . . . Ruth, even Toril.

Did I just say I fancied Toril? I wasn't so sure of that. Was I just in wanting-to-shag-anyone-who-lets-you-rest-your-head-in-their-lap mode? After a second's careful pondering I decided that I did fancy Toril but that Ruth's ebullience, verve, and outgoing nature won by an enthusiastically enquiring nose. There was something defeated about Toril. Her cautious reserve, like with me, held her back from life. I needed a Ruth to meet me more than halfway. What did I know? I wasn't sure about anything.

But this uncertainty was leading to honesty. I had been having heterosexual impulses and unexpected hard-ons, all focused on thoughts of Ruth. I might be from Hastings originally but I can be dead Californian when I need to be. I can listen to my body. Usually it's saying, 'Sit *down*, have a tinnie, what's on the box, look at *him*, he's all there, isn't he?' Now, it seemed to be saying, 'Ruth, please.' It seemed to be saying:

WOMEN.
WOMEN?

Don't analyse, I told myself, don't be an over-educated wanker. Since my life was becoming one of doubt, I decided to Ricki Lake it into one of possibility. If everything is uncertain then anything is possible, right? I was a master of the universe after all.

I caught myself looking at women in the street. I mean, *looking* at them. If I can divulge yet another Magic Circle secret, when gay men look at women, they do not think about women's sexual organs. At least I never did. When a gay man meets a man, the first things to check out are the face, the body and the package (I have a friend who checks out the shoes and the fingernails first, but that is just deviant behaviour). When a gay man meets a woman, he looks at hair, make-up and dress sense. I had a thread-bare working knowledge of female anatomy from my VI Form, but in my adult life, as far as I was concerned, women were like shop-store mannequins, smooth and solid. I had no dealings with female genitalia therefore they became like the Lake District: I knew it existed, I knew it was a really great place and had even gone there as a very small child, but I had no desire to visit again. I thought about vaginas as much as I thought about Lake Windermere.

Then suddenly I wanted to go hiking, stay at that mythical five-star youth hostel, maybe get a boat out, follow the river to its source. I was living in Pheromone Central, the High Street was choc-a-block with female genitalia (it hadn't been the previous month, where had they all come from?), and some women were looking very different to me as I imagined what they looked like naked. How do straight men get through the day?

I was reacting to some women as I had reacted for years to thousands of men. I looked and a few of them twinkled back. One woman even started to chat me up but I wolfed my prawn baguette and ran back to work. I started to include women in the Escalator Game on the tube: I look at the people on the other escalator and make an instant decision whether or not I would shag them. I think everyone plays it but I'm not sure: tube stations are so cagey. I used the same sophisticated, highly attuned mode of selection for women as well as men: 'Him, not him, no *way* him, not her, him, her, not him', and so on until the ticket barrier wisely suggested that I seek assistance.

The ticket barrier was right. It always is, that's its job. So I called Callum, him being the most heterosexual heterosexual I know. His ultra-liberal mother used to beg him to experiment with other boys but he had had none of it. He knew female anatomy like the back of his hand, while I knew female anatomy like the back of my head. I wanted information and when he stopped laughing, it turned out Callum was exactly the sherpa I needed, if unnecessarily vulgar.

'You think you're going straight so you want to know what a cunt is like? *Fabulous.* Whatever will Toril say? I'll be there.'

We met up in an Aroma café in town and he gave a

masterclass on the female sexual organ. I tried to maintain a sophisticated café-society veneer to match my surroundings as I was told the female facts of life, but in reality I was agog. Truth really was stranger than fiction.

Callum adopted an earnestness of Open University proportions.

'The most important thing to realise is that all women are different. No two are alike and all respond in different ways to the same techniques. That's not like men – our sex drives are much more simple and direct. We are like bicycles, we vary a lot but we are all bicycles. But every woman reinvents the wheel, every women is a new mode of transport. With every new woman you have to go to square one and start again.'

Square one, that was good, that was where I wanted to be. I needed a notepad or a tape recorder or something. I concentrated.

'And the reason every woman is different is because no two cunts are the same and women have such a weird relationship with them. I slept with one girl from work and hers was a work of art, just like a flower, such a beautiful thing. I never give red roses in the same way now. Anyway you can get others that look like the loose skin under your gran's jaw cut up and ready for stir-fry.' He paused for laughter; none came, I was listening far too hard. I nodded slowly.

'Stir-fry.'

'Simon, that was just an image, you don't need to remember it.'

'Right, right.'

I was dimly aware that a waitress had been clearing a nearby table for far too long. Perhaps a busy café was not the place for this. I realised I had been drifting.

'Cunts are like a box of chocolates, Simon, you never know what you're gonna get. Looks upstairs are no guarantee of looks downstairs. You have to forget what it looks like and remember what it is *for*, then just get nose-deep in it.'

I was entranced. I was in the army now. This was riveting stuff: all my imaginings when I had been looking at women in the street had verged on the fantastic with complete personalities lurking under every skirt and gusset, like gynaecological versions of the Seven Dwarves. All that Callum was saying seemed to confirm what I had thought. Then something he had just said struck me.

'*Nose* deep? I only ever did it twice way back when and I never got *nose* deep.'

Callum smiled at me indulgently. 'Nose deep is a must but you mustn't get rough with it, unless she wants you to. Now, do you know how to find the clitoris?'

'Intellectually,' I said defensively. 'I don't think I ever found it in practice.'

'How long did you go out with that girl in the VI Form?'

'Eighteen months.'

'And you never found it? Poor cow.'

'Well, I may have done. I read a book saying a clitoris was like a small penis and could get erect but another said it was like a baked bean.'

'And that confused you?'

'Well, I thought I was the only one with a penis like a baked bean.'

'*Ah.*'

Is Simon joking? I could see Callum thinking. We both kept poker faces, Callum nodding sagely.

'Well, you've got to be able to find it,' Callum continued

smoothly. 'Perhaps in the dark, perhaps only with your tongue.'

'What about your fingers?'

'You might be tied up.'

'Wow.' Callum was so wise. The eavesdropping waitress was now staring and caught Callum's eye. She blushed to her roots and tried to smile. He ordered two more cappuccinos.

I leaned forward and said, 'So you can find it with only your tongue?'

Callum puffed his chest. 'Oh yeah. Famed through Greater London. Hackney gave me a grant for it.' He was looking very sure of himself.

'Tell me how to do it, Callum.'

'Say please.'

'Tell me how to do it, Callum, please.'

'Well, you sad man, here's what you do. You get your tongue underneath the outer lip and work your way up the crack between the lips and when you get to the top—'

'You plant a flag.'

'Listen. When you get to the top, you find a sort of hood thing and underneath that hood is the clitoris.'

'You are putting me on. It sounds like Dungeons and Dragons.'

'This is gospel truth, Simon. So you keep separating the lips and the hood and probing around the clit.' All these technical terms.

'Hang on. You don't actually go for the clitoris *itself* once you've found it.'

Callum pondered what he had said. 'It's difficult. I don't as a rule. Remember that every woman is different. Some won't let you go down on them at all.'

Stop press.

'But I thought it was the expected thing these days.'

'Not always. Sometimes they say it is too personal, too intimate. "You don't know me well enough", they say.'

I was gasping for air. Too much information. 'So, most times, you have penetrative sex with a woman *before* you get to go down on her because she thinks actual sex is less intimate.'

'Well, maybe not *just* before,' Callum winced. 'That would be gross. Different dates, I mean.'

Men were very different. Gay sexual etiquette is a Chinese meal: you get to oral sex at about the same time as crispy duck, just after the spring roll but before the beef with ginger.

'Oral sex for a woman is more of a commitment,' confirmed Callum. This was all pure gold.

'You're getting your feet under the table,' I said, grasping the point.

'Your nose in the trough.'

'Wow.'

This was so *abstract*. There was a whole mindset and philosophy to be taken in, like a zen of cunnilingus: ducking and diving, bobbing and weaving, ready for any eventuality and turn of events, like free-market capitalism. You never knew what was going to be around the corner. It felt like being a secret agent: 007, licensed to lick. This was all much more complex than with guys.

Callum continued. 'Recap time, we'd just found the clitoris. Little test, where was it?'

'At the top of a crack, under a hood.'

'At the top of a crack, under a hood – and what else?'

I panicked. What had he said? What had he said? Then I saw the corner of his mouth twitch. I said, 'At the top of a crack, under a hood, *sir*.' His mouth twitched again and we both collapsed into giggles. Men just don't talk about such things, not even when they are best friends, and particularly when one of them is gay. The whole café regarded us for a while, decided we were on drugs and went back to its business. Our cappuccinos arrived, as if to shut us up. Callum tried to keep it together and warmed to his theme.

'The idea, once you've found it, is to skirt around it. You don't push on it or go for it directly. It's difficult to explain . . .'

'It's like if you're touching someone's prostate, you have to be careful.'

I realised that Callum had gone very quiet and was looking a little frightened.

'You've touched people's prostates? Why do you have to do a thing like that?'

I couldn't tell him that I never had, so I toughed it out. 'It's great. You should get someone to do it to you. Keep talking about cunnilingus, Callum, stick to what you know.'

'That's rich, coming from you,' Callum said, recovering and sprinkling sugar carefully over the foamed milk of my coffee. 'Time to practise. Try to lick off the sugar granules without dislodging any of the foam.'

I poked my tongue out and darted it around the coffee. Callum sighed and pushed my head down into it so that my nose was in the coffee. I squawked. It was boiling hot. I was going to die by drowning in a milky coffee while practising cunnilingus. Not the epitaph I was looking for. While I lapped and probed, Callum carried on talking.

'It's like trying to get hundreds and thousands off an ice

cream or picking up wet soap. You have to creep up on it a bit. But remember the Golden Rule. Simon, tell me the Golden Rule.' I came up for air with a gasp and a whoosh. I had chocolate and sugar over my nose but I knew the answer now.

'Every woman is different, sir.'

'Like Cream Eggs: how do you eat yours?'

'That's right, sir. I get it now, sir.'

'Like those little cars.'

'What's yours called, sir?'

'Exactly. I'm proud of you. Not bad for a young 'un. One day all this will be yours.' Callum cast his hand in the direction of a group of women by the door. They were looking at me aghast. I wiped my face and considered the various women in the café. It was as if I were seeing them with new eyes. *They were all different.*

'So how do women react individually to their fannies?'

Yes, I really did say that. An older gentleman sitting alone at the next table put down his paper and began openly listening. Callum said, 'Well, it's weird. Some have bought in totally to the male fantasy and they objectify themselves when you're making love.'

'And that's . . .' I tried to read Callum's eyes. Failed. Flipped a mental coin, '. . . really *bad.*'

'Of course it is. It's such a turn-off to get all that bad dialogue coming at you. "You're so big, fuck my pussy, fuck my pussy."'

The older gentleman with the paper leaned over and interrupted. 'Excuse me, I couldn't help overhearing.' He had a soft Scottish brogue.

'Oh, am I shouting?' said Callum, flushing slightly and glancing at a couple of forty-something ladies-who-lunch. They smiled broadly and nodded. Our conversation dropped to a hushed tone. The older guy, a City gent by the looks of him, told us about his approach to cunnilingus.

'I absolutely agree with your hypothesis and *modus operandi* as to the actual physical process of . . . er . . . pleasuring a lady orally,' he whispered. 'However, I have discovered that there is a deal of mental preparation necessary to the . . . er . . . act itself in the same way that the act of . . . er . . . penetration itself for some men can require a degree of forethought.'

'Allegedly,' said Callum, his eyes like plates.

'No indeed,' the man continued. 'I *know*. Concerning the acts of cunnilingus and, to a lesser extent, annilingus, which *some* women and certainly most *men* enjoy, I find that I have to play a mental trick on myself or play a game, if you will, and imagine that I am a deep-sea diver or somesuch. I construct an alternative reality out of it, otherwise in the dark, I become more and more aware that it is just this great wet patch on my face.'

With this he bade us farewell and left the café, having carefully placed a thirty-pence tip by the sugar bowl. We watched him go.

'Wasn't that the Foreign Secretary?' I said.

'Could have been, mate. Could have been,' said Callum, suddenly serious.

Chapter 6

'No, it is "Fanny" that I think of, and dream of all night'

Jane Austen

Never mind Fanny, I was thinking about Ruth all the time. I was thinking about her so much I was forgetting her, like when you say 'tanktop' too many times and it becomes meaningless. I was afraid I would misremember her and start having only a Ruth-in-my-head rather than a true memory of a Ruth-for-real. Sure, I was looking at women differently since Callum's love-lesson and knew a bit more about them, but only Ruth was exerting the same pull on me as any good-looking guy in the street. Ruth, miles away in Manchester, was having the same effect as some phenomenal Brad lookalike I happened upon at the swimming pool. That is to say, a very profound effect. I was still gay but falling in love with a woman and being very turned on by it.

And it was confusing me something rotten. After Callum drew back the veils of mystery that swathe the clitoris, I had a traumatic four days, for reasons which will become clear. The four days of tension came to a head in a very strange dream I had while napping on the couch in my office one drizzly Tuesday afternoon. Martin Luther King would not have bragged about this one.

I was a New York traffic cop trying to control all the vehicles at a busy intersection. All the cars were mauve, which upset me for some reason, but I was doing really well; the cars were all going where they should. Then they all gradually accelerated more and more until my arms were in fast forward and the traffic was a mauve blur whirling around me. A car drew to a sudden halt beside me and Toril, dressed as Lauren Bacall in To Have and To Have Not, *threw open the passenger door. 'Get in, quick,' she said, but I couldn't. I shouted at her above the roar of the cars but couldn't make myself heard. She slammed the door shut and raced off. As she slammed the door, all the other cars disappeared and all I could see was her car speeding away. A yellow cab flew past and I flagged it down and told the driver, who I think was Callum dressed as Bruce Willis in* The Fifth Element, *to follow that car . . . The cab turned into a running track and Ruth and I ran round the track in countless circles, always the same distance from each other. The relay baton felt very familiar, what was it, what was it . . . The circles gradually turned into a waltzing crowd at the ball from* My Fair Lady. *Patrick and Ruth were dancing together, Ruth in white tie and Patrick as Audrey Hepburn. I pushed through the crowd to split them up, waved the orchestra silent, and I did not know which one I wanted to dance with. So I did what all good homosexual characters do in Hollywood movies and withdrew a small silver and ivory pistol from my jacket and shot myself in the temple. As the shot ricocheted around the ballroom . . .*

I came to having had the first wet dream of my life. *In my office.* Either that or the tzatziki fairy had visited my underpants while I slept. It was all becoming a bit of a problem. I did not know how to jerk off any more: me,

the master of the hand shandy. It's not good to bottle
things up, especially semen. I had had so much backed
up, I hadn't dared blow my nose. I couldn't believe I'd had
a wet dream. Would I get zits next?

My problem was that thinking about men still worked
technically but it was not the same now. And thinking
about Ruth was a work of fiction, not a memory of an act
of friction. I had never slept with her and I did not know
enough about women to fantasise properly. I was losing
my frames of reference and not replacing them with anything. It had never been like this before. I had always
been able to bring myself to boiling point within about
five minutes of feeling the urge, like any self-respecting
male. Also, I was eroticising cappuccino since seeing
Callum and drinking far too much of it. I-was-feeling-
very-tense.

I walked carefully to the staff loo and cleaned up. I
looked at myself in the mirror. Perhaps I was a lesbian. It
would solve a lot of problems and be just a little shift of
category. I could still be gay and could legitimately sleep
with women. Ace. But I would have to keep my sense of
humour and *not wear the clothes* and only sleep with
straight women. Maybe I could keep my penis and still be
a lesbian, in some ways the perfect lesbian. Why don't I
shut up? *Smart-alec wanker, Simon.* How was it that I was
in a room alone and it was crowded? Can I state that I
know I am not a lesbian?

I AM NOT A LESBIAN.

At last a shred of certainty. I looked around me quickly.
No fly-on-the-wall documentary team. Thank God. Oh,
thank God.

My body was being Californian again, it was talking to me and I should listen, I decided. The wet dream meant I had to ring Patrick, sort all that out with him, then stride confidently on with a clear conscience and the clean slate I wanted and re-establish contact with Ruth. Whoever would have thought there could be so much meaning in a thinly spread teaspoon of semen? It was a sign, I tell you.

I rang Pat. I had no clue what to say to him. It was a strange situation. He was straight but when he'd been frying his brain on something he'd made a sort-of pass, which I had kind of reciprocated, and not much had happened except for my expensive breakdown. Oh, and I had gone sort of straight. Patrick didn't have to know this last nugget. I dialled the number, expecting a machine, but to my surprise Patrick answered.

'Claire, is that you? I can't find that fucking cardigan she wants anywhere . . .'

'No, it's Simon, Pat.'

'Oh, I thought you were my sister, oh *shit*—'

I got the impression he had dropped the phone. There was much scuffling and a slamming of a door then nothing but the crackle of the line.

'Patrick, are you still there?'

'Hi. Sorry, I'm packing a bag and dropped the phone. Phew. Sorry I haven't got back to you. I got all your messages.'

I remembered his mum was ill. He had never told me what with, events having rather overtaken us.

'How's your mum?'

'Not great. It's definitely the big C but we already knew that. Couldn't be anything else. Did I tell you this?' I told him he hadn't. Poor Mrs Reive, she was a nice lady. He recited the current gospel from the doctors. 'They don't think it's spread to the lymph glands so it might just be a lumpectomy. That's the best scenario we're rooting for. Mum's being incredible.'

'How are you bearing up?'

'Not *bad*. I tried to keep work going but I've got compassionate leave now so I can be here all the time at the moment, not long enough, though . . . Um, I'm sorry, Simon, but I've got to pick up my sister and take some stuff over to the hospital. Mum likes having some of her things around her.'

'Of course. We'll speak soon, yeah? You know my number.'

The line crackled emptily again. Were we not going to refer to what happened?

'Simon, are we still friends?'

'You shouldn't have to ask.'

'It's just stuff like . . . *that* . . . can muck up friends, you know . . .'

'Not us though, eh?'

'I've got to go.' Then he said, 'I love you, man.'

'I love you too, Patrick. Bye.'

'Bye.'

The 'I love you, *man*' spoke volumes. It wasn't a sixties hippy 'man'. It was a modern, male and very heterosexual intimacy. It was dorky slang but it was useful. It was completely platonic and removed any confusion. It allowed Pat to say 'I love you' to me after all that had occurred. We were back on track, my friend Patrick and me.

And that was the easy phone call of the two. I'd have had a lie down if I hadn't thought I might nod off and ejaculate again. I popped my head into the shop to see if my new but boring deputy needed me. She was so unoccupied she needed resuscitating. I grabbed a coffee, told her that I wasn't to be disturbed and closed the door firmly.

Ring Ruth, Simon. You've sorted out Patrick, now talk to Ruth. It's just a chat, nothing crucial.

I could try and convince myself of that, but it was crucial. I had to see her again and perhaps exorcise her from my mind. If it turned out that I was attracted only to the idealised Ruth-in-my-head then I could go back to being a happy homosexual and everything would be *normal* once more, thank God.

I dillied around picking up the receiver and putting it down again for about forty minutes, then ambushed myself and dialled really quickly. I shut my eyes as it rang. It was an answering machine of course so I left a message for Ruth to call me back. As I replaced the handset I realised that my heartbeat was deafening me. I gulped at my coffee to calm me down. Then I opened my eyes again. I caught sight of myself in a pane of glass. I looked bad in the old-fashioned sense of the word; you know, *bad*. Whenever I imagined Ruth and myself together, I was not like this. Me-in-my-head and Ruth-in-my-head were fabulous creatures. In fact I did not know which of us I fancied more, not that me-in-my-head would have looked at me twice. He always looked great, fresh out of the make-up trailer with never a hair out of place. In the reflection, I had a massive cowlick at the front that was pointing north. I smoothed it down, it sprang back up. I smoothed it down, it sprang back up. I smoothed it down, it spr— THE PHONE RANG. IT HAD TO BE RUTH. My answer phone kicked in:

'Thank you for calling Lyndontravel. Please leave a—'

'Hello, Simon Lyndon speaking.'

'Hello, Simon Lyndon-Speaking.'

'Ruth! Hi! What a surprise!' *What a surprise? I just called her. Good start.*

'But you just rang me.'

'Yeah! Great to hear your voice! How's it all going? Are you really clever now?' *Too many exclamations. Nobody talks like that.*

'You mean I wasn't clever before?' *Not good, not good. Wriggle out of it.*

'Einstein, darling. More than Einstein. Tell me everything about your life.' *Keep it light. Gay Best Friend. She doesn't know yet. Gay Best Friend.*

'Things are great, Simon. Coming here was the best thing I've ever done.' *In translation: leaving your poxy travel agency was the best move I ever made, tell me what you want and sod off.*

'How are the girls?' *Boring, boring, boring.*

'They're fine. They're taking a while to settle into their new school, Sarah especially, but they're fine.' *So Sarah's unhappy and Ruth feels guilty . . .*

There was a pause. Ruth and I had never had an uncomfortable pause before. She broke it.

'Did you ring for any reason?' *So now I need a reason? Because I can't jerk off properly and it's all your fault; good enough reason?*

'Just a chat, Ruth. The place isn't the same without you, you know.'

'That's nice to hear.' *Ruth probably barely remembered me. Why did I ring . . . This was awful. She was talking to me like she was stopping to chat to a* Big Issue *salesman.*

Another pause. Longer than the first. I broke it this time.

'I'm sorry, I feel a bit shy with you. Silly.'

'Thank God you said that, Si. Me too. We are funny. Can we start this conversation again.'

'Please.'

'I'll ring you back,' and the phone went dead. Oh boy. Empires rose and fell as I waited. It rang.

'Hello? Simon Lyndon speaking.'

'Hello, Simon, it's Ruth. How the hell are you? Long time no speak.'

'Rubbing along. Or not. How about you?'

'I'm great. Slightly sick of baby twenty-somethings, truth be told.'

'At their sexual peak, though.'

'If you can get past the Clearasil. The course is fantastic, though . . .'

She talked enthusiastically about her work. She sounded so motivated. I did not remember being so mad-keen on my studies during my degree but I guessed that you are always more of a zealot about something if you come to it later in life. Let me read that back. Slowly.

You are always more of a zealot about something if you come to it later in life.

Wise words, Simon.

She did not talk properly about the kids being unhappy but sort of mentioned it in passing, knowing I had picked up on it already. 'The kids love seeing their father a lot, of course. Imagine *him* being a silver lining.'

'He's around a lot, is he?' *Get your hands off . . .*

'Yup, like the proverbial, and he's even more attractive than the day I met him.'

'You don't mean that . . .' *Please don't mean that.*

'That's *right*. God, it's good to talk to you, Simon. I haven't really found anyone here to talk to like this. There's Paul, but it's not the same.'

'Paul?' *Paul . . . I hate him already.*

'Paul's a sweetheart. He's in some of my lectures. But he's no competition for you in my affections, Simon.'

'Why?'

'He wants to get into my knickers, that's why.'

'Maybe I do as well.' *Well, that was subtle.*

'*Sure*, can you imagine? Who does what and with what and to whom. Where was I? Anyway, Paul's only twenty, it's out of the question.' *It put him firmly in the frame in my book, but there you go, I wasn't complaining.*

'Floppy blond hair, minor public school, great smile, perfect teeth, off the wall sense of humour?' I enquired.

'You've met him?'

'Just guessing. I think I shagged his big brother when *I* was at university. Or maybe I just wanted to. So when can I come and see you?'

'Really? Great! That would be brilliant. I've really missed you, Simon. What are you doing this Friday?'

'One guess.'

'Eating Pringles and watching American sitcoms.'

'Our survey said: "Eating Pringles and watching American sitcoms".'

'Tape them. Paul's having a party at his house. *Please* come.'

'Will I be the oldest person?'

'Oh yes. It's why I'm asking you. Otherwise I am.'

'I'd love to come.'

'It's compulsory fancy dress and the theme is "Heaven or Hell".'

'I think I knew that.'

'What? Paul is coming as . . . this is really funny, listen . . .' she was nearly screaming with laughter. He must be bloody gorgeous. 'Paul is coming as a very small amount of sperm.'

'The Second Coming?'

'That's *right*. How did you guess? *Really* funny, isn't it?'

'Fucking *hilarious*. I can't *wait* to meet him.'

'You'll love him. But hands *off*, if anyone's having him, it's *me*.'

'OK.'

He sounded like a prat. No worries.

As I put the phone down, I felt bizarre. I could not figure it out. It felt like my eyes were wide open and that the top of my head was open to the sky with none of that fogginess and closed-in feeling you can get. I was so awake. I was going to see Ruth *in three days*. I was nervous, excited, I had butterflies.

'I'm happy,' I whispered to myself. '*This* is what it feels like to be happy.'

I rang Toril. I rang Callum. They were both out so I left them messages saying that I felt *happy*. I could expect concerned phone calls within the hour.

Chapter 7

'You've sung your song, you call that doing,
You've sung the song, then dance the dance'
Alexander Kuprin

Heaven or Hell? Which was it to be? Difficult choice or what? Ruth would not tell me what she was going as to the fancy dress party, saying it would be a surprise when we met there. I was working a full day in the shop, then travelling to Manchester, so I was going directly to the party from Piccadilly. I tried on lots of costumes in a theatre wardrobe that hired out stuff and opted in the end for a pragmatic Heaven in the form of a vicar's outfit, the full works: grey shirt, dog collar, black suit, crucifix, white vestments. I would be able to travel up in the suit with the rest packed away in my overnight bag.

I planned all this with over-meticulous precision, in the three days leading up to the party, just like my grandmother does when she packs in late November to come to us for Christmas. In my bedroom, I tried on the costume and looked at myself in the full-length mirror. Did I look sexy? I had to look good. Are vicars sexy? I decided that I looked damn fine and that the white robes swished really nicely.

The three days inched by. I was hardly sleeping and

trying not to abuse myself too much to keep the old tanks full just in case the best of all possible worlds came to pass. Insomnia and abstinence are not happy bedfellows at four in the morning. Also, I did quite a few sit-ups, about sixty over the three days. Not bad for me. By the time Friday arrived, I was a bit knackered to tell the truth, but high on life and raring to go.

It might have been the outfit but it was with an evangelical fervour that I boarded the train to Manchester. I was on a mission, perhaps not from God, but I could not help but think that He might approve for once. I was certain that I loved Ruth, that I wanted to be with her and tonight I was going to tell her.

I was on the 19:30 departure out of Euston but it left eight minutes late because of a signal failure in the Milton Keynes area. I can even recall the pattern of the coffee rings on the table at which I sat. A sort of Olympic pattern. A woman who sat diagonally opposite me had highlights and a leopard-print scarf fastened with an enamel brooch. She was an air-stewardess type who got on at Birmingham International. I remember every detail of that day as if I were still living it.

Having been in a rush, I only had the Bible that came with the clerical drag to read on the journey, so I contented myself with pure thoughts all the way to Manchester. That Job guy had a tough time, didn't he? As we drew out of Stockport, I got the dog collar and grey shirt out of my bag and popped into the loo to put them on. When I came out I saw the leopard-print scarf lady smile to herself. She caught my eye so I smiled back. Vicars *were* sexy, it seemed.

'I knew you were a vicar,' she said in a husky, knowing voice.

I went along with it and chuckled in what I imagined was a vicarly way; slightly forced, polite and wise.

'Ha-ha. Ha-ha. People always do,' I said. 'How did *you* know?'

'Well, the Bible.'

'Of course,' I said, suddenly serious.

'And you've got an air about you. Do you have a parish in Manchester?'

'No, down south.' I decided to push my luck. 'Actually, I'm going to Manchester to declare my love to someone. I'm rather nervous. Ha-ha.'

'How romantic!' she exclaimed. 'That's so *lovely*. How long have you known them? Are they in the same line as you?'

The train drew into Piccadilly so we moved towards the door. I said over my shoulder, 'Oh no, Ruth's not a vicar. I've known her about three years, I suppose. Ha-ha-ha.'

The leopard-lady laughed too. 'Well, it just goes to show,' she said, shaking her head.

'What?'

'You never can tell. I could have sworn you were gay. When I saw you, straight away, I said, "Gay vicar". Hope you don't mind me saying that.'

I said nothing in reply. I was furious. The train drew to a halt and the spotted bitch waved me a cheery goodbye and clacked along the platform. I queued for a cab and endured the nods and smiles of an elderly couple in front of me. The vicar outfit was a big mistake. During the ride to the party, I tried to calm down and get my head back together. The cab driver attempted to engage me in a conversation about the Pope's health so I told him I was a Baptist, which shut him up. I knew we were getting close to the party when I saw a couple of cherubim clutching cans of draught Guinness get off a bus. I took some deep breaths and wished I had done some more sit-ups. We arrived and the cabbie apologised for offending my faith. I told him it was fine and tipped him fifty pence. The sound of muffled dance music filled the air.

The windows of the small terraced house were steamed up and glowing red. It was a *student party*. My heart sank. What was I doing here? Why hadn't I said we'd have dinner or something? A monk and Satan were sitting on the wall outside smoking roll-ups. They were giggling uncontrollably as I put my white vestments on.

'You coming to the party, vicar?' snickered Satan. The monk snickered too. In their fancy dress, I could not tell which one was Beavis and which one was Butthead. I decided that sarcasm was the best route of reply.

'No, I'm not coming to the party although it looks a lot of fun. No, I have to deliver last rites to Mr Hollerinshaw in number 27.' I looked suitably pious. Satan looked embarrassed and stubbed out his cigarette. He nudged the monk to stop giggling.

'Stop it, Tobes. I'm sorry, vicar. I was just joking.'

'I know, I was j—'

'We just thought it was a really great coincidence when you drew up in the cab outside this party. Ironic, when you think about it.'

'Post-modern,' the monk said earnestly.

'Yes, but . . .'

I was not quite sure which end of which stick Satan was getting now. Friar Toby said I should come to the party after I had consigned Mr Hollerinshaw to his just reward.

'You're dressed right for it so you've got to come,' begged Satan.

'It would be really cool if you did. It might be a bit noisy for you, though,' the monk continued.

'I bet you haven't been to a party like this for a while, vicar,' Satan remarked good-humouredly. I looked at them both closely. Nineteen if they were a day. I felt like I was a hundred and two. I was far too depressed to come up with a retort so I picked up my bag, hitched up my vestments and stomped into the house. I heard an explosion of astonished hilarity behind me and decided to ignore it.

They were right: I *hadn't* been to one of these in a long time and it *was* too noisy and crowded for me. I was so pissed off. I had chosen this outfit because I thought I looked quite sexy in it. Instead, I looked like an ageing, gay vicar. Nice one, Simon. I put my bag down on a pile of absurd faux fur coats and tried to see if I could find Ruth in the crush of unwashed young intelligentsia.

The house was packed cheek by firm, young jawline with vicars, imps and angels. I can honestly say that I have never felt a group of people's hormones whizzing around quite so fast. People were rushing past me trying to find a crotch of gold at the end of the rainbow, and I realised that I was doing the same thing. Where was Ruth? I found out from two nuns making out on the draining board that she was dressed as the Virgin Mary; I think at least one of the nuns was a man but you can't tell with the younger generation these days. Disgraceful behaviour.

The third Virgin Mary I tapped on the shoulder turned out to be Ruth.

'Simon! You made it!' she screamed and flung her arms around me. We hugged for the longest time and just when she was about to stop hugging, I hugged her again. She had on Renaissance blue robes, which went round her head, her hair in a centre parting, a white dress with embroidered flowers and a blue neon-effect flashing halo. I could not have been more glad to see her if I were a Catholic.

'You look fantastic,' I said, meaning every word. 'I guess this makes you *my* boss now.'

'Or at least your boss's mother.' She stepped back, nearly falling over into the group of people behind her. She gave my costume the once over. 'Good vicar's outfit. Very classy. Let's get you a drink.'

Top idea. I was going to need a bit of courage for tonight. Dutch was as good a brand as anything. We edged our way through the cream of England's youth to the drinks table and I opened a can of lager. Ruth grinned like an idiot at me. God, she looked amazing.

I was definitely attracted to her. *Me, fancied her.* Turn-up or *what*.

'Good journey? It's so good to see you! I can't believe it's been such a short time. It feels like a different century. Where are you staying? Are you coming back to mine tonight? The kids are at their father's until tomorrow afternoon, my mum's at my brother's for the weekend, so we can be naughty and noisy. No worries.'

Good. Naughty and noisy.

'That's great,' I said. 'Perfect. If I stay longer, I'll book into a hotel or something. I've got something really important to tell you.' *Oh, that was so smooth. What a neat link.*

'You might stay longer? Fab. You can see the girls . . . there's Paul! You *must* meet Paul. This is his party. Paul! Paul!'

If she said his name once more . . .

'Paul! Come and meet Simon. The one I told you about.'

The one I told you about. The arse-bandit. Paul gave me an unmistakable up-and-downer and obviously decided I was not an obstacle to his trying to sleep with the woman I was now positive I adored. After my fiasco with the monk and Satan outside, my self-esteem was a little low but I was not at all downcast by Paul's dismissal of me as a rival. For one thing he was dressed as a teaspoon containing a small amount of semen. It was such a bad costume, made out of cardboard with silver foil around it. The bowl end of the spoon had a hole cut in it for Paul's face, which was made up with white greasepaint. Ha-ha-ha. On the credit side, he was wearing a black one-piece under the teaspoon and he had an amazing body. But hey, if you can't look good at twenty then you shouldn't be allowed out. Damn his teaspooned, tight-butted, twenty-year-old, probably slightly tanned hide. I decided to go on the attack. I was starting to enjoy myself. Ruth introduced us.

'Paul, Simon. Paul Simon! That's funny,' she laughed. I was slightly appalled at her finding that joke humorous in any way. I hoped she was pissed. I rallied.

'Hello, matey, how's it going?' Paul said cheerily. *Oh, he was so posh. Body of a god, blond, clever and posh. This was going to be tough, I might have to move fast.*

'Paul, good to meet you. Thanks for letting me crash your party. What the fuck have you come as?'

Ruth looked at me. Had I forgotten what she had said on the phone? I felt like John Malkovich gunning for Keanu Reeves in *Dangerous Liaisons*. Paul, for all his youth and beauty, was not getting past this line of death. Paul smiled stoically as I asked him to tell me all about his costume. He turned to Ruth.

'This was such a stupid idea, Ruth. I've had to explain it to so many people.'

'I think it's great. Really witty,' comforted Ruth.

'Half the people don't get it even when you explain it to them, I expect,' I offered helpfully.

'Right! But you understand it, don't you, Simon? You seem like a clever chap. Please say you understand,' moaned Paul in mock-angst as Ruth looked on enchanted. That public-school thing gets me every time as well.

'Don't worry, Paul. *I* understand,' Ruth comforted in her best Claire Rayner voice. Paul smiled, pulled Ruth to him and kissed her. Ruth put up the briefest token protest. Was I more jealous of her or of him? Whatever, I was the quintessential spare prick at a party for the twenty seconds the kiss took. Ruth disengaged with a wry look on her face.

'You are a *very* naughty boy,' she said, 'taking me by surprise like that.'

'Sorry,' Paul said winsomely. If I didn't shag him first, I'd rip his throat out.

Feeling better, Paul asked Ruth when she wanted to do her routine.

'Routine?' I said. 'What routine?'

'In about fifteen minutes. You'll see,' said Ruth and made eyes at me from behind her blue wrap. She looked so alive. I told her so. Paul glanced at Ruth fondly as I said student life must suit her. Ruth beamed.

'It's like I started again, Simon. I'm back on track and I know I can do or be anything I want. I've got my potential back.'

'Sky's the limit,' I said, smiling at her smiling.

She corrected me. 'No limits, Simon. You can't give

yourself limits.' She looked at me as if I should understand. What did she mean?

'Go Ricki, go Ricki,' Paul said drily.

'Shut up, Paul, you don't understand yet,' said Ruth.

'I think I probably could try,' he retorted, 'but I could always just crawl back into my playpen.' They shared a private look, locking me out of the moment.

'I'm exactly where I should be,' Ruth stated. 'With the people I should be with and doing what I have to do.' And she touched the end of Paul's nose. *She touched the end of Paul's nose.* It went pink as she took the white make-up off it. I felt so jealous. Ruth must have ESP'd something because she touched the tip of my nose too, just a beat too late for it to be properly genuine. I said I was glad for her, to let her know I didn't mind not being one of the people she thought she should be with. I lied. I minded a lot. The three of us were being so surface-gorgeous to each other but I was aching for Ruth now. Teaspoon Limpet Person was resenting my being there at all, and Ruth, well, what *was* Ruth thinking?

Now, Simon, now.

'Can we go somewhere quieter?' I shouted in Ruth's ear as some bright spark turned the music up even louder. I felt like such an old fart.

Paul scoffed, 'Aren't you having fun?'

'No, it's *great*,' I shrieked at him with as much sincerity as I could. I was quite rude and turned so that I excluded him from the conversation. Being a well-brought-up boy, Paul backed off with a bemused but indifferent expression and went to get another drink. I was no competition, it seemed, and could be left alone with Ruth. If he thought that, it was fine with me. Ruth pulled me out into the hallway. It was about two decibels quieter there.

Deep breaths, deep breaths.

'It's just that I've got to say something to you and it can't wait.'

A flutter of concern went across Ruth's face.

'What? There's nothing wrong, is there?' she asked, drawing nearer.

'Everything's fine.' I had to speak much louder than I wanted to. 'I've got some news. I've gone straight.' *So subtle, Si, such nuance.*

Genuine surprise is a great emotion to watch. No airs and graces, no sophistication, no seen-it, done-it. Just good old-fashioned 'What the fuck?' making the eyes bulge slightly.

'And I came up here . . .' I tried to continue but Paul returned with another Virgin Mary in tow, who said that Ruth was needed to get ready for the routine. Ruth hurried off with her, looking back at me with an extraordinary look on her face. 'We'll talk,' she mouthed to me.

Paul watched her huddle with her fellow conspirators in a hush-hush manner. He got another can for himself and handed one to me. We locked eyes for a second, nothing to say.

Paul said, 'She's wonderful, isn't she?' I dinked my shoulders, it went without saying. He asked, 'How long have you known her?'

'Three years or so. She worked for me.'

'Right, right. In the travel agency.' There was the slightest trace of condescension. 'This routine was all her idea, you know. You're gay, yeah?'

He did not know me half well enough to ask that. I was polite.

'What's in a name, Paul? To be honest I don't know

any more. No limits, like the lady said.' Then I made a
mistake. 'I know I'm in love with Ruth. What does that
make me?'

Paul looked slightly fazed.

'It probably makes you very sensible, matey,' he
answered, thinking fast. Another Virgin Mary pulled him
away and said he had to introduce the act, being the host.

It took a while for the whole party to make its way to
the back garden, where a floodlit area marked out a little
stage on which were five tables laden with props and costumes. Some of the guests ran upstairs to get a better view
out of the back bedroom windows. I saw Paul to one side
talking with Ruth, who looked round sharply trying to see
someone in the crowd. I should not have said anything to
him. Was she looking for me? I went on Red Alert, my
paranoia making me think ten steps ahead to the very
worst case scenarios.

Paul stepped forward, his outfit a little crushed by now.
A few wolf-whistles greeted his attempts to gain silence.
He grinned at someone in the crowd and bobbed a curt-
sey. He seemed like a very lovely man and I was not
surprised Ruth was good friends with him. I began curs-
ing myself for coming at all, trying to compete with the
likes of Paul. *She must be thinking I'm barking mad.*

Paul introduced the routine in a cod American accent,
Las Vegas meets Radley.

'Lay-deeeez an' jennulmennnn, Lovin' Spoonful
Productions is veh', veh', *veh*' proud to present "The
Immaculate Virgins"! I *thang* you . . .'

The five Virgin Marys trooped out to wild applause
and not a little ironic laughter. They waited in a pious
freeze for a playback to start, perfectly still, their breath
curling upwards in the cold night air. Ruth knelt in the

front of the group, her hands reaching up to God. An eighties medley boomed out from an amp, 'Like a Virgin' first, of course. Throughout the complicated routine, the five Virgins metamorphosed from character to character, lip-synching brilliantly. They must have been rehearsing for ages. Each costume change, invariably taking something *off*, of course, was greeted with a cheer by the audience. They changed from Virgin Mary to Madonna, to the Spice Girls to Margaret Thatcher to Princess Diana and then, incredibly, to Jesus complete with beards, before finishing as little devils with red basques, fishnet tights, toasting forks and pointy tails. As Ruth completed her change into Diana she caught my eye in the crowd and looked at me with her eyes downcast, just like the princess used to do. Whirling away, she blew Paul a kiss as she stuck the Jesus beard on. I shot a glance in his direction but looked away as he looked at me. Ruth was really good and by far the best performer out of the five. She was so damn sexy. I cursed myself for not facing up to what I had been thinking about her way before this. The sexy little devils hit their final pose and basked in the adoration of their peers, who were going crazy now. The crowd invaded the stage area and the Immaculates were left in no doubt of their success.

Eventually, Ruth pushed her way through to me, a Playboy vision of Hell. I did some 'we are not worthy' acting. I was feeling very sick. I like to feel that a situation is under control and this was not. I had no idea what Ruth was thinking. Some music started thumping out again.

'I told you, Simon,' she said, collapsing on the grass with me as the party went up a gear around us. We sprawled on the ground in our own little world, with people standing all around us. She stretched out, resting her head on my legs, looking up at me. The last time I had been sitting with someone like this, I had been lying with my head in Toril's lap, Toril running her hands through my hair. I banished Toril from my mind, lovely as she is; I had more immediate priorities.

Ruth was still talking, '. . . I told you, I can do anything now. I couldn't have done that a year ago.'

'You could.'

Maybe Paul hadn't told her what I'd said. Maybe he had.

'I'd have wanted to do it,' said Ruth. 'Not the same thing at all. There's no point just wanting something, you've got to make it happen.' She prodded me playfully with her toasting fork.

'This isn't a rehearsal, is it?'

'Damn right, Simon. Will you answer a question if I ask it?' she said. I nodded, my heart thumping hard enough to break my ribs. She played with the ends of her toasting fork. 'Do you want to kiss me?'

She said it in a 'So how's your day been?' tone. She was so full of herself now. Like the old Ruth but so much more. And this Ruth-who-could-do-anything was infinitely preferable to that imaginary Ruth-in-my-head. The situation was perfect as well: I don't think she would have asked me that question if she had not just done that dance routine and was feeling great about herself. I certainly would not have been able to answer so easily if the situation had not been so crazy, if I had not been dressed as a vicar, if she were not now a little devil with a beard and toasting fork. Real life had just left the building and we could talk behind its back. I love parties. It all happens, doesn't it?

Then Ruth changed her mind, sitting up as she said, 'No. Let's make it a harder question: *Why* do you want to kiss me, Simon?'

Tell the truth.

'Because I haven't stopped thinking about you since you left.'

Ruth blinked at this. 'Something big happened, didn't it?' she said.

'Yeah. Something . . . happened that made me rethink . . . things. That made me see you differently.' My voice died in my throat. I'm no good at talking about myself.

'Will you tell me it all later?' *We had a later . . .*

'Yeah.'

There was a world of trust in that one word. I would tell her about Patrick and what had happened and it would be fine. It had been a while since I had trusted anyone enough to talk like this without paying them a lot of money for the privilege and stumbling out into a waiting room afterwards. Like Ruth had said, right place, right time, with the right person. Ruth was looking at me very closely. She sat up and murmured, 'Well, it just goes to show.'

'What?'

'God knows.'

'Do you want to kiss *me*?' I asked.

Ruth kept staring at me, clearly thinking very fast and very hard. Just like Paul had. Students obviously thought in a different way to my day. It was quite unnerving. I had a hunch that Ruth was weighing up the very small pros of kissing me against the vast cons.

'What if I don't want to kiss you?' she asked back. Seriously. My heart went into my boots.

'I'll cry,' I said, adding with a flip glint, 'and you'll miss out and it will be your own silly fault. Don't say I didn't warn you.'

'But we'd still be friends if I didn't?' she insisted.

'After my therapy has been completed, the scars have healed and I've come off the medication.'

'Has it been horrible?' Ruth asked, reaching forward and stroking my cheek. It felt great.

'No. Not at all. It's been fine.' I paused, pushing myself against her hand. 'I'm hoping it's about to get better.'

Shaking her head in disbelief, she put her arms around my neck. I was about to kiss her when I realised that something was really wrong.

'Beard.'

'What are you talking about?' The music suddenly got louder again.

'Beard!' I shouted at her.

I gently peeled off the beard that she still had on a part of her devil costume. We both started laughing. A very Ruth and Simon moment. Ruth and Simon. It had a ring to it.

'Ouch.' The glue was quite strong.

On a normal night I quite liked beards but this was an extraordinary night. This moment had to be perfect. Proper. We stopped laughing. Looking carefully into each other's eyes all the while for the slightest trace of doubt, our lips met.

Heaven.

Chapter 8

'. . . a little star-dust caught . . .'
Thoreau

We kissed . . . It was quite similar to kissing men. I was tongue-tied. I wondered if all women's mouths were smaller than men's mouths . . . or if Ruth just had a small mouth . . . her tongue was quite pointed . . . her long hair kept getting in the way . . . is that why lesbians have buzz cuts? Double amounts of long hair would be a problem . . . I shifted position to compensate . . . I could not quite decide if I liked her hair or not. I played with it, grabbed handfuls of it as I kissed her, like I'd seen in the movies, and decided there was potential . . . The party roared on around us . . .

I remembered a pot-boiler novel I had borrowed from my grandmother when I was about fourteen. A man pays for a hooker to pile her long, dark hair up on her head with lots of kirby grips. Then she goes down on him. He's holding her head and feeling for the grips as he nears climax then pulls them out as he comes so that her tresses tumble down as the earth moves for him . . .

So long hair had potential and Ruth's had always been

very beautiful. I remember noticing some split ends. Such a heterosexual thing to notice, I don't think. One step at a time, I guess. Maybe one of those hot-wax treatments would be good . . .

I was very aware that she smelled differently to men I had slept with. *Would she hate me for having slept with more men than she had? Why was she doing this?* She had a deeper scent than a man, which was heavy and stifling. A closed and finite smell that I dimly recalled from my VI Form escapades with one Catherine Cartwright. I had not thought of her in a while . . . twelve years and a small battalion of men later, I'm still fumbling like a dyslexic virgin. Everything changes but everything stays the same. I suddenly understood this. This musk was particular and exclusive, containing something unfathomable and irrational (it was probably the spirit gum from the beard, but let it stand that this is what I thought at the time). I found it terrifying and approachable, like a red carpet that leads to the north face of the Eiger: if I'm going up there I'm going to need equipment, I thought. I had brought condoms, hadn't I? Maybe Ruth had some. Would we go that far on a first night? Do heterosexuals go all the way on a first night? Do Popes shit in the woods? Was Ruth going to sleep with me at all? I might be jumping the gun here. Was it all a joke? If it was, I'd have to pretend to be really pissed. I'd pretend to faint, I decided. Heck, I might even faint for real.

I was letting her lead, her tongue twirling mine round and round. Something made me pull back; it was Paul, not best pleased. He melted back into the crowd. I can honestly say I did not give two hoots. Ruth pulled me back and I put my hands round her waist and worked my fingers between the fasteners in the basque. I was fine with basques because I'd worn one once to a party. She adjusted her position and stretched to give me more room. This was no prank . . .

I started thinking about how I felt about her having had babies. Did I find her:

a)   as attractive
b)   more attractive
c)   less attractive, or
d)   none of the above.

It was a fact that I had never caressed in this way a woman who had given birth. I had hugged female relatives of course but usually as a ruse to stop them asking me if I was courting. 'Courting disaster at the moment, Auntie Carole, thank you for asking.' What the fuck was I doing?

My mind turned into a TV screen of static. It is time for me to close down now and call a cab. All rise for the National Anthem. God save this queen. Elvis Presley trivia floated unbidden and unwanted into my head. He hated women who had given birth, found them physically repulsive (what did stretch-marks look like? I'd never seen any). Instead, the King liked girls in white knickers with their pubic hair curling coyly around the gusset. Gusset is *such* a great word. Leonardo DiCaprio first came to prominence playing Johnny Depp's backward brother in *What's Eating Gilbert Grape?*, for which he received an Oscar nomination for Best Supporting Actor. Why, why, why did I think that? I'm going crazy. I'm in an asylum. Find the connection . . .

Elvis to *King of Rock* to *King of the Jungle* to *Lion* to *Leo* or alternatively *Courting* to *Courting Disaster* to *Titanic* to

Leonardo. I'm not insane, just excited. Good. The other ninety per cent of my brain and my body certainly did not find Ruth repulsive. I would have made love to her (and it would have been making love, even then) on the grass in the back garden of Paul's house if not for the eighty or so of Ruth's friends in the garden with us. Had they all been complete strangers to Ruth as well, it might have been a little easier. I have always been able to lose inhibitions in front of strangers and now that I was behaving like a stranger to myself I was heading into uncharted territory. Yes, there had been Catherine in the Lower VI but that was in another country and, alas, the wench is a lawyer now. For this journey, I needed new maps. I explored. I felt I could do anything . . .

In truth, I found it slightly unbelievable that babies had come from so small a place as Ruth's body, that this narrow waist had once had to expand to make way for new and growing lives. Incredible and exciting. Her skin was pale, like moonlight or pearls. I understood all those references to porcelain skin now. It was a moment of breakthrough and an understanding of a completely different eroticism. I liked hairy men, for Christ's sake. Apparently, I now liked porcelain moonlight women . . .

I started laughing at myself in my head. It seemed easier than letting genuine thoughts slip by unchecked. Being too self-aware is sometimes the only way to get through a moment like that.

Post-modern-retro-kissing. I had seen too many movies (not *quite* this situation) not to know all the angles on this scene. I was ten steps ahead of myself and heading into a divorce court and it was only the first kiss. This would never work. Was it worth going round the loop just to find that out? I had no fucking idea what to do next. I must stop swearing if I'm going to be around lay-deez and not jennullmen. I think I'm in love.

All in the first sixty seconds of kissing a woman since my late teens.

Chapter 9

'. . . She my mind hath so displac'd
That I shall never find my home'
Andrew Marvell

What a *great* party. Students are fantastic.

After Ruth and I had stopped kissing (the more accurate word would be snogging and I was listening to the Human League the last time I said that), Ruth pulled me up and we danced and danced and danced. Thank God I'd done all those sit-ups. A bottle of vodka appeared; students either had lots more money these days or they were prioritising a lot better than I ever did. On an emptyish stomach, I was one arseholed vicar within a short space of time. By which I mean I got very drunk, just to be clear, rather than immediately reverting to old habits. Too drunk, in fact. By about four o'clock that morning, I was barely standing but still bopping away and using Ruth as a crutch rather than the object of my affections. It was as if having said I wanted her and then having had a bit of a kiss and a cuddle, that was enough for now. A principle had been established.

A fleet of cabs was turning up at the house and hovering

like flies around a dead dog. One of them was for me and Ruth apparently. She was pissed but organised. We (plural! note the plural!) piled into a cab having said a brief farewell to Paul, now only in his black bodystocking. He had found another little devil in fishnets (they came along every five minutes at that party) and seemed happy enough under the circumstances, if a little grumpy. Ruth promised she'd ring him the next day. In the cab, we hung on to each other like lifebelts, hoping to remain conscious until we got back to Ruth's. This was not quite what I'd had in mind on the journey up but it was fun.

It took a long time to get to Ruth's, which was on the other side of the city. We drew up outside a very big house. I handed the cab driver what I thought was a tenner and made what I thought was a polite request for a receipt (as you can tell, Ruth and I were consumed with passion), but what I said could not have contained enough consonants. The cabbie looked at what had to have been a twenty I figured out later, looked back up at me, narrowed his eyes, said thank you very much and then went into warp drive before I could raise an objection. I was suddenly bereft, like when the train you've just got off leaves you on an empty platform. A pissed Ruth was next to me doing a Laurel and Hardy routine with a dropped set of keys. I looked down at her scrabbling around on the ground, cackling madly to herself. If I was wrong about all this then I was fucking up bigtime. I looked at the stars and thought that this would be a good time for lightning to strike. No decisions, no worries, only questions that never got answers and a sad loss to the travel business.

'There's no lightning. What are you going on about?' slurred Ruth. I had been thinking out loud. Insane wanker.

We trudged up the gravel drive. Leafy and affluent suburbia surrounded us: every house had two cars, front gardens with all the natural spontaneity of Trooping the Colour and curtains that twitched so much they had been diagnosed with Parkinson's.

The wind whispered in the trees: '*Go on, my son, get stuck in, all this can be yours one day if you are a good lad and do the deed, do the deed, do the deed . . .*' Even the breeze was straight around here, it seemed. However, I had drunk a lot of Smirnoff so my suburban destiny was going to have to wait. I really hoped that Ruth was not expecting anything from me once we got in since no oak trees were about to grow from this acorn tonight.

Ruth eventually got the key in the lock (you always miss the first time) and stood in the open doorway like a diabolical Mae West, jiggling grotesquely.

'Come on inside, you dangerous heterosexual,' she purred, admirably keeping a straight face.

'By the 'eck, chuck, y' gorgeous.' When in Manchester, woo like a Mancunian.

'You are so smooth. I bet you say that to all the girls.'

'No, just one.'

Ruth pondered this, looking at me. I hoped this was not the start of the 'big chat'. I was in no condition for it. It was not the time and me freezing my crucifix off outside the front door was not the place.

'I bet you say that to all the *boys* then.'

'Have said it, but not lately, and I'm not planning to at the moment.'

I could feel my eyes take on a don't-push-it glint. This was the point we could have had the huge talk. Perhaps we should have done. Ruth decided against.

'Your vicar's costume's ruined.'

I looked down at myself. Grass stains, mud, booze, food and a mystery substance. If there had been blackcurrant, I could have made a soap-powder advert.

'So it is.' I looked back up at her. We could move on. 'Can I come in now? I'm cold and I think I'm sobering up.'

'We don't want that, we might have to talk about something serious.' A little warning shot across my bows in return.

I stepped into the hall of Ruth's mother's house. Middle-class seventies chic (the kind that is *never* coming back) wrapped itself around me and tried to strangle me again. Beige, eggshell, chocolate, magnolia, mocha: the house was an orgy of *brown*. I had left somewhere a long time ago that looked very similar.

'You look a bit green,' Ruth said. *Oh no, did I clash?* 'Do you want to throw up?'

'I've gone straight, not bulimic.'

'*Bolshie* heterosexual.'

I tried to kiss her again because I thought I should. It wasn't genuine so the timing was all wrong. She wriggled free.

'We've plenty of time for all that.' Not tonight, Napoleon, in other words. *Fantastic.* 'You'll stay the weekend, won't you?'

'I'll think about it,' I said, playing mock hard-to-get.

'It's a good job I know you. Do you want a cup of tea? Or some water?'

'Ooo lovely,' I said, then realised it probably was not the straightest way in the world to accept a beverage. Old ladies make that sort of comment just before eating a cream cake: *Ooo lovely*. Would I have to be butch now? Even kick a ball about in the garden with Ruth's feminist daughters? I slumped on the stairs, the picture of a sexually unaroused clergyman.

'I am fucked.'

'Or not,' Ruth said, her laughter receding down the hall as she went into the kitchen.

'I'll loves ya tomorrow!' I shouted after her.

'I don't think heterosexuals quote musicals,' came the disembodied reply.

'Sorry.' *They did now.* 'Perhaps I could start a trend.'

'You could try.'

I wandered down the hall and found a knackered devil in laddered fishnets putting teabags in mugs. I took a glass down from a shelf and crossed to the sink to get some water. Ruth looked at me and yelped.

'Eek. Not that glass. It's Mother's best. Have one of these,' she said, passing me a plastic beaker that said 'Hannah'.

'Sorry. Like that with your mum, is it? Little boxes for pieces of string too short to be tied?'

'Ohhh yes. You've never met Mother, have you. A treat in store. Big tip – don't put the butter knife in the jam. There's no telling what might happen.'

'She sounds great.'

'She *is* great. I couldn't be doing the degree without her.'

'"Y' need a wife when you're a mother",' I quoted in my best *Coronation Street* accent.

'Too right. *Oh*, my head. I think I'm sobering up too.' She crossed to a cupboard and found some painkillers. As she handed me two, she smiled and kissed me on the cheek before going back to the kettle and making the tea.

I suddenly twigged what she was doing. We could just as easily have gone into Rhett and Scarlett mode but she had chosen not to. She was letting me sleep on it. She'd asked me to stay longer but she was giving me the chance to run away just in case I'd been shooting my mouth off. What a gal. It must mean she was still thinking seriously about what had happened. *Golly*.

We took our mugs of tea up to Ruth's room, which evidently doubled as her study. Books, notes and laundry festooned it. I was ecstatic it was so untidy. Her Brighton flat had always been pretty tidy but that was more to do with it having been quite small and two small children having a lot of toys. Prior to Ruth, more relationships of mine had broken up over The Tidy Thing than I care to mention. With me the washing-up gets done, but not five minutes after I've finished eating. Fairy Liquid is not a chic *digestif* in the circles in which I move. I have a punctuality fetish but I've never been a tidy-freak. However, I usually attracted them, the kind who said, 'I've had a good old clear-out', and then had houses that looked burgled rather than spring-cleaned. They dive for Kleenex *while* you ejaculate.

Ruth did not even bother to apologise for the mess. Marvellous. Things were looking up, or at least they would be able to when the vodka and the headache wore off. We crashed out on the bed and talked about anything but the topic *du jour*. I have never felt less sexy in my life but I loved being with her again. Just us, no students, no Paul, no kids – just us, chatting about naff all, knackered, pissed and giggly, with Ruth snuggled into my shoulder. After a little while, she slipped out to the bathroom and, while she was gone, I took off the vicar's gear and slipped under the covers.

I heard some birds start to sing outside and drifted off into that halfway house between being awake and being properly asleep. I had a dream about milk floats and demons. The demons wanted to drive but the milk floats could not get up the hill and probably would not have gone fast enough for the devils anyway. Crates of vodka clinked disconsolately as the milk floats revved in vain. Whatever would it all have meant? Just when you want your subconscious to be profound, you let yourself down.

I came groggily back to consciousness as Ruth tiptoed back into the room, dressed in a baggy T-shirt with all her make-up taken off. No more pretend, just Simon and Ruth after the ball was over, a little bit shy and very tired, wondering what to do next. Ruth knew.

'Errol Flynn to Kevin Costner. Connect the Robin Hoods,' she said, playing our cinema buff game again, joining our past friendship to this present moment. Clever woman.

'O-K,' I said, waking up again with effort and jutting out my lower lip to consider the task. 'Difficult one, Ruth.'

'I think you'll be fine.'

'Are you sure?'

'Practically positive.' I *think* we were still talking about the game. She slipped under the covers. What could have been a massive moment just happened, it passed. We were not lovers yet but we had made the decision that we probably would be. Tomorrow. Or the next day. I barely registered the moment as I strained for connections.

'Right. Errol Flynn was in *Robin Hood* in the thirties and was also in *Captain Blood* with Olivia de Havilland, who co-starred in *Gone With the Wind* with Vivien Leigh, who was the lead in *Lady Hamilton* with Laurence Olivier, who was in *Sleuth* with Michael Caine . . .'

'Oh, well done,' Ruth breathed as I leapt into the modern cinematic era. I could tell she was impressed.

'Thank you . . . and he's coming round the final bend, it's a gold medal for Great Britain, Michael Caine was in *The Man Who Would Be King* with Sir Sean Connery, who won an Oscar for *The Untouchables* starring Mr Kevin Costner, who was in *Robin Hood: Prince of Thieves*. And another one bites the dust, no flowers please, donations to Mensa.'

'Not bad, you clever old heterosexual.'

'Less of the old.'

It was strangely sweet and chaste behaviour from the both of us. We played the game for another couple of rounds each, getting worse and worse at it. Ruth fell asleep first. I heard her breathing even out.

It felt so right, it was odd.

Chapter 10

'Provided one has plenty of bread, butter, milk and eggs, there is no need for much else except for variety'
Walter J. C. Murray

'You smell funny, Simon. Get up. It's two o'clock in the afternoon.'

I woke up thinking I was having a heart attack and had gone snow-blind. Instead I had an eight-year-old on my chest and a piece of A4 taped to my forehead, covering my eyes. The paper was ripped off and held up for me to read. 'I've gone to fetch Hannah and Sarah from tap-dance class. Sleep as long as you want', it said. I had entered the Twilight Zone and had lost my memory for a decade: it seemed I was married with children. What time was the PTA meeting? The paper was screwed up and thrown away. A gap-toothed little girl slapped me round the face. Was there no respect any more?

'Hannah,' I said, uncomfortably aware that I had my getting-up hard-on and that Hannah was sitting on top of me very near to it. For the first time in my life I was thankful that my penis is not unfeasibly large, otherwise Hannah would have been even closer to it. If you see what I mean.

'Hull-oooo. You've woken up. I thought you were dead,' she said, pressing her nose right up to mine, enjoying having an adult in her power. 'Pooh. You have stinky breath.'

'Do I?' I said and exhaled in her face to get her off me. It was the first time I had been glad to have halitosis. It was going to be a day of firsts, I could tell. Hannah scrambled off me, coughing.

Hannah was quite right, as always. I stank of beer, mud, farts, sweat and for all I knew snails and puppy dogs' tails. Somebody had left something awful and gelatinous on my tongue. Spit or swallow? As always, I swallowed. Hannah was looking at me with unease.

'Are you all right? Should I get Mummy?'

'No, no need. I'm fine. Just waking up,' I said quickly. Ruth was *not* going to see me like this.

'Why are you in Mummy's bed?' I coughed at Hannah's question then belched, bringing up a little bile. It was like battery acid on the way back down. Hannah watched intently again as my face screwed up in pain. I realised she was waiting for an answer.

'Why am I in this bed? Well, we fell asleep talking last night after the party.'

No word of a lie there, big old *satiable* stud that I am.

'Paul's party?'

'Yes.'

'Do you like Paul?'

'Yes, I do.'

'Did he dress up as a teaspoon? He said he would.'

'Yes, he did.'

'I like Paul a lot.'

'Everybody does.' *Snarl.*

'He always has lovely breath. Minty-fresh.'

'Not today, Hannah. Call me psychic.'

Hannah looked unconvinced. Her brow darkened.

'So why are you in Mummy's bedroom at all?' she said, continuing her in-depth study of adult behaviour. 'I thought you wanted a boyfriend. Sarah thinks you want a boyfriend even more than Mummy does.'

I was not at all sure I wanted to know that Ruth was desperate for a boyfriend. I had a coughing fit that lasted a while. This was far too difficult.

'We were just talking and we were a little squiffy, to tell you the truth.' Hannah looked blank. I explained myself. 'A bit too much to drink, Hannah.'

'Oh, I *see*,' said Hannah, nodding her head as if that was what she had suspected all along. These adults are crazy, you could see her thinking. She started practising a tap step, humming to herself. Thankfully the room was carpeted.

I swung my legs out of bed and groaned as the full force of my hangover hit me. Thank God I had taken those painkillers; I'd have been in Intensive Care if not. Money saved for the NHS. Hurrah. However, there was no cause for celebration in the fact that my morning stiffie was going nowhere fast.

I hate my morning stiffie. It's rubbish. Nothing to do with being turned on at all. If I had a pound for every morning I've stood in front of a loo trying to slap down a meaninglessly rigid penis so I can urinate, I'd have about £5,840 plus change for leap years. My immediate problem was that my boxers were visibly tenting into a turgid wigwam. Before Hannah could glimpse anything, I grabbed a pillow and holding it in front of myself, I walked to the door. The dancing stopped.

'You've got a hairy chest,' came a little voice.

'There's no fooling you, is there?' I turned in the doorway. 'Where's the bathroom?'

'We've got two,' bragged Hannah. 'One's just next door.
It's funny you've got a hairy chest.'

'Why?'

'Because I didn't think you were allowed to have one.'

'Why?' I had an idea where this was going.

'Because you want a boyfriend.'

'And men who want boyfriends can't have hairy
chests?'

Hannah pursed her lips in concentration.

'It's just that Daddy doesn't want a boyfriend and he is
really hairy, much hairier than you, Simon, and he used to
like Mummy and now he likes Michelle.'

So, Daddy liked someone called Michelle now. How
truly *fantastic*. Good old Michelle.

'I don't think the two are connected, Hannah. People
with hairy chests can want boyfriends. It's allowed.' I took
a deep breath. 'Sometimes people change, though, and
people with hairy chests who wanted boyfriends *before*
want girlfriends *now*.'

'So Daddy wanted boyfriends before he met Mummy?'
Saints preserve us. Move fast, move fast.

'No, no, *no*, no, no. Your daddy's *always* wanted girlfriends. I think so, anyway.'

'Have you met him then?'

'No, but I've heard lots about him.'

Hannah subsided, not sure what to say next.

That all went well . . .

Hannah stared very hard at my chest, then looked with
curiosity at the pillow covering my erection. I decided to
escape before she asked me any more difficult questions,
and headed into the hallway.

I ducked back into the bedroom straight away. Hannah had not moved, still perplexed.

'Your grandma isn't in, is she?' Semi-naked, smelly, unshaven and hungover with a hard-on would be no way to meet Ruth's mother for the first time.

'She's back from Uncle Pete's this evening.'

I dived quickly into the hallway, turned left, opened up an airing cupboard, then doubled back to the right and locked myself in the bathroom. An avocado suite; what a surprise. An ageing mildewed shower curtain; what a shock. I heard footsteps. There was a knock on the door.

'Go *away*, Hannah,' I wailed. Another knock. I opened the door a crack. It was Ruth. She was holding out a towel, with Hannah laboriously doing a timestep in the background. We locked eyes. Had either of us changed our mind? I hadn't.

'Have a bath, stinky,' Ruth said. 'There's plenty of hot water.'

'Oh. Hi.'

'Hi. And you are.'

'I am what?'

'High.'

'Oh.' I took the towel from Ruth and gave her a goofy grin, hoping that goofy might be sexy. The grin subsided as Ruth said nothing but suddenly looked near to tears and on the verge of saying something. We both started to speak. She moved towards me and stopped herself. My breath caught in my throat just like on that night months ago when she spilled the wine on herself. I could not hear anything. I could only see Ruth. She has such beautiful brown eyes. We had ourselves a little moment and nearly kissed, but I pulled back because Hannah was there and I had halitosis. Ruth looked hurt for a split second then masked it. I nodded towards the mini Bonnie Langford on the landing.

'Hannah's there.'

'She's busy.'

'OK.' Our eyes locked. No going back. I leaned through the door, the pillow falling to the floor. We kissed lingeringly and Ruth reached round the door and brushed her hand against my wigwam. For the first time in my life I was glad of my morning hard-on. I was shaking, Ruth was shaking and Hannah was being Ginger Rogers in front of a full-length mirror.

'Oh boy,' I said. 'Bathtime.'

'Bathtime. Brunch in twenty minutes.'

'OK. This is different in the daylight, huh?'

'It's better.'

'Oh yeah.'

'There's toothpaste.'

'Bad breath?'

'Yeah.'

'Thanks.'

I shut the door again. I could hear Ruth breathing on the other side of the door. Hannah stopped dancing and I heard her ask Ruth if she was all right. Ruth said something in reply that I could not quite hear. The taps on Hannah's shoes clattered down the wooden landing and became duller thuds as she and Ruth went down the carpeted stairs.

I bathed quickly but thoroughly as only men know how to do. This was not a day for long soaks in the tub. I even found more painkillers in the bathroom cabinet. Dripping my way back into Ruth's bedroom, I found that my bag had miraculously reappeared. God knows how it made it back from the party. Smelling like a fruit salad from all Ruth's Body Shop produce, I put on jeans and a T-shirt.

It's strange to say this but I would have dressed more smartly and made more of an effort if I had still been calling myself gay and had just come up to see my old friend Ruth. As it was, old faded jeans and a big T-shirt: just as contrived an outfit as the vicar's outfit had been the previous night.

I padded barefoot downstairs to the kitchen. The girls were tap-dancing still. I vowed never to show them a trumpet. Sarah, whom I had not seen yet, ran up to me and hugged me hello. She looked more solemn than I remembered. Ruth looked at my pristine condition with approval. She was sitting at a long refectory-style table and reading what I assumed and hoped was her mother's *Daily Telegraph*. She seemed very poised and in control but if she was feeling a quarter of what I was, then she was anything but.

'Morning all,' I said and crossed round the table to say hello to Ruth. 'All clean and fresh now.'

'Good job,' puffed Hannah, concentrating on her step-ball change.

I stood behind Ruth and put my hands lightly on her shoulders. Without words and not looking at her, I tried to tell her that everything was going to be fine. She arched her neck slightly as I touched her, perhaps from annoyance. I could not imagine what she was thinking. We had to be alone again to talk everything through and go to bed together. Should we talk first? Was that a really bad idea? Talk, *then* make love or vice versa and vice first? I could not decide which was better.

'Orange juice?' Ruth asked, rising suddenly. 'Be careful where you're standing, Simon. I broke a glass earlier.'

'One of Nanna's best ones?' asked Sarah in mid-step.

'No. Another one. It was just where you are standing, Simon. Hold still.'

She dropped to her knees by my feet and her long hair brushed my toes as she mimed picking up an invisible piece of glass.

'While you're down there . . .' I murmured, so that the girls would not hear.

'I think I've found a piece,' Ruth said, resting her forehead against my crotch, her hand up my left trouser leg trying to pull a hair out of my calf. My heartbeat was going through the roof.

'A piece of glass?' I gasped as she succeeded in removing a hair. I knelt by her to help look for non-existent shards of tumbler.

'A piece of glass,' Ruth confirmed loudly, handing me my plucked hair. Dropping to a whisper, she hissed, 'Here's the plan: you go to a hotel, I join you this evening.'

'It's inspired. It's brilliant. *It will work*,' I replied in a B-movie way and we both stood up quickly, looking like meerkats on sentry duty. All clear, the girls were still dancing.

'Oh no, there's more glass on the floor,' I intoned solemnly.

'No, there's not, you're imagining it,' Ruth answered with finality and a warning glare, and went to the fridge to get me that orange juice.

'Spoilsport,' I said, just a little too loudly. The girls stopped tapping.

'Why is Mummy a spoilsport?' asked Sarah.

I floundered. 'What? Oh, nothing, just something that happened last night.'

'What happened at the party? Was it funny?' questioned Hannah.

'Nothing happened at the party, Hannah,' said Ruth, testing some sausages under the grill. 'Simon's just being silly.' She added meaningfully, 'Absolutely *nothing* happened at *all*. Anyway, I think we're ready to eat now. Up the table, you two.'

We served up the food. I sat at one end of the long table and Ruth at the other, too far away to play footsie. The girls sat between us, chattering about how they wanted to redecorate their bedroom. Ruth and her mother were obviously working hard to settle them into Manchester. I asked them about what they were reading, who the latest teeny-bopper heart-throbs were. Both of them stared at me in pity as I uttered the phrase 'teeny-bopper heart-throb'. I avoided talking about school in case it was proving difficult for them.

A second, wordless conversation was happening with Ruth at the same time. I was still here with Ruth, I had not made my excuses and run away. My presence was the answer to her justifiable caution and unspoken question of the night before, 'Are you serious? Is this for real?' For me to tell her properly, we had to be alone again. Sarah unknowingly arranged the details of Ruth and mine's first night together, asking carefully, 'Are you staying the whole weekend?'

'Until really early on Monday morning, then I've got to try and get back home in time to open up.'

'Ouch,' said Ruth, grimacing at the prospect of my early start. To my surprise, Sarah's face had fallen at the news I would stay. Why didn't she want me here?

'Are you staying with us then? In Mummy's bed again?' said Hannah, looking instinctively at Ruth. Sarah looked down at her plate when she heard I had slept in Ruth's bed. I was starting to upset an already unhappy little girl.

'No, there's not enough room,' I said. 'I'll only get in your granny's way.'

The girls did not disagree. Granny was obviously quite a piece of work.

'Don't call her "Granny". It makes her feel old,' Sarah said with sudden vehemence. Ruth stretched out a hand and stroked Sarah's arm.

'I'd call her Mrs Whittaker to her face anyway, Sarah. How's that? *And* I'll move into a hotel this afternoon just as soon as I've found a free room somewhere. When is your *very young* nanna back?'

'About six fifteen,' said Ruth. 'I've booked you into the Thistle already. Is that all right? It's handy for the station.'

'That's great, thanks.' When had she booked me the hotel?

'And a friend of yours rang to say they can meet you tonight.'

'Did they? Who—' I said in surprise. Ruth rolled her eyes. 'Oh. *That* friend.'

'Who is your friend?' asked Sarah, her dismay at my presence all weekend lifting at the thought of my absence this evening. What was the matter with her? She seemed far too serious for just eleven or whatever she was now.

'A very *old* friend,' I said.

'They didn't sound old,' said Ruth, with an edge in her voice. 'They sounded rather lovely.'

'Is it your boyfriend?' asked Hannah.

'No.'

'Just a friend?' Sarah said, disappointed.

'Not quite,' I replied, confusing the girls completely. 'We've lots to catch up on.'

'They said seven o'clock on the phone,' Ruth interjected.

'Seven?'

'Seven.'

'Really?'

'Really. They're getting someone in to cover for them from about a quarter past six.'

We were almost giving ourselves away now, our subterfuge swiftly turning into a music-hall routine. Hannah and Sarah were like a Centre Court crowd as Ruth and I twinkled at each other across the table. We finished our brunches and the girls went into the TV room to watch a video.

Ruth and I seized our opportunity and had a little clinch there in the kitchen. She ran to the door and peered out into the hallway to see exactly what the girls were doing. Closing the door gently, she ran back, pulling me into an old-fashioned walk-in larder and shutting us both in. The afternoon light shone through a small stained-glass diamond-pattern window in the wall, dappling us in scarlets and greens. There was just about enough room for one person to put away or fetch down food so it was intimate, to say the least, with two people jammed in by spaghetti hoops, onions in bags hanging from hooks and cling peaches in heavy syrup.

I felt fifteen years old again instead of double that. After all those men, I was now positively virginal. As if to prove the point, I tried to get my hands up Ruth's T-shirt as we kissed. I wanted to see her breasts, to hold them. I'd have settled with just holding one. I was turning into a tit-man, it seemed. How straight is *that*. She was not wearing a bra and I managed to momentarily touch the right one. Ruth was having none of it.

'No, no, oh *no*. I've waited for this for two years.'

She undid my belt, looking at me, suddenly kissing me as she did so, flipping the top button of my jeans open and unzipping my fly. She moved so fast I had no time to register what she had said. Ruth kissed me again as her hand reached inside my boxers (fresh on, thank God). Her hand moved up and down, pulling the foreskin back roughly.

'Woah, be *careful* with that,' I objected as quietly as I could.

I was learning all the time. I had not expected that. Men are always quite good at the ceremonial pulling-back-of-the-foreskin on this side of the Atlantic, usually having personal knowledge of a foreskin's highly individual qualities. Some foreskins can hardly move at all and you have to be quite gentle with them for fear of rips and tears before bedtime; can you imagine anything worse? Others shuck back into place as easy as you please. Mine is fine once it gets there, you just have to be careful en route.

'Sorry,' said Ruth, sinking to the ground, clearly not sorry at all.

She stared eye to eye at my penis, like Lord Nelson seeing no ships. It was momentarily quite intimidating. I could not guess what she was thinking but had a trio of guesses. It could be the confidence-building and flattering Daddy Bear option or the vaguely disappointing 'I'd say you were average but just right for me,' Mummy Bear scenario. The Baby Bear choice was not even in the running, I hoped and trusted.

Ruth went to work with enthusiasm and ever-increasing expertise. At one point she did something phenomenally novel and I deduced she must have played a brass instrument in her youth. A master of the art acknowledged a mistress of it. My orgasm hoisted sail and hove into view on the horizon, full speed ahead.

Suddenly, the two girls came out of the TV room and erupted into the kitchen shouting for Ruth to get them a drink. We froze. I had a bet with myself that this had never happened to the Queen and the Duke of Edinburgh. Never an interrupted blow-job in fifty happy years. Ruth muttered a muffled expletive.

'Don't talk with your mouth full,' I said under my breath. We held still for about ten seconds, listening to Sarah and Hannah move about the house, trying to find Ruth. I gently withdrew and tucked myself away, just to be on the safe side. A mental picture flashed up of me involuntarily ejaculating in surprise over their kneeling mother as the girls suddenly opened the larder door. I lost it completely and started giggling uncontrollably.

Ruth stood up, in that cramped pantry her face only an inch from mine, plainly terrified that the girls would discover us, tears brimming in her eyes.

'Shut up. Shut up, Simon! They can't see me like this. Oh my God, I'm so fucking stupid. I'm so fucking stupid.'

I tried to stop laughing when I saw she was upset. I think it was Sarah who came back into the kitchen, went to the fridge, got the drinks herself and returned to the TV room. Ruth was rigid with fear the whole time. We slipped out of the larder and Ruth quietly opened and then slammed the back door, saying loudly, '. . . yes, Mother was a very keen gardener. She and Father worked like slaves in that garden for decades but—'

'Well, it's certainly worth all the work. It's magnificent,' I interrupted keenly.

Ruth winced and pointed into the back garden. It was

nearly all a patio and where it was not, it was neglected. Obviously, Mrs Whittaker gardened no more.

'. . . magnificent-ly paved,' I continued. We both watched my improvisation fall gasping to the floor, twitch and die. Ruth shook her head in despair and walked through to the hallway where we discussed for the girls' benefit my going to the hotel to check in and that perhaps we should all go out somewhere the next day. I had ordered a cab, packed my bag and left all within ten minutes of the larder incident, having poked my head into the TV room to say goodbye. The girls were too engrossed in a Disney video to notice. At the door Ruth had confirmed the arrangement.

'Seven o'clock,' I had agreed. 'You OK?' She had nodded and shut the door quickly.

At the hotel, confusingly but pleasantly enough, I flirted openly with the dishy and plainly gay check-in clerk. I think I was emitting 'I want sex' signals on all frequencies at that stage. I waited in my room for Ruth to arrive, channel surfing impatiently and trying not to jerk off.

I thought about what Ruth had said: 'I've been waiting for this for two years.' All the time she had been working for me, she had been attracted to me? I recalled a few comments like 'You're such a waste being gay, Simon' and suchlike, but that is all standard fare for a Gay Best Friend. The GBF's BF always says it at some point, but she usually never means it. Who would she talk about make-up and boys to then?

Having said that, Ruth had not had any significant relationship while working for me. There had been a few disastrous dates and abortive set-ups with friends of friends but nothing approaching a 'real thing'. I had always assumed the divorce had hurt a lot and that working a full-time job as well as bringing up two kids made her too busy even to think about a serious relationship again.

So, she'd been waiting two years. *Fantastic.*

At five to seven, Ruth knocked at the hotel-room door. At one minute to seven we were naked and in the shower. At six minutes past we were falling dripping on to the bed and a minute later I was putting Callum's cappuccino training to the test (with a small degree of success and a large amount of trepidation), and by about 1912 hours I had a condom on and was finally going to get to make love to Ruth. Alarmingly, she had brought a packet of ten with her and I had another three in my bag. Unlucky for some. What was I going to do? At this rate we would have run out by about twenty past eight.

I checked all the pressure gauges, scanned the radar, got a thumbs up from ground crew that everything was tickety-boo and chocks were away. I taxied down the runway.

Chapter 11

'How you got her, to me, I must own, is a wonder!
When I think of your natural aptness to blunder'
Anthony Pasquin

It is so easy (relatively) to get one's penis inside a vagina.
Sorry to be anatomical, but it's a miracle of engineering.
When making love to a man, spit, polish, creams and
embrocations have to coax and cajole the barricades into
submission. Repeated attempts are repelled until, with
only partial success achieved, Kenneth Branagh rides on,
his horse rears up like the Lone Ranger's, he screams,
'Once more into the breach . . .' and finally entrance is
gained. There is no need for Ken (as Emma discovered)
when getting a penis into a vagina. Like a cup of tea, if it's
wet and warm, you can't go far wrong. The difficult bit was
getting the bishop poised and primed just outside; never
mind finding the clitoris in the dark, let's find the vagina in
broad daylight. Women appear to have so many openings,
I expected to find some C-list celebrities eating canapés
down there. But once pointed in the right direction, my
vast Machine was all systems go. Odd to report, I never
doubted I would get an erection. It was always a dead cert.

I was intent on having a good time. I had never taken sex to be a sacred rite like some people do and I tend to laugh a lot during foreplay, if not the act itself (one does have to concentrate). Whatever, I was not about to turn this into a major existential event . . . *much*. The only pre-coital agreement I made with myself was that by fair means or foul, and by whatever technique necessary, Ruth was going to have an orgasm. That was important and would be some kind of self-vindication: there was no point in stopping being a rather good homosexual if it turned out I was going to be yet another dreary het.

If this had been a movie, harps would have played softly as fountains tinkled in the background and sunlight diffused through muslin. If a choir had been just outside, they would have had to sing in celebration: in purely physical terms some terribly fine love was made. Well, I enjoyed it anyway. A lot of pipe was laid that night, as I believe the saying has it. Moveable parts worked to demand, all was fab and gear.

The huge impact on me was to do with something that Ruth could not have suspected. I was aware of it almost immediately, as the part of my brain men usually use to recite Wisden during sex to prevent a preemie was being used to work out why it all felt so different. Why should it be different making love to a woman rather than a man? Sweat, juices and friction, what was there to be different? But it was. Everything seemed out of proportion. I'm nearly six foot (in height, I add for clarity) and the men I liked were always about the same build as me but with forty-eight-inch chests, size eleven feet, legs for days. Ruth was tiny by comparison; she was by no means a petite woman, but when put beside the lunks I was used to, she was diminutive.

Her smallness triggered two instincts within me; both were disappointingly, thrillingly conventional hunter–gatherer stuff, which contained no element of the impulse towards the joy of similarity and equality I felt with men. Firstly, it seemed I needed to protect her, and secondly, I needed to physically overpower her.

I think I just repeated myself.

Either way, I did not feel good about these instincts and felt them to be alien to me. But because I could dominate, I had to and, strangest of all, she appeared to expect and want it. I did not want to take over but it looked like neither of us was giving me a choice. In black and white, it all looks like a caveman mentality but, in the moment, with Ruth wanting me and digging her nails in, the love-making became ever more violent or, to sugar the pill, passionate. I was expecting at any moment my free subscription to cable sports channels for successfully fulfilling at least a dozen heterosexual clichés in as many minutes. There was a very normal lad deep within me itching to get out. I had not seen him going in. Where had he come from? *Please God, don't let me turn into my father.*

I was somewhere outside myself, watching me inside her. I reached up to touch her breasts at last, mimicking what people do in movies when they touch women's breasts. Tim Roth and Gary Oldman types are always rather repulsive, clawing and squeezing as if to puncture the woman. Kevin Costner always seems rather good at it, so I tried to remember what he does in the back of the limo to Sean Young in *No Way Out*. Hard but fair, rough but tender. I never believe the levels of ecstasy women attain on celluloid from a flaccid caress of a breast and I certainly did not help Ruth that night to any new plateau of pleasure with my obtuse handling of her. I felt like I was trying to find a ripe pink grapefruit in Asda.

As I pushed my desultory trolley round Ruth's fresh fruit, I tried to work out in what way I was turned on.

Damn it, this is getting existential after all . . . perhaps I'm not having fun . . . it feels like fun . . . or am I so shallow I can get aroused by any flesh . . . she's biting my nipples again . . . can I get aroused by any flesh in close proximity to mine, no matter whose it is?

To answer this from a more distant point of view, I probably *am* that shallow but not that first time with Ruth. To continue my search for profundity that night:

. . . Am I just an indiscriminating . . . I've got my tongue in her navel . . . indiscriminating, selfish . . . maybe I should do a nipple thang myself . . . am I an indiscriminating, selfish, untrustworthy bisexual?

From this far from omniscient standpoint I can answer . . . I can answer . . . uh . . . can I pass on that one? It's kind of the point of the book. Was I indiscriminating? I could place an ad: 'Looking for person with limbs (up to and including four), skin, orifices, non-smoking.' Was I turned on because I was with *a* woman or this one in particular? In the moment it was difficult to tell. This could not be about our past friendship, Ruth had said as much. My back was *bleeding*, this was not *chummy*.

This was strange. This was fucking strange. This was strange fucking. I did not recall this violence from my VI Form affairettes. As Ruth cried out for more, asking me to stop while throwing herself against me, I kept slamming away. It was all so *butch*. This was not subtle stuff, this was not sultry shieks with bowls of goldfish by their beds. And although I was being far rougher than I had ever been with a man, although I was dominating, there was no clear idea of who was in the driving seat.

It was becoming clearer to me why those date-rape court cases are always so foggy. 'It's too much' in the middle of sex like that, with a man feeling as I was feeling, *is* an ambiguous statement and no amount of 'Just answer the question, yes or no' renders it any the less double-edged. She was actively urging me on with stuff like 'I can't take any more'. She was giving me permission and, I suspect, telling me that I was doing OK for a first-timer. I don't know how straight men know when they are getting the green light in this way, but this new straight man only could hazard a guess, because I had said the same things when men had roughly made love to me. My ignorance was woeful. The more atypically violent I became, the more effect she was having. That choir outside kept singing the final bars of Pavarotti's World Cup song in an endless loop of sexual Muzak.

When Ruth was on top, I felt the same as when a man made love to me. The power was all hers, she was taking charge of herself as well as me. She decided the gear changes and it was her femininity that let her do this. This must sound very obvious to anyone out there in Hetland but it was a revelation to me. It is the polar opposite to me making love to a man who is riding the range. He is still giving me his masculinity not affirming it. I take what is his, she was taking what was hers. She enhanced her femaleness. She looked into my eyes as she moved up and down me. I had no idea what she was looking for, I had no idea why she was here with me. But my eyes sought hers for the confirmation I sought from men when they made love to me. Being *made* love to for a man is a search or a question; the focus of it is in the mind and the eyes, believe it or not. When a man *makes* love, it is a statement that concentrates in the stomach, the penis, the legs: the head is not involved.

That first time, I came quickly, having had a month's build-up. That's enough teetering on the brink for any man. The second time was much more leisurely.

And this time Ruth came as well.

When I read in novels or erotica about the female orgasm, it seems kinda dainty, intense but ladylike. 'Lady Harriet clung to the groom, spending copiously as waves of pleasure flowed through her and gradually subsided.' Things flow, things subside, they wave, you wave back. I've never gone for that Victorian female ejaculation business that New Age people insist happens but nothing prepared me for the force of what happened to Ruth. Hurricane Ruth hit town that night; there was only one survivor and it wasn't me. None of this OTTness about Ruth's cataclysmic climax is to claim that I was an astounding lover on my first time out, like a new international cap scoring a hat trick. I could tell that this happened to Ruth a *lot*. Having said that, I was proud of myself: as Glenn Hoddle would have said, 'The lad done well. He's only a temporary transfer from Ancient Greece but we hope to make it permanent. Tonight was a big night and he rose to the occasion repeatedly. Let's hope he can do the same next Saturday, Brian.'

May I make a statement? If I were to have access to orgasms like that, I would put up with lower rates of pay for my gender, periods *and* childbirth without pain relief, and do so with a Cheshire Cat smile. It made my puny five seconds of scrunching my face and spurting look like a sneeze. A man builds to a mini-nova of pleasure but Ruth just kept on going, peak after peak, her body bucking and contracting. It did look like a series of waves but the tide was definitely coming in by the looks of things. This was voracious, full-fat, all the calories, would-you-like-cream-with-that-madam orgasming. I made do with what I now knew to be a carrot-stick dipped quickly in Cum-lite, the mayonnaise for men.

If that choir had been outside the door, one of the elder ones would have turned to a distressed little treble as Ruth came and would have said, 'Don't worry, Timmy. He's not hurting her.' I was not so sure what was going on myself. I was as dumbstruck as Timmy, only slightly less terrified and infinitely more jealous. I made a Faustian pact with God as Ruth went ape-shit in my arms: '*Take my soul, let me keep my penis and let me have orgasms like this.*'

If every man could partake of such climaxes, bedrooms would be filled to the light-fitting with jissom every time, breaking the door down as a still-entwined couple surfed the stairwell on a breaker of sperm with the choir scattering for their lives as they sang the Old Spice theme. The man would be a hollow husk afterwards, drained and bravely smiling, able only to eat a bland diet, swallow vitamin pills and watch daytime TV. The main global effect of this male über-climax would be that there would be no war. Why bother when you have Armageddon in your underwear?

I won't tell you about my orgasms. Sniff. They went OK.

But in the days and weeks following that first time with Ruth, I understood why straight men do not riot in the streets demanding these strange and wonderful Nagasakis in their nether regions. The straight male has a big secret that goes way beyond the enormity of the female orgasm and he keeps his cards close to his chest.

Chapter 12

'*A changeable man is not one person but several, for-
ever about to be what he has never been . . .*'

La Bruyère

The only time I ever got fired from a job, my boss was
French. The two facts, that I was fired and that he was
from France, are not necessarily connected. I have a great
regard for the French nation and from my readings of the
historians Uderzo and Goscinny have long held the fight
of the Gauls against Roman invasion in high esteem.
However, I would support the school of thought that says
there has been a decline since the heroism of yesteryear,
which resulted in that greasy, onion-selling scumbag calling me into his office and telling me that since I was the
last in, I was first out and that he was very sorry but he
had to make 'Great changements'. I think the fact I slept
with his son had something to do with it as well.

'Great changements' was a phrase that stuck with me in
the weeks following that first night with Ruth and my
departure from the sexual shadowland *demi-monde*
through which I had moved for so long.

These changes showed themselves in small ways.
Because we could only get together at weekends, Ruth

and I developed slowly as a couple, two steps forward then one step back during the weeks apart. This pattern took a little getting used to and initially I was very careful around Ruth, to the extent I went a little overboard on the etiquette for gentlemen towards ladies. A couple of weeks after the fancy dress party, Ruth and I went to a busy restaurant: I held the car door for her (even though she was driving), I did 'after you, no I insist, after *you*' acting as we went into the restaurant, pulled Ruth's chair out for her. I had become one of those 1930s English gent characters Leslie Howard specialised in. I was loving playing the man. I've a feeling it got on Ruth's tits and it was a phase that thankfully soon passed because of what Ruth did about it.

We were perusing the menus and I was wondering whether to risk the *moules*. I was so macho now, I thought I just might. Suddenly—

'Kiss me, Simon.'

'Hmm?'

'Kiss me.'

'Right here, right now? I haven't even decided what I'm eating yet. Have you no sense of priority? What's the special?'

'I am. Rare. Kiss me.'

'Ruth . . .'

'Just *do* it.'

I heard an unmistakable tone of command and obeyed. And do you know what? We kissed for about fifteen seconds and nobody in that restaurant batted an eyelid.

It was almost impossible for me to assimilate this. It was something I had never been able to do with a decade's worth of boyfriends. I know that some gay men do the holding hands, kissing in public schtick but I have always

been more of a Sir Michael than a Sir Ian in that respect.
For me, kissing is not a confrontational political act and
never will be. I'll stand on a soap box to kiss a man if he
is really tall, and that's your lot. That said, of course the
kiss in the restaurant was deeply significant and political
for me way beyond 'Oh how lovely, I just kissed Ruth
and the indifferent waiter had to hang around and smile
indulgently before he took our order'. I did have the
moules in the end.

That public kiss with Ruth was a much bigger statement for me than coming out had been a decade before.
'I'm different' is what you *should* say at nineteen in whatever way you do it. But to say

I BELONG

at the age of thirty is enormous. It means you've done it,
you survived, you're a big person now. You get the luggage
with the little wheels; it doesn't feel an imposition to wear
a tie, in fact you quite like it and have forty-five silk ones;
you completely miss a youth phenomenon and don't care.
In my case it was Nirvana: I didn't even know Cobain
had existed and by the time I did, he didn't. Whatever, a
subscription to *Auto Monthly* was a must. I could not wait
to check a dipstick and wipe it clean with an oily rag.

It was at this point I began to understand the appeal of
fascism. I clicked that it is A Good Thing to believe that
you belong to the dominant group in society. Three great
big old cheers for Simon:

> Simon's white!
> Simon's male!
> Simon's straight!

Don't tell me you're surprised I'm white because I don't believe you. *I was even solvent.* I was so far from being in an oppressed minority, you could have put me in a government building in Jo'burg and called me Pik.

An almost tangible and embraceable sense of serenity descended upon me as a result. I saw it, I touched it, I held it close to me and almost smelled it. I was no longer an individual because I did not need to be. Fantastic. I had jumped back into the closet and shut the door behind me but the back of the wardrobe had opened up to reveal a Narnia where it was not necessary to prove myself as anything other than a part of something greater than myself. My little self-employed business had been bought out by a huge multi-national corporation. Suddenly I was one of the big boys, strutting through the endless corridors of HET plc, the newest Vice President on the top floor.

I reckon Tom Cruise is the ideal casting to play me in this part of the film of my life. It depends on my mood as to who plays me. Tom is about as good as it gets. If I'm depressed, I cast either Charlie Sheen or John Goodman. If I'm suicidal then Rob Lowe's agent gets the phone call. Anyway, the Cruiser strides down the corridor, the camera in a tight shot on his handsome face, his eyes shiny with the joy of being *him*. He flashes smiles and good-mornings to people and more than a couple of secretaries exchange knowing and longing glances before they go off for a quick Diet Coke break. This part of my life was in fact the start of any Tom Cruise film.

I would often surprise Ruth after that by trying to kiss her in department stores, in pubs and even at the cinema.

'Simon, I'm trying to watch the movie.'

'Kiss me.'

'Simon, you're spilling your popcorn.'

'You bet I am. Kiss me.'

'Oh, for God's sake, *all right* then . . .'

Holding hands at the flicks was no longer a punishable offence. I used to detest boyfriends who tried to insinuate their sweaty palms into mine as we watched. Now I quite liked it, liked it a whole bunch in fact, although it irritated the shit out of Ruth. Did she have no romance? And the more I confirmed in front of an indulgent but indifferent world that I was with Ruth and demonstrated our item-ness, the more I felt great about myself and who I was.

I have no notion of whether all straight men know they have this endless sea of tranquillity to swim about in. You can call it what you like, but they, excuse me, *we*, have access to a feeling of complete calm and self-belief simply because of who we are.

THIS IS THE BIG SECRET YOU NEVER HEAR ABOUT.

That seismic female orgasm is the consolation prize by comparison. I have a hunch straight men do know about it but are barely aware of it. Just as when breathing becomes a conscious act so a straight man gets a glimpse of his total belonging in the world only occasionally. A fish does not think about water, the Pope does not think how to get his whites whiter, a professional footballer does not think. It is a wonderful thing to be at one with the world and oneself and I strongly recommend it to everyone. Straight males only need apply.

In fact, my being at one with the world lasted only eight weeks but those eight weeks were the happiest of my life. I was so confident. Even the words to describe confidence also describe male heterosexuality: I stood up *straight*, my bearing was *erect*, I looked the world *square-ly* in the eye. As a man who had loved loving men for nearly all his adult life, I can safely say that in those two months, a few moments excepted, I was actively glad not to be gay, gleefully swapping my humble, hard-won and home-grown notion of individuality for a shiny, shop-bought sense of how I now fitted in. And God, in His infinite wisdom, had designed half the world's popula-tion so that I could *literally* fit into them.

Having said that, there is a catch.

The big 'but', the leviathan 'that notwithstanding', the huge 'however' now follows. Notebooks out, lick your pencils.

For a man to feel like he is at one with the world and experience the calm and serenity that follows, he must be loved by The Right Woman. They are the key (the key-hole?) that opens the door in the back of the wardrobe. My tragedy in my first career as a rather fine, if quiet, gay man was that I was always looking for the right *man* to give me this completeness. Silly old me. It is only women who can do this magic trick of making a man truly belong in the world. A man can make another man feel loved and they will of course be happy together and belong together. This is completely different to the effect a woman's love has on a man, completely different to the effect Ruth's love had on me.

A Lady's Love, hereafter known as ALL, validates a man in the world's eyes *and therefore in his own eyes*. A whole official civilisation tells us that the combination of a man and a woman is the only proper and natural union of two people. Sorry to state the obvious but the only creature more peripheralised in straight society than a homosexual is a middle-aged straight bachelor. *What has he done with his life? He must be deviant in some way. Why does he keep his cellar locked? Does he ever look at little girls? I've heard he's a satanist. Run him out of town. While I'm helping run him out of town, I'll leave the kids with that nice gay couple next door. The things they come out with, they make me laugh.*

But a man loves a woman and the world turns.

For me, Ruth's big attraction was not only that she was beautiful, witty, clever, resourceful, courageous blah blah, although all those things were and are true; as those first weeks went by, I grew more and more close to her because of the way she made me feel about myself. I was *valid* without having to do anything except be loved by Ruth and to love her in return. Because I had ALL, because I felt the world now accepted me, I stood taller, I was better at my job, I was one serene mutha. Since I loved Ruth and, crucially, she loved me, I loved myself. I gained my approval.

As a result of this having to do nothing, a gradual change came over me. I cracked fewer jokes. My line in banter withered on the vine because I did not need it any more. I barely noticed the process until it was almost complete. I had no need to defend myself with humour and caustic one-liners because I had no vulnerabilities to defend. Being excluded is the origin of gay and Jewish (and Liverpudlian, come to think of it) senses of humour, and explains why the New Testament has fewer laughs than the Old Testament; also, the reason why Jesus was a carpenter and not a stand-up comedian. God is a boring straight man, the Devil the colourful funny one. God is Ernie who sets up the gag and Eric is Satan who delivers the punchline. God doesn't have to make Himself laugh or say funny things. He *knows* that everyone likes Him because they are like him. I was now a minor deity myself because I was like other straight men and they were like me.

I was not, however, one of the heavyweights. The alpha males of the human gorilla troupe are the happily married men; the men who not only have ALL but have it on a *piece of paper*. Happily married men are the gods of this planet, they know it and always look like smug bastards as a result. It's a man's man's man's world but it ain't nothin' for that man's man without a woman's love. It gives men the backbone to live their lives.

Fast rewind back to that first night with Ruth. I was light years away from godlike oneness at this point. I was cock-a-hoop that all had gone swimmingly and my mind was racing with the sheer excitement and newness of it all. All I knew was that I wanted to keep her, so from the beginning of being with Ruth, I tried very hard to be as honest and open as it was possible to be. I had never been like this with anyone before but, lying there in the darkness of that hotel room on that first night (the first *proper* night) with my head on Ruth's shoulder, I talked about what I was feeling and *why* I thought I was feeling like this. It was more important for Ruth to hear it than it was for me to say it. God knew I'd been thinking about myself enough lately. Ruth had to hear this because in the end it was her decision if the two of us were going anywhere together, if we were only a weekend break or a holiday of a lifetime.

Some people love that kind of conversation. I find it an ordeal and can only stop becoming Pathetic Man Who Weeps Like a Child by taking one step back from myself, not letting my emotions get in the way of talking about my emotions. I think I'm trying to say I'm a middle-class Englishman. (If it is an additional surprise that I am not only white but also middle-class, you must now pay close attention: *get out more*.) I find it easier to crack a joke or crack open a bottle than to crack the mask I present to the rest of society. People might find out what I'm like and we wouldn't want that. But that night I tried to tell Ruth nothing but the truth, warts and all, so help me God.

I don't want you to think I'm going all squishy. One has to be careful *how* the truth is told. There is always a little spin-doctor inside your head saying, This could be a good way to say it, this makes you look generous not desperate, tell a joke now so you'll sound relaxed and self-deprecating. It's a tough thing, being honest.

If you are lucky, you have a Labour spin-doctor in your head rather than anyone else's, so you can wade through three feet of sin and shit but still come up smelling of the reddest of roses, which you then proceed to give to your beloved. Having been in opposition for so long, it was a difficult policy to sell to my electorate of one (on whose breast I lay, which was a good start, my opinion polls indicated) that I had successfully crossed the floor of the house and could now take up a position as a junior minister. In my favour, I had just memorably won two by-elections with my electorate's help in the last couple of hours and had every intention of standing for another.

Our discussion was much more to the point than I had thought it would be. Ruth listened to my history of strange and unwelcome hard-ons, the night she resigned from the travel agency being the prime example. The fact I had been a secret admirer for some time was received by a hand rested on my chest, gently stroking the hair this way and that in an encouraging way. I love playing with men's chest hair too.

The spin I gave my sexual conversion on the road to Didsbury was that the Patrick episode was the last straw for me as a homosexual rather than a very sudden switcheroo and ricochet into liking women, which is what, in my heart of hearts, I was suspecting it had been. I told Ruth it was the culmination of a long process blah blah. True enough to be not quite a lie, which of course, is the best type of lie. Why couldn't I tell her everything? Instinctively, I had lied, and lied well.

'But you would say you were bisexual now, wouldn't you?' asked Ruth.

I sensed that my patented 'what's a label, who's to say' reply would not quite do. I tried it, however, as a flip joke in case it did not work.

'Well, aren't we *all* to some degree or an—'

'*Simon.*'

'Just joking, just joking. Uh . . . I dunno . . . I guess so . . . Yes.'

Ruth threw my dumbness back at me, repeating in a Bill & Ted voice, 'Er . . . I . . . er . . . dunno . . . I guess . . . er . . . so . . . yes.'

'Well, sorry, but that's as good as it gets at the moment, I'm afraid.'

'Uh-*huh*,' said Ruth and waited for me to continue.

My spin-doctor was passing messages on mental Post-its like there was no tomorrow: don't tell her you schtupped the intern; oral sex doesn't count now so that's OK; *really* don't say you flirted with the check-in clerk five hours ago. Ruth waited.

'Oh . . .' I very nearly said something. 'I'm trying to say . . .'

'Mmm?'

'. . . that I'm here. With you. Because I want to be. With you. And no one else. That's what I do know, right here, right now.'

'And tomorrow?'

'One day at a time. No promises. I can't do that.'

A silence.

I realised that it sounded like I had just used her for sex and she could sod off back home now. We'll be in touch, thanks for stopping by. What an irresistible hunk I am. I added, 'But I really want to see you again. Like this.'

I had done the honesty thing after all. That was as near as dammit all my cards on the table. The reality of the situation was that Ruth had all the aces and she was in charge.

I waited for the jury to return.

'And it's OK I don't have a nine-inch penis?' Ruth said finally.

'Well, not many people do.'

'Ain't that the truth,' Ruth said meaningfully, as I absentmindedly massaged my little general underneath the bedclothes. He did not know what had hit him.

'Careful what you're saying, the male ego is a fragile construct.' I had learned a lesson from all those girlie self-help books over the years: I turned the tables. 'And why are you here, Miss Ruth "I've been waiting for this for two years" Whittaker?'

I could almost hear her blush.

'You remember that?' she said, a little groan escaping.

'Oh yeah.'

'Nnnnn . . . well . . . *Simon* . . .'

'*Ruth* . . .'

It's strange when people you know use your name like

that. Something huge is around the corner. Ruth was about to tell me she had always loved me, that was what she had meant in the pantry. We had spent two years secretly fancying each other. In my case, mostly subconsciously. How extraordinary. She said, 'To be utterly, utterly, *utterly* honest, it's not what you think.'

'And what do I think?'

'That I've harboured a passion for you ever since I met you.'

I did a very bad impersonation of somebody denying something. 'Ha! You think that's what I was thinking about what you said? Ha! That's funny. Oh . . . that's . . . that's *funny*.' Once I'd started I could not stop. 'No, no, no, I wasn't thinking *that*. No, no. No.'

In my mind, my penis, which had been ready to metaphorically double in size as Ruth declared her secret love, shrank to microscopic proportions.

'Oh,' said Ruth, not believing a word. 'So what did you think?'

'I don't know,' I spluttered. 'I was curious to find out. That's why I brought it up.'

'Wee-e-ll. It was all more concrete than perhaps, just perhaps, you thought. What I meant was, and I was talking to myself really, was that I had not *been* with a man like that—'

'Sucking him off in a pantry?' I clarified.

'Indeed,' she giggled. 'I hadn't sucked off a man in a pantry or anywhere else for that matter for two years. That's what I meant.'

'Oh.'

'So there you go.'

'You mean you haven't had that Paul boy?' I asked in wonder. He was obviously gagging for it.

Ruth scoffed at the thought. '*No*. He's great but he's too young. In a couple of years maybe.'

'You're insane. I'm glad you're insane but you're insane,' I said, remembering Paul in the bodystocking. Disturbingly, I felt myself stir at the thought. The world really isn't black and white, is it? I asked, 'So why did you come over to me after your dance routine then?'

This was starting to be like the end of an Ellery Queen mystery. We had gathered at the scene of the crime and Mr Queen was asking us to explain ourselves. But I did want to know. Ruth started to laugh, twisting round and poking me in the stomach.

'You vain bugger. You really want me to tell you, don't you? First, you looked very horny in your vicar's outfit, especially when it was really dirty and stained. You looked like a naughty choirboy. It was *great* to see you. What else, you're not nineteen . . .'

'Who told you?'

'Your secret's safe with me. You've always been a great friend, I was quite pissed, I love you a lot anyway, and so when Paul told me at the party, just before we did that *fabulous* routine, you'd said you weren't necessarily gay, I thought something must be up . . .'

'As 't were.'

'. . . and I suddenly felt like kissing you because . . . I felt like it. There you are. I don't really know, I fancied you.'

'Good enough,' I said, stretching around to kiss her again. Ruth pulled away first, her own spin-doctors going to work.

'I mean, thinking about it, I must have fancied you a *little* back at work.'

How swiftly history can be rewritten.

'Really?' I said, far too quickly. I made a face, to tell Ruth I was being flip and only pretending to be pathetically eager to be chuffed. She saw through my scrawny little double-bluff immediately but carried on.

'When I first met you, I thought you were a lovely, cuddly homosexual.'

Cuddly, the cruellest word in the Solar System.

'. . . Then I thought you were kind of cute . . .'

Cute, the second cruellest word in nine planets.

'Then I got to know you and, this will sound silly, but I really fancied the back of your head . . .'

'The back of my what?'

'Your head. It's lovely . . .'

I was not sure what to say. It's a useful place to admire if you're shagging me from behind but that did not do Ruth much good, unless she had a strap-on accoutrement in that untidy room of hers that she was not telling me about. She was still talking about me, how exciting, don't *drift*, Simon.

'Then after the first few months I just sort of put fancying you to the back of *my* head, you being a quote, self-confessed notorious homosexual, unquote.'

'I thank you.'

'And I was your friend. That was that. End of story.' She settled back.

'Sad celibates together, watching ER,' I said.

'Well, some celibates are more celibate than others,' Ruth said pointedly.

'Straight for the jugular,' I said with a nervous laugh.

'Have you been tested lately?' And she turned the tables right back.

There it was, in the middle of the room, blinking malevolently, the question we had hedged around for two days. Do I risk getting a terrible disease from you because you are an untrustworthy bisexual?

'I haven't had a test for two years. No occasion to.'

Ruth waited for me to go on again. She was good at that, an old BBC interviewing technique.

'No point. I haven't had unsafe sex in that time.'

True enough. I had had Benny from *Crossroads*'s sex life for eons. Ruth waited. I said, 'I'll have another test, if you like.'

The 'if you like' was vile of me. I should have just said 'I'll have another test' but this time I waited for her to speak. I really did not want to have a test: that man behind the desk with the printout and the clipboard. Yeuch.

'*Could* you have another one, Si? I've got children, remember.'

The 'Si' was crucial. An endearment to sugar the pill and make me do it.

'Yeah, of course. Whatever you want.'

It was all suddenly formal. Please sign here and we'll be able to give each other orgasms. The edge was certainly off the romance of the moment. But it was very nineties to have safe sex, tacitly accept that the risks existed and only afterwards talk about the four-letter word. Safe and instant gratification, then clinical pillow-talk.

Ruth shifted position suddenly and straddled my stomach, changing the subject beautifully. She leaned over and brushed my face with her nipples. Good trick if you can do it; I've never quite managed it. I tried to catch them, apple-bobbing with my mouth. She said airily, 'Anyway, my dad always told me I was more like a boy. That's why you like me.'

'You've the best tits of any boy I've seen,' I retorted,

catching hold of a passing breast and teasing the nipple erect with my teeth. Ruth started issuing instructions.

'That tickles . . . actually that hurts . . . that's better . . . a bit harder . . . that's it.' She certainly knew what she liked, adding, 'Dad always said I had a boy's sense of humour.'

Did she have to talk about her father while I was doing this?

'Mmfwoargheffmoeklndsgaiz,' I said.

'Pardon?'

I stopped suckling at her breast.

'I *said*, weren't you *listening*, I said that probably makes you a homosexual man in disguise.'

Ruth thought about it and shrugged.

'Whatever makes it work, Simon, *whatever* makes it work. *Down* a bit . . .'

Cut to: waves crashing on a shore, dusk over a palm-tree islet, a lone bird flying across an empty, epic sky. Fade to black.

Chapter 13

Fade up three weeks later on me and a close friend having
a problematic sensual experience.

'What I'd really like is one of each, of course.'

'Why not have both?'

'Is that allowed?'

'I'd not tell anyone. You're looking great. Go on, fill
your boots.'

Watching Toril dither about whether or not to have
both kinds of cream cake I had bought in for dessert
(because I'm crap at dinner parties and can never be
fagged to actually make anything), I began to wonder
how I would tell her about Ruth. I knew she would be
fine about it, everybody else had been, so it was almost a
game deciding whether to slip it into the conversation,
make a big announcement or just tell her.

'Oh Lord, I'm such a glutton,' she moaned, lifting a
calorie bomb to her lips. 'I'm looking at it, I know that the
second I've eaten it I'll regret it, and I even know that I'm

eating it because I'm not sleeping with anyone at the moment.

'So why are you eating it?' I asked her as she bit into the cake.

'Because it's fucking exquisite, that's why,' she said, swallowing with a shudder of pleasure. She shut her eyes, fanning her face tensely in anticipation. 'And, yes, here it comes, a wave of guilt.' She opened those blue eyes and looked at me, at her most spontaneous and charming. I loved her in this unguarded mood, so unlike her everyday mask of chilly irony. Like me, Toril knew herself far too well and she always put barriers between herself and the world for protection, but when she lowered those defences, as she sometimes did with me, she was truly delightful. But it was never very often, or for very long. I hadn't been able to go up to London and this was Toril's only free evening, but she'd volunteered to drive down straight away, saying, 'Any chance to see you, Simon, you know that.' I had been quite touched.

She picked up the plate of cakes and offered it to me. 'Are you not having one?' Wot larks. Here was my chance to tell her. I'd drop a big hint and see if she got it.

'No, I'm not having one. I don't really feel like one,' I said carefully.

I was actually on a 'look more svelte when in the buff with Ruth' diet at that point but, like everyone else, I always lose weight when my love life perks up for any length of time. Then when I've lost quite a bit and I'm looking leanish and meanish I start worrying that the weight loss is due to AIDS because I've been shagging. I start eating to stop the worrying, balloon and then get dumped because I suddenly have the Statue of Liberty's waist measurement. That's the usual cycle. It's important to be paranoid about something.

My main reason for paranoia that evening was that people's reactions to my born-again heterosexuality were so nonchalant and positive. It was a mixture of surprise, curiosity and indifference but very little else. For obvious reasons, I had been most nervous of telling my gay friends. I was most fearful of telling Truman the policeman, my ex, because he was the nearest person to a boyfriend I had to whom I was still speaking. We had enjoyed a civilised arrangement since our split where we met up every now and again for lots of mutual affection: no emotional strings but good food, good conversation and classy, down-and-dirty sex. Before Ruth, I had believed that this was as good as it was going to get. I had been especially nervous of telling Truman, but his reaction was fairly typical: 'What? Really? *Oooo* . . . I don't know what to say.'

I may have been fantasising it, but I detected behind Truman's and other, mainly gay, eyes the belief that sad old Simon was going to fall on his face this time. Truth be told, I was slightly disappointed that none of my gay friends had had an overtly negative reaction because that would have made them easy to walk away from. They're just as trapped into stereotypes as any old straight bigot, I could have thought as I walked into the glorious dawn of my new life. As it was, I liked them even more and really enjoyed their company. Life's never easy, is it?

I was longing for someone to be less than supportive. Then I could let fly and show just how committed to Ruth I really was. No such luck with Toril, I thought as I dropped my hint about not needing comfort food at present; she was going to be true to her Norwegian Social

Democrat roots and be a proper Scandinavian, anything goes, let's-beat-each-other-with-twigs-and-roll-in-the-snow kind of person.

'Have a bloody cake. Keep me company here. They're so, what do you Brits say, "naughty but nice".'

Toril's English, as well as her surprising knowledge of 1970s Milk Marketing Board ad campaigns, is flawless apart from a tendency to make the word 'nice' sound almost too nice. She also occasionally puts ritzy five-dollar words next to profanities, 'Fucking exquisite' being a prime example.

'They're vuh-ree nai-ce actually. I've had them before,' I said in my best Muppet Swedish chef voice. I repeated, 'I just don't feel the need for one right now.'

The kröne dropped.

'You love cream cakes but you don't feel the need for one right now. You are having regular sex and you haven't told me, you duplicitous tart.' She had another revelation. 'And that's why I've dragged myself all the way from London on a work night and you couldn't see me at the weekend. Where are you going?'

'Manchester.'

'You filthy hound. You went there last weekend as well. Is it love?'

'I *think* so,' I said slowly.

Toril widened her eyes in tabloid shock-horror.

'Oh, I say. That's bad. You've been thinking about it, that means it *is* love. Oh my God. Tell me all about him.'

Here goes.

'Well, for starters, it's not a him.'

Toril, to her credit, kept smiling but the smile became fixed and the mischief in her eyes faded to a grey lifeless-ness I had never seen there before. She looked away from me, her smile sliding off her face, and for a half-second I thought I saw a flash of anger, which she swiftly concealed. 'It's a woman?' she asked.

'Yep. You remember Ruth, who used to work for me?'

She passed a hand across her face, brushing non-existent hairs out of her eyes.

'Oh . . . *Ruth* . . . she's nice,' Toril faltered. 'I remember her now. She's . . lovely. Long, sort of red hair. Quite clever.'

'That's the one.' I was half offended on Ruth's behalf: '*sort of* red hair, *quite* clever.' I knew faint praise when I heard it.

There was a short silence as Toril stared at the pepper mill in the centre of the table. Why was this such a big deal? My ex, Truman, had disguised his possibly sceptical reaction by being excellently upfront, vulgar and bitchy after his initial surprise had worn off. I could not be angry with him, as I was certainly going to be with Toril if she did not shape up in a minute. Truman and I had sat in a naff caff near my shop and the volume of his comments rose and fell as people he had arrested, relatives of the aforementioned and colleagues from the cop-shop came and went.

'You'll miss dicks, Simon. Once you've had black, you never go back, and once you've had a dick in your mouth, you're just waiting for the next one. You'll be back, I prophesy it,' Truman had said in a brisk undertone.

'Truman, you are so rude. When have you ever slept with a black guy?'

'Obviously I haven't because I was sleeping with *you* every now and again until quite recently. I feel responsible, that's all. I obviously haven't been man enough for you.'

'Oh, you *were*, too much.' Not far wrong; he packed a punch, did our Truman.

'Thank you for that, anyway. I'll start a sweepstake for everyone who knows you, Simon,' Truman had brain-waved. 'I'll call it "How long will he hold out before he nibbles a nob again?" Tickets from ten minutes to ten years. Bags I don't get the one for ten years.'

His big smile and the warmth of his hug as he said good-bye had been his real reaction. As he broke away from the hug, Truman told me that he was always there if I needed him. He knew that everything and nothing had changed: I was still me. I had very few gay friends because I had never been that much of a scene queen and had often had argu-ments about the notion that a separate gay identity existed outside ten cappuccino bars on Old Compton Street. I've never drunk a gay coffee in my life. As a partial proof, put me next to a acid-tongued body-fascist disco bunny from Trade or G.A.Y. and just watch me have fuck-all to say to them. So I valued Truman's friendship all the more.

The odd thing was that I only really gained a sense of 'gay community' after I had told my gay friends that I had a lover who was female. I could not say to them that I was attracted to Ruth *while simultaneously* liking men. It sounded dazed, dishonest and confused even to me, and anyway I was enjoying my heterosexual ring of confi-dence far too much to verbalise such weakness. Suddenly my gayness existed only inside me and was not reflected back at me by friends who were gay. I was not fully a part of their conversations: it was not that they ignored me, far from it, but I was no longer part of the charmed circle. It was as if the passwords and secret handshakes had changed and I was never told the new ones. It was all to be expected and I accepted it reluctantly, knowing that getting your bread buttered at both ends of the loaf at the same time just ain't sportin'. I loved my gay friends the most even as I became distanced from them.

However my most immediate and pressing problem was coming from a very surprising source. Toril was still toying with that stupid pepper pot. What was she thinking? She knew more about the situation than most, having actually been in the room with me and Patrick that night. In fact there was nothing about me of any significance she did not know. I got a little edgy.

'You can have the pepper mill if you like it so much,' I said to break the silence.

Toril looked up at me, her face breaking into a big smile. Her eyes were just a little behind the smile but they soon caught up.

'I'm sorry. That took a bit of time to sink in. When did all this happen?'

We talked for a while, me telling Toril all about Ruth and the kids and what Ruth was doing up in Manchester, Toril listening intently.

'Isn't this rather sudden?' she said unexpectedly. She would be asking for a ticket in Truman's sweepstake, I could tell.

'Uh . . . "sudden" . . . I don't think it's *too* sudden. At the moment it's feeling just about perfect.'

Toril ploughed on, ignoring my warning remark that things were 'perfect' so she should not rock my boat.

'The children, instant family, it's all very *convenient*, isn't it?'

'I'm not looking for a family.' *Is that true? Not sure. Pass.* 'I want some happiness . . .'

'You want happiness so much that you think a woman can give it to you?'

Wow, below the belt. I said, 'Please don't say that this is me settling for second best.'

Toril looked surprised. 'I don't *think* I did . . . but . . .' she left 'if the cap fits' unsaid. 'Is this what we were meeting up for tonight? So you could tell me this, this *news*?'

'Well, it's big news, isn't it? I wanted to tell you in person.' I was trying to be very upbeat here, to tell her how I wanted her to react.

'Oh yes, it's big news, changes a lot of things.'

'Not for us though, Toril, eh?' I was a bit confused. '*We'll* be just the same as before.'

Toril almost laughed. Almost. Even for a Scandinavian, she was looking pale. 'Won't we though. I think *that's* the truest thing you've said all night.'

The truest thing? Did she think I was lying? I decided to try and cut this conversation short. There is no competing with Toril in full flow.

'No, *this* woman, at *this* moment is perfect,' I insisted. 'It had to be a woman to make me feel this happy. I don't know why but it had to be. But more importantly, it had to be Ruth. It feels so different with her—'

Toril pounced on this, looking for weak links. *Don't be like this, be happy for me.*

'Different how, Simon? You've got to be so careful you don't confuse . . .' she searched for the right word, '*novelty* for—'

The phone rang. I frowned, wanting to hear what Toril had to say but I knew it would be Ruth. She always rang about this time, sitting by the phone in her mum's hallway, having just got the girls to bed. I stood up and crossed to the phone, saying, 'I'll just get this, *if* you don't mind. It'll be Ruth.'

Toril shrugged and nodded. Graceless cow. I picked up the phone.

'Hello you,' I said.

'Hello you' is a quote from *The Philadelphia Story*. James Stewart says it to Katharine Hepburn while he's drunk at a party. God, we were *sickening*. We had favourite films coming out of our ears.

'Hello you,' Ruth said back. I smiled as she spoke. That's a good sign, isn't it? I thought to myself, her voice makes me smile. Toril was getting me very het-up.

'Kids all asleep?'

'God no, I think Hannah must be on speed tonight. Do you know what she did . . .'

Aware that I was coming on like a new family man and that Toril would be picking up on all this, I turned slightly to see how she was reacting. Out of the corner of my eye I saw her take her pager from her belt loop, press a button and look at the display, holding the pager up to the light to see better.

Ruth and I prattled on, Toril enduring the conversation, then I told Ruth I had better get off the line because I had company.

'Daftie, you should have said. Who is it?'

'Toril, an old friend.' I smiled nervously at Toril, who was sitting on the edge of her seat. At the mention of her name, she did that 'I can't talk because you're on the phone but you're talking about me' thing where people move their head from side to side with a 'That's me!' expression on their face. People usually smile and look goofy when they do it but Toril just looked taut and wired.

'The Danish one?' Ruth asked, trying to remember.

'Are you Danish?' I called out to Toril as jovially as I could.

'Certainly not!' Toril replied loudly enough for Ruth to hear. At least she was being polite within Ruth's earshot.

'Toril's Norwegian,' I told Ruth. There was an indifferent '*nuls points*' noise from the Manchester jury. 'I've just told her all about you, she can't wait to meet you.'

With this lie, I tried to put a full stop on my disagreement with Toril: 'Be loyal, be a pal, don't rip me apart'. Toril raised her eyebrows at the news of her enthusiasm for Ruth and smiled briefly.

My voice dropped to a hush as I said, 'I got my test results back, by the way. All fine.'

'Thanks for doing that, Si. I'll let you get back to Heidi or whatever her name is. Call me tomorrow.' I said my goodbyes and put the phone down.

'Ruth says "Hi".' She hadn't at all but it seemed the thing to say. I was trying to build bridges here. Where was Mo Mowlam when I needed her?

Toril stood up, something on her mind. 'Great,' she said, not saying 'Say "Hi" back'. 'Can I use your phone, Simon? I just got paged for something that looks quite urgent.'

'Sure, go ahead.'

She knelt to get something out of her bag. I went through to the kitchen as Toril punched a number, looking at her pager again. As I stacked some dirty pots, I heard her say something in German. From the tone of her voice she was talking to an answering machine. She was trilingual, I was bisexual. Everyone's good at something.

After a short silence, I heard her hang up and she walked through to the kitchen. I looked round from my stacking.

'Everything OK?' I said.

'I think I've got to get back to London,' Toril said with

a rueful look. We had arranged that she would sleep over and drive up early next morning. 'It's something with one of the foreign buyers and it sounds like I should get back.'

'Really? It'll keep, won't it? I wanted to talk a bit more—'

'Surprising as it may seem, Simon, the world's financial markets will not hang fire while you talk a bit more. Galileo was right, as it turns out. Look, will you ring me? I'll be in all tomorrow night and I'm not up to much over the weekend. Oh, you've got to go to *Manchester*, haven't you,' she said, turning on her heel and stalking back into the living room to get her bag.

'You're going right now?' I said, following behind as Toril went into top gear with lots of 'must dash, terribly busy' London behaviour, plucking her coat from the rack.

'Sorry. Look, call me. Promise? Ignore everything I said. I'm happy for you, really.' Hrrmmph, I thought.

And with a quick peck on the cheek she was gone.

The flat was suddenly like the *Mary Celeste*, Toril's coffee cup still warm to the touch, the other coats on the rack still swinging. I had a neurotic suspicion at the back of my mind. Hating myself for having such a thought, I went to the phone and, even as I watched Toril get into her car and sit there for a brief moment with her head against the driving wheel before driving off at top speed, I hit last number redial to find out who she had called.

I felt like such a traitor but, as I had suspected, I got Toril's answering machine. I put down the phone before the tone went. She had not been leaving a message with someone to do with work. She had rung herself and left a bogus message in German, which she knew I did not speak. The whole pager, hold-it-up-to-the-light business had been a charade to get her out of my flat and on the road back home. I was livid. I rang her back and left a message for her to call me when she got in.

Toril's reaction to my little piece of news, I came to learn over the next few weeks, was completely unlike any other straight-friend-who-happened-to-be-female's reaction. They all seemed quite glad to be getting one man back for their team for a change, but they too treated me differently as a result. I was no longer one of the girls so I was cut out of that loop as well. Physical contact with them became more proscribed because an arm around the waist, a hand on the shoulder now had a sexual charge.

Maybe they thought, as Toril did, that I was making a big mistake and just did not feel they knew me well enough to say anything. None of them was suddenly clamouring to take Ruth's place in my affections. After all, when a new model of car or computer comes on the market, you don't rush out to buy it; you let others take the brunt of all those start-up problems.

Toril rang back just after midnight. By that time I had stewed and fretted my way into a standard army-issue self-righteous tizzy and was ready to go fifteen rounds with anyone. No close friend of mine was going to treat me like this.

'Toril,' I said frostily, knowing it would be her. On a normal night it could have been Callum but he was away on holiday with his latest flame. *He* had been fantastic about it all.

'Hello you,' Toril replied laconically. Sarcastic bitch.

'Good trip back?'

'Fine. Did I leave something behind? My remote thingy for my—'

I interrupted. 'I wanted to find out what you didn't say

to me, because you had to rush off. There was something, wasn't there?' There was a small silence.

'You're so perceptive. It's your best quality.'

'Tell me. What's your problem?' I said this as lightly as I could under the circumstances. I genuinely wanted to know what she was thinking about Ruth and me getting together.

'It's not a problem, Simon. It won't keep me awake at night.' As if I was thinking it might. 'I think I said my piece, I've got noth—'

'So why did you leave like that?' I butted in again.

'You know why. I got paged and I must talk to someone bef—'

'In *Germany*?' I said pointedly.

'Yes. Is that OK with you?'

'You left a fake message in German on your own answer phone. I bet you didn't even get a page.' I was on my high horse now.

'How nice that you trust me, Simon,' she said evenly. The 'nice' was perfect.

'You're jealous.'

'Mmm?'

'Of *me*, Toril. Of what I told you.'

'*Jealous* of you. Jealous of *you*. Do you know, you couldn't be more wrong,' she said in an infuriatingly airy tone. 'Quite the reverse in a way. I was a bit upset—'

'Why can't you be happy for me? Everyone else is—'

'Maybe that's because they don't . . .' her voice tapered away, then regained strength, still sounding lame, however, '. . . they don't *know* you like I do.'

I was not impressed by this at all. 'So what are people like Callum missing that you are picking up?'

'*Callum* knew before me? When did he know?' She

sounded very pissed off to have been out of the loop. But tonight had been the earliest she could make.

'Does it matter? Just tell me why you're so upset about this.'

There was a silence on the other end of the line. Bind-weeds blew across the empty streets of Dodge as Toril's and my high noon approached.

'I don't think . . . er . . . what's her name?'

'Ruth.'

'I don't think Ruth is the right woman for you. That's all.'

This was the point I really fucked up. I saw red and went a bit fruit-loopy and TV mini-series.

'Don't you *dare* say anything against Ruth.'

There was a squawk of protest from the other end which I ignored.

'You're not *listening*, Simon, you have never *properly* listened to a w—'

'Toril, I think you *are* jealous of me finally being happy with someone. It suited you that we both became old maids together, didn't it, and you can't bear the thought that I've now got someone in my life and the fact that that person is female makes it all the more real to you. Such a *fag-hag* reaction . . .'

I called her a fag hag and an old maid *in the same breath*. Just the memory brings me out in a cold sweat. I was protesting too much and in my heart-of-hearts I knew it, but I had my heterosexual fancy-dress on and I was 'defending the woman I loved'.

But I had not finished yet. Oh, no sirree Bob. Once you've taken a crap on your own doorstep, it's *important* to slip in it. So I strode confidently on.

'You think you know fuck *everything*, don't you, Toril?

You always have done. "I think it's a bit fast", you pompous cow. How the hell would you know? You know fuck-*all*.'

'*If you'll let me speak!*'

She was pissed off now. I half managed a defiant tone of voice.

'What?' I improvised.

'Firstly, never *ever* call me a fag hag again. It's the *last* thing I—'

I was feeling bullish. In for a penny.

'If the cap fits, Toril—'

'*That's it.* I gave you a chance, you self-obsessed prick, which is more than you gave me. She's welcome to you. Don't bother to call again. Just fuck off.'

And the line went dead. I had always been so careful about what I said to my nearest and dearest, to Patrick, to Callum and to Toril, because I knew how the slightest knock of criticism from them sent me flying. Callum was the one I needed to talk to but the bastard was away. He would have been able to figure out what was going on. The other one who always knew was Toril.

I had to sit down, feeling like I'd been in a fistfight. Why had Toril been so *stupid*, why had she let me down like that? Surely people like Callum and her, even *Patrick* loved me for reasons other than I was gay. I deserved better than that. The whole evening made me feel very sick and lonely. Toril and I were too close and had known each other for too long to argue over Ruth.

This *Mary Celeste* feeling was the low point of my fabled eight weeks and it happened more than once. In the middle of feeling triumphantly 'at one with the world', I none the less had these strange moments, not of doubt but of isolation when I was away from Ruth during the week. It was not just that I missed Ruth, although I did. The strange result of telling people about me and Ruth was that my relationships with them changed, very slightly, but they changed to something a smidgen less intimate just because my lover was a woman. I was no longer one of the girls with either my gay friends or my women friends and I missed that easiness. Just like Ruth with her new life in Manchester, I wanted it all. It had to be possible. Perhaps it was also a matter of me not being certain how to behave now around my friends and being too careful and wary. If so, that would be easier to solve.

But if it came to it, and people as precious to me as Toril fell by the wayside, that was too bad.

Chapter 14

'Deeper, and deeper still, thy goodness, child, pierceth a father's bleeding heart'

Thomas Morell

'Iss zair a passvurd?' I said quietly. This was quite frightening.

'Zair iss hno hneed. Ve ahr ohld ememeez, ziss man und myzelf,' Ruth replied, the cold January wind driving her deeper into her heavy winter coat.

The Checkpoint Charlie handover venue of the precious objects was by an ornamental pond in the park near Ruth's house. At this time of year, even on a Sunday, the park was deserted; as we approached the point, I saw that it was a huge and perfect circle, drained for the winter, with a forgotten rowboat on sentry-duty in the centre, covered in silt and grime.

Two adults and two children emerged from a light mist about forty yards away, all dressed in muted winter shades.

'Eet iss they,' I said. 'Do just ass ve haff discussed. Put the briefcase on zuh ground, step back and ask for zuh cheeldren to valk slowly over to you.'

'But vot do I do,' muttered Ruth, 'eef the lying bastard

tries to duppelcross me as he hass done so often ven ve vere married?'

'Tell hees girlfriend he hass herpes. Zat alvays vurks.'

The atmosphere of tension was exaggerated by the fact that Ruth and I were still not a public item in Manchester after quite a long time of going out with each other. Well, a long time for me. The girls still didn't know and I hadn't even met Ruth's mum. If Ruth's house was empty then I stayed there when I came up at weekends, but otherwise I was getting to know Manchester's mediumly expensive hotels very well. I did not mind it because I was enjoying my heterosexual glow too much, although I found it a touch bizarre to be to all intents and purposes in the closet again.

Ruth was being cautious, I could understand that. As a result, Christmas had been a complete non-event and I'd thought that had been a real shame because we could have had a lot of fun as well as have seized a chance to be together for more than two days in a row. Not that I had said anything even when an offer to go on holiday some-where had been firmly declined. So, I hadn't seen Ruth at all at Christmas and New Year, had done all my usual family things, had seen Callum a lot, hadn't seen Patrick, who was looking after his mother. Toril and myself had not been on speaking terms since that dreadful row so I didn't see her either. Hadn't done very much at all. Ruth had been with her extended family the whole time and had said it would be too much of a big deal to introduce me at Christmas. It had mystified me, to be honest, but I'd pushed it to the back of my head: who was she more ashamed of, her mother or me?

Today, I was undercover. Ruth's ex-husband didn't know who I was but I suspected I was here today specifically to piss him off: I was Ruth's new mystery man. It was a big deal I was here at all.

For all that this was a regular ritual, there was an unexpected moment of confusion. The two couples stood for an instant at a stalemate, facing each other across the pond, wondering who should move or blink first and cross round to join the other pair. Was there a protocol for this? Does the divor*cee* or the divor*cer* feel more obligated to make an effort?

Ruth was the one to blink. Nice touch, I thought. Make him think you don't care, that you're casual about this.

'Hello, how are you both?' she called out. 'Have you all had a lovely time? We'll come round to you. Isn't it cold? *Brrr.*'

'Brrr? You actually said "Brrr"?' I asked under my breath as we walked around the pond's circumference.

'Fuck off, I'm being friendly,' Ruth managed through gritted teeth.

'But I thought this was the Cold War all over again.'

'That's why I'm pretending to be friendly. It throws him off the scent.'

'That's *deep.*' I was impressed. 'This really is a sixties spy film.'

'Or a spaghetti western,' Ruth said out of the corner of her mouth, waving to Hannah. 'I'd *love* to gun him down.'

'It might upset the children,' I pointed out.

'That's right. *That's* why I never killed him. I remember now.'

I could make out that Ruth's ex was wearing some sort of track suit. We had so much in common.

'Can I talk about sport to him? Man to man.'

'Whatever lights your candle, honey-bunny. He supports City.'

'*Loser.* Even I know that much.' I knelt to tie a shoelace. 'What's she like?'

I looked in the other couple's direction. *She* was Ruth's ex-husband's new girlfriend, Michelle. They were talking out of the corner of their mouths as well. *Fabulous.*

'She's far too good for him,' Ruth summarised, eyeing her ex with barely concealed hostility. 'Come to think of it, Rose West would be too good for him.'

Hannah and Sarah started shrieking around the edge of the pond on the opposite side to us. 'Careful, you two,' Michelle called out, then caught herself and glanced towards Ruth.

'You're being friendly,' I reminded Ruth, who then suddenly smiled inanely and put her head on one side. 'Not too much, love.'

'All right, all right. God, I hate this.'

We got to Ruth's ex and Michelle. A gnat's whisker of a pause. Then:

'Darren.'

Half a gnat's whisker of a pause.

'Ruth.'

'This is Simon, my friend,' Ruth said with a rictus of friendliness on her face. 'Simon, Darren and Michelle.'

I muttered something amiable, extending my hand. Darren shook hands slowly with me, his eyes narrowing as he clocked a southern accent. I can't help it, it's not my fault, if you prick me do I not bleed? Michelle filled an uncomfortable vacuum by telling us what the girls had been up to that weekend. Ingesting additives and watching videos by the sound of it. Good on 'em, I was jealous. Darren stared at me. I stared back benignly for a moment, then looked at the girls playing on the other side of the pond.

I have been in a lot of bars where men look at each other with much less naked curiosity than that with which Darren examined this new boy on the block. Who was he, this 'friend' of his ex-wife? Darren was thinking. He had a real eye for detail, I could tell. Not having a clue about the etiquette of this situation, I kept looking away. It did not do for straight men to stare at each other, that much I did know, but in this divorced couple scenario, it was advanced nuclear quantum heterosexuality and I was still at GCSE level.

Anyway, I did not need to look at Darren. He was a type I recognised instantly: he had had the pick of the girls at school, had been king of the sports field, ruling the roost until the end of the VI Form, when he left and went straight to work and never moved a mile from the house in which he grew up. He was everyone I had known at school and, in my arrogant 'I'm off to uni' way, had not wanted to ever see again. I was not surprised Ruth had fallen for him; Darren had retained his sporty build and must have been dreamy eleven years ago. He had a great head of hair, dark and wavy like Hannah's, while Sarah had inherited his green eyes and was getting his lanky build. He had snake-hips and did not like me at all. He had snake-hips so I didn't like him either.

'They've had a big Sunday lunch and shared a Twix and a can of Coke about an hour ago,' Michelle finished efficiently, and with that and the passing over of an overnight bag, the technical part of the handover was complete. Just some conversation to be made and then we could all flee, saying variations on 'Thank fuck for that, is *Masterchef* still on?'

There was a pause begging to be ended. 'So, how about United then?' I offered.

Darren's eyes narrowed. 'I'm a City man myself,' he said.

'*Really?* They're not doing so well, I've heard. But I'm not really a football person. More tennis, me.'

I saw Ruth bite her lip. Darren said, 'Me too, actually. If you're still about, we could have a game in the summer.'

If you're still about . . . bastard. Fifteen-love to him.

'You'd thrash me,' I answered. 'I haven't played seriously for a long time.'

'I played for Cheshire,' Darren stated. Of course he had.

'Wow. Cheshire. Is that near here?' Let's push it a little too far.

Darren opened his mouth to reply but Michelle interrupted brightly, '*What* a cold day.'

'*Isn't* it,' agreed Ruth. 'Too cold to be standing around in the park talking about tennis.'

They both laughed in a girltalk way and then we all went into an extraordinary ballet of 'right then, let's go' moves.

'Where *are* those terrors?' Ruth said, looking around. She never spoke like a clichéd parent usually. Spotting the girls, she shouted, 'Come on, you two!'

The girls walked over to us, Sarah holding out her left hand.

'I grazed it. It stings,' she said, trying to be brave in front of so many authority figures but still wanting the attention.

Instinctively, Darren and Ruth both knelt by their daughter and examined her hand. Darren licked his finger and wiped some dirt out of the tiny graze, while Ruth smoothed Sarah's hair back out of her eyes. Darren and Ruth were a good team. While they concentrated on her hand, Sarah looked up at Michelle and me with a devil-child, Omen-ish look in her eye, as if to say, 'Whatever you might do, *I* bring them back together again'. Sarah had not officially been told anything yet, I was just Simon up on a visit, but I knew she knew. I had been warned.

Hannah, following behind, regarded the four adults, trying to understand the complexities of the situation. She joined her parents, looking at Sarah's enormous wound, thus completing the group and unconsciously locking Michelle and me out totally. They were a family again.

Michelle glanced at me and smiled quickly. We had absolutely nothing to be talking to each other about apart from the dissolved marriage of our respective parties. Nothing to say to each other whatsoever. So we had a chat.

'Have you come far?' Michelle said.

There was no question in her voice. The remark was just a way to exist through the time it took to say it. Michelle did seem really pleasant, a person with her head screwed on. Come to that, Darren seemed like a decent sort, if understandably a little hostile; Ruth talked about him like he was the Anti-Christ. There had been a lot of acid under the bridge, I guessed. I went along with Michelle's conversational gambit and attempted to pass the time.

'I'm just up from Brighton. Mind you, with the trains like they are . . .'

I wittered on for a bit about journeys, Michelle nodding and saying 'Yes' at five-second intervals. I trailed off and stepped back as Ruth and Darren stood up, Sarah being safely off the intensive care list. Michelle and I instantly forgot the conversation we had been having and reverted to our mannequin status.

Darren hugged both his daughters, staring at them so intensely it was as if he were trying to make each final second with them last an hour, freeze-framing each instant until he saw them again.

'I'll be around in the week to see you and I'll ring Tuesday. *You* take care of your hand and *you* finish that story we started. I love you both lots and lots.'

The girls clung on, saying goodbye. I was stunned by the unconditional love suddenly pouring out of this taciturn man. The look in Darren's eyes as he said goodbye to his children was something of which I had no knowledge. It was obvious that he would willingly die for them and, thinking about it, I did not feel that for anybody. I was not sure I was even capable of such emotion, but I knew I would want to be one day. In Darren's eyes was a trailer for one of my potential futures. But not yet-a-while.

If you have to think about it, you don't feel it. If you had asked me a year earlier, I'd have said I would 'die' for Toril, Callum, Patrick and the rest, but I certainly did not feel that for Toril now that we had rowed and weren't speaking. And even though Patrick and I had made up, and his mum being ill notwithstanding, he wasn't exactly battering my door down or ringing my phone off the hook since our escapade. I did not feel so close to him now. I would not die for anyone. I might consider getting injured.

With Darren and the girls, it was the blood-of-my-blood, fruit-of-my-loins factor and I had no access to that. Darren and Ruth had buried years of mutual differences and hatred to look after a non-existent graze on their child's hand. *Of course* they had, she was their daughter and their love for her outweighed anything else. It was a universe a million miles away from where I presently was.

As he straightened up, Darren's smile faded to nothing and he said goodbye to his ex-wife.

'Ruth.'

A fleck of dust on a gnat's whisker of a pause.

'Darren.'

'Nice to meet you,' said Michelle, shaking my hand.

'Likewise,' said Darren, his eyes cold again.

We went our separate ways at last, exiting in opposite directions out of the park. Thank fuck for that. Is *Masterchef* still on? I wondered. A black cloud forming about her head, Ruth slipped her arm through mine and we strolled back towards the main gate along a path bordered by bare trees and benches. Some insane death wish made me ask the stupidest question.

'Do you do that "Darren-Pause-Ruth" thing every week?' I said as the girls ran ahead to look at some ducks.

'Yep. Lovely, isn't it? After five years of marriage and two children, it's all we can do to say each other's name,' Ruth answered, grim-faced.

We walked on in silence. Ruth suddenly stopped and said. 'Could we *not* talk about my marriage, please?'

'We were?'

'I think we were just about to. It's absolutely none of your business, you know.'

We eyeballed each other, stalemate again. Were we going to have a fight? I heard myself say, 'Fine, just don't ask me along when you pick up your kids so you can show me off to your ex-husband. I'm bound to be curious.'

Only grown-ups talked like this. I was getting old. Ruth dodged and weaved.

'Showing you off? Is that what you think I was doing? You are so full of yourself.'

'You know that's what you were doing.'

'*Prick.*' With that emphatic uppercut, she walked on ahead, fuming, and started shouting at the girls, who had cornered a duck and were trying to stroke it.

I had to step on it to catch up with her for fear of speaking too loudly and the girls overhearing us quarrelling. Ruth had just stopped the girls trying to feed Rolos to the poor bird and marched off as I approached. I accelerated some more and said quietly but firmly in her ear, 'Do not take out your bad mood on me. Don't even begin doing that.'

If there is one thing I cannot stand it is people treating their nearest and dearest like emotional punchbags. 'I love you and therefore I am entitled to make your life hell' holds no water for me. Life is way too short for that kind of shit; I had tried not to take it from men and I was not about to accept it from Ruth. So she gave me some shit.

'You fancy Darren, don't you?' Ruth said.

Too easy, far too easy.

'That's right. I want him to fuck me up the arse. Right now.' Was that too crude? Probably. Backtrack, just settle for being nasty. 'As a matter of fact, I don't fancy him, at least not as much as you still do.' Too easy as well, but perhaps accurate judging from the flush rising in Ruth's cheeks. I continued, 'Anyway, I've never fancied anyone called *Darren.*'

'Snob.'

'Chippy bitch.'

We were having an honest to goodness *row*, it dawned on me. I had never had one before where I was not crying. This was Life in the real world, I thought, where people row and it does not mean they have to split up afterwards. Since I was enjoying myself, I carried on. 'Actually,

I fancied Michelle more than I fancied him. Which makes
you feel worse, Ruth, me fancying him or her?'

'I don't believe you *did* fancy her, not that I give a toss.
You can go to hell.'

'I'm going there anyway. What is this? I walked with
you to a park. End of story.'

Ruth stopped again and put her hands over her eyes.
She's going to cry, I thought. Oh, bugger. Now I'll have to
say sorry. But she wasn't crying, she was just counting
to . . .

'. . . ten.' She uncovered her eyes. 'Sorry. I get so het-up
meeting Darren. Please can we not have a row?'

And there we were: we had made up again. Now that is
magic. I love being an adult if it is like this all the time. No
simmering grudges, no underlying tensions that last
weeks. I had never known anything like it.

'But I was just starting to enjoy myself,' I protested.

We started to nostalgise over our first and hopefully
not our last row.

'You called me . . . what was it?' Ruth tried to remember.

'A chippy bitch. Sorry, it just came out.'

'Never row with a queen. Big mistake.'

'Vast,' I agreed, remembering some royal altercations of
my own from the not-too-distant past. 'Sorry.'

'Do you really fancy Michelle?' Ruth asked, forcing me
to look her in the eyes.

'Yeah,' I said as seriously as I could.

'*Bastard*.' Which is a surprisingly juicy and effective
word when used as a term of endearment.

'Do you really still fancy Darren?' I said, more for the
sake of completeness than anything else. I did not want to
know at all.

'Of course,' Ruth replied, eyes wide with sincerity.

'*Cow.*' Which is a crap word at the best of times, and this was close to being a best time. I felt exhilarated and very turned on by the row. It was a revelation how purifying arguing could be. Both of us were closer than we had been ten minutes before as a direct result of having had a barney. So we had a making up, everything's-all right-again kiss (very nearly my first), our cold noses rubbing against each other as we tried to find any sensation at all from our frozen lips.

Two startled little girls watched from a few yards behind us, mouths open in surprise, showing half-chewed Rolos, their cornered duck seizing its chance and escaping.

'Audience,' I whispered. Ruth swivelled round to look at her daughters.

'You'll haff to meet my muzzer now,' she said in her Cold War voice. '*Sheet.*'

Chapter 15

*'Tell me, tell me, smiling child,
What the Past is like to thee'*
Emily Brontë

Ruth turned towards her daughters. 'OK, I guess I should let you two in on a little secret.'

'Simon's your boyfriend,' Sarah stated. Hannah looked genuinely taken aback.

'Thank you for telling me,' Ruth answered. 'You're a very clever young woman.'

'I've known for ages,' said Sarah. She looked less than thrilled.

'Really?' Hannah said to her sister. Her sister muttered something about not wanting to upset Hannah. Hannah turned to me. 'Is that why you've been up to see us so much, Simon?'

'Yes. Is that OK?'

'So it wasn't to see Sarah and me as well?' Hannah said, trying very hard to understand how the world worked. Me and her both. I awaited my answer to her question with interest. Ruth and I steered the girls to a park bench and we all sat down.

'Well, you and your sister are so busy, I hardly see you anyway. Tap dancing, seeing your daddy . . .'

'And Michelle,' said Hannah.

'And Michelle, and school as well hardly leaves much time for a friend of your mummy's. No, I come up to see your mummy and, if I'm lucky, I get to see you two as well. An added bonus.'

I saw a lightbulb form over Hannah's head.

'Cherry on the top,' she said.

'That's right. Big tick. Ten out of ten,' I said, smiling at Hannah to get a smile back. Very slowly, she did so. Sarah, meantime, still looked stony-faced.

'And you too, Sarah. Icing on the cake,' I said, trying to find a bridge to this morose young lady, who I now knew so closely resembled her father both physically and temperamentally.

'My daddy's *lovely*,' she blurted out and burst into tears.

Ruth went into a well-worn pick-up-the-pieces mode, trying to comfort her stricken elder daughter. This was a big deal.

Sarah angrily shook off her mother. 'Go away. You hate Daddy,' she said. Hannah looked traumatised. Ruth started to speak but Sarah cut her off. 'You said to me that you loved Daddy still because he gave you me and Hannah but you don't even love him for that now.'

Ruth put her arms around her elder daughter and this time was not rebuffed, although Sarah remained as rigid and tense as before.

'I love your dad because he loves you and Hannah so much. But you're right and you've known for a long time that I'm not *in* love with him any more. Not the way I now . . .' *what would she say, what would she say?* '. . . like Simon. Sometimes people change and they fall out of love. It's sad but it happens,' said Ruth, losing control of her voice as she saw how much she was upsetting her daughters. This was why she'd kept us under wraps.

Ruth and I had not yet said the 'L' word to each other in earnest. The girls were accelerating everything for us. Hannah scrambled round to get some hugging action herself from her mother. Sarah stared grimly down at the gravel path. I did not know if I should say anything else but I did anyway. It had to be good, however, because Sarah was going to remember this for the rest of her life.

'Can *I* say something?' I said.

Surprised, Ruth looked at me in curiosity. Sarah nodded quickly. I took a deep breath.

'Your daddy *is* lovely. I could see that from the way he said goodbye to you and the way he said he loved you and the way that he looked after your hand. And because of that I don't want you to be scared of what I might do now I'm your mum's boyfriend.'

Fuck, this was difficult. Ruth watched, wondering what I might say next. Sarah nodded again for me to continue, Hannah wide-eyed now.

'I would never even *think* that I might take your daddy's place. I wouldn't even want to . . .' Sarah looked at me suddenly, tears still enormous in her eyes and on her cheeks. *Easy, Simon, but you do like them, yes?* 'I haven't finished. I wouldn't even want to, because he loves you and Hannah and you both love him far too much. But I can be your friend and someone to have fun with, someone who will help you if your mum or your dad or your nan aren't around. I'm a friend and that's all I *want* to be.'

Keeping an eye on Ruth throughout, I realised that this was our conversation about 'the kids and Simon and how he fits in'. We had not got to this point yet. Ruth had been listening very hard so I had tiptoed my way through that little speech like it had been a UN peace initiative.

'But you wanted a boyfriend like Mummy where we lived before,' Sarah said.

Without knowing it, Sarah hit the nail on the head. I had wanted a boyfriend exactly like Ruth and had never found one: one who laughed at things in the same way I did, who saw the world in a similar way, who was like the 5th of November in bed. Ruth.

'Like your mum said, people change.' That made it sound a cinch. 'But you're right that we both wanted the same thing, and when your mum and I clicked that that could mean we wanted each other, then we, sort of, fell in . . .'

I said 'fell in . . .'

Because I'd said 'fell in . . .', I now had to say 'fell in love' because you can't say 'fell in like' or 'fell into deep affection', even though that is what people do all the time and believe that they have fallen in love. I could say something else, that we 'fell into each other's arms', that we 'fell into a chasm of passion' or even 'fell in-tuitively for each other'.

I edged out on to the plank. I prodded myself. *Jump, you bastard, jump.* I jumped.

'. . . *love*,' Hannah, Ruth and I said simultaneously. I landed in the water and was in over my head.

'That's right, we fell in love,' I said, trying to stay afloat and keep my eye on the ball all at the same time (I guess this is a water-polo figure of speech). This was not about me, for once. It was not even about me and Ruth. I had to keep focused on the fact that a ten-year-old girl was understandably horrified that I was perhaps about to become her father.

I could not look at Ruth, even though I had just said 'I love you', not in so many words, but nearly.

'So people can change like you have?' Sarah asked slowly.

'People *always* change, Sarah,' said Ruth. 'You're different to how you were two years ago, I am, your dad is and Simon's changed too.'

'Nanna doesn't change at all, *ever*,' Hannah pointed out.

Ruth considered her mother's permanence with a wry grimace.

'I think you're right, she doesn't. But she did change a lot after my dad died.' Ruth looked at me here as she spoke of her father. 'So maybe she's just like everyone else after all.'

Sarah's head suddenly popped up.

'What was your dad like? Nanna never talks about him.'

Ruth's face had a radiance and happiness I had never seen before and she hugged her children to her. This was a *big* family day, all the main topics of interest at once.

'He was . . . he was . . . Pop was *funny* and he loved me and your uncle Pete just as much as your daddy loves you.'

They played 'I remember' for a little while, Ruth talking about how she used to go for walks in this park with her father and how they had played bat-and-ball, tag and hide-and-seek in the summer. I guessed this conversation was what Sundays were invented for. It all sounded too perfect, too good to be true.

'Can we go back now? I'm cold,' Hannah said.

'I'm cold too,' added Sarah, a huge drop of tearful snot still hanging, nearly frozen now, from her nose. We all looked at it.

'Yuk,' said Hannah.

'Sniff,' instructed Ruth. 'Or blow. Whichever.'

Sarah, recovering her sang-froid a little, gave her mother a mischievous sideways look, and wiped her nose on the sleeve of her coat. We edged out of the unforgettable lifetime trauma zone and back into the disposable everyday as Ruth coached her daughters on the intricacies of the handkerchief. The relief amongst us all was palpable. Crisis over.

We walked back to Ruth's. I was able to go round to the house because Ruth's mother was visiting her other grandchildren again. The legendary and unchanging Mrs Whittaker was assuming epic proportions in my mind. I still had not met her after nearly eight weeks but that would have to be remedied now that the girls knew, like Ruth had said. Not today though: I would be on a train bound for t' South when Granny got in. I was looking forward to falling asleep on the train. Nobody had told me that heterosexuality was a full-time job.

'How did we do?' I whispered to the expert.

'We did fine,' she answered. 'Just fine.'

Ruth sounded a little bleak. I glanced at her; she looked distant, even as she held tighter on to my arm. She knew I had looked at her and was thinking of what to say.

'No, it *was* good and thank you for talking to the girls like that. It makes us all know where we stand . . .' Ouch. She continued, 'and that is valuable to know.' Valuable? These were grown-up words. Technical talk.

'But you never thought I could be anything else for the girls, not with Darren around?'

Ruth shook her head, her eyes dulled with reality. I was amazed that we were now talking about this and not about the fact that we had sort of said 'I love you' to each other.

'Of course I didn't,' she said. 'We're nowhere near anything like that and now . . .'

'We won't be,' I finished for her. I had meant what I said. Toril had been dead wrong when she accused me of looking for a ready-made family. There was no doubt in my heartless little mind that life with Ruth would be simpler without these two little girls, but they were a fact, they were mostly delightful and that was the situation. Most days I just about got by looking after myself and I was not going to inflict that on a child like Sarah. It was vital that I remained as peripheral to their lives as possible, for them and, much more importantly, for me. I was not capable of being a substitute for that serious man who so obviously loved them with an intensity I had found almost shocking. One day I could imagine having my own children, having the same look in my eyes when I looked at my babies as Darren had had. But not now, not this way.

It came to me why Ruth was unhappy with what I had just said. I had as good as told Sarah that my love for Ruth was not unconditional. I had just placed conditions on it to protect myself: 'I love you *but* I will not love your children just because I love you'. I was distancing myself from a commitment that placed obligations on me while making a commitment that benefited me: a completely male reaction, just as Darren's complete and unconditional love for his daughters was also. My impulse for self-protection did not stop me *eventually* wanting what Darren so obviously had, just as he would see no illogic in occasionally missing a monthly payment or two. So maybe 'I love you but' stretched into Darren's world as well.

'I love you but' is not a great line in any movie and certainly ranks below the simplicity and charm of 'I love
you'. The reason that Ruth was a little blue was that I
had said 'I love you but' when I had thought I was saying
'I love you'. And she had realised it first.

It was the 'but' that made an ounce of spontaneity ooze
out of Ruth's and my relationship even though we had
both known from the start that we were not Clark and
Vivien on a velvet staircase or Leo and Kate clinging to
wreckage. It's the only time in my life I've known I had a
great 'but'. It was not a good feeling. Men know just as
much as women when they are shite at commitment and
in a secret recess of our hearts we feel bad about it as
well. But the pain is less intense and passes faster. The
pros outweigh the cons.

We got to the park gate. It was getting dark.

'No, we did fine,' said Ruth, forcing herself to perk up
again. 'Sarah's been low for ages. Perhaps this will help.
Thank you, you . . .'

'. . . full-of-himself prick?' The row had been the high
point of the afternoon. Let's talk about that again.

'Did I say that?' Ruth crinkled her nose in dismay. Cute,
very cute.

'Yes, you did.' I was not about to let her off the hook,
however cute her nose-crinkling was.

'Oh well, *c'est la vie*,' she said airily.

Toril had said I was self-obsessed, I recalled. A self-
obsessed prick, to be precise. No smoke without a grain of
truth, as they say. I started to worry about how much
time I spent thinking about how self-obsessed I was.

We got to a crossing and waited for the green man to
give us the all-clear. As Ruth and Sarah chatted about this
and that, Hannah tugged at my coat.

'I want to tell you a secret, Simon. Bend down, I'll whisper it.'

I bent down. With a face that said she was bestowing an enormous honour on me, which she was, and doing me a huge favour, which she was not, Hannah said, 'I don't mind having two daddies. I don't mind at all.'

She rejoined her mother, giving me a confidential nod and smile. Appalled, I stood up. We waited for the green man. I looked at Ruth.

'You don't really think I'm self-obsessed, do you?'

'*No*, no, no, no, *no*,' she replied briskly, keeping her eyes firmly fixed ahead. The green man flashed at us.

We made sure that the two children got across the road safely and then went home and prepared food for them. Ruth washed up the dishes from their dinner and I dried them. I then read Hannah a story as Ruth helped Sarah with her maths homework.

Mmm. This was going to be complex.

Chapter 16

'People who have no weaknesses are terrible'
Anatole France

The week following that very het weekend was not the most straight one possible. Something had *sort of* happened and I had not been able to tell Ruth about it on the phone: she was too busy writing an essay on revenge tragedy, bringing up children, being a student and, most terrifying of all, organising for me to be introduced to her mum and her brother Peter the next weekend. Nightmare Scenario No. 341. Either way, she was too busy. We talked twice, maybe three times, always too briefly.

The visit was all fixed. I was arriving at Piccadilly and she would pick me up, then we would all congregate and be one big happy family back at Ruth's. That was the theory.

As the train drew in to Manchester, I vowed that I would tell Ruth all my sins of the week. None of my sins were mortal sins; indeed all of them were only mental but that had made it worse. Nothing lubricious had gone on, except in my head, but it had not been a celibate straight week at all.

Ruth met me on the platform with loud hellos and

hugs, having just dropped the girls off at their father's. It was going to be just grown-ups for afternoon tea. Great. We walked to Ruth's car, holding hands. This moment of seeing Ruth again after five days away was so strange as she became real again. I was always a little shy and stilted at first, no doubt appearing cold and austere to Ruth. A rule for life is that if a man you know well appears aloof and chilly he does not know what the fuck he is doing. I lectured myself to loosen up. I was like a boxer warming up before a fight, throwing fake punches into the air: *Tell her the truth, Simon, before you meet her family, tell her what you thought, now, as you're putting your seatbelts on.*

Clunk click.

'I need to talk to you about something . . .'

The key froze in the ignition along with the expression on Ruth's face. I could hear the slightly hysterical tone in my voice that was ringing alarms in her head.

'About something that happened to me this week.'

Ruth looked warily at me, knowing what this could be about. She kept one hand on the steering wheel and one on the ignition as if she was going to accelerate away at any second. She said slowly, 'Oh God, is this dreadful, Simon? What are you going to tell me?'

It felt like I had made a bad beginning and that everything was suddenly much worse than it actually was.

'It's not as bad as you're thinking it is. Honest.'

'So how bad is it on a scale of one to seven?' she asked.

'One to seven? Why not one to ten?'

'Seven's my lucky number. How bad? *How bad?*'

'It's a three,' I whined.

'But it might be a four, right, Simon?'

'Depends.'

Any moment now I might actually get to tell her what

my news was as opposed to merely assessing my news's screw-up-Ruth's-life factor. Ruth's voice was spiralling into a mass of detail that neither of us needed.

'Will it take long? Because I have to come straight back here to pick my brother up because his car's broken down and he's maybe leaving a message at home saying what train he's getting—'

I grabbed her hand and held it, staring at her, trying to get her to calm down enough for me to talk to her. This seemed to petrify her even more. It really was not as bad as she was thinking. I changed my mind and resolved not to be honest ever again if it was going to have this effect on people. Ruth was suddenly showing just how fragile her cool exterior was. We were building on very shaky foundations, Ruth and I.

'It's not as bad as whatever is going through your head.'

'How do you know? Why do you look like a frightened six-year-old? Just tell me.'

I told her about my week. It had been composed of countless little jaunts up to London for the business and I had ended up staying over at Callum's flat one night, as I always did if I had an overnight in the smoke. Callum had given me keys to his gaff, as he called it, years before and I came and went as I pleased. 'If I've got someone staying with me and you're there, I'll just take her straight to my bedroom,' he had said. I was doing him a favour, he reckoned. If no girl was on the scene we invariably had a laddish time in front of late-night TV. Since his incarnation as my sexual guru, it was especially good to see him.

What I didn't tell Ruth was pretty crucial. Callum had rung me early in the week to tell me that Patrick had bought the flat across the hallway and was soon moving in.

'He was staying with me for a couple of nights and he

saw the sign up. It's a repo' and he's not in a chain so it's all happened really fast. He moves in in a fortnight, I think. It'll be weird having Pat as a neighbour.'

'That's great. How is he?' I asked carefully.

'He's all right. You never can tell with Patrick these days, can you? He was always a cagey customer at the best of times, and he's worse since he got back from Hong Kong. And the thing with his mum isn't about to go away.'

'Is she all right?'

'Not sure, Simon, you'd probably get more of an answer out of him on that front than me. Look, I've got to run – I'll see you in the week? I'll be in late most nights. Remember to buy some bog-roll and milk.'

'You're such an old smoothie.'

'You see right through me, don't you? Bye.'

I had not seen Patrick since the creaky futon fiasco that had started all this off. We'd had that long chat on the phone afterwards but we had not met up at all to go to the cinema or the pub, the normal things we would have done if nothing juicy had happened that night. Callum remained in the dark about that night. It was just me, Pat and Toril who knew.

At about seven o'clock on the Thursday of that eighth and last week of my being serene and complacently happy at being straight, I let myself into Callum's building. I was not expecting to find Callum, him being a madcap socialite and ligger extraordinaire. Soap operas and dinner on a tray were not his style at all. I took the little lift up to his flat, although it was only two floors, because it had been a day and I was shagging a lot at weekends. I had to conserve my energies. If God was in His heaven, there would be enough hot water for a bath.

The lift took its customary age to climb two floors but

I forgave it this once because I saw that the lift had had quite a day as well. An all-too-familiar sight of cardboard-box hell on Callum's floor said that Patrick had completed his flat deal early.

As I picked my way along the jam-packed corridor, Pat, dressed in dirty jeans and a denim shirt, cigarette hanging from his mouth, came out of number 12, the flat opposite Callum's. His hair was longer than when I'd seen him last, unkempt and curling. He looked wild but he looked wonderful. He stopped when he saw me.

My heart started pounding. *Keep cool, Simon, you can do this.*

'Simon. Bloody hell,' said Patrick. 'Are you crashing at Callum's? I don't think he's in.'

'I've got keys,' I said, jangling them in the air. 'It's great about the flat. I didn't know it was today. Callum said you were moving in in a fortnight or something.'

'The mortgage came through early.' Patrick swallowed and nodded. 'Good to see you, Si. It's been too long.'

We shook hands very formally. It was all rather sweet, like we were reintroducing ourselves and starting over. The unmistakable whiff of sweaty man reached my nostrils. I took in a lungful just for old time's sake and tried not to fall over.

'Quiet day then,' I said looking around at the boxes.

'Yeah, just me and the afternoon movie. Nothing special on,' he smiled and passed a hand over his tired, grey eyes. It was quite a shock to discover that *I was not in love with him*. I loved him as a pal and a part of my life; I *fancied* him but I was not head-over-heels for him.

'Hey, too bad I've missed all the hard work,' I said, looking over Patrick's shoulder into his empty flat. 'Can I see your flat? How exciting.'

I went to take a step forward but he stopped me with a wave of his cigarette.

'It's just like Callum's except it's just me and a sodding *huge* sofa. It was a nightmare getting it up the stairs.'

'I'll bet,' I said, trying to be upbeat. So I was not welcome, it seemed. How silly. My bath was calling to me. I jangled my keys again.

'Well, best of British with the new place, Pat.'

'Thanks, Si.'

'Excuse me, could I . . .' and I had to squeeze past Patrick to get in the little vestibule between Callum's front door and his. Patrick flattened himself against the wall to let me through a mite too quickly. I glanced at him with just a trace of scorn.

'I wouldn't touch you up in a corridor, Patrick.'

'No . . . I was just getting out of your way,' he said hastily.

I searched for the right key to Callum's flat. Beam me up, please.

'Callum says you're going out with a girl,' Patrick said, his words tumbling out over each other.

I looked back at him, feeling quite shy. 'Yeah, she's more of a *woman*, actually,' I said, rolling my eyes. 'Two kids.'

'Really?' Patrick looked shocked. *Poor kids*, he was probably thinking.

'Yep. How's your mum?'

He took a big drag of his cigarette before replying, a shadow coming over his face. I hadn't been around for him, had I? Not at all. After all that I had promised.

'We-e-ll, she had the op three weeks ago—'

'Just the lump?'

'The whole thing. It was pretty difficult,' Patrick said, English understatement rescuing us both.

'But she's on the road back?'

Pat touched his head, 'Touch wood,' and smiled at me. He'd had to cope with all of that alone. He looked like he needed some attention himself.

'See you later perhaps?' I said. 'I've *got* to have a bath. Give me a knock, yeah?'

Patrick's smile faded. 'I might do that. Thanks.'

I shut the door behind me as he carried on humping boxes through to his flat. He *might* knock on the door later? How times change. If that was what he wanted, I could get by. Not good, though.

Of course, there was no fucking hot water. I put the pre-Victorian immersion system on, Callum's flat not being quite the hymn to matt black, bachelor interior design one might expect. I settled in front of the television, having decided not to open any cupboard or fridge door in the inferno of bacteria that was Callum's kitchen. I'd find a take-away after my bath. I watched a British sitcom that made me laugh out loud, giving me certain proof that I was tired and braindead.

I stiffened as I heard Pat's front door slam and his footsteps recede down the stairwell. I'd been on edge waiting for him to come over without realising it. So he'd gone out; big deal. I'd find a way for us to be friends again. Just not today, it seemed. I watched the news, worried briefly about global problems and then went to go and test the water. There was a knock.

It was, of course, Patrick, smiling his most winning smile and holding two bottles of Moët & Chandon.

'Hi, it's me,' he said.

'Hello you,' I replied, instinctively using Ruth and mine's special greeting. I felt a thin bat squeak of betrayal just for doing that. How odd.

'Sorry I was a bit strange earlier,' Pat said. 'It was a bit of a shock to see you.'

'It's OK. Considering the last time you did see me, you—'

'La, la, la, la, la . . .' Patrick sang tunelessly, blocking his ears with the bottles. 'I can't hear you *at all* . . .'

'Oh, fine,' I said. That's how we'll play it then. The ostrich manoeuvre.

Patrick proffered the bottles again. 'Help me christen my flat. *Please*. It's just too godawful sad opening one on my own.'

He showed me the bottles like he was an advert, all prominent label and toothy smile. He added, '*Go on*.'

I pretended to be reluctant, whining, 'But there was a documentary on transport policy about to start.'

'Really. Well, you'd better watch that then, of course,' Patrick nodded earnestly.

'Oh, let's do it, you twisted my arm.'

We beamed at each other, friends again, Patrick looking relieved.

'Thank you, you're saving my life. I was just about to put on some sad songs.'

'You don't want to do that,' I said, as we crossed into his flat.

The empty apartment seemed enormous but it was the same size as Callum's, just cleaner and not cluttered yet. A truly enormous sofa on a skew whiff angle dominated the centre of the room and a large ornamented mirror leaned against a wall, swathed in bubble wrap. Other than that it was boxes, boxes, right on till morning.

'So what's her name?' Pat asked, searching for and finding two coffee mugs in a box. 'These will have to do.'

'Ruth,' I replied. 'She's called Ruth.'

'You could have told me, you know. Not left it up to Toril,' Patrick said, sitting on the edge of a packing case.

'Toril told you?'

'Yeah. Are you talking to her again?' So he knew Toril and I had argued.

'No. It was all pretty stupid. It'll take a little time, I think. Is she well?'

Patrick shrugged. 'She wasn't great when I saw her. Don't leave it too long.'

'OK.'

'So, Ruth isn't a transsexual or anything? Nothing kinky?' Patrick said with a waggle of his eyebrows. What *had* Toril told him?

'Nothing kinky,' I confirmed.

'But that's quite kinky in itself, isn't it? For someone like you,' Patrick said darkly, pointing a mug at me.

Much too close to the bone. I crossed to him and took the mug from him to change the subject. 'Where's that drink? Let's wet the baby's head.'

Patrick hesitated then said, 'You don't have to answer this. Is your being with this woman anything to do with what . . . happened . . . with us?'

'La, la, la, la, I can't hear you.'

'Is it?' he insisted.

'A bit,' I conceded. 'But nobody's forcing me to go out with Ruth, she's *great*. That night was a jump-start for it all. Perhaps. So thanks, I guess.'

'My trauma,' he said. 'I mean, my pleasure.'

I felt that oneness-with-the-world a last time. It had been a great eight weeks and I was not to know that it had just come to an end. Pat handed me his mug to hold then struggled manfully with a cork. The cork popped and I quickly got the mugs under the champagne.

'Congratulations, Patrick,' I said, trying to be bouncy for him. 'A new start. I can recommend them, they're pretty fucking spiffy.'

'Pretty fucking spiffy, huh?' Patrick brightened up. 'OK, that's the toast, to "Pretty Fucking Spiffy New Beginnings".'

We downed the mugs of bubbly in one. I felt the shock of the alcohol ricochet around my empty stomach and shoot straight to my head in about ten seconds. The walls revolved a little. They were a really horrible colour.

'You've *got* to redo the walls,' I said. 'What an awful colour.'

Patrick looked downcast. 'Oh, I like it. Don't you like it? Duck egg.'

Precisely. Duck egg. He might as well live in a TB ward. He *was* straight, not a clue. Trying to shift the topic to something I did like, I looked around the empty room.

'I spy with my little eye something very *classy* beginning with "M".'

'M-M-M-M, whatever could you mean? I love it, don't you?' said Patrick, pouring me more champagne and crossing to the m-m-mirror.

'I've never seen one as big as that before,' I said with relish.

'Fnar, fnar,' Patrick replied. 'It's been in storage for *years*. I've never had anywhere to put it until now.'

'Wa-*hay*,' I sniggered, finding another *double entendre* as the champagne shot through my system.

'Easy, tiger, watch it, you're straight now. No, it was my grandmother's, she left it to me about eight years ago. She hated it, said it made her look fat, but she knew I always loved it. It's Edwardian, I think.'

Patrick squatted by the mirror, touching the glass. He

suddenly stood up, holding the champagne bottle out in front of him.

'Nanna!' he toasted and swigged direct from the bottle.

'Nanna!' I said, then stopped. 'What was her name? She wasn't just a grandmother, was she? She must have had a name.'

'What *was* her name?' Patrick said, looking perplexed. '*Phyllis*! Her name was Phyllis!'

'Crazy name, crazy lady,' I said and we toasted Phyllis and her mirror all over again, Patrick pouring me out yet more champagne. The alcohol took hold. Patrick was swiftly turning back into Michelangelo's *David*. Bad news. I started having a little rose-tinted moment, remembering Patrick from when I'd first known him as a fresh-faced undergrad: in cafés cracking jokes and holding forth, on a demo outside a Barclays Bank, beating Nigel Havers in a fabulous race around a crowded courtyard. Ooh, I was pissed, I was getting him confused with *Chariots of Fire*.

We moved on to the second bottle and neither of us having eaten, we got pie-eyed very fast. I cleared a space on the big sofa and stretched out. It was so big I felt like I was a kid again. Resolving to buy a sofa like this pronto, I must have passed out, because when I opened my eyes again the bare lightbulb in the middle of the room had been turned off and replaced by candles. Incense was burning in a little holder. Patrick? Incense?

From some hidden music system, I could hear new-age whale-music type sounds. Patrick was sitting cross-legged in front of the mirror. Golly, perhaps he'd become a Buddhist in Hong Kong. He suddenly leaned forward and pulled back the folds of bubble wrap further to get a better view. He drained the second bottle and put it to one side. Looking round quickly to check I was asleep (I shut

my eyes just in time), Patrick stood up and undid his
jeans, letting them drop to the floor. Then he eased out of
his boxers and stood there contemplatively stroking his
balls and looking at himself. He had a great bum but he'd
got an evil-looking scar on his left thigh. When had that
happened? With one hand be began stroking his cock to
life, his free hand undoing his shirt. He wasn't a Buddhist
at all.

Trousers round his ankles and his shirt now hanging
open to reveal a hairy torso just starting to put some
weight back on (he'd been far too thin that night I slept
with him), he sat down and leaned back against the end
of the sofa, out of sight to me. Fuck, I couldn't see a thing.
Shifting quietly, I could see everything again in the reflection, and because of the darkness in the room, Patrick
would not see me moving. How convenient.

With the expert coaxing of his right hand, Patrick's
penis grew hard, to a respectable six inches or so. Like a
finger of fudge, it was just enough. I had not seen
anyone's erection but my own in months and stared in fas-
cination as he spat into his hand, and, always looking at
himself, used the spit to take back the foreskin, his mouth
opening in contentment as he did so. He kept staring at
himself, stroking his chest, murmuring to himself, pulling
at his nipples with painful tugs. He was really going for it
tonight. The whale music was replaced by wind through
the trees and birdsong music. He whispered in a bizarre
American accent, '*Oooh, birdie, birdie, come and perch on
me, ooh, birdie, birdie.*'

My friend Pat was a kook of the first water, I realised.

'*Little tweety, come to Momma, ooh, birdie-pie, big birdie-
pie, lick it all up, look at this present for my girl, big present
for the big birdie-pie, ooh tweety . . .*'

A freaking whacko in fact. People always say that you don't know someone until you sleep with them. But I *had* slept with Patrick and this sub-Jack Nicholson/Dennis Hopper routine was a new one on me.

Not that I disapproved. I could feel my own cock pressing against my trousers, but I did not dare move. I really wanted to join in, to sleep with my potentially psychotic pal who just happened to be naked and aroused in front of me. He was accidentally turning me on, he was deliberately turning himself on, and nothing, least of all me, was going to stop him doing that.

If the mirror had made his grandmother look fat, it was doing wonders for Patrick's self-esteem tonight. He was having a high old time and loving himself with a passion, never unlocking eyes from his reflection, drinking himself in. He squeezed his balls gently as the rhythm of his strokes gathered pace. Suddenly he grabbed the champagne bottle and started feeling that as well. Now *that's* a twist, I thought. The music looped back into the whales whistling and fluting.

'Oooh, thar she blows, harpoons, corks going to go.'

Concentrating now, with short, feverish strokes, he placed the bottle on the top of his dick. What a *deviant*. These heterosexuals, what are they like? I found myself thinking about how I wasn't thinking about Ruth, about how she did not enter the equation. I surreptitiously succeeded in rubbing myself through the material of my trousers. It was safe to move slightly now; Patrick was far too deep into his personal cabaret and would not have noticed if I started playing the tuba let alone the pink oboe. He stiffened suddenly, and as he came, gasping and wheezing the phrase '*Who's the fairest of them all*', he tried to catch the arcing spume *in* the bottle, like a fast rewind of the earlier uncorking. An imaginative variation on an old theme, I thought approvingly, good for Patrick. I do like my friends to be original. At the time it was certainly slightly David Lynch-frightening but quite beautiful. In the moment, like most things sexual, it had almost seemed like Art. Only in retrospect did it seem like a naff wank in front of a nice mirror.

Breathing heavily, Patrick relaxed, put down the bottle, saying something that sounded suspiciously like 'Boxes, boxes, boxes'. Strange man. In time-honoured fashion, he took off a sock and mopped up some of the debris on his stomach that had not got into the bottle (not much had, it has to be admitted). He stood up, and in the trousers-round-the-ankles shuffle that is the trademark of *Homo sapiens post masturbatus*, he waddled to his bathroom to clean up properly, giggling insanely to himself as he saw me still asleep on the couch.

Ruth exploded back into my mind. I had to get out of there.

While he was out of the room, I made lots of waking-up sounds.

'Pat?' I called out.

He stuck his head round the bathroom door *very fast*, reaching into the living room and switching on the central light again. Mr Hyde was gone; that lovely Dr Jekyll was back.

'Hey! You really zonked out. Big day too, huh?' A trace of his serial-killer American accent remained.

'Sure was,' I unconsciously mimicked back. 'Look . . . er . . . thanks for your . . . hospitality, I had a lovely time.'

Run, run for your lives. As I stood up, I glanced at the bespattered bottle of château Patrick. He saw the look and was back in the living room like a bullet, doing up his shirt and kicking the bottle into touch in one fluid movement. Quite a lot of fluid actually.

'Brilliant to see you, Simon. Too long for us not to see each other.'

'You've only got one sock on, Pat,' I said innocently as I could.

Patrick ground to a sudden halt and looked down at his one bare foot.

'What?'

'One sock. Only one. You had two,' I repeated carefully.

'Yeah? I was just about to . . .'

'Wash your feet?'

'Wash my *socks*,' he corrected me, nodding his head vigorously.

'Oh, I see.'

'You watched me wank.'

'Yeah.'

'*Bastard.*'

'Sorry.'

My poker face disintegrated and I burst out laughing. Patrick's face went the colour his penis had just been. Only to be expected; it was the same blood. He threw himself on his sofa and curled up into a foetal position, banging his head against a cushion.

'You bastard. I thought you were asleep. *Bollocks, bollocks, bollocks, bollocks, bollocks.* Nnnngh. . .' and so on and so forth.

'*Nice* bollocks though, Patrick. Very *full*, I thought.'

'Stop it, stop it, I hate you.'

I thought I'd push it a little too far. The big state secret among men is how big their dick gets when it's hard, unless it's enormous of course, in which case you find a piece of high ground and shout about it. The added frisson here was that I was the only man who had held Pat's, apart from him. He was moaning now.

I said, 'Great *cock*. *Very* thick. Congrats.'

'I do hate you, I fucking do.'

Suddenly he leapt up and began forensically examining the couch.

'Did you jizz on my new couch? If you have got spunk on my new couch, I'll swing for you.'

I was choking by now. He was such an old nelly. *Semen on my loose covers! Semen on my loose covers!* I became hysterical and had a warm sensation.

'I've got to go to the bog, I'm peeing my pants,' I gasped.

It was the jolliest pee I'd had in a long while, just me and a soggy sock in a corner, laughing insanely. Just me, not the sock as well. When I came out of the loo, Patrick was sitting up on his sperm-free sofa and clutching a cushion to himself.

He vowed, 'The next time we meet, if we meet, and at the moment, it is definitely iffy, I'll try not to get my dick out.'

'No need to bother on my account,' I said, sitting beside him on the sofa and starting to laugh all over again. 'I have to say, that Moby Dick tweety routine is something *else*.'

'Aaaargh!' shouted Patrick, stopping his ears and starting to laugh himself now. He'd forgotten about that. I repeated choice bits of the '*ooh birdie-pie*' stuff to him. After about five minutes of this we laughed ourselves to a standstill.

A breathless silence reigned. Patrick turned to me to say something just as I turned to him and our gazes locked for the longest, longest moment. Something almost happened.

I jabbed a finger at him to break the bubble.

'Time for me to go.'

'Time for you to go,' he agreed.

Simon, *get out*. I practically ran for the door, but could not open it because the latch was different to Callum's.

'Let me, let me. This happened before. I think it's stuck,' Patrick said as we both scrabbled madly at the door. I thought lightning wasn't meant to do this. The door finally opened and with an exultant gasp, I erupted into the vestibule. Now there's a phrase you don't see too often.

'Thank you for coming,' Pat said.

'No, thank *you*,' I replied, right on cue, setting both of us off again.

'Goodnight, Simon.'

'Goodnight, Patrick. Lots of love to your mum.'

'OK.'

I went back into Callum's flat and ran a bath, the water by then being scalding hot. I poured in some of Callum's Matey bubble bath (you don't have to clean the bath, remember? *Very* Callum).

I calmed down, undressed and sat on the loo, waiting for the bath to fill up. It seemed right that the person who had propelled me on the road to heterosexuality should be the one to put a spanner in the works. Settling back into the bubbles, I looked at my dick, wondering why it did things like this to me. If Patrick hadn't been Patrick and hadn't been deranged, I'd have been fucking him at that moment, no doubt about it. So much for my promises to Ruth. Some heterosexual I was. But in the moment, if the other person is on for it, there's nothing you can do. Man is a social animal, as an old, probably homosexual Greek said.

Suddenly Callum burst through his front door, nearly tripping over my bag, judging by the clatter.

'Simon! Are you here?'

'In the bath.'

'Can I come in, I'm busting for a piss.'

'Make yourself at home,' I said, arranging some bubbles over my half-erect penis. I had not wanted to jerk off thinking about the out-take from *Se7en* I had just seen. It had felt wrong.

Callum darted in and unburdened himself in full view of me.

'Sorry about this,' he said as a very big evening in the pub endlessly coursed out of him. I looked away.

Penises, penises everywhere and not a drop to drink, I thought. Callum glanced at me.

'Is that my Matey you're using?'

'Is that a problem?'

'No, it's fine, just don't use too much, that's all.'

Heterosexuals can be such queens sometimes.

'You haven't made up with Toril yet, have you?' Callum grunted.

'Will you guys stop telling me that?' To move the subject on, I told Callum that Patrick had moved in ahead of schedule.

'Oh yeah? How is he?'

'Bit of a wanker, to be honest,' I said and sank despairingly under the water.

Chapter 17

'I want my daughters to be beautiful, accomplished and good; to have a happy youth, to be well and wisely married, and to lead useful pleasant lives with as little care and sorrow to try them as God sees fit to send'
Louisa M. Alcott

Back in Ruth's car, I finished my dismal little tale and waited for Ruth to reply. She looked relieved and mystified, probably because I hadn't quite told her everything. The way she heard it, it wasn't Patrick, it was a stranger who turned out to be kooky. I also told her I had only woken up as the guy actually came, not stuck around from adverts through the trailers and stayed in my seat until the end of the credits and the lights came up. I had censored myself as I went along, trimming and editing so that Ruth's panic would not be justified.

'So nothing happened with this psycho Buddhist who came in a bottle?'

'He wasn't a Buddhist. I think he was a bit low,' I protested, sticking up for my mythical stranger. I was going mad.

'Whatever. But nothing happened. Simon, you're *bisexual*, you get turned on by men. What else are you going to think if a man jerks off in front of you? Even if he is Hannibal Lecter? This is not a shock to me. I might get turned on if I watch a woman having a wank. I *might*. It's not necessarily a bad thing.'

Ruth leaned over and gave me a kiss. 'Please don't scare me like that again. Thank you for feeling bad enough to feel guilty.'

'Pleasure,' I said.

Fuck.

Ruth had missed the point because she didn't know the whole picture and I couldn't start the conversation again. The point was that even if I did not go out of my way to find men to sleep with, the opportunity might present itself, as it would have done if Patrick had been gay. Such an offer was going to be difficult to turn down however much I wanted to be with Ruth.

'By the way, I told Mum all about you being gay for ten years,' Ruth said, negotiating her way out of the car park.

I had a coronary.

'By the way, *by the way*.' I was incredulous. 'How can you tell me something like that "by the way"?'

'I had to tell her. She knew as soon as she realised you were my ex-boss. And, anyway, the girls know. Mother's fine with it. No problems.'

Fantastic. What a lovely weekend this was going to be. As we drew up in Ruth's driveway, her mother came to the door. She looked very smart – in pearls with a light cardigan round her slim shoulders. She seemed quite nice from a distance, if a little proper. Ruth without Ruth's warmth, but I hoped not ruthless. I could see her breath in the cold air.

'She's breathing flames,' I said. Ruth told me to calm

down and grow up. I was shitting myself. Ruth made the introductions, lit the blue touch paper and stood well back. We exchanged pleasantries. Ruth's mother's voice was posh northern, Alan Bennett-ish. She seemed fine.

'I'll make some tea. You must be parched, Mr Lyndon,' she said and went through to the kitchen. It was strange that this house, where I'd been quite a few times now without her direct knowledge, was actually hers.

'Do call me Simon,' I said, but got no reply.

Ruth crashed out in an armchair with a long sigh. She did not take her coat off because she was waiting for her brother to call.

'It's good you two have met. I hated not telling her.'

So why didn't you? I thought. We had never resolved the proper reason for all the secrecy.

'We are meeting,' I corrected her grammar. 'It's not finished. It ain't over till the fat lady sings.'

'Mother's not fat,' said Ruth, seemingly confident that all was well.

'Whatever,' I said, not so convinced.

The phone rang. Mrs Whittaker called out from the kitchen. 'That will be Peter, could you get that, Ruth?'

'Ruth the Minicab,' Ruth said in a Welsh accent as she answered the phone. She started laughing at something her brother said back. 'OK, I'll be there in about ten minutes.' She put down the phone. I was horrified.

'You're seriously leaving me with her? I'll come with you. Why can't he get a cab?'

'You'll be fine,' she mouthed at me and laughed at my terrified expression. She grabbed her keys and headed for the door, giving me a thumbs-up from outside as she passed the living room.

Mrs Whittaker came through with the tea. The best

china was indeed on display. This could be a good sign. It could also be a bad sign.

'You haven't met Peter, have you?' she asked, putting the tray down.

'First time today.' I was so sodding upbeat.

'Peter's quite a few years older than Ruth. He has three children; the eldest is in the VI Form doing biology, physics and chemistry,' she recited.

Faaascinating, I thought. She poured the tea. We talked about the travel business, the Euro (she was against, surprise, surprise), the weather in the south. This was a snap; the old lady would be darning my socks by the end of the month and saying 'Oh, Simon!' at my risqué jokes. I finished my tea. There was a pause, a decision was made and then she said, 'Ruth tells me you were an active homosexual until two months ago, Mr Lyndon.'

The sky was blacked out by the megaton shockwave of what this suddenly formidable older version of Ruth was saying. How un-English. How not cricket. Having thought that we would all have afternoon tea and begin the uneasy process of my being welcomed into the family, it seemed that war was about to be declared. There was something about the clinical way she enunciated 'active'. Why did Ruth leave me with her? Somewhere, Freud was having a field day.

Thinking about it much later, I realised Ruth's mother must have been terrified. She was putting the wagons in a circle and preparing to defend her family. At the time, however, she was one scary lady.

My tongue turned to shoe-leather. Keep calm, keep calm, cool wet grass, sunlight on water. Shakespeare says something about however bad a day is, time still passes and the day ends. I think Shakespeare is more pithy but he was still dead wrong. This was the longest stretch for a teapot of my life. Every tenth of a second was a millennium. If I did not drink something, I would not be able to speak.

I contrived a smile. Robert Downey Jr opened an envelope: 'And the Oscar for Best Actor in A Tight Spot goes to . . . Simon Lyndon for *Alone With Homophobic Old Lady*.' But my hand trembled slightly as I poured the tea. She noticed, of course. I was caught in the crosshairs of her gaze, she was on full alert. Be urbane, I told myself, be charming.

'Call me Simon. Would you like another? Cup of tea, I mean? No? Well, to answer your question, it kind of depends what you mean by "homosexual" and "active".'

I flashed her a smile, the full personality haymaker, a glance in search of a friendly glint of recognition. *Big mistake. Huge.* She passed me the milk and said flatly, 'I think we both know the meaning of those words. You far better than I.'

Ouch.

'Biscuit?' she added.

'I'd choke.'

Ding ding. Seconds out.

'Why are you here? What are you doing here?'

'I was invited.'

'Don't be glib, Mr Lyndon. This is no—'

'I'm sorry. I apologise. Glib is sometimes all that works. I'm here because I thought we should get to know each other.'

She said dimly, 'Did you.'

'Yeah, I just thought you might be more . . . oblique. Less direct.'

At this, there was the first glimmer of a smile. Perhaps it would be possible to communicate.

'I have only met one other homosexual.' It was as if she was saying 'disinfectant'. 'He was, I have to admit, a very pleasant man. But he *was* homosexual, whereas you, Mr Lyndon, are not quite homosexual or anything else.'

Ouch. I was on the canvas and the referee was counting me out. Somehow I recovered and met her eyes. She continued smoothly, distancing herself from every word she uttered. She was getting clear water between herself and the fear and anger she felt. English reserve can be such a wonderful thing. I was scraping the barrel of mine for every last drop. My face shut down. She would not know what I was thinking, nor I her. Her fear was revealed in the clarity of what she said and the straightness of her back. She was magnificent.

'If you are a homosexual then you are the cruellest man I have ever met. If you have been lying to yourself until two months ago, then you are a sad, confused soul who has no business being near anybody, much less my daughter. Ruth loves you or is very close to loving you. You must not experiment with her.'

'This isn't an experiment—'

'Of course it is,' she cut in. 'I cannot believe that people can change in the way that you say you have. The world does not work like that.'

We stared at each other. I put my teacup down too hard and knocked the milk over the table. I said 'Jesus!' far too loudly and sensed her stiffen in fear as this strange man in her house suddenly became angry. A high note of frustration remained in my voice as I tried for about the third time in my life to say what I really felt.

'Isn't it possible, just *perhaps*, that I could be all that you think of me, but at the same time I'm not anything like that . . .' *So eloquent, Simon, good old me,* '. . . and that

life is about shades of grey. Just perhaps, I could want to
be with Ruth because of who she is and not which sex she
is. That I am attracted to her because . . .'

'. . . she makes you laugh. She is a true and wonderful
person. She is not like anyone else you have ever met.'
The cynical blade of her voice was devastating.

'Yes, but—'

'But meantime, you can look at men and want them.'

'Life isn't as simple as we both want it to be, Mrs
Whittaker. This is all new for me and I'm taking each day
as it comes.' She breathed in sharply at this, startled. She
said nothing, so I continued. 'All I know is that I want to
be with Ruth.'

Incredibly, she laughed. She spelled it out for me. 'But
you can look at men and want them.'

A statement not a question. *You're bisexual, Simon. You
get turned on by men.* Ruth's and now her mother's words
rang around my brain. I became aware of my breathing
and tried to keep my head together, staring at the grain of
the coffee table, at a knot hole waxed and polished to a
bottomless infinity. My eyes swam. The truth always
sounds so banal but it sets you apart. *I looked at men and
wanted them.*

'I want Ruth . . . as well. I want Ruth . . . *more*. I know
I must not try to have them both.'

Did I mean that?

'But you will try. Men always do.' Ruth's mother sagged
suddenly, ageing before my eyes. After a little while, she
spoke in a quiet tone that was sympathetic but implacable.

'You are not cruel. No, don't get your hopes up, Mr
Lyndon, you're worse. You genuinely "want" Ruth but
you also "want" to sleep with men. If you do betray her –
and you will – you would be able to square that with

yourself, wouldn't you? Have twenty reasons why you were right to behave in such and such a way. If you were with a man, you would persuade yourself that you still cared for Ruth and that somehow by dividing your life into compartments, you were helping her. Men find ways to get what they want, just as you are doing now. You are the worst sort of man: you're a good man capable of hypocrisy, capable of destroying lives. Except your kind of destruction takes years and decades. While you convince yourself that you are ultimately honourable and truthful and that deception is the way to protect Ruth and keep her happy, she will *know*, she will know somewhere deep in her soul, that soul which you say you value so much, Mr Lyndon, that something is decayed and rotten. And decades of my daughter's life will pass because *you* are taking *each day as it comes*. You will destroy my daughter atom by atom. And I hate you for it already.'

The contempt was limitless, each word was clipped, precise and prepared. She got up suddenly and I flinched away. I had never known anything like this. My adult life had been about being true to myself, granting myself liberties and pleasures and therefore being *more* true to myself. Now I was being told that trying for happiness in this new direction was not allowed. She was saying that the world had no room for what I was doing.

She crossed to a small table on which were several silver-framed photographs of children gleeful on beaches, uncomfortable in Sunday best outside churches, or wild-eyed and screaming on roller-coasters. A few were black and white but most were in colour. She picked up a frame, her back to me. We were silent, minds racing. I tried to speak, failed, then managed to say, 'Ruth is not going into this blindfold, Mrs Whittaker. She knows about my life before we got together and I am being as honest with her as I know how.'

She turned to look at me, for the first time genuinely amused. 'But how honest *is* that, Mr Lyndon?'

'As honest as I can be, everything up front.' *Except I had not been today, not totally.*

'So she walks into a disaster but that's fine because she knows it's a disaster.'

'You must let her make her own—'

'Mistakes?' she interrupted.

'*Decisions.* Ruth is not you.'

'But you are just like her father.'

She passed me the photograph in her hand, saying, 'Why else do you think she likes you?' It was a studio-taken family group in black and white, a pose reproduced a million times. The photographer had probably just cracked a joke as everyone was laughing. It was a photograph of something I had scorned for years, that I had rejected last week. That I knew I would want one day.

A young Mrs Whittaker sat with an infant Ruth in her lap. She looked pretty and proud, presenting her new baby to the world, her hair resolutely late sixties. Ruth's brother Peter stood by his mother, his neck straining at an unfamiliar tie. Mr Whittaker stood by Peter with an arm resting lightly on the nine-year-old's shoulder to keep him still while the picture was taken; protective, caring. Ruth had inherited her thick hair and lively eyes from him as well as her slim build. He was a neat man with an open, humorous face, like Hannah's. I liked him. I passed the picture back and wondered if Mrs Whittaker meant what I knew she must mean, saying, 'I'm like her father? I don't see the resemblance.'

'Don't pretend to be stupid. It never suited him and it doesn't suit you. For all that the world has changed so much, it seems that the only difference between you and him is that you are deceiving yourself that you are honest. At least he never did that. Do you know we were the first people we knew to get an automatic washing machine? Do you know why? I was so sick, physically sick, of washing other men out of his clothes. He thought I would not notice . . . it. So we got a machine to make it all just go away. And for months at a time, it did, but it always came back.'

We did not say anything for a long time. I finally said, 'I'm sorry. I didn't know. Ruth didn't—'

'She doesn't know. Nor her brother. You are the first person I have ever told. Perhaps now you understand why you fill me with such horror. She will become me.'

Sitting again as suddenly as she had stood, she was silent a long time. My thoughts tumbled over each other. If Ruth was seeing her dead father in me, did she want me *because* I had been gay all my adult life? I suddenly remembered Ruth talking about her father that first night together. My brain went into meltdown.

Ruth's mother spoke softly again, her experience giving her the right to talk to me like this. She was a wasted woman but, to some degree, she loved it: it was her life, it was her Purple Heart, her cross to bear. And this afternoon she was indulging herself and in a sick way I was getting off on this absurd melodrama as well. It was too extreme to be real.

'The world is built around opposites like black and white. Men and women, black and white, love and hate. It is people like you who muddle things and make it grey just as he made me grey. You never use the world "love", do you? I noticed that as you spoke. You *want* her, to *have* her the way you still want to have all those men . . .'

These last words were drawn out, vowels evaporating slowly: 'all those men'. I stared at the floor, just like young Sarah in the park. I had no moorings, no certainties.

'. . . you don't use the word "love" because you can't. Because you split yourself in two, you can never be entitled to use a word that should be said to only one person.'

I was not sure who was being spoken to. She was looking at the photograph, her eyes on her dead husband smiling back at her. She looked as proud now as she looked in the photo: she was defeating him at last.

A car drew up in the gravel driveway. Sarah was back with her mother. Not before fucking time. Mmm, another relative to meet. Couldn't wait. Mrs Whittaker picked up the tea tray, noting the spilt milk.

'You must never tell either of them about this. Agreed?'

I nodded, struck dumb now.

She *still* had not finished. I was out for the count and needing surgery but she decided to slip a knife between my ribs anyway. At that moment, I hated her so much.

'Ruth does not love you for *your* soul. She loves you for her father's sense of humour, the way she thinks you understand her just as he did, the way you are masculine without actually being a real man. But you only think you understand her because men have made love to you the way you make love to her.'

I flushed and caught my breath. This could not be happening. Old ladies love me, I'm funny, they don't talk about fucking and semen stains, they don't treat me like this. I detested her for knowing what I had never admitted: that for a long time I had loathed myself. Not for being gay, life really isn't that simple. I had set myself impossible targets like Callum or Patrick falling in love with me because I had thought *nobody* could. Then Ruth came along and the world looked different suddenly and I started liking myself. Because Ruth loved me.

And Mrs Whittaker was ripping that to shreds before my eyes. She was so wrong and so right: *the way you are masculine without actually being a real man . . . you fill me with such horror . . . all those men . . . you are deceiving yourself.* There was nothing in what she was saying I had not thought at some point.

'I should be grateful to you, Simon.' I looked at her warily. What now? She smiled almost jauntily. 'This honesty business is quite satisfying, isn't it? I've wanted to have this conversation for thirty-five years.'

She disappeared through to the kitchen with what looked suspiciously like a spring in her step as Ruth's key turned in the front door.

Chapter 18

*'It was routine that consoled her grief which nothing
else could mend'*

Alexander Pushkin

Threatened by impossible odds, groggy with fighting and
weak with fatigue, our hero (ideally Harrison Ford
c.1983–4) appears to be facing the end of the road. Events
have overtaken him, he is only one man and he is surrounded by his many foes. This is the moment he can give
up and we will understand. He has done his best.

But, what's this? The background music has returned
to a major key, Harrison is raising his bloodstained face
from the dust and struggles to his feet with a superhuman
effort and a roar of pain. He assesses the threat about
him and despatches the oncoming hordes with an ironic
wink, a cunning plan and a well-timed deployment of a
popular catchphrase (in this case the immortal 'Fuck you
too, Mrs Whittaker!'). Oh, and he gets the girl in the
end.

After Granny's all-out nuclear strike, running away was
a serious option; running away, going home, getting very
drunk and weeping was a very serious option. And I won't
deny it was considered. But to my great surprise, I fought

back. I rallied. I am that intrepid sexy archaeologist with the neat hat. Just when, by rights and being true to past form, I should have dissolved into a tearful puddle on the Axminster to be mopped up along with the spilt milk, Simon (I shall speak of myself in the heroic third person) found some good-old fashioned British spunk and backbone. I was so proud of him. Me. So what if the perfect Pop in the photo had been a toilet-trader, I was *not*. Well, not for years anyway. I was younger then, I was Interrailing.

Alone in the living room, I got my shit together. Not as messy as it sounds, I was very calm. In the hallway, assembled Whittakers were doing your basic higher primate greeting rituals, rubbing lips against faces, clasping each other's upper bodies, emitting small sounds of welcome and non-aggression. I was so eerily tranquil, I did not even feel the same species as them any more.

'Hello, Mum, how are you? You're looking well,' a man's voice said. Peter the Brother. Lovely.

I heard the rustle of an embrace and Mrs Whittaker replying, 'I'm feeling fine, actually. Rather bouncy.'

Of course you're feeling bouncy, you witch, you just tried to destroy my life. I was having some terrifyingly standard mother-in-law reactions, not that I cared. This family thing is vastly overrated anyway, I mused in my composed, Mr Spock-like way. Why did I have to meet the organisms to whom Ruth just happened to be genetically linked through some massive galactic coincidence? What did they have to do with Ruth and myself? The situation was illogical, Captain.

Here we go, Simon, I told myself. Go into the hallway and meet Ruth's brother. Keep it light, be charming.

I still treasure the expression of total surprise on Mrs

Whittaker's face as I strode confidently into the hall and pumped Ruth's brother's hand, to all intents as butch as a butcher. Ruth seemed delighted by my zappy persona, assuming that all had gone well with her mother since she had left. After a bit of introductory chitchat, as Peter popped upstairs to the loo and Mrs Whittaker retreated into the living room with kitchen roll to mop up the milk, Ruth and I had a quick, whispered conversation.

'How did it go?'

'*Great*, what a lovely person your mum is. She told me *all* about herself. We had a lovely chat.' I wondered if I should say 'lovely' again. Go for it. 'Really lovely.'

'O-kaaay,' Ruth murmured back, wrinkling her brow. This was not sounding like the mother she knew. Ruth tried out for a size a phrase which she obviously did not associate with her mother. 'She told you all about herself? I didn't know her generation did that.'

'Neither did I. We really opened up to each other.'

Ruth looked very confused. Out of the corner of my eye, I saw Mrs Whittaker coming back into the hallway. I deliberately moved closer to Ruth for a kiss. Ruth was about to respond when she saw her mother coming as well. She gave me a perfunctory little peck.

'Give me a proper kiss,' I wheedled and put a hand in the small of her back to bring her closer.

'*Simon*,' Ruth said uncomfortably, nodding towards her approaching mother and wriggling free. A toilet flushed upstairs. Whittakers converged from all directions.

'God, that's better. At least seven pounds lighter,' said Peter emphatically as he stomped down the stairs. He was a bluff, no-nonsense type with a rugby-forward build and what looked like the *de rigueur* rugby broken nose. The Whittaker mane of hair was, alas, not for him, Peter being a classic case of male-pattern baldness. Quite how he had sprung from the loins of the dapper man in the photo and steel magnolia Grandma here, I did not know.

'Peter, I wish you wouldn't talk like that,' Mrs Whittaker said indulgently. He was obviously the apple of her jaundiced eye.

'I'm nearly forty, Mother, I'll talk how I want,' Peter replied, smiling at me.

He was an ageing rugger-bugger. How weird. I wondered if perhaps some of the sperm from Mr Whittaker's sodden clothing had rubbed off, producing Peter while Mrs W was doing her anguished handwash prior to the purchase of the washing machine. What a pathetic detail that had been. Touchy-feely bollocks. As you can tell, I was feeling charitable towards Ruth's mother at this point. Peter continued, 'Anyway, I'm sure Simon can take rough talk, can't you, Simon?'

'Anyway you like, Peter,' I said, glancing at Mrs Whittaker. She looked rattled, her bounciness disappearing. What a bastard I can be when I have to.

'That's what Ruth just told me about you, you old arse-bandit. Call me Pete, only Mother calls me Peter. You do right by my sister and we'll have no complaints, isn't that right, Mother?'

We all looked at Mother.

'Yes,' Mrs Whittaker managed. Very quietly.

'Pete knows too?' I whispered to Ruth. She never told me anything.

'In the car coming over. He doesn't give a toss,' she whispered back.

'No whispering!' exclaimed Pete, as we all went into the living room. 'No secrets in this family. Can't *bear* secrets. Isn't that right, Sis?'

'Too true,' Ruth said stoutly. If only you both knew, I thought, risking a peek at Mrs Whittaker, trooping in behind us looking like a tweedy block of granite.

'Anyway, live and let live, hey?' said Pete, unlike any rugby player I have ever met. 'I'm fairly sure one of my kids is a lesbian. The girl. I don't give a toss.'

'Told you,' Ruth said under her breath.

'Peter!' said Mrs Whittaker. She had transformed into a little woman capable only of uttering one-word exclamations in front of her son. Where there had been strength, there was now an inbuilt deference to the male head of the family. It was an antique crock of crap, but I was deeply grateful to it at that point: her tragedy, my salvation. With one bound I could be free and clear. I began to realise the enormous courage she had shown in attacking me head-on. It had been a one-off. Her eloquence and determination seemed all the more remarkable. Peter bulldozed on.

'What are you upset about more, Mum? That a grandchild of yours might be a lesbian or that I said "give a toss"?'

'Peter!'

'Honestly, Simon, she's thirteen, looks like Sporty Spice's little brother, me and the wife can't get her near a skirt or a frock and she's got three identical little friends. You're a man of the world, what's your verdict?'

All eyes swivelled towards me.

'Maybe it's just a phase she's going through,' I said as seriously as I could.

'Is that a technical term?' said Ruth, joining in.

'*Very* technical. It sounds to me as if your daughter . . . what's her name?'

'Caroline. But she answers only to Cazzer,' Peter said with a grimace.

'Well, it sounds as if Cazzer will discover lipgloss and boys in about six months' time and never look at a shell-suit again.'

'All change,' agreed Ruth.

'So, did you discover lipgloss at fourteen then, Simon?' asked Pete.

'Peter!' exclaimed you-know-who. I slowly began liking Mrs Whittaker now she had been neutralised.

What a great guy Pete was. Still is, for that matter. Ruth had not told me her brother was such a diamond bloke. I love blokes because they make the world go round. There are some moments when only a bloke will do, usually moments that require a Makita cordless screwdriver as well, but also occasions like this when some big, bluff *chap* blows away the cobwebs and breaks through all the rubbish; a talent I sometimes have but did not possess in that personally uncertain situation. Pete was a happily married man, sorted, kids: he had all that serenity I had just lost. Pete was a god and did what he wanted.

'I'm as dry as a bone,' he declared and his mother jumped up like Pavlov's dog and scuttled off. I watched her go out as Ruth and Pete curled up on the sofa together.

'I'll just go help your mother make tea,' I said, standing up on an impulse, knowing what I should do.

'Arse-licker,' Pete called out after me and exploded into *double entendre* laughter, Ruth hitting him in mock anger. My past was going to haunt me as a source of many good-natured brotherly jokes at Ruth's expense, I could tell.

I did not need to help in the kitchen. If Mrs Whittaker could do one thing by herself, it was make a pot of tea. But I needed to see her alone again, now that I could see she was not the demon I had briefly turned her into. We had a conversation to finish.

In the kitchen, Mrs Whittaker was sitting down at the long table, the kettle on. She looked ashen, driven once again into silence by a man in her life. I sat down beside her and saw her eyes were brimming.

'Please don't be so worried . . .' I began.

She broke in immediately, talking in a fast, ardent undertone. 'Look after my daughter. She *must* get this degree, she *must* be happy, she *must* be able to have more of a life than I had,' then she corrected herself, '*am* having. It's not over yet, is it?'

'Not by a long chalk,' I said, trying to be positive, but not at all sure that was the answer Mrs Whittaker wanted to hear.

'I never had the chances Ruth had. I never had the education, you see. I'm sure I was clever enough but in those days, girls weren't meant to be . . .' she trailed off and dabbed at her eyes with a sheet of kitchen roll. 'I'm sorry, it's so difficult *talking*.'

'I'm just the same,' I said.

'Are you?' At last some common ground: neither of us could communicate. It was a wonder we'd found out. She went on. 'I must try to say this to you, to explain. Back then you left school, you found a man, you got married and stayed at home with the children. You didn't have to think about it, that was what happened. It was even what I wanted, I thought. I found out I was wrong. So I buried myself in the children. I wanted Ruth to be different to me but the same thing happened to her when she fell pregnant with Sarah. She was married at eighteen. *Eighteen*. too early, even earlier than me and I was a *child*. I forced Ruth to retake her A levels the next year, though. And she did well.'

I nearly fell off my chair as she said this last heart-stoppingly proud statement of fact: *My daughter did well.* The look in her eyes was the same as Ruth's ex-husband in the park saying goodbye to Sarah and Hannah. That crazy love. Like him, Mrs Whittaker would die for her children at a moment's notice, without hesitation. And had, for years and years.

'Now she has to get this degree. It's important,' she repeated. 'And I want Sarah and Hannah to know just how important it is. They think I'm strict with them about their homework but it's the only way. The rule is that Ruth can't become me and they can't become Ruth. One of us will get it right. And you won't break that rule.'

I remembered that Ruth had said exactly the same thing to me months before.

'So promise me, Mr Lyn— *Simon*, promise me that if you find yourself running the risk of making Ruth unhappy, as *he* made me unhappy, that you will leave her and stop history repeating itself. If you can't make her happy, you can't have her.'

I opened my mouth to speak as Pete stomped into the kitchen, calling for his tea. He stopped when he saw us, then went to make the tea himself.

'Oh, you two having a moment? What about, let me guess . . .'

I stood up to cover Mrs Whittaker getting herself together.

'I was just promising your mother I'll make Ruth as happy as I possibly can. Nothing huge,' I joked, trying not to be too serious about it all. What a day.

Pete grinned at me, a hard, wry look in his eyes.

'Too right, cocker. But it *is* huge. If you make her unhappy – ' he jabbed a finger at me, ' – for *whatever* reason, not necessarily the one Mum's worried about, I'll fucking *kill* you. Sorry for swearing, Mum.'

'Not a problem for once,' said Mrs Whittaker, twisting round to look at her son with a small smile.

Pete smiled back at her then looked at me. 'What a woman, hey? Do you take sugar?'

'One.'

'I'll give you two. Don't stir it too much if you don't want it but you look like you need it.'

Fair enough, I thought. After the day I had just had, Pete's warning of the circumstances under which he would find himself provoked enough to murder me had been of very small impact. It had seemed almost routine. The tension in the room lessened as Pete handed us mugs of tea. No best china this time: it seemed I was almost a Corleone now. Thank the Lord for that.

Ruth appeared in the kitchen, wondering what we were all doing, and the four of us got on with having as pleasant an evening as possible. Mrs Whittaker turned out to be very reserved, with a laugh that, when it happened, transformed her. Her face lit up repeatedly as the Pete and Ruth sibling show dominated the proceedings, trading repartee and family jokes. Nobody mentioned Dad though, the spectre at the feast.

Ruth and I had no time alone and as a result I hardly spoke to her; as we both went upstairs to bed at about midnight, there was an odd atmosphere between us, of many questions being unanswered. As casually as I could, I said, 'Well, that was a day.'

'Wasn't it, though. I think Mum likes you. That's great, that's wonderful,' replied Ruth, slipping her arm around my waist and leaning her head on my shoulder as we walked along the landing to her room.

'I think she's scared stiff of me as well.'

'Of course she is. I'm her precious daughter. And she's thinking about Dad as well.'

Careful, Simon, careful.

'Really? What about him?' I asked far too cautiously.

'She told you about him, didn't she? I could tell. You probably know more than me now. No need to tell me anything,' Ruth said, sitting heavily on the edge of the bed and looking up at me with her honest, clear eyes. She looked troubled, toying with the lid of her Pandora's box. I thought about the day I had had and saw red.

'You know? *You know?* And you left me *alone* with her? Is all this why I wasn't allowed to meet her? It was, wasn't it? What kind of sadist are you? I had the worst thirty minutes of my life while you were taking the scenic route back from the station. Jesus!'

Ruth was trying to interrupt me throughout my outburst and managed to cut in as I caught my breath and stalked to the window, my back to her. Fuck Ruth being an experiment, I felt like a lab-rat myself now. 'Simon, I'm sorry, you said it went well, what did she say?'

'She warned me off. I'm not fit to touch you. She thinks you're with me *because* of your dad. Because *I'm him* or some corny shit like that.'

'What do you think about that?' she said. I swear she held her breath. Not an answer, Ruth, not an answer.

'I don't know – you tell me, love. It's your fuck-up for once, not mine.' I wasn't at my most benevolent. I took deep breaths, trying not to completely blow my stack, still too angry to look at her.

'If I'm with you because of Dad, then it's not conscious, I swear it, Simon.' Ruth came up to the window and stood beside me.

'Why did you leave me alone with her?' I said quietly. *Make it good, make it good, my Ruth.*

'You're so good with people, Simon, I didn't think it would be a problem. I didn't think she'd dare say anything.'

'She found a reserve of courage,' I assured Ruth. 'She dared. She loves you. She'd kill for you. Pete threatened to kill me as well if I hurt you.'

'Did he? You've been through the mill today, haven't you? If it's any comfort, Pete threatening to kill anyone is a bit of a concept. He's such a softie.'

'So the fact he said it at all makes me think he meant it. Oh, I didn't *mind*. He saved my hide as well today. I think I won your mum round a bit, by the end.' A thought struck me. 'How do you know about your dad?'

'I overheard a row once I wasn't meant to hear, when I was about thirteen. Just before he died. Mum doesn't know I know. Pete knows too.'

'"No secrets in this family",' I quoted.

'I think Pete was being ironic,' Ruth said, slipping a hand through my arm. 'I want Mum to feel as good about us as I do, then maybe—' And she brought herself up short.

'What?'

Ruth looked caught out. '*Then* she'll maybe rest easier about Dad. Not think about it so much.'

I closed my eyes. So it *was* conscious, at least on some level. I was bringing Ruth's parents back together in her head. We would succeed where they failed. I couldn't decide if it was better or worse than the fag-hag cliché: Ruth didn't want to cure *me*, she wanted to cure her *father*. I could barely speak.

'What else did she say?' Ruth asked.

'That was the main idea. History repeating.'

Ruth let out a frustrated yell, clapping her hands to her face and pushing back her hair from her face. She was trying to gee me up now, looking on the bright side. 'But I don't think that's *true*,' she said. 'This isn't the same situation at all. I'm not as naïve as Mum was, I'm certainly not as long-suffering, you're not as two-faced as Dad must have been . . .'

You're not *as* two-faced? Thank you, Dr Freud. I wouldn't be pursuing that one after the lies I'd told her today.

Ruth continued. 'Times have changed. It's *different*.'

'Your mum's afraid I'll go cottaging or something.'

'Then that will be the end, won't it? You won't have to stick around, like Dad did. It will just be over.'

Ruth sat on the bed and collapsed back, staring at the ceiling, thinking hard. I turned round to look at her. Her face was screwed up in concentration. There was a silence. I sat on the bed as well, with my head in my hands.

'Are you with me because I was gay, Ruthie?' If the answer's 'Yes', in any way, it's over, I thought. But I can live with it if it's not verbalised.

Ruth shifted, untucked my shirt at the back and slipped a hand on to my skin. We made up well after rows, me and Ruth. I twisted round to look at her, lay back and kissed the side of her neck. She liked that, I knew. She sighed, the unmistakable sound of a small sob in the sigh, pushing her chin up and out like a cat. I pulled back her collar and gently bit her shoulder. She groaned and slipped off the bed, kneeling before me, unzipping my fly and coaxing me to life. Eventually she said, 'I'm with you because you are a very sexy man, Simon, pure and simple. Please don't let all this get in the way.' It was what I needed to hear. Love-making seemed to be the antidote to our day.

We were wrong. Just as with our very first time together, I found myself having to prove myself to both of us. No, this was different to the first time: we were *both* having to prove now how we felt about each other. And the inevitable happened. I began to think about men as Ruth and I made love. Not Brad, Mel or Leo thoughts, but images of sleeping with that neat man in the photograph, of Patrick in the mirror. Tell someone they can't have something and they'll want it. Even as I pictured her father's face as I kissed Ruth, I knew these thoughts weren't real. They were fabricated, as if the revelations of the day were making me think these things rather than the reality of how I felt about Ruth. I was thinking about men because Mrs Whittaker had said I would. If you know about History, it stands a better chance of repeating itself.

Since Ruth and I both thought that her father being a grubby little man should mean something, it did. As we made love, we knew that the other was thinking about Ruth's father. I imagined me sleeping with him, Ruth sleeping with him. Somewhere in the seventh level of hell to which they have undoubtedly been consigned. Freud and Jung were giving each other high-fives and celebratory blow-jobs to mark one of their finest hours. Bastards.

Instead of relaxing, we both became more and more tense and after I had huffed and puffed my way to a lonely, cheerless climax, Ruth turned away from me. We might as well have been in separate countries. I was still thinking about sleeping with men, my head full of Mrs Whittaker's and Peter's words.

It seemed very British that I was being defined by what I had renounced rather than what I now said I was. I was even doing that to myself, I realised. We all look back, we don't live in the present and look to the future. Sometimes that can be a good thing but mostly it inhibits us and prevents us from branching out, making us believe that leopards can't change their spots, that you can't teach an old dog new tricks, life is just repetition, the same old same old.

Ruth and I had been going great but it seemed the past was too much with us, ghosts kept getting between us just when we should have been closest. Lying there with Ruth a million miles from me, I resolved that the past would not be an obstacle between me and the possible life I had lived for the previous eight weeks. *I wanted that peace of mind back.* If I was going to look to the future I had to face my past and Ruth's past, not fear it. I had to exorcise her father from our minds. I could not choose to spend my life with a woman if we were both always thinking that I could be with men as well. Not fair on Ruth, not fair on me.

I made a decision. That was quite butch for a start. Just as when I had had to become Harrison Ford to be brave enough to pick myself up after Ruth's mum's onslaught, I was now having to become that adventurer-archaeologist again: a sexual archaeologist. I was going to go back home and excavate my past. Adjusting my hat to a rakish angle, my conclusion was that in order to stay with Ruth and be certain it was the right thing to do, I had to sleep with some men in the coming week before I saw her next. I had to relive my past in order to reject it. All in the cause of science.

If I still preferred men, if they seemed to give me as much or more of a chance of happiness than Ruth, then I would keep my promise to Mrs Whittaker and leave Ruth and never go back. But if I had some really *bad* sex with men in the next few days then everything would be *great*.

'Are we going to be OK?' asked Ruth. She sounded so low.

'I hope so, baby, I really hope so. Go to sleep,' I answered.

It all seemed to make perfect sense at the time.

Chapter 19

'... the word has gone mad today, and good's bad today
and black's white today ...'

Cole Porter

How many times in one life could it feel like I was losing
my virginity? This was at least my fourth.

I rang up my ex, Truman the policeman. He did not
seem surprised to hear from me until I told him what I
wanted him to do. A stunned silence was broken by me
repeating what I had just said.

'Will you come around and sleep with me so I can be
sure I want to be straight. Please.'

'So-o-o . . .' Long silence again. Finally, he said in an
undertone, 'I wish you hadn't rung me at work. The desk
sergeant's staring at me. He knows this isn't business.'

'Is he good-looking?'

'Bloody ugly. Here he comes.' Truman suddenly
switched into an official tone. 'As to your request, sir, I'm
sure we can send a squad car round.'

'I only want one of you, Truman.'

'You can't be too careful, sir.' His voice dropped to a
hush again. 'Simon, I sense a big feeling of rejection
coming my way.'

'Only *hopefully*,' I said with a grimace.

He eventually agreed, much against his better judgement. We arranged for him to come round the next evening. What began as an experiment fast became a potential night of shagging. Simon was on a promise and looking forward to being in bed with a man again. Not a good sign.

But it was all so that I would stay with Ruth, so that made me feel better. I had to keep remembering that. What had Ruth's mother said, . . . *you'll be able to square it with yourself, persuade yourself that you still care for her.* Mmm . . .

I spent the following day at work psyching myself up to seeing him, to grappling with a man again. Truman rang me in the middle of the day with cold feet but I managed to re-persuade him. I do hate having to beg for sex I'm hoping I'll hate. After a whole day of winding myself up, magnifying everything in my mind, the actual moment of his arrival was an anti-climax. Instead of the Ally McBeal-esque huge walking phallus I was expecting to turn up on my doorstep, it was Truman, looking tense but handsome, clutching a bottle of shiraz. Just like old times, and a very odd sensation as a result. I had just entered a home-made contrived and customised Twilight Zone. I hoped I didn't look as bemused and nervous as Truman.

Things were very stilted at first, neither of us knowing quite what to say. The unspoken conversation was that Truman was doing me an enormous favour and we both knew it. What we actually said was 'so' and 'well' a couple of times. We went into the kitchen to find a corkscrew.

'Wow! You've tidied up!' Truman exclaimed in shock. It was a rarity, I had to admit. I'd been obsessively tidying the flat since I got back from work, more for something to do, so the kitchen looked like I'd had an anal-retentive seizure. Which I had. I opened his wine and we loosened up as we chitchatted. Alcohol and sex as a prelude to sex, you can't beat it. However, a gap eventually yawned in the conversation. Down to business.

'So-o-o . . .' said Truman, lifting his eyebrows questioningly. 'What do you want to do?'

'I don't know,' I replied, smiling restively. 'Not really.'

'Er . . . are we going to, y'know, *do it*?'

'Y-you mean . . .' I stuttered. What I was trying to say was 'You mean you thought we wouldn't?' But that wasn't the way it came out.

'Am I going to screw you?' Truman blurted impatiently, then looked taken aback at himself. How blunt.

'Er . . . I think we should. I mean, *you* should. If that's OK with you?'

'Y-e-ah. *Yeah.* No problems. It's not like it's the first time with us two.'

'That's right, that's right.'

We nodded formally at each other. Well, *that* was erotic. A good start for some really bad sex. Perfect.

'You have to know that I wouldn't do this for *anyone* else,' Truman said. 'I'm not even sure why I'm doing it for you, to be honest. I still haven't really got the point of this. Do you want me to fuck you *badly*?'

I looked at him. He looked so hot. He was wearing a tight white T-shirt and jeans. I could see his nipples under the T-shirt. Quite the young man about town. You know you're getting older when the policemen you're sleeping with look younger and younger. What was he, still twenty-six or something? He was fiddling nervously with a frond of chest hair curling over the top of his T-shirt. Thunderbirds were go. Yes, I wanted him to fuck me.

Badly. Oh, Simon. I had to swallow in order to speak because my mouth had watered.

'I want you to be your usual phenomenal self,' I said with a cool smile. Rather, with what I hoped was a cool smile. Truman was thinking too hard to even notice.

'Bu-u-t . . . it would be great if you hated it,' clarified Truman.

'Liked it *less*.'

'Tha-a-n . . .'

'Women.'

'I've got it now,' he smiled at me in confirmation.

'Sure?'

'Yes.' Truman looked at me pityingly. 'You complete warpo.'

My exterior crumbled slightly.

'I know, I know, you don't need to tell me.'

I blinked back tears furiously. I was spending my life trying to calm down. This could be awful.

'All right, OK. Let's do it, let's do it,' Truman said suddenly. He put his glass down, took my glass out of my hand and, Lord love him, he took over. Greater love hath no man than one willing to appear to be crap in bed for his ex-boyfriend. A new rule for life, everyone.

'Do you want to dance?' he said unexpectedly.

I looked at him in surprise.

'*Dance?*'

'Oh yeah. We can't just shag. It would be good if we had a nice time, wouldn't it? Let's woo.'

'*Woo?*'

'Woo,' affirmed Truman.

As we went through to my living room, I reflected that this was only the second time Truman had ever surprised me. The first time was the 'What flashbacks?' sketch at

Pulp Fiction. But what had split us up in the end was that Truman bored me as well as being on endless night shifts. He has a fab body, much better than mine, dreamy hazel eyes with flecks of green, buns of steel (not that he ever let me near them), and he was a great lover – but he had never surprised me. If people didn't keep on surprising me then I didn't want to be around them for the rest of my life, thank you very much. If they ran out of surprises after a month, then I'd likely be with them for that one great month followed by a tortuous six weeks as I tried to let them down gently. If they hadn't dumped me first, of course.

In my living room, Truman was looking through my CDs.

'*Songs for Swinging Lovers?*' he suggested with a tremulous laugh in his voice. I could tell he was not wanting to do this. Fine, it just meant that the odds were stacking up in my favour a bit more. It would not be a great night, all would be well for Ruth and me.

'Sounds perfect,' I said, half smiling. I had never seen Truman like this, being quite so adorable.

As Francis started singing, Truman stood up and faced me.

'"You make me feel so young . . ."' he crooned along, swaying half-time with the music.

'You *are* young. I feel so old, Truman. Too old to be like this.'

'I know, I know.' He crossed to me and put a finger against my mouth. 'Sssh. May I have this dance, Mr Lyndon?'

'Only if you take me to the Policeman's Ball, constable.'

'"I'm such a happy individual . . ."' carolled Truman. He had a really nice voice. I had never known that while we were going out. 'I'll think about taking you, Cinderella. Whatever would they all say? Who's that handsome man with Truman, probably.'

'You are so sweet,' I said and really meant it, for once in my life. I was feeling very inadequate and Truman, in a very weird situation himself, was looking out for me. When in doubt, ask a policeman.

He took me in his arms and we just stood there for a while, breathing carefully. He was wearing a sandalwood cologne. He knew it was my favourite. Bastard. Then he started dancing, taking the lead, guiding me expertly through the steps, neatly avoiding bumping into the furniture.

'I didn't know you could do this,' I laughed, feeling dizzily like Audrey Hepburn. I could have danced all night. Let's just flirt and foxtrot. *Much* nicer.

'There's lots of things you don't know about me,' Truman said pointedly. 'Kent Junior Ballroom Dancing Champion 1987. I danced with my little sister.'

'Wow, I'm impressed.'

And I was. With our hips tantalisingly locked together, Truman made me feel human again. As the track finished, he even dipped me. I nearly came there and then. I was being ginger in more than one way that evening. The next track started and we began dancing again, slower this time.

This was far too enjoyable. What a disaster. The last thing I wanted was for Truman to turn out to be *interesting*. Life as a ricocheting bullet was not what I wanted. Simon Lyndon Inc. was striving to possess continuity and this evening had to contribute to that. But the music was great and Truman was *so* charming.

You are the worst sort of man . . . a good man capable of hypocrisy . . .

We danced cheek to cheek for a while, listening to the song. Apparently, something had happened in Monterey, a long time ago. I had forgotten how great five o'clock shadow against five o'clock shadow is. How could I forget that? The sandalwood was driving me insane. I stopped dancing suddenly. It had to happen now.

We had both calmed down, the situation not feeling so contrived or formal. I looked directly at him, giving him the go-ahead. He was looking at me in a half-regretful, half-tender way. He stroked my face.

'Is Ol' Blue Eyes back?' Truman said.

'I don't know if I am. I hope not. Thank you for this.'

'What for?' Truman said. 'I haven't done anything yet.'

Here we go. He kissed me. I do love it when people just hoover in and take charge.

'We need the wine,' Truman said, breaking away and leading me back to the kitchen. It was like I was one of the doomed passengers in *The Poseidon Adventure*, just following blindly. Frank sang blithely in the background about wanting the things you love. In the kitchen, Truman ignored the wine and pushed me up against the wall, kissing my neck.

'Truman, I have got a bedroom.' *It might be less exciting there. Let's go there. I've tidied up in here.*

'We're doing it in the kitchen,' Truman said firmly. 'My cock. My fuck. We're doing it here.'

'All right. *Wow*. What has got into you? Have you been promoted?'

'People can change, Simon. You're not the only one.'

Why did everyone think I was egocentric? I felt very put in my place.

Truman was being incredible. Maybe Truman was the one for me. *Truman*. This new improved one. This version might even watch a film with subtitles. Was Ruth a blip? Surely not. Surely not. Truman undid his jeans, adjusting so that I could unzip him. Straight down to it, very different to Ruth. As I slipped my hand into his boxers, I reflected that Ruth might be a blip. *In that moment*, I thought she *might* be.

That's all. I swear it.

After this lead-up, it took me no time at all to become aroused. A little pot is soon hot, as they self-deprecatingly say. Truman took a little longer. This was obviously difficult for him but he was covering it well. He rolled a condom on to himself as expertly as the Queen putting on her tiara before a state banquet. And then Truman did my old team proud.

Team: I really hate that phrase, I'm sorry I ever used it. Sex becomes all about winners and losers and *opposing*. My days of blue-sky serenity were well behind me so I wasn't looking to *win* anything, just to know which goalmouth was definitely mine. And if that sounds desperate, well, there was a reason for that. I wanted my life with Ruth back, but back without the complications of the world obscuring my view of her. With Ruth, there was a chance for something I had not even glimpsed before: the big, lifetime commitment chance. I had not realistically thought in those terms about anyone else in my life. Ruth was not special *because* she was a woman. When I was in bed with her, she excited me more than Truman ever had because when I made love with her, it meant something. That in itself was sexy. Even as Truman sweated and heaved over me, I knew it was just a physical release. At most, we serviced each other. Nothing wrong with that and plenty right with it, but I wanted something else now. I was ready for more. Even when the actual sex with Ruth was awful, like the other night after her mother's onslaught, two people were still trying to say *something*, to be a statement of faith in themselves. And that was thrilling and new to me.

With men, with each different man, it had been wonderful and interesting because new bodies are exciting, *by definition*. Making love with Mikhail Gorbachev for the first time would have some redeeming quality. If you lick that birthmark on his head, does it change colour, maybe go slightly darker? Stuff like that can fuel any one-night stand. For me, the men I had slept with over the years had been like bar snacks, by which I mean they were moreish. Having slept with a man, it made me want another one, but not the same one *again*. Who wants to see a bar snack after you've eaten it? And in the end, that was why Truman could not be Mr Right because he had been Mr Right-Away in too many moments of need. That said, he did seem different and more dynamic, but I would find a way for it not to work, for me to become disenchanted. New and improved Daz is still washing powder.

When I was a younger man about town, all that bar-snacking was fine; it was almost a philosophy. It was all about trying things out, good times, walking borderlines between taboo and disapproval, thumbing noses and asserting the me-ness of me. But that makes sex into a young man's game where you reach the limits of acceptability very fast. I would get older, but the men I wanted would stay the same age. I could not spend the rest of my life chasing men in their twenties. I hate those old men who do that. I did not hate myself *that* much to go up that blind alley until kingdom come. Youth can't be the only truth. Increasingly futile attempts to find the Adonis who could make me feel so young did not equal happiness, but

I don't fancy men over forty or, perish the thought, over fifty either, and I knew I would not even when *I* was over fifty. Joint prescriptions for Viagra are not an aphrodisiac.

I was side-lining myself while being side-lined.

Even as I loved the rough feel of Truman's long legs against mine, the strength of his mouth against mine, the weight of him pressing me into the kitchen floor, I realised that I would end up yearning for the joys of a hard, young, male body *whether I remained gay or straight*.

This was crucial. How brilliant that it perhaps did not matter that I wanted to sleep with beautiful young men. Wanting that was like a creek that was about to dry up and I didn't have much of a paddle left anyway. Therefore, it was old news, yesterday's noodles. And maybe, just maybe, I *preferred* my beautiful young men either out of my league, like Ben Affleck, or beyond my grasp, like Patrick. After all, that's what Heaven's for, right? And maybe, just maybe I had Heaven-on-earth within my sights with Ruth and I shouldn't lose the chance to be with a wonderful person who made me happy. Or who wanted to make me happy. Or who I wanted to make happy. Whichever.

I pushed out of my head all secret, not-quite-admitted thoughts of settling for less or for second best. That wasn't what I was thinking at all. There was no point in even contemplating going back to men if all I was looking for was what I already had with Ruth. If I seized this moment with her then I could be fine. I was not going through a phase. A phase was going through me. If I did not move on, I would be moved on anyway. And I now knew that wanting men would never go away. Maybe that was OK. *Perhaps* it was liveable with if I knew it was inevitable whatever I decided.

I tried to imagine what Ruth would say now seeing me with Truman as he sensed himself getting near to orgasm; he suddenly withdrew, leaving me gasping, and knelt between my legs, whipping the condom off and throwing it to one side. Perhaps Ruth would say, *'I really admire you for what you are doing to preserve our relationship. How brave of you.'*

I imagined Ruth's father watching as we helped each other to climax, Truman coming over my chest: *'Now that's what I call heterosexuality. Look at the cock on him. Fancy a beer, prospective son-in-law?'*

It had felt great letting Truman call the shots, pushing me around with his big hands to where he wanted me. He was rough in a different way to Ruth's violence in bed. He was more methodical, more calculated for his pleasure. But she was wilder, her strength lying in how unpredictable she could be. I loved the fact that I still did not know how she would react.

Somehow, Truman and I had ended up braced against a corner cupboard. The saucepan one. The kitchen was like a trainwreck. He rolled away, his heavy intakes of breath slowly easing. Duty done.

To my horror, I started shaking and crying and had to turn away. I knew that this had to be the last time I could be with a man if Ruth and I were to stand a chance. Ruth was now my hope for happiness, the real go-the-distance, long-term, not-lonely version of my future. Men and me worked in bed but only Ruth and me could work in Life was well. I had to have both Love and Life. But . . .

The idea of not being with a man ever again froze me with fear. My body told me to do this, that I liked this. My head was telling me that men were a big part of my life but that it had to be over. Why was I having to choose *now*? I felt emptied and alone. I wanted Ruth and I wanted my friends even more. I had not even spoken to any of them for weeks. I wanted Toril most of all. She would know what I should do. I did not know what I should do, so I wept. I missed Toril, so I wept. And I mourned the end of my prime, the one I'd wasted behaving and feeling middle-aged and adolescent by turns. Going nowhere as a result.

Truman pulled me to him and my tears ran down his body. Why could I not love him as I thought I loved Ruth? As I *knew* I loved Ruth? It would all be so simple. Truman reached up a hand and ruffled my hair.

'It's OK. All over now. All over.'

All over? Did he think he'd 'cured' me or something? Everyone was wanting to cure me. What was I, bacon? He reckoned that twenty minutes of Truman was enough to banish every straight thought out of my head? Impulsively, I twisted round to face him and kissed him far too hard, my tongue forcing deep into his mouth. I could make Ruth happy and I wanted Truman to know that. He pulled his head to one side.

'Simon, not so rough, huh? That's *it*. Over. I've done what you—'

I kissed him again, pushing him over and holding him down against the kitchen floor so that he was pinioned into place. I rolled on top of him, getting myself between his legs, trying to hoist his legs on to my shoulders, whispering into his ear, 'Let me do this, let me show you.' I knew he didn't ever let anyone do what I was trying to do to him. But I wanted him to know how I had changed.

Truman wrenched his head away.

'Simon, stop it, you know I don't do that—'

I tried to stop his mouth with mine but his head was free now and Truman was having none of it. He was very angry now.

'I'll brain you, Simon. I'll fucking *hurt* you if you try anything.'

I remembered that policemen are trained in self-defence-type things when he headbutted me on the nose. Not that hard but enough for me to see little stars. Like Billy Zane and Ethan Hawke.

'I said *stop* and I mean it!' he shouted, pushing me away with all his strength.

I flew back and cracked my head on the corner of the kitchen table and lay stunned and prone as Truman stood up, groping for his clothes as he did so. I wanted to apologise immediately but could not say anything as my mouth was filling up with blood. It had been one of those unambiguous 'No means No' moments, hadn't it?

Truman looked at me in disbelief as he pulled his trousers back on.

'What were you trying to do, Simon? Show me what a *man* you've become? I'm nearly a blackbelt, you silly sod, I could have killed you.'

Blood was pouring out of my nose. I started whimpering.

'Oh, for fuck's sake,' muttered Truman. '"Gay Police Constable in Brawl With Lover." Perfect.'

He rifled through my freezer and found a packet of peas. He threw them at me and they landed on my stomach. They were bloody cold. I yelped.

'Doh, diddums,' Truman said unsympathetically. 'Keep your head lifted and clamp the peas to your nose. You'll be fine.'

His mobile rang. Muttering expletives, Truman tracked the sound through the rubble of my kitchen. He found it and impatiently flipped it open. 'Uh-huh . . . hey, *hi* . . .' he said, his face brightening. He padded into the hall for some privacy but I heard him organise a date for the following night. Absurdly, I felt a twinge of jealousy. He came back in, shaking his head when he saw I had not moved at all.

'Poor ickle sorry-for-himself Simon,' he mocked, and picked up the rest of his clothes. I managed to ask a question through my pink-misted haze.

'Who was that?'

Truman gave me a derisive stare. 'Looking for the latest goss, Simon? Nothing tops you at the moment, believe me. For your information, that was Rob, my newie. I've been with him about a month. I'm the older man, would you believe it.'

Truman had a new boyfriend. That was why he seemed different: he was in love. And he'd still agreed to this fiasco. And then I'd tried to assault him. Gorgeous. I groaned and wanted to die.

I said, 'Why didn't you—', then had to stop to spit some blood out of my mouth. Truman watched me with disgust written all over him.

'You look so-o-o sexy,' he said drily, 'I will always remember you like this. Why didn't I what? See if you can say it this time.'

I shifted position and looked up at him as he sat on my kitchen top and put his socks on. When had he taken them off? What a *gent*.

'Why didn't you tell me about Rob?' I croaked.

He looked uncharitable for a second. 'Well, you never asked, Simon.'

Oh. That will be me being selfish again, then.

'But if you're with someone, why did you come here tonight?'

Truman considered his reply, searching for the kindest words. I hoped he failed.

'Because I felt sorry for you, because I wanted to help you, because I think you're a bit of a fuck-up . . .'

I nodded glumly. He could stop any time he liked.

'. . . And I love you a lot, for all that.' His tone hardened. 'But at the moment you're pissing me off something rotten.'

'I'm sorry,' I said thickly, tears springing to my eyes again. The peas were not helping at all.

'It's OK. I'm trying to forget it.' He knelt by me and held the peas in place a lot tighter. My hands flopped to the floor like a rag-doll's. We contemplated each other.

'I'm *really* sorry,' I repeated, starting to hyperventilate. 'I'm really sorry.'

'OK, OK,' said Truman. 'I accept your apology. Will you promise me something? That you'll get some professional help.'

'Ok-a-ay,' I said slowly. A policeman thought I needed professional help. That's *bad*. 'But I'd hate talking about myself like that.'

'Yeah, *right*. You'd hate paying for it, you mean.'

I summoned up the last shred of my courage and asked Truman if he thought I was gay or straight. He gave me a strange look.

'Well, that's a toughie for me to answer, Simon, if only because I just fucked you and you just tried to fuck me back. But if you *really* want to know what I think . . .'

I nodded miserably again. Truman took a deep breath.

'I think that when you sleep with a man, you like being the woman, and when you sleep with a woman, you like being the man.'

'Oh,' I said. I had not counted on Truman coming up with anything quite so thought through. Bugger.

But you, Mr Lyndon, are not quite homosexual or anything else . . .

Truman looked about ready to go. I did not want to be by myself yet.

'Are you in love?' I asked.

Clouds went across Truman's face. 'Don't know. Maybe. Are you?'

'I want to be,' I said slowly. 'I think I am. She's great.'

'Is she a psycho underneath, when you really get to know her? That's what scares me about people.'

It's what just scared you about me, you mean.

'No, she's not a psycho,' I replied. That's not to say Ruth didn't have issues . . .

'Stick with her then. Non-psychotics . . .'

'. . . like hens' teeth,' I completed for him.

'Huh? But hens don't have teeth,' Truman said, confused.

See what I mean, see what I mean? It could never have worked with Flashback Boy.

'Do you want kids, Simon? Is that why you're suddenly with women?' asked Truman, his eyes narrowing.

Was it? It couldn't be.

'Do you want them?' I asked back. I had no answer to give.

'Kids? Nah.' Truman was musing aloud. He didn't even think about it yet, far too young. 'I'd be a good dad, I know that just from meeting dreadful parents every day, but you just accept it, don't you? They'd be great but they're not for us. Well, me. So you want to be a dad?'

'Not really.'

A *child*. Thirty, thirty-one's a good age to become a father. The classic age, really. And that look in Sarah and Hannah's dad's eyes when he'd said goodbye to them had been a good look. It had been a great look.

Truman stood up and put on his shoes. 'Can I go now? Anything else I can do?'

'Stick the kettle on,' I bleated pathetically.

'Jesus, I feel like kicking you, you wanker,' Truman exclaimed, eyed me for a split second then dead-legged me. I didn't say anything, I deserved it. But he filled the kettle up. He put on a talking-to-the-deaf voice. 'Now, are you comfy just lying there, Mother? Do you want a blanket? Do you need to go to Casualty?'

I told him I'd be fine but I was not certain I would be. I watched him leave. He turned back to me when he reached my front door.

'Be happy,' he called out and smiled at me.

'OK,' I shouted back. Easy-peasy.

He had even put an Earl Grey teabag in my favourite mug. What a guy. The door clicked shut.

This was the low point. This was rock bottom. It *had* to be.

I was naked and half-unconscious on the floor of my trashed kitchen with a packet of Birds Eye peas on my face. I was covered in my own blood. The back of my head was bleeding as well and I was sure it would need a stitch. And I had a policeman's spunk drying on my chest, from the man with whom I had just enjoyed making love prior to an attempted sexual assault on him. And I loved my girlfriend very much. Topping. A saying of the other great patriarch of the nation (apart from Captain Birdseye) came in to my head: *I have nothing to offer you but blood, sweat, toil and tears. Oh, and semen.* I started laughing but stopped because it hurt my nose, and clambered to my feet like a frog from a tadpole pond. I had to move on and do that rest-of-my-life thing. Dammit.

The phone rang. My machine clicked in then beeped.

'Hi, it's me. I've just got the kids to bed. I've been think-ing, a lot actually, about what happened over the weekend . . .'

Oh, please don't leave me, please don't leave me, I need you.

'. . . um . . and we should see each other very soon, but away from here, yeah? We'll organise something. Where are you anyway? . . .'

'I love you,' I whispered. 'I won't let you down, I promise.'

'. . . er . . . call me tonight up until half-eleven or tomor-row morning, I haven't got a lecture 'til midday. Comedy and Tragedy. Bye.'

Move on, Simon, move *on*. We were going to be just fine. No doubts at all. Hardly any. I now knew for certain that men were becoming a part of my past. Of my youth. They had to. God knew how, but they had to.

My nose eventually stopped bleeding. My head seemed better once I stood up. It was just a bump. I set the furni-ture straight, made the tea Truman had set up for me, took a shower and then rang Ruth back.

Chapter 20

'I laugh when I hear that the fish in the water is thirsty'
Kabir, the Weaver Mystic

'Why don't you all stay with me?' I had said. 'It'll be a tight squeeze but we'll be fine.'

'Are you sure?' Ruth had replied cautiously. 'You know what the girls are like.'

It was half-term and Ruth was bringing Hannah and Sarah back down to Brighton to see some of their old school friends. I made up a bed in my tiny second bedroom for the girls. A tadge of tactful clearing away was necessary. I moved various incriminating pictures, postcards from friends, magazines and books into the dark recess of a drawer and generally made my flat suitable for an eight-year-old to go snooping around in. It was an odd feeling to lock a drawer on old worn-out copies of *Mandate* and *Colt*, a treasured picture of Keanu Reeves naked on a highway I'd ripped out of a magazine years before, volumes of erotica I knew by heart.

I told myself this wasn't about closet doors creaking and slamming shut. Magazines devoted to people such as Mitch Bravo, who was 'ready, smilin', waitin', wantin'' and had something in his hand 'standin' straight up 'n' throbbin'', should not be within reach of people such as Hannah and Sarah. It was not lost on me that I liked that picture of Keanu's butt too much, that I locked rather than threw it away.

Ruth and the girls arrived on the Saturday at about three in the afternoon. I heard Ruth honk her horn, looked out of my window and waved down to them all. Operation Embryonic Family Man was off and running down the stairs to help with luggage. Hannah was jumping up and down on the pavement, obviously excited, and Sarah was stretching some kinks out of her back. Hannah ran up to me.

'Simon the Pieman, give me some *skin*,' she said and proffered a hand for a high-five.

'Yo, sister,' I said, slapping her hand. Since when had Spike Lee been directing *Grange Hill*? Ruth got out of the car looking a bit frazzled after the drive, but gave me a big wave hello. The big shock was that she'd had her hair cut. Really short.

'*Hair cut*. Wow. You didn't tell me about that,' I said. 'It looks *great*.'

And the Sean Penn Memorial Award for Telling Your Beloved She Looks Great With Her New Look Goes to . . .

'Don't you like it?' said Ruth.

. . . *Someone Else*. How had that worked? I said she looks great, she said, 'Don't you like it?' When we had been best friends, she'd have taken me to the salon and got me to help pick out the style from the magazines. How times change.

Ruth handed me a couple of bags, 'Well, I *love* it. It's so much easier to look after.'

'Mum just washes and goes now,' remarked Sarah.

'Does she now?' I said. Sarah nodded.

'Nanny Whittaker said it was *too* short,' stated Hannah.

'It looks so *chic*,' I said. Ruth grunted disbelievingly. 'Any more bags?'

Grandma was right. I had loved Ruth's hair being long. It was . . . well, feminine, which meant that I was . . . so if she had short hair then that meant I . . . *Simon, don't go there*. I started talking myself into liking Ruth's new look straight away. It gave her a fresh, modern feel, gave her a real make-over and made her look . . .

. . . *boyish*.

There, I said it, Boyish, just the quality a recently retired homosexual needs in a girlfriend. Discuss. I was going to have to get her naked very quickly in order to check she'd retained everything else. I liked her being *womanly*. Not that gettin' nekkid, smilin' 'n' throbbin' was going to happen with Hannah and Sarah around. I felt like a crotchety caretaker in *Scooby Doo*. Pesky kids, darn tootin'. When were they going to visit their friends? Soon, make it soon. Then I remembered that I was being a family man today.

'Hey, how was your *journey*?' I suddenly gushed at the startled girls. 'Was it really *long*? I used to *hate* long car journeys when I was your age. Have we got *all* the bags? I'm on the *first* floor, have you been here before? I can't *remember* . . .'

'Are you OK, Simon?' Sarah interrupted, exchanging glances with her sister. Ruth stood behind them with a surprised look on her face.

'I'm fine,' I said, my happy-face slipping a notch. 'Why?'

'It's just that you're talking in a funny voice all of a sudden.'

'And your smile's all different,' added Hannah.

You're trying too hard, dickbrain, just cool it.

'My smile's different? I don't know what *that's* about. Anyway, I've got some orange squash upstairs. Who wants some?'

Ruth jumped up and down, waving her hand. 'Oooh, me, sir, me, sir.'

I flicked two fingers at her, repeating to her daughters, 'Who wants some?'

'Haven't you got any Dr Pepper?' Hannah demanded. 'Orange squash is for *children*.'

'You are children, aren't you?' I asked back. Ruth sucked in her breath and leaned on her car, waiting for the fallout. Sarah looked very offended.

'Hannah is. I'm not. Hannah can have squash.'

Hannah socked her sister in the arm. Oh-so-grown-up Sarah twatted her back, causing Hannah to yelp and turn to her mother for support. Never tell children they are children. I could remember that. Ruth split them up.

'If you start that again, we're going back to Manchester.' *Oh, don't do that.* The girls ganged up on their mother.

'Well, you can't mean that, because we just got here and you want to see Simon,' said Sarah.

'And I don't mind orange squash,' said Hannah winningly, looking at me.

'Say sorry to Simon. We've only just got here and you're causing trouble,' Ruth instructed.

They mumbled at me. 'No worries,' I said. 'I've a nasty feeling it was all my fault anyway. Should we go inside? I could always pop out and get some Dr Pepper, if you wanted.'

'Don't you dare, Simon,' Ruth said darkly. 'They're fine. They shouldn't be too hungry yet, we ate something on the way down.' The girls ran ahead of us and up to my flat. 'First floor, first door on the left,' I shouted out. Ruth gathered up some bags of books and games and started to troop in behind them. I accosted her. 'Where are *you* going? Good afternoon.'

'Afternoon,' she answered. I tried to kiss her but the bags got in the way. I put the bags down for her. We had a little moment alone but were soon distracted by the girls banging on my window to get our attention. Ruth waved them away.

'I hope you put the Ming vases in storage,' she said. 'Are you really sure we're welcome? I can still find a B & B.'

'I'm looking forward to it. Honestly.'

'Say it again like you mean it this time.'

'*I'm looking forward to it.*'

'Better. They're both devil-spawn when they want to be. They get it from their father. You have been warned.'

'How is Duane?'

'Darren.'

'Whatever.'

'Who cares? You hate my hair short, don't you?'

'I *love* it. It looks great.'

'Say it like you mean it.' We went inside bickering gently and I got us all some drinks. Orange squash was drunk and was even enjoyed. Sarah rang up one of her old school friends and they spoke shyly to each other like lovers talking for the first time in a while. I knew *all about* that intense friendship thing. Ruth took over the phone eventually and arranged with the other mother that we'd take Sarah over the next day.

In the midst of all the preparations, I was the only one to notice Hannah grow pale and start to tremble. Spotting what was about to happen, I scooped her up and tried to get her to the toilet in time. Too late.

She threw up just a little on the floor in my hall but a huge amount on both walls and over me as well. Remarkably, Hannah moved her head about as she vomited, managing to achieve an even coverage on either side. Ruth quickly put the phone down and came running, Sarah hanging back and looking on in concern, waiting for her mother to be fantastic. As was I.

'My tummy hurts,' moaned Hannah, hanging like a dead weight in my arms.

'It's OK, Hannah. Mummy's here. Thanks, Simon, I'll take her.'

'I can do it,' I said.

'*Let me take her.*'

'I tried to get her to the loo,' I said, handing Hannah to Ruth, who managed to drag her into the bathroom. I rinsed my hands and cleaned up a little as Hannah leaned over the toilet pan briefly then exploded again. All through this, Ruth was stroking Hannah's back and making calming sounds of encouragement as her daughter nearly succeeded in turning inside out.

'What's she eaten?' I asked, hovering uselessly like a Tory ex-cabinet minister. No one listened to me so I said it again. It seemed relevant.

'Uh, not much,' said Ruth. 'Some cereal and toast and she had . . . *oh*, she had a prawn sandwich on the way down.'

'That'll be it then.'

'Watch Sarah, would you? They shared the sandwich.'

Oh, *good*. I whipped round to see Sarah taking a step into the bathroom only to retreat again as a complete Tex-Mex refried meal for two came out of her sister.

'I thought the sandwich tasted funny. That's why I left most of it,' Sarah said, looking a touch pale herself.

'Why didn't you *say* something?' Ruth said in despair, glancing round from looking after Hannah.

'I tried to but you were in a rush. You didn't want to be late for *Simon*,' Sarah nearly shouted, starting to cry. 'Is Hannah going to die?'

'She'll be fine,' I cut in. 'She's just got to get it out of her system. Come into the living room with me and I'll get you a bowl to sit with in case you feel ill too.'

The living room was stoutly defended by a small moat of orange squash populated with shellfish. Sarah jumped over it as I went to get the bowl and some cleaning stuff. I was almost doing this from folk memory, remembering primary school afternoons off sick, watching *Houseparty* and *The Galloping Gourmet*, curled up in a sleeping bag on the sofa with a bottle of Lucozade and the washing-up bowl close to hand, feeling like the Little Prince and saying 'I'm ok-*a*-y' in a doubtful tone to any enquiry after my health. Great days. Vaulting the moat myself, I handed the bowl to Sarah who took it and walked to a chair holding it carefully in front of her. She was like Marie Antoinette going to the guillotine.

Ruth came through from the bathroom. 'I'm going to ring Mum. Hannah looks awful. Keep an eye on her, would you?'

'It's cordless,' I said, handing Ruth the phone and putting a protective arm around the dormant Sarah. I preferred the devil I did not yet know to the three-foot-eight stomach-acid volcano in the next room.

Ruth gave me a scornful look. 'Coward,' she said.

'Press the green button to get a tone,' I replied with a grin.

'Can't say I blame you,' Ruth sighed, taking the phone into the bathroom, going into hyper-efficient this-is-what-I-must-do mode. She got through to her mum.

'Mum, it's me . . . yeah, the journey was fine . . . I think they've got food poisoning . . . Hannah's being sick, Sarah's fine at the mo' . . . prawns . . . I know, I *know* . . . Don't tell me off, Mum, just tell me what to *do* . . .'

She listened hard, me hearing her make sounds of agreement every now and again. She said goodbye and the phone beeped as she turned it off. Hannah and Ruth emerged from the bathroom, Hannah like the Queen Mother coming out of hospital after her hip operations.

'Mum says we don't necessarily have to get the doctor out. We need to get lots of fluids int—'

Sarah interrupted her mother, sending Hannah flying as she got in on the act with a sudden attack of the squits. The bathroom door slammed shut as Ruth tried to help Sarah on to the loo. I called through to see if there was anything I could do. Hannah picked herself up and tot-tered through to the living room. I put the bowl on her lap again but while I was doing that, I missed Ruth's reply.

'What did you say?' I asked, knocking on the door.

'*What?*' Ruth replied, sounding exasperated. 'No, there's nothing you can do. Look after Hannah.'

'She seems fine now. Can I get anything?'

There was a silence as Ruth obviously attended to something diabolical happening with Sarah.

'Simon, are you still there?'

'Yeah?' I almost stood to attention.

'Go to the chemist for me. Get me . . .' and she reeled off a whole list of things.

'I've got quite a lot of these already. Look in the cabinet. Do they still *make* Milk of Magnesia?'

'It's chalk. Chalk doesn't change.'

'Should I get some Lucozade?' I added eagerly. I could *contribute* here. I knew about Lucozade.

'Whatever you think,' Ruth called quickly. Leaving Sarah combusting in the bathroom and Hannah glumly staring at the bottom of the plastic bowl, I ran to the nearest chemist, half expecting that, on my return, I'd find Ruth cradling two pairs of charred Reeboks with a faint smell of Sandwich Spread in the air. The woman behind the pharmacy counter seemed well used to people covered in vomit running in for Alka-Seltzer and Milk of Magnesia and was not overly impressed by my dramatic account of events.

A young woman waiting for a prescription nodded wisely. 'You have to be careful with seafood,' she said.

I sprinted back. In my absence, things had calmed down a little. My flat stank and had turned into a field hospital. Sarah and Hanna were under blankets on my couch in the living room, green and shivering, and Ruth was in the middle of mopping up the hall.

'I got everything.' I was panting for breath, feeling like the Fourth Cavalry saving the day. 'How are things?'

Ruth mimicked my breathless tone. 'Fantastic, thanks. It's really exciting, isn't it? How do you think we're doing?'

'Huh?' *That was a bit rough.*

Ruth angrily threw a J-cloth into a bucket of soapy water, splashing water on the carpet.

'I've nearly finished. You might have to get someone in for the carpet,' she said, leaning back on her heels. 'I suppose something had to happen.'

'After twenty minutes though? Extraordinary.'

I finally got a smile out of her.

'What are you two laughing at?' wailed Hannah.

'Nothing, Han. Are you all right?' Ruth called back.

'I th-i-nk so.'

I went and peeked at the walking wounded. They looked very sorry for themselves. I squatted by the couch.

'Hey, I got you some Lucozade,' I said. 'They were out of Dr Pepper. Lucozade's better for when you're ill.' I called to Ruth to ask if they could have one of the glucose sweets I'd bought at the chemist.

'I suppose so,' she said, straightening up from wiping my hall carpet. 'See if they want one.'

'These are good for you,' I said solemnly. 'Eat them slowly so you don't surprise your stomachs. Just one each. And a moist wipe as well.'

'I *love* moist wipes,' said Hannah, nodding fervently. That was why I'd got them, it seemed. She got a consumer glint in her eye. 'Two moist wipes each.'

'One should do,' I said frugally.

The girls took the sweets and nibbled on the corners. I laid out moist wipes like antimacassars on the back of the sofa. Ruth finished sluicing the hall and was taking the bucket of water into the bathroom to empty it out. I followed her in and sat on the loo to talk to her. She grunted, 'I wouldn't sit *there*.'

'Ugh.' I perched on the bath. 'How long will they be sick? I take ages getting over food poisoning.'

'Don't know, a couple of days?' said Ruth, pouring away the dirty suds. 'Don't worry, it shouldn't be long.'

'As long as it takes,' I said hastily. 'It doesn't matter.'

Ruth gave me a sideways glance. 'You're so noble.'

'I'm not being *noble*. They're fine staying here. Everyone's entitled to get food poisoning. You just have to put up with it.'

'"Have to put up with it"?' she threw back at me. 'Don't think you *have* to *put up* with anything, Simon. Don't do me any favours, OK?' She rinsed out the plastic bowl. I'd get another one for the washing up, I decided.

'Well, I'm not *putting up* with it,' I said. 'I'd just like them to get better, then we can have some fun.'

'You like the good bits, don't you?' Ruth said. *What did she mean?*

'Mu-u-u-m.' It was Sarah this time.

It was like a siren for nuclear attack going off. Ruth winced, shut her eyes for a second, opened them. Within five minutes, the bathroom was radioactive again. Ruth wanted Sarah to lie down properly after this so she took her into my bedroom. Not what I'd had in mind when I changed the sheets that morning. I found another bowl so both of them had one now. I put on the TV for Hannah, who bravely watched some racing from Haydock.

Ruth came into the living room, looking knackered. 'One prawn sandwich, what a pain.'

'How's Sarah?'

'You don't want to know. The Gross National Product of Belgium just came out of her, by the look of it.'

'Do you want anything? Class "A" drugs, grain alcohol, cup of tea?' I asked Ruth.

'The manager of that bloody transport café's testicles between two slices of brown bread,' muttered Ruth, so Hannah would not hear. Louder, she said, 'I'm going to sit down, you'll bring me a tea and then I'll apologise for being so crap,' and collapsed into an armchair.

'Coming up,' I said jauntily. Ruth didn't look me in the eye. I'm trying, I thought, can't do more.

I went to make some tea, stripping off my shirt as I did so. God, what a stench. I opened a window in the hallway to air the flat. I threw the shirt back into the wash along with some rancid towels Ruth must have put in there earlier. After some effort, I finally managed to open a sky-light in my kitchen as well. I got some clean towels from by the hot water tank and put them in the bathroom, calling out to tell Ruth what I was doing. No answer. Poking my head around the door, I saw that both Ruth and Hannah were asleep, Hannah more fitfully than her mother. It had been a big day and it was only ten past five. I left them to it. Sleeping or being in a cranky mood ain't puking. It could only be an improvement. I switched off the TV.

Sneaking into my bedroom to get another shirt, I tried not to disturb Sarah, who was shifting uneasily, with a nasty sheen of sweat over her. I found a T-shirt and was putting it on when I heard a little voice.

'Can I have a drink?'

Sarah had not moved but was looking at me, her big green eyes slightly bloodshot.

'Yeah, of course,' I whispered back. 'Just water, yeah?'

She nodded. 'Where's Mum?'

'She's asleep. All that driving, I think. How are you feeling?'

'Horrible,' Sarah replied with a scowl. I beamed sym-pathetically at her. She stared back then added, '*Can* I have some water?'

'Coming right up,' I said hastily, then added in my best French waiter voice, 'Still, o' wiz gas?'

'Still,' Sarah said, without smiling at my gag. What a young woman of taste and discernment. I went into the kitchen and poured out some water, then took the bottle back in with me so she could have it near her. Lots of fluids, Ruth's mum had said.

'It's Evian. Only the best for you.'

'Nanna calls it frilly water,' Sarah said, carefully taking hold of the glass.

'That's a good name for it. Do you want a cup with a handle?' I said, seeing the glass tremble a little.

'No,' said Sarah. 'The glass is nice and cold. Can you shut the curtain? The sun's in my eyes.'

She sipped at the water. As I shut the curtain, Sarah said, 'You met Nanna, didn't you?'

'Yes, I did. We got on quite well, eventually.' I turned back to look at her, my eyes adjusting to the darkness. Sarah looked very beady, thinking hard.

'She's a tough cookie, Uncle Pete says.'

'He's not wrong there.'

'That's good, being a tough cookie, isn't it?'

'Ye-e-s. But you need to know when not to be,' I replied. Sarah waited for me to go on. 'To know when to be gentle and kind to people.'

'I think Nanna's like that too,' Sarah said after a moment's consideration.

'I think she is. She's got a great laugh, hasn't she?'

'She doesn't laugh much, though.'

'That's why it's great. You know it's real.'

'Bowl, where's the bowl!' Sarah said urgently, her face contorting.

I scrambled for the bowl by the side of the bed and got it to her just in time. I rubbed her back as she threw up the water she'd just swallowed. There wasn't much but it left her winded. She leaned against me, breathing hard. She felt very frail as I supported her. I didn't know what to do.

'Do you want your mum?'

'No, she's sleeping,' Sarah whispered slowly. 'Nanna says we shouldn't disturb her when she's sleeping.'

'You all look after each other, don't you?'

Sarah nodded, her eyes closing. I could feel her heart-beat, too fast for how tired she was.

'Daddy was asking me about you the other day.' *Was he now.*

'What did he ask?'

'Not much, what you did, how you knew Mummy.' She adjusted to get a more comfortable position against me, wrinkling her nose, then rubbing it.

'What did you say to him?' I asked quietly.

'I didn't tell him about . . . you know . . .'

'You could have done.'

I hated that she'd had to make that sort of decision. She was *eleven*.

'Daddy wouldn't have liked it if I'd told him. He might have argued with Mum.'

'Ah.'

'Nanna says that Life should be as simple as possible.'

'Your nanna's very wise. But it sometimes doesn't stop Life from being complicated. Unfortunately.'

'I told him you were nice . . .'

And she fell asleep against me, her eyelids flickering.

I looked down at her, feeling an inkling of what Darren had felt talking to his daughters in the park that day. I got it for the first time. This person asleep against me could be my child. The thought astounded me. I tried to imagine what this obligation would be like for real. One false word, one false move and the shine is taken off the child, they get a glimpse of their future's fragility and it tarnishes them. No wonder so many people are bad parents; it's *difficult*. Sarah wasn't mine, but right at this moment she felt like she was.

This felt right. It was a good, positive thing to have a sick child trust you enough to fall asleep on you, for you to honour that trust, to feel rewarded by it. I sat there listening to Sarah breathe, dipping in and out of sleep myself.

'Hey.'

My head jerked up. It was Ruth, standing in the bedroom doorway.

It was getting dark outside. The curtained room was murky, making Ruth look like a hazy charcoal drawing of herself. My alarm clock said it was twenty past seven.

'We all fell asleep,' I said, looking down at Sarah now sound asleep on my chest, her arm across my stomach. I looked back up at Ruth and said fondly, 'I could get used to this.'

'You didn't say that before,' Ruth said.

'I know. A girl's allowed to change her mind, isn't she?'

'Is she? Why doesn't it feel like it?'

'*Oh yeah*, changing your mind is great. I'm the living proof,' I said comfortably. 'I had a great chat with Sarah. I think she likes me again.'

In the shadowy light I thought I saw Ruth smile.

'The good parts are always good,' she said. She'd said that earlier, hadn't she? Or something like it.

'How do you mean?'

'Never mind.'

'How did you do it, Ruth?'

'What?'

'Bring them up to be such good people. You were a baby yourself.'

Ruth did not move, thinking. I wanted her to come and join me and Sarah on the bed, for us to be together.

'I had lots of help. Mum was and is a miracle and Darren's mum was great too. My grandparents helped with money. It was still really hard. I wouldn't recommend it to anyone.'

'Not that young. No way,' I agreed.

But maybe now, Simon, maybe now. Or in a couple of years' time.

'Darren was fine, at first,' Ruth continued wintrily. 'Then he got scared by it all. He ran away.'

'I'd have been scared too, if I was him.'

'But you wouldn't have run out on me?'

'How do you know that?'

'No, I was asking you.'

'Oh. I hope not, Ruth. Maybe then, but not now.'

Had she registered that? A first little warning shot about what I wanted for us, for our future? I could not tell what she was thinking at all and something stopped me from asking. I was bathed in a warm glow of paternity, feeling doors opening up to me. Whatever Ruth was thinking now behind her inscrutable, shadowy mask, if it was bad, I'd be able to talk her round. We loved each other, we were a great team, that was all that mattered.

'Maybe you wouldn't have run away,' Ruth said. 'But then you are quite strong, Simon. I needed a strong man to look after me then and Darren was as weak as I was.'

'I don't think you're weak, Ruth. It's the last thing you are.'

'Oh, I *am*, Simon. I need so much help just to get through, from Mum, Pete, my friends, I need to get this degree just to feel *worthwhile*, so I uprooted my children from their home. I even used *them* as a crutch. They look after me as much as I look after them.'

She spoke with a tone so emphatic it had to be the truth. It was a truth I had known when I was her best friend, before I was her lover. Then our relationship had been about laughing at our flaws, making fun of how silly we could be about men, cheering each other up. After we got together, I lost interest in Ruth's deficiencies. Most of her problems had been to do with not having a man: now she had one. Me. How could she possibly be unhappy?

And university had changed her so much, made her seem so much more confident. She had reinvented herself. We had both reinvented ourselves.

So what did she want from me? It sounded like she was asking me to help her as well, to look after her. I could do that. I *wanted* to do that. I'd look after Hannah and Sarah too, as much as I could.

I looked down at Sarah again as she stirred slightly.

'She's spark out,' said Ruth. 'She can't hear us. Hannah's the same.'

I glanced up to catch Ruth's eye but the gathering darkness defeated me. 'I hadn't realised you still thought like this,' I said.

'Oh *God*, yes. Where have you been? I couldn't doubt myself more.'

'Jesus, why are you with *me* then?' I said as a joke.

'I don't know, Si. Why are you with me?' she replied seriously, catching me on the back foot.

Good question. Why had she never asked it before? Make this a good answer, Simon.

'Er . . . I love what you're doing with your life. You keep on wanting to learn and I adore that. You can talk to me about things you've read or seen that I know sod all about and you could do that before you went to college. You surprise me all the time. When I'm with you, I surprise *me* and I hadn't surprised myself for a long time before all this happened. It's great that we can talk like this without me breaking into a sweat. I've never had that before. You're my friend.'

'Do you love me?'

'Didn't I say that?'

'You didn't. I was listening *very* hard.'

Say it, klutz, say it, she wants to hear it.

'I do love you. It runs underneath everything I just said. I loved you before I was *in* love with you.'

I was almost fainting, I talk like this so rarely. I carefully eased Sarah off me. *Gently, Simon.* I crossed to Ruth and kissed her, a soft, almost chaste kiss that I wanted to mean everything I had just said.

'Simon, I—' She tried to pull away from me.

'I know you do, I know,' I said. I *knew* she loved me, she didn't have to say it just because I'd said it. I hate feeling *obliged* to say stuff like that; why should Ruth have to do it for me? I kissed her again.

'Can I just—' she said. *She's trying to say it again.*

I cut her off. 'I've got to have a shower and so have you. Care to join me?'

She sighed and leaned her forehead against mine. I felt her shoulders slump.

'I'll just check on Hannah.'

I went into the bathroom and switched on the shower. I was euphoric, I was closer to Ruth now than I had ever been to anyone before. Ruth came in and shut the door behind her.

'Is Hannah asleep?'

'Rock solid,' said Ruth, looking upset. End of a terrible day, I guessed. 'Oh, *Simon.*'

I held out my hand to her and she took it, holding it to her face.

'*Be my friend, be my friend,*' she said.

'I always have been. I always will be. Don't worry. I'm here. We look after each other in this family,' I said and slowly undressed us. Ruth must have been so tired because she felt almost stiff in my arms. Stepping under the jet of the water, she stood still while I soaped her and washed her hair, so short now. We kissed only occasionally, me whispering over and over again that I loved her, that I loved her so much. I lingered on her breasts, her stomach, I knelt to kiss her legs. She said hardly anything as I towelled her dry, except that she was tired and had to get to bed. She curled up beside Sarah on my bed and shut her eyes immediately. There was no room for me so I ended up sleeping in the bed I had made up for the girls in my study. It was still incredibly early. I read for a while but couldn't concentrate on anything.

As I went to sleep that night, I knew that being in the shower with Ruth, just kissing her and talking to her, was the best love I had ever made to anyone in my life.

Chapter 21

'What is love? A passion which sets all the universe in
one scale and the loved one in the other'
Napoleon Bonaparte

I was on the brink of something phenomenal. A small
bacillus in a suspect sandwich had set off a chain of events
that had propelled me to the brink of finally becoming an
adult and wanting what adults want at the ripe age of very
nearly thirty-one. It was like Victor Kyam was holding up
a mouldy crustacean and saying, 'Chaos theory can work
for you too! I liked it so much I bought the galaxy!'

However I had arrived at it, the previous night in the
shower with Ruth had been a unique experience for me,
a wordless *communion* almost, two people giving themselves up to being with each other. That's what it had
been like for me and it had shown me what I had to do
today. I spurned the blandishments of my wake-up hard-
on and refused even to think about jerking off, I was so
fucking *tantric* now. Today was going to be a *big day*, I
needed all my masculine juices coursing through me.

I bounced out of bed to find Ruth and the girls already
up and doing. Walking into my living room and watching
them all – Ruth on the phone talking to the mother of

Sarah's schoolfriend again, the girls looking much more chipper and playing with my old set of Connect 4 – I got butterflies. Was this my wife? Were these my step-children? Was this what every morning would be like if things went well with Ruth?

'. . . like I say, they both seem fine now and they can't wait to see Bethany again. If you're happy to cope with them, that's great. I'm sure they'll be OK . . . That's right, nothing rich to eat. See you soon, bye-bye.'

Ruth put down the phone and announced to the girls, 'Bethany's mum is coming round to pick you up at half-eleven.'

Hannah gave a little cheer and Sarah nodded eagerly. She still looked pale, I thought.

'Are you sure you're well enough?' I asked.

The three women in my life looked at me and I was patently found wanting. Ruth seemed strained; maybe she'd been up in the night with Hannah. Sarah shot me a dangerous and guarded look, as if to say 'Don't rain on my parade, you *adult*'. Ruth came to my rescue, 'I said they couldn't see Bethany unless they got better and whaddaya know.'

'We feel *fine*,' Hannah said with a self-satisfied smile.

I went to give Ruth a good-morning kiss, but she was moving round the other side of the couch and down to the kitchen, taking some used cereal bowls with her.

'Morning!' I called out pointedly after her.

'Oh, hi,' she said from halfway down the hall, turning back to look at me. I waved at her and smiled, trying to re-establish the intimacy of the night before. Ruth was thinking about other things. 'Did you sleep all right on that put-you-up?'

'Fine,' I said, thinking that once I'd seen the osteopath

I'd be as right as rain. 'How were they during the night? I didn't hear anything.'

Ruth was being very polite, as if she was still talking to Bethany's mum.

'They were fine, thanks. Slept the clock round.'

Thanks? I'd helped look after them yesterday, it hadn't been an idle enquiry. I followed her down to the kitchen.

'So what are *we* up to today?' I said, catching her by the waist as she put the bowls down. 'Have we got time off for good behaviour? I missed you on my put-you-up last night.'

I tried to kiss the side of her neck. Ruth wriggled free, saying, 'From half-eleven until three the girls can vomit elsewhere, not that I think they will.' Then we both said simultaneously, 'I thought we could . . .'

'What?' I said.

'No, you first,' Ruth said.

'*Well*,' I went on, taking her hand and looking at her, 'I'd like us to talk.' I tried to make what I said as pregnant with meaning as possible.

Ruth's eyes widened. 'Yes, that would be good. I've been wanting to talk as well. Things got a bit busy yesterday, didn't they?' She nodded at me and went back into the living room.

She was so amazing. I tried to be cool about things and failed miserably. Excellent. I looked at the kitchen clock: twenty-five past ten. Let's get these children packed off and then Ruth and me can *talk*. About the *future*.

The next hour was interminable and my anxiety levels shot up as the time wore on and on. What was I going to say? I had to talk about how I'd changed my mind about the children, about how I was going to fit into her family's life, into her life. The more I thought about it, the more sense it made. Ruth and I both needed permanence and security; we always had done. I could give Ruth that solid base while she was studying and, eventually, here my heart started pounding, *eventually* we should have a kid of our own. Ruth wanted to talk as well and she had been so wonderful last night, I was sure she'd been thinking along the same lines.

The crisis of the moment, however, was that Sarah was not happy with the clothes that had been brought down from Manchester. She was nervous too – she wanted to look her best for Bethany. How was I looking? I wondered. I checked myself out in a mirror. A hairy *thing* stared back at me. My hair really needed a cut – it looked like my vibrator had exploded. No wonder Ruth hadn't wanted to kiss me. I dived into the bathroom and tried to turn into somebody Ruth might want to marry. I could not believe I was thinking of doing this. The question was bursting to get out of my head, pressing against my forehead and soon she would hear it. I shaved too quickly and cut myself on my chin, having to spend ten minutes staunching the blood. Brilliant, I didn't want to be still bleeding when she said yes. I started laughing at the thought. I was insanely happy.

When I came out of the bathroom, Ruth was making sure the girls had their coats done up. Sarah was fighting against such an unfashionable and practical measure.

'Hey, you two look *great*,' I burbled.

'I look like I'm eight or something,' Sarah said, plucking unhappily at her coat. 'I might as well be wearing long white socks and a dress.'

'You look fine to me,' I beamed. Sarah threw up her hands in sartorial despair and looked at her mother as if her point had been proved.

'What's the matter with being eight?' peeved Hannah, looking up at her sister.

'Everything, when you're eleven,' Sarah said cuttingly. Oh, the humiliation she was going to go through, it was written all over her face.

I was still smiling. 'I think you'll be fine,' I said. 'Bethany's probably just as nervous about seeing you again.'

Error. System malfunction.

'I'm not nervous about seeing *Bethany*. Don't be stupid,' Sarah jittered, staring at me like I was a Martian.

'Simon meant "excited" perhaps,' soothed Ruth, raising her eyebrows at me with a grimace. A car horn tooted. We all moved on with great relief. Ruth gave the girls a last little checkover, I said I'd see them later, and then Ruth took them down to the car. As the car drove away, Ruth waved it off, then sat heavily on the wall outside my flat, her back to me. She was obviously thinking pretty hard. This was a big day for her too.

It reminded me of Toril, that night we had the row, just sitting in her car, her head against the wheel for a couple of minutes before suddenly starting up the engine and shooting off back to London. I hadn't seen Toril in ages, I realised, neither hide nor hair. I hoped she'd be happy for me and Ruth. Ruth squared her shoulders and got up. As she walked up the path, she glanced up and saw me looking at her. I smiled and she gave me a smile back. Her new short hairstyle looked great.

I told her so as she came back into the flat. She adopted a very broad northern accent, 'You can't get round me that easily, young man. Anyone would think you were after me for my money.' She tapped me reprovingly on the shoulder. I caught her hand.

'Are you rich then?' I said, mock-swinging her hand.

'I have a ten-pound note in my bag,' she bragged, moving away.

'Ice creams on the beach are on you then,' I said. 'Do you want to go? It's a nice day.'

Ruth hesitated momentarily then said, 'Why not? The beach will be good, won't it? Where we used to go after seeing a film, just there.'

'Perfect.' Joining up past and present and future on one strand of beach. I loved how clever she was. We grabbed a couple of jumpers and wandered down to the beach in silence, enjoying the liberty after the previous day. We made straight for the less busy part, just up from the Grand and Metropole hotels. It was a grey day and there was a slight breeze that made it not a day for ice cream. The derelict West Pier had lots of scaffolding on it now, men in hard hats examining it, making it live again. The sea looked great, brooding and choppy. There was a kiosk open for business but Ruth decided she didn't want anything and went and sat on the stones while I went and got a coffee. I didn't really want one but I needed just a moment to think about how I was going to do this. I had to be right. As I turned from the kiosk, I could see Ruth sitting on the top of the slope of stones that goes right down to the sea. She was almost hunched into herself, her knees drawn up to her chin.

Was this the right moment? *No time like the present, Simon. She said she wanted to talk. Don't bottle at the last second, go on.* I lurched forward and had to dodge a rollerblader to avoid spilling my coffee.

'Sorry.' He smiled apologetically. We made eye contact. A bit of a dish. He skated on, pirouetting to look back at me a couple of times as I crunched my way over the stones to Ruth. *Thank you God, impeccable timing, just impeccable.* Ruth didn't look round as I approached, perhaps thinking it was someone else.

'Maybe this wasn't a good idea,' I said.

'What?' she looked up sharply.

'It's *freezing*. I got a coffee instead of an ice cream,' I joked and sat down on the stones beside her. She returned to looking out to sea, pulling her jumper up over her nose. I could see only her brown eyes; she looked exactly like Hannah.

'I'm sorry I was a bit of a cow yesterday,' she said through the jumper.

'It was a high-pressure day. You were great, I thought.' I slipped my arm around her and fished for a compliment. 'Sorry I got in the way all the time.'

'You were fine.'

I was *fine*. Well, it was something. Slightly crushed, I sipped my coffee, furiously trying to think how to engineer this conversation. It wasn't a candlelit dinner, it wasn't what it should be like.

Maybe we should go back to mine, make love again like last night, then I'll ask her; that might work.

Ruth said, 'I always came to this beach to think about how to get away, how to get myself out of the rut I was in . . .'

'You've managed to do that,' I said, 'You're doing brilliantly, I think.'

'It's strange though,' Ruth was speaking very carefully now. 'Although I wouldn't give up university for anything, I sometimes miss all that routine, the easiness of how things were. The easiness between us.'

'It wasn't *that* good,' I said firmly to wrench the subject to where I wanted it. 'But I know what you mean. This is more serious.' I took the plunge. 'I've been wanting to talk to you about this.'

Ruth looked earnestly at me. *She knows where this is going,* I thought.

'Really? I've been dying to talk to you like this since we got here,' she said. 'It's why I wanted to come down. The girls seeing Brighton again was just an excuse, really.'

'But the girls are all a part of it, aren't they? They are for me.'

'They come with the package, that's for sure,' she conceded. 'It's difficult for someone walking into it. I always knew that.'

'But I've coped. I learned a lot from watching you with them.'

'No, you're great with them. I hope you still will be,' Ruth said and smiled at me. She was looking a little happier now, like a weight was being lifted off her. 'I hope you still will be.' Was that the green light to pop the question? I wasn't sure.

'Of *course* I will be,' I said, turning so that I could see her face properly. *You can do this, Simon, you can.* 'I think the last few weeks have been pretty intense, don't you? All that business with your mum. It could have been awful, but I really want something great to come from it.'

Ruth nodded her head vigorously. 'Absolutely, it was a big shock to the system. I'm so glad you can see it like this. It could have been such a negative thing for you. Well, for both of us.'

'But then, last night, the shower was just the most—'

'I know, I *know*, you don't need to tell me. I just let you push me around and I shouldn't have done. I should have *done* something, *said* someth—'

'No, Ruth,' I interrupted her, I was on track now. I put

down the coffee and shifted so that I could hold her hand. *Go, go, go.* 'It really changed things for me, changed how I saw *us*.'

'I'm glad we can talk openly, Si, because things changed for me a while back. It's great we can talk like this again, just like before.' She gripped on to my hand and smiled.

I had to ask her to marry me now. Now or never.

'It will be *better* than before, Ruth, it *has* to be. I promise. There's no way it can't be. Now I know that this is absolutely the right thing for both of us to do, and that's why – why are you laughing?'

A big idiot grin crept over my face because Ruth was suddenly smiling at me so broadly, shaking her head in wonderment. She let rip with a huge cry of joy, relief and liberation. Words bubbled out of her.

'Simon, only *you* could break up with someone like this. You are *amazing*. You make it sound like the most positive thing in the world. I've been agonising over this for days now, thinking about how I could tell you. Then last night in your bloody awful shower was so terrible, like you said, you trying so hard, me so unhappy and tired I could hardly move. I didn't know what to do . . . Simon, Simon?'

The blood had drained from my face. *Only I could break up with someone like this.* In the middle of proposing marriage to them. She must never know. Ruth must never know what I was going to say. *How To Make An Exit With Dignity: A Beginner's Guide.*

'Me? I'm fine. Yeah, yeah,' I said. Keep it light, Simon. When suddenly in huge amounts of gut-churning confusion, keep it light. 'It's just so cold, isn't it? Should we wander back?'

Ruth looked a little nonplussed. It wasn't that cold and we hadn't been out twenty minutes. 'If you like,' she said. She took my arm as we walked back up the beach. I was poleaxed.

'So when did you know things weren't quite right?' she said, looking at me. She was looking at me properly in the eye, I was now realising, for the first time this weekend.

'It crept up on me really. Imperceptible.'

'Thank God we haven't been together too long. That would have made things more difficult.'

But you changed my life, Ruth, turned it upside down.

'No, it hasn't been any time at all. Not really.'

We got on to the prom and started to walk back to the main road. I was very close to running away from Ruth as fast as I could. If she had not started laughing back there, I would have proposed in the next breath. Was I truly so stupid? How had I missed what she was thinking, how could I have misread the signals so disastrously? All my adult life, I had prided myself on how well I got on with women, how I empathised with them, how I knew what they were thinking. I couldn't say *that* any more, could I? I was such a heterosexual now: all of the shortcomings, like being thick about women and not having a girlfriend, but none of the advantages like . . . like . . . tell me what the good points were again? I was damned if I could remember. We stood at the crossing waiting for the little green man. Tardy little bastard.

I asked the only question I had left in my head to which I wanted to hear Ruth's answer.

'So when did you start having second thoughts?' My voice was like a rock, not a tremor, but I had to pretend to be looking at the traffic, waiting for it to stop in order to be able to speak at all.

Ruth said nothing at first, then said, 'That day in the park, when you told Sarah and Hannah you weren't going to become any sort of father-figure for them. At first I was disappointed because I'm not getting on with Darren, but then I realised how pathetic that was. He's their father, not you. You were completely right.'

We crossed the road. At the other side, I said, 'So if I had felt differently about kids, even wanted some of my own eventually, that wouldn't have made a difference.' *Playing it so safe, Simon, a statement not a question.*

Ruth's forehead wrinkled, 'God no, I'm never having another child *ever*, you know that . . .'

I didn't know that. *I didn't know that.*

'. . . No, my brood-mare days are over. This is my second chance, I'm not ballsing it up with another baby. I love Sarah and Hannah but I don't want any more.' She looked at me in curiosity, completely academic curiosity. 'Do you want kids then? I didn't think you did, really.'

'No, can you imagine me being a dad? Jesus.' I forced a laugh.

'I think you'd be great. Truly.' She squeezed my arm. I felt so much better immediately. 'You have to know this isn't about you, you know. It dawned on me slowly after that day in the park that I don't need any boyfriend at the moment, I don't need ties or security. I thought I did and I don't. I'm studying, I'm starting again, I'm a mum, that's it.'

'So me coming up every weekend was a bit much.' *I had got in the way.*

'A little,' she admitted. *I had bored her senseless for weeks on end.* 'But not at first, Simon. Honestly. I just want my time back. I'm sorry. I don't need a man in my life.'

'Not even a retread like me,' I tried to crack a joke but

it fell flat. Just a glimmer of what I was going through
came out.

Ruth stopped. '*Don't* say things like that about yourself.
This isn't about you becoming straight. You must know
that this is nothing to do with my dad or anything like
that.'

'I thought we were reuniting your parents somehow,' I
said airily, like it was an obviously trite thing to mention.
'Making them work in retrospect.' I was trying to provoke an answer. I needed to hear this.

'Well, that was true that night I said it,' Ruth said
uneasily as she started walking back to mine again. I kept
pace alongside her, watching her face closely as she spoke.
'But I can't live my mother's life for her, can I? And Dad's
been gone a long time now. Pete's managed to move on. I
should as well. I've got to find what my own goals are.
Use the next few years to define what the rest of my life
is.' A flush rose in her cheeks as she said this and betrayed
her white lie: not quite the truth, not the whole truth,
nothing like the truth.

Own goals, how apt. I had a net full of them, Ruth having
lined up several balls for a penalty shoot-out. My being
bisexual had brought us together, indeed she wouldn't have
touched me if I had not been gay – *bam!* back of the net.
I had been left alone with Ruth's mother and crucified by
her, then I laboriously won her round to make her *mother*
feel better – *bam!* it's another one. I had been warmed up
on the sidelines as a Darren substitute but then, *oh*, I
wasn't one after all – *bam!* it's a hat trick. Then Ruth
realised she needed more time for herself – *bam!* – and I
wasn't going to resolve her psychosis about her faggot
father after all – *bam!* Five-nil, it's all over, good night
children everywhere. My face betrayed nothing but I was

becoming angry as well as very confused and upset. If all
men are bastards and all women are no better, what's a girl
to do? I really regretted not having that wank, I needed to
have had a high-point somewhere in my day before I stuck
my head in the oven.

Ruth was still talking; fuck knew what she'd been
saying since I'd tuned her out in order to fume.

'. . . and you want to split up too, don't you? That's why
this will work and we can still see each other.'

I never wanted to see her again. I was in full retreat. I
could feel the defences going up, a familiar sensation.
The drawbridge was being raised on Lyndon Towers.

We arrived back at mine at last, thank God. As soon as
I got back in the flat, I went to my cutlery drawer and
rooted out a spare set of house keys. I gave them to Ruth.

'Take these. You're welcome to stay as long as you like.
I've . . . I've got to be on my tod for a bit and I'm not sure
when I'll be back so if I'm not back by the time you have
to leave tonight then I'll call you or you call me. Give my
love to the girls . . .'

At this point I nearly lost it. Last night, I had been
mentally preparing to become some sort of *father* to them.

'. . . and tell them I'm sorry I wasn't here to say goodbye. Post the keys through the door as you leave, in an
envelope or something. I've got to go, sorry. Bye.'

As I dived back through the door, I glimpsed Ruth
looking dumbfounded. She had no clue what was in my
head now and I had no idea what she had been thinking
for weeks. We had assumed that we knew each other
inside out, that the changes we had both gone through
to become new, improved people were the only new
things we needed to find out about each other. But best
friends don't know each other properly because they

never got to the last ten per cent, the vital ten per cent, that is only for lovers.

THIS WAS OUR BIG MISTAKE

My heart ached it was beating so fast. I thought it was going to implode or something. Somehow I got to the railway station, bought a ticket for London and raced to the end of the empty express platform, flung myself on a bench and cried and cried and cried. What had she said? *It's not you, it's what I need*, or something. And what she didn't need was clingy, sloppy-seconds me sniffing around her, trying to get a cliché life on the cheap.

Chapter 22

*'Beneath the calm surface of the waters . . . the mêlée of
the creatures in the sea'*

Vercors

I fucking hate the British. Just when I wanted someone to
come up to me and say, 'What's the matter?', no one did.
But then, no one ever does at times like that. An entire
carriage kept their heads down as we sped to London.
'There was a drug addict weeping and wailing on the
train, dear. I steered *well* clear.'

But I could see why no good Samaritan was edging
closer to check on me. Having come out in a rush, I had
no handkerchief and had to cope with ropes of snot of
biblical proportions emerging from my nose like French
knitting. I wasn't sure where the loos were on the new
express trains and I didn't want to maraud around looking
like a swamp-thing in search of a Kleenex. By the time we
got to Victoria, I was one godawful mess. I dived into the
loos at the station and cleaned up as best I could. Drying
my face, I felt marginally calmer.

I had to talk to someone. Callum was impossible to
track down on any of his numbers or just wasn't answering his phone. I thought of Toril. She knew me, she was

the one who, as it turned out, had been right all along. Maybe I *had* confused novelty for the real thing, got so caught up in what I was thinking for the first time that I mistook it for divine inspiration. She'd known what I was doing from the second she heard about Ruth. Toril, I decided, I had to find Toril. I got her machine, which had her pager number on the message. I paged her as well, saying I was coming round and I needed to see her.

A taxi discharged into Toril's terraced backwater of Shepherd's Bush a shadow of the fizzy wannabe family man who had woken up in Brighton that morning. I knocked at the door but she wasn't in. I peered in at her front window but there was no one around. Maybe she'd be back soon. Deciding to wait it out, I sat in Toril's door-way, my head in my hands, following the fortunes of some ants as they marched in and out of their nest. Obviously, in some cosmic context, what I was going through was as unimportant as the ants but, to be honest, *I didn't buy that*. The last few months were *big stuff*, up there with Saul on the road to Damascus, water turning into wine, Jon Pertwee turning into Tom Baker.

What I didn't get was that I had apparently become more *stupid*. Is it the rule that men lose five IQ points every time they just fuck a woman and get, say, one point back every time they *make love*? It would explain a lot of the Neanderthals you meet. Had my going straight meant that I understood women less? While I had been going out with Ruth, *I had never known what she was thinking*. I realised that now, far too late. It was as if there was a direct causal link: the way to a man's ignorance is through his girlfriend's vagina.

But no. Life is full of Catch-22s but they are not as easy to work out as that. If there had been a Catch-22, it had been that while she was going out with me and having second thoughts from a fairly early stage, Ruth was not about to tell *me*, her boyfriend. Obviously. She probably had told half the English department at Manchester but in the old days she would have told her Gay Best Friend. Me again. With my GBF hat off and being the cause of her ramshackle, phony love life, we couldn't really discuss it.

'Have you been here long?'

It was Toril, looking down at me in surprise, holding her doorkeys. I hadn't heard her car draw up. She was in a track-suit top and shorts, carrying a sports bag, her short blond hair wet and combed straight back from her head; she had been to the gym or something. I shook my head in reply, unable to say anything for fear of crying again. She could see I was in pieces.

'Come on in.'

I had been afraid that she might tell me to leave, after what had happened between us before. I had called her a traitor more or less, then a fag-hag, then, worst of all, a spinster. But she unlocked the door and went in. She dumped her bag at the bottom of the stairs and went through to the kitchen to put the kettle on.

I sat at her dining table. The place was as spotless as ever, not a magazine out of place, the flowers on the table fresh, not a speck of dust to spoil the view. Toril was something else, everything under control. The whole house smelled of vanilla, as usual.

Toril came back through, pulled out another chair from the table and sat down next to me so that she was facing me, our knees almost touching.

'Tell me what's happened,' she said. She must have guessed already.

Amazingly, I didn't cry as I haltingly explained to Toril what had gone on that day. She did not blink as I told her I had been trying to propose to Ruth, she did not even seem surprised about Ruth's father. Her sky-coloured eyes kept their steady grip on me. She asked me only one question.

'Why did you want to marry Ruth?'

I told her it was because I loved Ruth, I realised I wanted children and I had been positive Ruth wanted more eventually as well.

Toril closed her eyes and exhaled, her escaping breath a long sigh of frustration and pain. When she looked at me, she gave me a world-weary smile coupled with a half-laugh to negate what she had just expressed, and her face resumed its mask of complete impenetrability. Something enormous had just happened and I did not have a clue what it was because I was only a thick heterosexual now, *Doh*.

'Tell me what you are thinking,' I said.

Toril shrugged and made a gesture to get me talking again. She leaned an elbow on the table and dug the heel of her hand into her cheek. She'd gone back to being a good listener, I could tell.

'*Please* tell me what you're thinking. I can't tell any more.'

'When could you?' came the crisp reply.

Good question. It was another point of view: I had always been a twat. Maybe gay men understanding straight women well is as much of a myth as straight men being dimwits about women. It's all a matter of who the women choose to confide in and lots choose their GBFs. It's simple to understand someone when they're telling you their innermost feelings; I was great at murmuring 'I know, I *know*', but the mistake was believing that I did. If women don't tell you their deepest thoughts, that's when you need male intuition. Male intuition: it even *sounds* wrong. Very *hot* ice, a *tasty* English wine: as a phrase, it's not a winner, is it? So, perhaps it was the fact that Simon Lyndon, individual in the world, had never had the slightest instinct for truly knowing his friends and lovers. A lifetime of incomprehension pretending to be effortless superiority.

'What was that sigh for?' I repeated. 'Tell me what you are thinking.'

Toril sat up, shaking her head and pushing her hair back with her hand. 'My thoughts are my own, Simon. You can't just walk in and demand to know my *thoughts*. You can have my advice, if you want it.'

Not the same thing. I pursued her. I wanted to know. If I'd asked Ruth for honesty more, instead of trying to make sure I was being honest myself so often, I'd have been less deluded, wouldn't I? I had assumed we were having a miraculously mutual friendship. Of course, Ruth never lied to me, she just kept some thoughts back, the most important ones.

Toril was doing the same now. I'd find Callum. I always knew what he was thinking. He was upfront about sex 'n' stuff: his doorbell played the *Jaws* theme these days. I stood up as if I was going, an implied threat.

'Tell me what you're thinking. I have to know.'

Toril walked to her front door. She was kicking me out?

'You don't *want* to know. You have *never* wanted to know what I was thinking before. You always thought you knew.' She exaggerated my Estuary English with Streep/Paltrow-like accuracy. '"You thinkin' wot I'm thinkin', Towiw?" Don't start asking now.' She opened the front door, saying formally, 'I'm very sorry for what has happened to you today. I think you should leave now.'

I was as angry at that moment as I have ever been in my life. Not at Toril but at a new world I suddenly did not *get*, just when I thought I had assimilated perfectly. I shut my eyes and shouted, 'TELL ME WHAT YOU ARE THINKING!' I opened my eyes and in the back of my head realised I had been an arse. '*Please*.' I sat down defiantly. I wasn't going anywhere. Toril looked at me incredulously. My face was quivering with the effort of trying to keep under control. The past few weeks had shown me that I had a violent streak I had not known was there, when I'd been in bed with Ruth, then, most appallingly, with Truman. I did not want to hurt Toril.

'You really want to know? Right now I'm thinking that you are behaving like a teenager. That you are being uncouth and aggressive. That you have invited yourself into my house, poured our your troubles and that now you are . . . what's the word . . . *venting* all your anger at Ruth on me.'

She was right. It was a fair cop. I threw up my hands, admitting defeat, and walked to the door before I did some damage. She slammed the door shut before I got anywhere near it.

'Where are you going?' she said. 'I'm talking now. It's what you want, isn't it? You asked for it, you're going to get it *all*. I'll never have another chance like this . . .'

Chance?

'You were talking about wanting children. I sighed like that because that's all I've ever wanted as well . . .'

I nodded. I *knew* all this. Toril looked at me like I was the stupidest man in the world.

'You *still* don't get it, do you?' She crossed to a chest of drawers and retrieved a large bundle of letters. 'This is what I've been doing since I last saw you. I've been writing these.'

She threw the letters on the table. All of them were addressed to me, all had stamps but none had been sent. I had heard nothing from Toril in all this time but she had been trying to find a way to tell me something enormous. To tell me what she was thinking.

The letters had fanned out across the table. Pick a card, any card. Toril did not stop me as I picked up an envelope. It was one of maybe thirty or forty. I opened the envelope and just as I was about to read the letter, Toril said, 'They all say the same thing, Simon. I've always wanted *you*. To be with you. To have a baby with you.'

I froze. I didn't know *that*. I had ended up having the baby conversation today after all but with the wrong woman. Perhaps Toril was the right woman, since Ruth had not exactly come up trumps. But I couldn't talk to Toril about this, not now, not after today. As always, Toril was correct. I didn't want to know what she was thinking, after all. She kept on telling me anyway.

'I've felt like this for ten years.' Her face clouded over after she said this. 'I have imagined saying that to you so many times but I never thought it would feel so *bland*. How disappointing.'

It was disappointing and bland because I received the news with deafening and numbed sweet FA. My deer-in-the-headlights impersonation was coming on a treat. Toril looked at me, one tear rolling down her cheek. She didn't know it was there. She said, 'And now I don't know what you are thinking. I've a feeling I don't want to know.'

She was right again. *Tell me this in six months, Toril, not today. I'm so sorry I asked.* I was bringing everything down around me. I reduced to dust every relationship I had ever had – in this case, before it had even started. It was amazing how fast Ruth was disappearing from my mind as I spoke to Toril. I can be startlingly superficial at times. There was a long silence. The tear hung from Toril's jaw, caught the light, then dropped to the carpet.

My eye followed it, the first words on the opened letter in my hand barely registering, 'My Simon, I'm so useless I know I'll never post this . . .' All of Toril's pent-up emotions had poured into these impotent pieces of paper. I was her Patrick. The pages of the letter fluttered to the floor and almost involuntarily I made a move for the door again.

'PLEASE DON'T LEAVE!' Toril only said it at normal volume, I think, but it sounded deafening as she broke the silence. 'I have to tell you now.' I dared to look at her. She wasn't crying any more. We were both beyond that. 'For ten years, I thought you knew, that it was assumed. But there was nothing to be done because of who you were. I wanted you, you wanted Callum, then Patrick, they wanted other people. That was the rule, wasn't it? Not that you ever knew. I tried looking for other men – I even went out with Callum to make you jealous. But I only ever wanted you. God knows why, looking at you now. But I still do.' She shrugged. 'Doesn't matter now, does it?' She continued cataloguing my lack of tact. 'Then you invited me down to tell me so . . . *triumphantly* that you were having an affair with a woman. And all I could think to say was "Why not me?"' She took a deep breath. 'So, why not me, Simon?'

I descended into one of those male, inexplicably silent moments. On the outside, the man is imperturbable but

inside he is fighting for his life. His back is against the wall
and the wall is moving towards the opposite wall. He's
potted meat in two minutes unless he can find a way out. I
was going through a million possible answers as to why I
had fallen in love with Ruth and not Toril, all of which Toril
could not hear. I had not even considered Toril, Toril was
not primarily a *woman* for me: she was a friend, a great
mind, a person I knew and loved. She had always been the
one close friend from way back I *didn't* have to have a
huge crush on, and I'd always had that stupid notion of
her getting back with Callum. I hadn't known Ruth half so
long, I saw her every day for years, she had always been a
woman friend, she had the kids, she was more *instinctive*,
that's not to say I didn't think she was *clever*, you see?
These things can't be said in any form that doesn't sound
crass and chauvinist. You can't verbalise the whys and
wherefores of what makes your dick twitch. Either it does
or it doesn't. I couldn't say anything she might want to
hear. I had to say something just to get out of the house.

'I'm sorry. I can't cope with that today.'

'You asked.'

Do you see? I had *agonised* to come up with 'I can't
cope with that today.' There had been no way out that let
me let her down gently, that let her feel better about herself. The only way was to make like a prick and shaft
myself. Which is a good trick if you can do it.

'I'm sorry I asked,' I said. 'Come here.'

'You come here.'

So I went to her. We held each other like babes in the
wood, lost in a big bad world. To all intents, we were still
the twenty-year-olds who had first met each other. We
had put ourselves on hold throughout our twenties; neither of us had had a lengthy relationship, we were still

looking for love. There had been some changes. We could get more money out of the cashpoint each day, we ate nicer food, our clothes came from better stores. Well, Toril's did. But the ten years had petrified us.

Inevitably, the hug became an embrace and there was a moment for something more. We had our heads on the other's shoulder, then as our heads came up, our cheeks brushed, one against the other and I could see her eyes, feel her breath. Toril angled her face towards mine and we kissed. Kissing for the first time is so much more terrifying when you're sober and it means something. Or, rather, it has to mean something.

It wasn't right. I had lost one of my best friends today, I couldn't start losing another. I was hopeless at Love, I had been target practice for that plump little fucker Cupid for too long. I'd just ruin everything. Me and Toril? It might work, but not today. I wasn't seeing anything clearly. Toril said she loved me but I could not be certain *now* that it was right. This was over-egging the pudding. Today was too rich. But, kissing Toril, it certainly *seemed* right. We fit together beautifully, Toril being that little bit taller than Ruth. I was rebounding from one old friend to another to another: I'd only just salvaged my relationship with Patrick, I couldn't envisage ever seeing Ruth again and . . .

Oh, Jesus, she's taking off her top, oh, thank God, she's not naked, she's got one of those Sloggi bra things . . .

I had enough adrenaline to light up the Empire State, I hadn't come last night in the shower, I hadn't jerked off this morning: my nuts thought it was Christmas. My flesh was ready and willing but my spirit knew it was wrong, wrong, wrong. Not today, I wasn't on for a first sighting of Toril's tits today; I should be tutting over the *Sunday Times* with a cup of tea. Hadn't she put the kettle on? It should have boiled by now.

I pushed her away, starting to say I was sorry, I couldn't do this now, it was too soon, it wasn't her fault, it was me, blah, blah, blah. Much the same steaming rubbish Ruth had dished up for me. Dumper and dumpee in one day; that put me at zero, didn't it? I wasn't rough at all but the push was unexpected. Toril stumbled backwards, lost her balance and landed hard on her backside. She wasn't hurt but she was surprised, a little winded at most.

In any other circumstance, it would have been funny. The old friends, Toril and Simon, would have laughed. But, in this situation, where we needed to be so careful with each other, where Toril had put so much of her much-prized dignity on the line already, it was *awful*.

Immediately, I darted forward to help her up. She could not bear to look at me. Toril brushed me aside and picked up one of the pages of the letter I had dropped. She looked at it, scrunched it into a ball and sat with her head in her hands. She did not get up. There was no point. In a voice I recognised, because it was exactly how I was feeling, she said, 'Just get out. *Out*, Simon.'

Chapter 23

'What I need is a prophylactic . . .
That thinly veneers the distress'
Brighton graffito

'OK,' said Patrick. 'We are going to cheer you up tonight, you unhappy, forsaken, strange *heterosexual* . . .'

'I feel better already,' I replied with a rictus of a smile. I'd seen him psycho-wank. Who was *he* calling strange?

Callum chipped in, 'A lads' night out will do you a power of good.'

'With just you two?' I asked, peering at them from under hooded eyes. I didn't want anyone else along.

I was depressed. I'd been like the Ghost of Orgasms Past all week and had eaten a packet of Kipling Fondant Fancies *every day*. A *bad* sign. Self-pity can be a very satisfying pastime. Nothing quite like it – moping around your flat still in yesterday's underwear and playing sad CDs to try to make yourself sob a little. Then you begin to realise that you're feeling better and the bastard/bitch (delete as applicable) wasn't worth it anyway. I wasn't quite there yet. I was still missing Ruth too much, or rather, missing being with her. I had got used to having someone in that empty space next to me. My girlfriend had prised herself away from me just when I'd wanted us to be Siamese. Joined at the neurosis for eternity. Ruth had left a couple of messages on my answer phone but I hadn't replied. I couldn't face talking to her and pretending that everything was fine between us.

And then there was Toril. We hadn't spoken since Sunday. I did not know what to think about all that. It was plain I had won 'Most Dense Homosexual' for years running and no one had told me. I'd wrecked her life, that much was obvious, but as to how I thought about her, I hadn't a clue. The other afternoon I had definitely *wanted* her. I had gone round looking for a comforting hug and had ended up with a whole lot more. My bodily travel agent had spoken to me again and had recommended Scandinavia: lovely this time of year, fjords can be fun, glaciers would melt at my touch. Did that mean I could *love* her? Pass.

When Callum had rung me up to ask me to go up to town for a Saturday night piss-up, I had not really been on for it at first, being Queen Victoria after the death of Prince Albert and still in official mourning. But maybe a laddy night out was just what the doctor might order if alcohol poisoning was good for you. I was sure a boys' night out would have done Vicky a power of good as well. So here I was, and Pat and Cal were sights for sore eyes. They were obviously enjoying being neighbours; they were very *bonded*, I noted.

'Just us,' I insisted again.

'Nobody else, just us.' Patrick ruffled my hair sympathetically. 'You are so *miz* at the mo'.' He was resorting to baby-talk now. I must be in such a bad way. I attempted to rally, trying not to be too much of a miserable sod.

'What shall we do then? Cheer me up, boys.' They looked at each other in satisfaction.

'A few beers obviously,' Callum said tweedledumly.

'Then back here to watch some videos and perhaps take some drugs,' chimed in Patrick tweedledeely.

'Ooo, I'm not sure I'd like that,' I moaned, sounding like my grandmother. 'I've never done any drugs, you know me.'

'Well, we think, don't we, Callum . . .' Patrick said with a slide of his eyes at his colleague.

'We do, Pat,' nodded Callum.

'. . . that you should chill out, look up at the sky, find out that there's a big world out there to make you happy with its many pleasures. Drugs might be the key to this.'

I was not convinced, asking doubtfully, 'Which drugs?'

'Not sure, haven't bought them yet. I'm waitin' fo' my man,' drawled Patrick. 'I *think* I can get some acid.'

Hallucinogenics. What a good idea for a man in the throes of depression. I'd refuse later. Beer, I could cope with that. I bounced to my feet, clapping my hands together.

'Pub!' I declared.

'He *is* better already. Attaboy! Or attagirl, depending on mood. Let's go,' said Patrick.

The pub was their local, a semi-trendy place on Church Street, packed to the rafters with a young crowd divided roughly down the middle between those who wanted to go to or had been to India and those who wanted to stay in Blighty and make pots of cash. The pub was OK, the music was a bit loud but not too much, I was feeling a bit better: this was a good idea.

'So what do you fancy?' asked Callum, staring with intent at Patrick and me. I looked around at all the happy people. They couldn't all be happy, surely?

'I don't fancy anyone really. Oh, he's quite nice,' I

mused, nodding towards a young City-type near the fag machine. 'The girl he's talking to is kind of cute as well. That's about it.'

Callum took out his wallet. 'To *drink*, Simon, to *drink*.'

'Oh. Guinness. Thanks.'

'You are *obsessed*. You're worse than me,' Callum said as a parting shot before he pushed his way to the bar. Callum thought *I* was obsessed with sex – him, the man who did not so much put notches in his headboard as whittle it to a toothpick. Patrick was saying something.

'. . . sking after you the other day.'

'What? Say again, it's noisy.'

'Toril was asking after you the other day.'

I'd have to talk to her soon. What was I going to say? I didn't shag you, sorry.

'How is she?' I asked faintly.

'Yeah, fine. Job's going well. She mainly spoke to Callum, was in his flat for about an hour. She seemed a bit upset about something. You should call her.'

'Great. I will,' I said with a croak and a sniff.

'Oh, cheer up, you tosser,' said Patrick, trying to ignore me, looking around at the sea of pulchritude around him.

'Good psychology, Pat. Is that what this "make Simon happy" night is going to be like? Standing in a smoky room with pissed hippies and capitalists while my friends shout "Cheer up, you tosser" at me? I'm really glad I came up to see you.'

'Get *you*. Just don't be miserable,' Patrick overrode me, obviously going for a tough-love approach. 'Snapping out of it, even if it's just for an evening, might make all the difference. That's all I'm saying. Don't bite my head off.'

'Sorry.'

'That's all right.'

'Love you lots,' I said.

'Love you too.'

'Mind out, man with pints,' said Callum, returning from the bar and handing us our drinks. 'What are we talking about?'

'If Pat is in love or not,' I decided.

'Not me, I'd rather stick needles in my bollocks,' Pat declared firmly. Unnecessarily graphic, I thought.

'Why?' I asked.

Patrick looked discomfited. 'There was this one girl in Hong Kong.' he said reluctantly.

'Just the one?' Callum said with a laddy wa-hay.

'Um, *yeah*, actually,' Patrick admitted. Callum's eyebrows shot up and he backtracked, obviously shocked by Pat's meagre turnover of women. Patrick continued, 'Anyhoo, this girl was fabulous, legs all the way up to her pelvis, the works . . .'

'Limbs and *everything*?' I said in wonderment.

'Hands, feet, knees, ankles, the lot.'

'Pubic hair?' asked Callum, in search of detail, I could tell.

'Bushy as a bush-baby, got in the way a bit. I even told her that I'd never been with a girl with such a lot of minge.'

'I've had a couple like that,' agreed Callum.

'Well, eventually she dumped me,' exclaimed Patrick. 'Said I was uncouth and inconsiderate.'

'No!' I said in disbelief.

'Mmm, she did. *Me*.' Patrick nodded slowly, evidently still not believing it himself and harbouring fond memories for this multi-limbed, if overly hairy miracle. 'Anyway, the moral of this story, Simon, is that even a Romeo like me can take losing his Juliet. And so can you.'

He looked to Callum for support but Callum

'Oh, cheer up, you tosser,' I said charitably.

Callum looked at me in annoyance. 'Yeah, yeah, I
just thinking about Bronwen.'

'Bronwen?' I racked my brains. 'Which one was
Bronwen?'

'Did you never meet her? Your loss, I'm telling you,'
exclaimed Callum. 'She was amazing.'

'Oh, she was *ages* ago. The Welsh one,' said Patrick,
nodding at the memory.

'No, the Swahili one. She was called *Bronwen*, you dick,
of course she was Welsh,' Callum said cuttingly, suddenly
pious as he revered Bronwen's memory. I couldn't remember her at all.

'How long were you with her?' I asked.

'The usual. Couple of nights. I remember waking up
after the second night, thinking "I'm in love", but she
woke up and said, "I'm emigrating to New Zealand."'

I burst out laughing. Callum looked hurt and Patrick
looked at me reproachfully, knocked back his pint and
patted Callum's shoulder, saying comfortingly, 'Wow, that's
really harsh, Cal, I'm sorry.'

Callum and Patrick ruefully smiled at each other,
having a men-can-have-feelings-too moment. They
stopped after about 1.7 seconds and sighed again. It
seemed all of us were victims of feminine good taste.

'So this is how you cheer me up?' I said, grinning at
their unhappiness. 'By getting suicidal?'

'Well, it's worked then, hasn't it? You're in a better
mood than we are now. It's all relative,' Callum puttered,
edging out of the way for a woman in a dress like a second
skin. We all stared at her retreating form, heading for the
ladies'.

'Nice arse,' Callum said to Patrick (cutting me out of the loop, I noted).

'No cellulite,' Patrick replied approvingly, then took a sudden deep breath and regarded me with the eyes of a weighty intellectual about to make a point of great importance. 'Pint of Tetley's,' he said and handed me his glass.

'Same for you?' I asked Callum.

'I'll have a Guinness with you actually,' Callum said intensely. 'It better suits my dark mood.'

'You're a man in touch with his emotions,' I complimented him, taking his glass. 'His feminine side.'

'I know, it's how I understand women.' Callum said.

As I moved to the bar, I heard Patrick say, 'You understand women? They *emigrate* to get away from you.'

'You can't even get laid, so don't start on me,' retorted Callum. They both roared with laughter. I looked back at them. My boys were either unparalleled masters of the piss-take or dorks. There was no in-between. I didn't fancy them any more, not really. We were brothers now. They saw me looking at them. 'Get the fucking drinks in,' Callum mouthed at me.

After an age at the bar, I brought the drinks back. I couldn't see Patrick and Callum at first for young hippy professionals, because they had grabbed a corner table that had come free. They were saying something in a foreign language about the Premier Division that sent me into a catatonic state. I started thinking about Ruth and Toril, how I could have been so wrong about them. I felt Callum kick Patrick under the table.

'Oh God, that's . . . *Josephine*,' said Patrick, pointing at a girl going through into the other bar. 'I went to school with her.' And he disappeared, taking his drink with him.

Callum rolled his eyes slightly at Patrick's excuse to leave. He had sent Patrick off and I knew why.

I turned to Callum and whispered fiercely, 'It wasn't my fault, you know.'

'What?' He looked taken aback at my getting straight to the point.

'The fucking fiasco with Toril. I just froze, Cal. I've never viewed Toril like that. She's *Toril*, you know . . . not . . .' The girl in the skin-tight frock walked back from the loo. I nodded in her direction. '. . . *totty*.'

'I've never heard you use that word before.' Callum looked appalled, shaking his head. 'Did you *really* not know about Toril?'

'But I'm even thicker than you and Pat when it comes to women.' Callum looked momentarily offended. I ploughed on. 'At least you can *tell* when a woman is attracted to you. I can spot a man coming on to me through a brick wall but I've slept with two women in a decade. I don't know about women. Not like that.'

'Toril's loved you for years, Simon.'

'But that was like me loving Pat all that time. I was gay, it was academic that Toril felt like that. I hadn't noticed and, anyway, it didn't count.'

'But then it did.'

'Yeah, I didn't know, I swear it.'

'So, there couldn't be anything there?'

'With me and Toril? God knows, *maybe*. Yeah. In time, Ruth dumped me last week, you know? I think I've fucked that all up with Toril anyway.' Callum shrugged at me and didn't say anything. I said, 'You saw her, didn't you?'

'She came round. Not the happiest woman in the world.' Callum got quite serious. 'She cried and stuff.'

'*Toril* cried in front of *you*?' I said aghast.

Callum nodded. 'She was a bit of a wreck actually, looked dreadful. Shit, Patrick's back, she didn't want him to know anything.'

No secrets in this family either. Patrick was weaving his way back with another round.

'Good to have the next one handy,' he said. *What did he mean? Was he talking about Toril or the pint of Guinness? My paranoia knew no bounds.*

'How was Josephine?' I asked drily, trying to get back into sociable mode again.

Patrick gave an elaborate shrug. 'I went through to the saloon and realised she didn't exist. But I found my main man with the gear.' He patted his coat pocket and went all London for a brief second. 'No probs. Sorted.' He looked at my and Callum's serious faces. 'Have you had your grown-up talk?'

'Yeah, we have,' said Cal and settled back in his seat, letting the conversation roll over him, thinking.

Patrick worked overtime to keep me buoyed up. We stayed for about three more pints each, by which time I was like the proverbial lord, newt and rat's arse. At closing time we hit the cold night air with an audible flinch and set off back to Callum and Patrick's building.

'I vote we watch the vid in Callum's. Mine's too tidy,' said Patrick.

'Vid? I'd forgotten you guys had a vid. What is it?' I asked. A film now would be perfect. Maybe a thriller or even a Meryl Streep-y weepie would be fine.

'*Lesbian Space-vixens Are Go!*' Patrick stated with gusto. 'You'll love it.'

'Porn?' I asked in surprise. 'You've got a *porn* video? Good-oh. Do you boys do this a lot?'

'Patrick loads more than me,' Callum remarked airily. 'More need, you see. Don't hit me.'

'You cheeky bugger,' Patrick said, trying to cuff Callum round the head as he dodged away and ran across the road to the corner of their street. 'It's just that I haven't quite hit my stride back here. I'm just settling in again.'

'It's been months, you monk!' shouted Callum. We caught up with him and Callum threw his arm around Patrick. 'You've probably seen *Lesbian Space-vixens Are Go!* before, haven't you, choochie-face? *Loads* of times, just you, Rosie Palmer and her five little helpers.'

'No, but the cover's always looked good in the shop,' Patrick admitted, pretending to be sheepish.

'So you guys have watched a lot of porno without me, haven't you?' I said, sensing I was being inducted into a charmed circle this evening.

'Hardly at all,' Callum said, scratching his nose shiftily.

Ruth and I used to watch Kate Hepburn and Carole Lombard films together. Now I was watching fake rug-munching porn for straight boys. See how the mighty are fallen. Oh, what the hell, it'd be a laugh.

Back at Callum's, I flopped on his mystery-stained sofa, throwing an empty pizza box on the floor. What a tip. Then I remembered my own flat.

Patrick schmoozed up behind me. 'Can I press something disappointingly warm into your hand, sir?' he murmured solicitously.

'Matron.'

Patrick gave me a bottle of beer. 'I forgot to put them in the fridge. Sorry,' he said and plonked on the sofa next to me as Callum put on the video. As the titles flickered, Callum came and sat on my other side. There wasn't really enough room but it didn't matter. I was feeling quite happy now, between my chaps. Nothing erotic, just happy to be with friends rather than being Sad & Solitary of Sussex on a Saturday night.

'A rose between two thorns,' I said, sipping on my beer. This was fun.

'A *lily* more like,' scoffed Callum. *Did that have an edge in it or not? Did he think I should have slept with Toril last week? Surely not.*

The film was crap. *Quelle surprise.* A group of lubricious ladies had been stranded in space for a long time without any men or communication with the rest of the universe. Judging by their penchant for backcombing, shoulder pads and blue eye-shadow, it had indeed been a while. So, anyway, they were all lesbian now. I glumly watched the taut, effective drama unfold. Such a distinctive running-bass soundtrack; I wondered if I could get the CD.

'That one's got a horrible bum,' said Callum. 'I wouldn't go near her.'

'But the one with the strap-on's nice,' Patrick answered earnestly. 'Great tits.'

'What do you think, Simon? Now that you're straight?' They both snickered into their beers.

'They're all horrible,' I said. 'Is this really a turn-on?'

'*Oh* yeah,' said Patrick, then bellowed, 'Space-vixens are go!'

I was feeling quite unhappy now, between my boys. This was no fun at all. Pat reached round my head and tapped Callum on the shoulder.

'I got some E's in the end. Keanu didn't have any acid. Want one?' he said to Callum, then looked at my expression. 'What are you staring at?'

'Your dealer's called *Keanu*?' I asked.

'It's a codename,' said Pat, looking a little caught out.

'Tell Simon *your* codename,' Callum interrupted smoothly. Patrick shook his head uncomfortably. 'Go on, you know you want to.' Patrick shook his head again. 'It's Che Guevara, isn't it, Patrick?'

'. . . Yes, it's Che Guevara,' he muttered.

'Tell Simon why,' urged Callum as I just kept my face under control.

'Keanu thinks I look like Antonio Banderas.' The burden of beauty was indeed heavy. Patrick had to speak up to be heard over my deeply satisfied laughter. He tried to get the conversation back on track. 'So, do you want an E or not?'

'And miss a second of this masterpiece, Zorro?' I nodded at the screen, where a space-vixen was rubbing space-soap into the space between her space-buttocks. 'No sirree Bob.'

Patrick got up and reached into his coat pocket. 'There you go, you wanker,' he said, passing a small white pill to Callum. 'What'd you have to tell him that for?' They washed their passports to paradise down and sat there in a state of anticipation, saying things like 'Oh, I can feel something,' at regular intervals.

Back at the film, men, who were *pirates*, had come on board the ship, the first men the space-vixens had ever seen, so of course some of the space-vixens were instantly *cured* of their perversion and became radiant with new satisfaction. Just like that.

You just wait, darlings, it's all downhill from here, I thought glumly. It's not as good as it looks.

Some of the male space-pirates were ordering two of the space-vixens to make love for their entertainment. The space-vixens went to it with a will, peeling off their tin foil catsuits, forgetting any element of narrative. Their mouths went out of sync with the soundtrack. At one point, with her mouth full of a nipple of improbable length, a vixen said without moving her lips, 'Oooh, yeah, I love your tits so much.'

'All *right*,' enthused Patrick. 'Is your E kicking in yet? Cal?'

'Not really.'

'Have you two got hard-ons from this piece of crap?' I demanded, pointing at the TV.

'Not me, I'm a bit pissed,' Callum said, disconsolately prodding at the empty folds of his trousers. He wasn't splitting any seams, it had to be said.

'Patrick?'

'Getting there, getting there. Look at her. Oh, oh, oh, 69-a-go-go.'

I regarded Patrick. He could be such a *lad*. He caught my eye.

'What are you looking at?'

'I was in love with you for *six years*.'

'You crazy, beautiful bitch.' Patrick belched and blew me a kiss. Then he smiled and leaned his head on my shoulder.

'What about *you*, Si. The vixens getting to you?' asked Callum, sitting up with difficulty and peering into my lap. Patrick had a stare as well.

'Don't look at my cock, boys.' All those years when they should have done . . . 'Too late for all that. Anyway, nothing's going on down there.'

'Not a sausage,' snorted Patrick, who toasted himself in the air in tribute to his wit and swigged from his bottle. He refocused on the TV and pointed at the screen. 'Stella's got a better fanny than Velocita. More personality.'

'These characters have names? When did we find that out?'

'You're not paying attention, are you, Simon? The blond one's Stella, the redhead is Velocita. I love 69s, don't you, Cal?'

What about me? Why don't you include me on that? I like 69s too, dammit.

'I could do it all day, old son. And do you know, I often have,' said Callum pretending to get a crick out of his jaw.

But as I watched the video, my dick the size of a wonton, I gradually felt the walls begin to spin and the room go darker. Only the screen remained, exploding with colour, a close-up of a tongue with a girl attached giving improbable amounts of pleasure to a clitoris with a girl attached. The sofa was strangely intangible beneath my bum. I swam around in the dark, getting nearer to the kaleidoscopic screen, then pulling away from it, and the girls metamorphosed. It wasn't Stella and Velocita any more, it was Toril and Ruth, dressed as space-vixens, climbing out of the telly and resuming the soixante-neuf in front of the sofa. 'Mind the empty pizza box, I don't think you two have met properly, do you need an introduction?' I wanted to say, but no words came out. They obviously didn't need an introduction. Slowly, luxuriantly, they stretched their legs wide to receive the other's mouth, tongues getting nearer and nearer. Space-vixen Ruth and Space-vixen Toril were about to provoke a mutual and deep sense of gratitude when they both did a double-take on the other's crotch. Suddenly the rinky-dink music stopped. They both craned their heads round to talk to each other. 'Where is it?' Ruth whispered to Toril. 'Yours has gone as well,' Toril said in a strangely disembodied I'm-a-bad-actress voice. 'It's just not there, baby. Our Love-Berries have disappeared. They are nowhere to be found. Oh God. What shall we do?' They resumed their search, looking frantically in cupboards and drawers for their missing appendages, the air filled with papers and clothes. Then a slow, mocking male laugh filled the room. Callum and Patrick, both dressed as thirties gangsters, were slyly looking at Toril and Ruth from under the brims of their hats. They reached inside their immaculate double-breasted suits and each produced a small pink object, which they rolled between their forefinger and thumb. In a Bogart voice, Callum said, 'Of all the Love-Berries in all the world, we just had to have yours.' They shot their cuffs like gangsters always do and threw the stolen property up and down like a dime. As the women ran at them, Callum and Patrick flipped the little organs high into the air, caught them in their mouths like peanuts and swallowed them. Toril and Ruth disappeared into thin air with screams of frustration. Then Callum slowly turned to me. 'And as for you, little lady . . .' Patrick reached into his breast pocket with a wolfish smile. With horror, I put my hands down my trousers. There was nothing down there, nothing at all. Patrick took something very familiar out of his pocket and waggled it at me. I shrieked in recognition and jumped at them, shouting, 'YOU CAN'T EAT MY CLITORIS, I ONLY JUST FOUND IT! AND WHERE'S MY COCK GONE?'

Chapter 24

'You and God both know I love you'
Janet Flanner

I woke up. I was still in Callum's flat, the TV was off and the main light was on, really bright. Patrick and Callum were standing over me looking concerned and amused all at the same time.

'AAARGH!' I screamed at their looming faces.

'We won't eat your clitoris, Simon. We promise,' Patrick said gently.

'Unless you really want us to,' Callum added with a straight face.

'And, to the best of our knowledge, we don't have your cock,' finished Patrick.

I stuffed a hand down my trousers. One of *my* hands, I add for complete clarity. I still had a penis. Thank God for small mercies.

'You spiked my drink with acid, didn't you,' I accused Pat. Callum looked pissed off. Pat looked sheepish and said, 'Nooo, I didn't, actually. I was sold some fake stuff.'

'He paid forty quid for some Nurofen,' Callum said disparagingly. 'Che Guevara or *what*.'

They were telling the truth. Patrick and Callum were shockingly headache-free. Unlike me. I needed drugs.

'Have you got any more? I begged. 'Two. Give me two.'

'So your dream about us eating your clitoris,' Callum pointed out, as I swallowed the painkillers, 'was completely unaided by drugs of any kind apart from alcohol. It was just you and your *mind*. What a worry.'

Then Patrick and Callum bounded around the room saying 'Don't eat my clitoris, I only just found it' and 'You've got my cock, you've got my cock' over and over again, throwing cushions at each other.

'I have something to say. Listen to me.' The mayhem continued. 'I said, listen to me.'

Panting heavily, Callum and Patrick stopped running about the room. Patrick pointed at me and said in a movie-trailer voice, 'Simon, the man with the edible clitoris we must protect, has something to say. Simon, take it away.'

'Callum, I don't fancy you. I love you but I don't fancy you.'

Callum pretended he was wounded and fell on the sofa, writhing.

'Patrick, same goes for you.'

Pat wiped a tear from his eye.

'In fact, I don't fancy *anyone*. I will never have sex again with man, woman or beast. I will have nothing more to do with libido and lubrication . . .'

'Fucking and fiction,' Patrick alliterated helpfully.

'I am an amoeba and proud,' I declared. 'I thank you.'

'Don't say that, Si. Not over a *girl*. You'll meet some . . .' Callum dithered, '. . . *one* really nice and it'll be great.'

'No, it's too confusing. I'm thirty-*one* next week, that's nearer to forty than twenty.'

'He's not far wrong,' said Patrick.

'But closer to twenty-five than forty,' clarified Callum. 'Never forget that.'

'. . . and I *retire* from the sexual fray,' I declared primly. 'I reproduce by fission at most.'

And with that I left, ignoring Callum's protests that I should stay, and high-tailed it for Victoria in a minicab, just catching the two-in-the-morning train. I had to stand the first part of the way and had a good view of all my fellow nocturnalists. I usually find someone beautiful to stare at.

And I didn't fancy *anybody*. What I had said at Callum's was true. Cameron Diaz and her old pal Matt Dillon could have asked me in for group sex with their friends Nicole and Tom and I would have said no, put it all *away*, the four of you, who do you think I am?

It was exhilarating to discover this, because it made my being single a positive thing. I wasn't a flummoxed homosexual, I wasn't a spurned heterosexual; I wasn't anything but Simon. And Simon didn't have to walk around with all his antennae out searching for his ideal person *any more*. Celibacy, how *exciting*. What a blessed relief. For a fleeting moment or two as we pulled out of Gatwick, I considered religious faith as a replacement for sexual love in my life but twigged as we drew into Hayward's Heath that it performs no such function in most Catholic priests' lives, so why should it in mine? And I'd have to be Catholic: all that *theatre*, bells and smells. I soon started worrying more about whether there would be a cab at Brighton Station to take me home. I couldn't be bothered to walk.

The train drew into Brighton. My oh-so-unattractive fellow passengers streamed out of the station into the darkness of the early morning. I considered joining them as they walked down the hill to the sea. As I hesitated, I saw the lights of a solitary boat far out in the deep. I'd get a cab, I decided, and walked over to the deserted rank. Prepared for a long wait, I rested my forehead against the cool metal of a lamppost by the rank. At that moment, a cab rolled into the station. Definite and certain proof of the existence of God, I decided.

It was one of the new London cabs, the TX1 bubble ones. I love them. I climbed in the back, congratulating myself on my good luck, and told the cab driver my address. He wasn't one of the regulars I'd got to know over countless trips between my flat and the station, so I didn't make conversation. In the rearview mirror, all I could see of the driver were his incredibly bright blue eyes. Really fabulous eyes, actually. I couldn't stop looking at them and the driver caught my eye.

'You had a good night, mate?' His voice was coming through the cab's intercom system, tinny and disembodied, but right next to my ear.

'Huh? Sorry, you made me jump. *Yeah*, actually. A *wonderful* night – I've decided something pretty enormous.'

'Really? Do you mind me asking what? It's been a bit of a quiet night, I could do with a story.'

His voice was honey-coloured somehow. There was just a trace of an accent but I couldn't place it. He seemed like a nice chap so I thought I'd tell him what I'd decided to do. Correction: decided *not* to do.

'I'm going to be celibate – that's the decision. No more angst, no more heartache. Just contentment, I hope.'

'Celibacy? You don't want to go in for that, it's a real mistake.'

I didn't want to hear this.

'Really? Expert on the subject, are you?' I said, nettled by his certainty.

'Because . . . how can I put it so you'll understand what I'm saying . . .'

'Try me,' I said sourly. I thought I might stand a chance of getting cabbie wisdom.

'Well, I've always found that we only become content and happy to *additions* to our lives, be it a lover, a vocation, a purpose. If all you're going to do is *subtract* sexual love from your life, subtract searching for a special person, then that's just a hole in your life. You'll end up trying to ignore it and hoping it goes away. What's your name, sir, if you don't mind me asking?'

'Simon.'

'Simon. I had a friend called Simon once, but for some reason we all called him Peter. Fuck knows why.' He laughed, a full-throated guffaw that made me want to hear it again. 'Do you want me to go via the front or through to the old Debenhams?'

'What? Oh, whatever will take longer.' I wanted to hear what he had to say.

'OK, Simon, you're the boss.'

Well, why does it never feel like that?

There was a silence. It felt like the driver was waiting for me to speak.

'So what's your advice then?' I asked Blue Eyes in the front.

We were driving along the front as I asked this. We came to a halt by the kerb and we both looked out into the darkness of the Channel. That one boat was still out there, its lights blinking. The driver turned his head away from the sea and spoke, not twisting round to look at me directly but looking at me in the mirror.

'My advice is – keep going. Don't get bitter, don't get jaded over one bad experience. I'm sorry, Simon, I'm presuming you've had a bad time recently.'

'You're right.'

'Don't close yourself off even over *lots* of bad experiences. That's the key.'

'Hope springs eternal,' I scoffed. A fat lot of good my sage in the front seat had turned out to be. I was about to tell him to take me home when I realised he was fuming. The blue eyes were like lasers now.

'That's just the kind of ironic, cynical shit I mean,' he snapped. 'It's too *easy*. The difficult thing is to stay hopeful. Your problem, Simon – you don't mind me talking to you like this, do you?'

'No, carry on, carry on.' *Slap me, hit me, beat me – why should you be any different?*

'Your problem is that you are embarrassed by how much you love people. You can love anyone, can't you?'

What did he mean? Did I have 'bisexual' written on my forehead in backwards ambulance writing?

'Um . . . yes I can. I love lots of people.' Tears sprang to my eyes and I looked at the single boat, far out to sea, trying to get myself together. The driver turned his eyes towards the boat as well.

I said, 'Sometimes you meet someone and you think they're the one, they're the one for ever. So you try to give them everything, give them what you *think* they want but they give you nothing back. Nothing at all. They let you down . . .'

'They don't. It means that you are not the one for them, that's all. Most times the net comes back on board empty, like that fishing-boat out there. He won't have caught anything tonight. He'll go back to Newhaven with sod all. But just when he is most tired, just when *you* are most vulnerable, honest and open, you will throw out your net and find that the net returns full. Fuller than you could ever have hoped for.'

I want that so much. I want a new haven, a new home. But it won't be with Patrick. Or Ruth. And after last week, it won't be with Toril. I loused that up good and proper.

'I'll get out here, look at your boat for a while.'

'Five pounds sixty, Simon, I'm afraid.'

'Cheap at the price, mate.'

I thought I saw his eyes crinkle in amusement. I passed a tenner through to him.

'Keep the change,' I said and added as sincerely as I could, 'Thank you.'

'Mind how you go, Simon.'

As I got out, I tried to get a better look at the driver's face but he shot off as soon as I slammed the door. The cab raced past the West Pier into Hove and disappeared from view. Thoughts of Toril crept into my brain and took up residence. I looked at the sky, just like Patrick had wanted me to, wanting to see a shooting star, but there wasn't one. I would have liked a shooting star.

The sleep of the innocent was mine that night, and I woke up next day with more energy than I would have thought possible after the combined emotional and alcoholic batterings I had taken lately. What had my divinely dreamy driver said? *The difficult thing is to stay hopeful . . . You're the boss, Simon.* If I could somehow have a go at combining those two, then I was in with a shout. I also took his advice and resolved just to have a break from the love thing. No angst for a while, no pain. I had no idea what form the love thing would take when I returned to the sexual front line, but that was a problem for another day.

I did something I had not done since the very early days of the business. I went in to work on a Sunday to catch up on the mountain of paperwork that had accumulated while my attentions had been elsewhere. I took in a CD player, had my music on in the background and had a productive time. The world felt like an easier place to live in. I only thought about sex a hundred and twenty times in the whole day.

Pages tore themselves off an old-fashioned calendar and fluttered towards the camera, then out of shot as whole weeks were spent in two activities, the first being a gradual realisation that I was capable of thinking about other people in more than a how-does-it-affect-me way. Viewing people as loves and even friends *might not be about me*. I was also reborn as the perfect boss, shocking my staff that I was capable of giving more than one hoot about them.

Cue Beethoven's Fifth: G-G-G, E flaaaat. What a revelation, so late in life and only possible because I wasn't considering myself sexually active at the moment. I even picked up leaflets for Voluntary Service Overseas: I looked into digging wells in unlikely places for grateful natives, then realised that digging was quite tough, so I pictured myself walking smiling through minefields raising world awareness instead. *Much better*. 'Lets fight the scourge of landmines together. Because I'm worth it.' Then I could toss my glossy hair and laugh an open-mouthed laugh until the freeze-frame. I had never known that putting other people first could feel so *glam*. Because it felt right.

But charidee begins at home, so I started small with every intention of building up to walking through a minefield. God knew I'd had enough experience of that lately.

The world is littered with abandoned heterosexuals just waiting to blow up in your face. Anyway, I concentrated on work, on being cynicism-free, and was so golly-heck nice to my employees, they got jittery and asked if I was softening them up for redundancy. I even spoke regularly and amicably to members of my immediate family, which was a major event for me and, I think, for them. My thirties would be perfect if I could keep this going: heaven is other people, contrary to rumour.

The second activity in this selfless orgy of celibacy was realising what a dumb-cluck I'd been over Ruth and Toril: moving far too fast with one and about ten years too slow with the other. Ruth left a few messages on my machine telling me to get in touch but, revealingly, never rang work when she knew I'd have to be there. I didn't know what to say to her and my mother always said not to pick at a healing wound. In those weeks I came to look at my 'I must marry Ruth and adopt her puking daughters' episode as temporary insanity, a rush of blood to the ring finger on my left hand. And in the midst of this, I tried not to think about Toril. It didn't work. *Toril Toril Toril Toril Toril Toril Toriltoriltoriltoriltoriltoriltoriltoriltoriltoriltoriltoriltoriltoriltorilto . . .*

Her name became surreal through repetition, turning into some kind of old-fashioned soft drink, Rilto, a blend of many fruits. Callum stopped talking about Toril to me although I had a hunch they were seeing each other a lot since her tearful evening round at Callum's about which Patrick had let slip. Maybe Callum and Toril would get together after all, just like I'd originally always wanted.

Perfect.

Problem solved. Everyone's happy, glorious sunsets all round and I could be a godfather yet again. Great stuff.

I discovered there was a limit to my selflessness. I did not want Callum and Toril becoming an item. No, no, *no*. In slow moments at work, or putting jam on my toast at breakfast or on my own in bed at three in the morning, I kept hearing what Toril had said to me: '*I've always wanted you. To be with you.*' And just as I was about to curse myself for my stupidity, for God's appalling sense of humour, for Toril's timidity, for mine, for losing such a friend, I would pull back and put the thought into the deepest recesses of my brain, where I keep the tough stuff, the hundred-pounds-an-hour psychoses. *Don't go there, Simon, be giving and gorgeous to people. It's so much easier.*

After about six weeks of this, feeling alright-ish about the world, I got in one evening from work to find a message from Ruth and another from Callum on my answer phone. Nothing from Toril. Ruth was first.

'Why aren't you talking to me? It's so unfair. I think we need to clear the air. Please don't ignore this.'

Soon, but not yet, Ruth, maybe soon. The next message beeped in from Cal.

'What are you doing on your birthday? Wednesday, isn't it? Come up to town and we'll go out. There's no point in being your usual thirty minutes early because I'll be delayed at work, so half-seven, mine, on Wednesday.'

He had this funny edge in his voice and I thought I knew why. It had sounded like the poorest, most blatant attempt at setting someone up for a surprise party I'd ever heard and because lots of us had turned thirty lately, I'd heard quite a few. I had a key to his flat, for heaven's sake: it hardly mattered if I was half an hour early. I played along and left a message for Callum, suggesting restaurants, should I book one and just meet him there? Sure enough, he got back to me sharpish.

Callum is one of the two people in the world who would never have to identify themselves when they call me. With these two people, I resume a conversation as opposed to start another one. Toril was the other one, but she didn't call me any more.

'No, come to *mine*,' Callum said. 'It'll be easier all round. I'll have to change and stuff.'

'Uh-*huh*.' *Right*, he always dressed for dinner. 'Or I could meet you somewhere at eight thirty say? Why don't I do that?'

'*No*, come to mine,' Callum insisted. 'I'll make margaritas or something before we go out.'

Now *that* was a desperate measure. Callum *ordered* margaritas, he certainly didn't make them. I let him off the hook; he was sounding strained.

'Hey, that sounds cool. Seven thirty, at yours, *on the dot*.'

I've rarely looked forward to a birthday more, even though thirty-one is a supporting feature of an anniversary compared to the glamorous star-studded première of the previous year. Making a meal out of it would be fun. I'd never had a surprise party before. How to react? Not camp, not too distant, touched, maybe a little tear to be wiped away? Or a full-blooded 'Yo! Party!' acceptance of the situation. I decided on the last route as a clear signal to the extended clan that the Comeback Kid was indeed 'back in the 'hood' and if he had changed it was just to become more of a *fun guy* to be with. Orientation *schmorientation*: who cared who he wanted to shag these days if he was in such *good form*?

I was still practising my delighted explosion of surprise and pleasure two days later as I walked along Callum's road, startling the shih-tzu out of an old lady walking her dog. I had my spontaneous reaction down pat by then, having been perfecting it all day at work: a milli-second of Utter Shock, followed by a Jaw Drop, with a touch of Eye Twinkle added in (to show that I could cope ironically and quickly with such surprises), followed by a Rumbly Laugh that slowly built to a one hundred per cent 'Let's *rock*' Group Hug.

From a distance, I could see the windows of Callum's flat. They were dark. *Nice touch.* I let myself in, spotted some second post waiting for Callum on the table in the hall (a *great* red herring to make me think he wasn't in yet), decided to take the post upstairs to make my reaction seem even more ad lib, and took the lift up. Even the timer-light in Callum and Patrick's hallway was off. How had they managed that? I tidged my hair, ran a finger over my teeth and opened Callum's front door. The flat was dark. I made lots of arrival sounds to stand everyone by and walked into the living room, Utter Shock then Jaw Drop into Eye Twinkle at the ready.

Nothing.

Empty. Tidier than usual, but empty. I went into Callum's kitchen where only washing-up greeted me.

Bollocks.

No surprise party then. Just dinner with Callum and he'd be here soon because he'd been delayed longer than he thought. Some birthday this was going to be. I could feel a bit of a pout coming on. I'd had a few cards but *nothing* from Ruth, *absolutely* nothing from Toril, even Patrick had forgotten and I'd *told* him. Thirty-first birthday, damp squib or what.

I heard a floorboard creak.

'Callum? I'm in the kitchen,' I called out, vowing to be as bouncy as possible tonight and not let on what I had been thinking. I wasn't disappointed, not me.

Some music started, lots of strings and wind instruments playing a slow melody full of huge, sweeping phrases. It was coming from the living room. Maybe this was a very enigmatic and classy lead-up to party-poppers and streamers. Unusually classy for something organised by Callum. Where had they all hidden if they were now all in the living room? The lush music swelled, its slow, insistent bass chords drawing me closer. I walked into the darkening room.

The music suddenly stopped. There was silence.

A woman, holding a remote control, was standing in the bay of the window, her short hair and slim frame silhouetted against the evening light.

'*Surprise*,' she said.

Chapter 25

'Lord, give me chastity and continency, but not yet'
St Augustine

She switched on a small table lamp.

'Toril,' I said. For a bizarre second, her short hair in the darkness had made her resemble Ruth. Thank God I hadn't said anything. It would not have been good to screw this up again.

There was a moment's silence as we stared warily at each other. She had come here for only one reason (she *might* have come to kill me, but I doubted it), so we both knew what we should be saying; we just couldn't find the way.

'Happy Birthday,' she said.

'It is now,' I replied a trifle over-earnestly. 'Happy, I mean. It *is* a surprise to see you.'

'I think you were expecting a bigger surprise,' Toril said evenly, stroking the underside of her chin back and forth with the tip of her forefinger. God, she was playing it so cool.

'No, this is a *big* surprise, rest assured,' I said and made to step forward to kiss her – just to kiss her hello, mind, but that forefinger stretched out and stopped me in my tracks.

'Stay where you are. You are going to talk to me this time,' she commanded softly.

Toril was in charge, or trying to be. Everything about the way she'd set this up said she wanted the control, not like the last time. She looked amazing: a crisp, midnight-blue suit, the cinched jacket tailored to fit, the skirt just above the knee, simple earrings glinting under her hair, which burned white in the lamplight. Her eyes were almost in shadow from the light hitting those cheekbones but I could still make out her grave, turquoise gaze.

My mind went speeding ahead as my face went into its patented expressionless mode. *Make-your-mind-up time, Simon, are you up for this?* Was I excited that Toril in particular wanted me or was I just plain thrilled that *anyone* still did? It was a tough call, made more difficult by the undeniable fact there was something profoundly erotic about going into a situation where I knew the other person found me attractive. Call me superficial. But what on earth was she bothering with *me* for? If I'd met a man as stunning as Toril was tonight, I would have assumed him to be way out of my league. But women, as I had always known but never seen, don't think like men. Thank God. And anyway, Toril was special to me, being a member of the inner circle from pre-history. That clinched it for me. True to form, I was falling for a friend.

Bother with me, Toril, I willed her silently, *bother with me*.

'How old are you today, Simon?'

'Thirty-one.'

'Thirty-one. *Gosh*.' The peculiarly English word sounded strange coming from her mouth. It wasn't instinctive, so it was loaded. With Toril, you always had to watch for every inflection, every possible level of double-meaning to get at what she really thought. That 'Gosh' meant 'Thirty-one and still a fuck-up' or 'Thirty-one: old enough to know better'. It didn't mean just 'Gosh'.

'Will you dance for me, Simon?'

Just like with Truman. How funny. I moved towards her but she stopped me again with an imperious wave of the remote control. I hadn't listened carefully after all.

'My English is good, I think. I didn't say "Dance *with* me". "Dance *for* me".' She pressed a button on the remote and more music played.

She'd really organised this: the trouble she'd taken was the true barometer for what she was feeling. It was different music to before, an aggressive floor-filler, all angry beat and no words. Toril turned it up and waved the control at me again, as if to say, 'I said, *dance*.'

The lady was in charge. Take it away, girl, tell me what to do. I had to be careful. It would not take much to bring this down around our ears. The unspoken assumption was that something was in the air between us, we had *potential*. Toril had to look like she was in charge, but she could tell me what to do only for as long as I wanted it.

Or so I told myself as I began to dance under her scrutiny, feeling like an arse of the first water. I've never been a spectacularly good dancer, it won't astound you to learn. I can't be accused of being a king of white rhythm, but I'm no Gene Kelly. I can jig about in a club, or disco-thèque, as I believe they are now called, but this was different: this was me on show. I cursed myself for leaving my seven veils at home (they were drip-drying in the bathroom), but the music was too fast for me to do any-thing sexy. Probably a good thing, as I wasn't sure the world was ready for me to do a lap-dance routine.

It felt foolish, it looked foolish and, by gosh, it was foolish, but Toril kept her poker-face. I beckoned to Toril to join me; she shook her head slowly. So I tried to just bop, to be as unselfconscious as I could. Which is to say, very selfconscious. Toril kept watching, turning the music up even more with a flick of the remote. I tried to dance closer to her but she waved me away. Humiliation was a bit of a turn-on, I had to admit.

Toril turned off the music. My ears rang; the only sound breaking the silence was me trying to catch my breath. Just paying gym fees isn't enough in itself, I guess.

'Why did you dance?' Toril demanded, walking over to me until her face was about eight inches away from mine. She was wearing Issey Miyake perfume as usual. The heels she had on made her a crucial little bit taller than me. She stood in front of me almost bolshily, her weight on one hip, daring me to say something wrong but still wanting answers.

'Why did you dance?' she repeated.

'You asked me to.'

'Why did you do it? you needn't have.'

'Because I wanted to do something you wanted me to do. I hurt you and I'm sorry and because . . .'

'Yes?'

I tried to put a hand to her face, to initiate a kiss. It was what she was here for, wasn't it? Toril immediately pulled away a step, her voice steady but only just, 'Don't presume to tell me what you think I want to hear.'

'OK. I don't think that th—'

'You have to deserve me. You have to *earn* me.'

And she slapped me round the face with all her strength. For the split second before she hit me, Toril's cool, collected exterior disappeared and her face was contorted with pain, shame and injured pride but mostly original flavour anger. My ears rang again. I just managed to stay upright. That was for the other day, I guessed. I had hurt her so much. How I had felt over Patrick was nothing to this. My cheek felt red-hot.

'I hope that makes us even,' I said, realised my error at once, and braced for another richly deserved sock in the chops. None came.

'It's a beginning.' She swallowed, inhaled deeply, trying to keep that icy mask intact. It was melting, it was melting, I was positive. 'Apologise for assuming I was a sure thing.'

'I Am Sorry.' I was big-time *apologising*, I was so *nineties*. I knew my assumption was correct though. So I wasn't really apologising, which was even more nineties. Call me arrogant, if you like. Call me arrogant even if you don't.

'OK, you're forgiven.' She smiled for the first time, quickly. 'Sit down, Simon, please.'

I sat down where Toril told me to: the lowest, deepest armchair in the room. She positioned a wooden table in front of me, unbuttoned her jacket, revealing a cream silk blouse that revealed in turn a faint image of her bra beneath. I found that exciting in a disappointingly schoolboy kind of way. She sat down, crossing her legs and resting her hands in her lap, all poise and dignity once more. She was significantly higher again than I was. I looked up at her from the depths of the chair. The angle was exactly the same as asking the ice-cream man for a 99 when I was ten. Maybe that was why I was feeling like a schoolboy. There was no way she was as calm as she looked.

'Is this how you interview people at work?' I asked.

'Of course not, it's far too intimidating,' Toril replied briskly.

'Oh, I see. Good psychology.'

Toril picked an imaginary piece of fluff from her left leg, dropped it on the floor with a just-a-pinch-of-salt gesture, sniffed and said, 'Tell me why you should have a second chance. Tell me why you are the man for me.'

What could I possibly say that would be the right answer? 'I don't want to be alone' was the only thought in my head, but it wasn't even an answer to the question. Call me psychic: I knew it would not be the ideal reply, it being only a pathetic shred of truth best not shared. I floundered.

'I'm such a bloody stupid hotch-potch of things, Toril, I don't—'

'Hotch-potch?' Toril interrupted, puzzled. 'What's that?'

'A mix-up, a mess, a confusion.'

'Oh. I thought it might be something I didn't know about you.' She whirled her hand around in the air for me to keep going.

I had a really stupid idea. It might just show her I was serious.

'I know how I can convince you,' I said, getting out of the armchair with no small difficulty. I crossed to the fire-place and kicked my shoes off.

'What are you doing?'

'What you did. I can make myself vulnerable. I can be a sensitive male. Then we'll be even for the other day,' I said, and pulled my shirt off over my head. Toril looked a little dismayed, I thought, as the grim reality of my body hove into view, so I decided to keep my T-shirt on. This was all quite a big deal for me, as I was not aroused at all at this point. I quite like my dick when it's erect, hell, I love him, and I fall proudly smack dab into the 'average' band of any 'How Big Is Your Boy's Best Buddy' table in *Marie Claire*, but when my little man is there for peeing, he's nowt to write home about. Plus I was nervous anyway. I stepped out of my trousers and handed them to Toril with a nod of thanks. She received them with the look of mystification Hillary must have when Bill remembers their wedding anniversary, as if to say, 'Why are you doing this? What do you want?'

I hesitated a second. Toril raised her eyebrows, but I trusted not her expectations, and I scooped off my boxers. I stood there droopy, with even one of my socks going to sleep, in a grubby BHS T-shirt, my knackers to the four winds. Toril was taking all this in her stride, if only because at that point there was not much to take. God bless her, she was looking me in the eyes.

'What were we saying?' I said defiantly, folding my arms across my chest in a wan attempt at a feeling of security.

'You were about to tell me why you are the right man for me,' Toril said, her voice going very high at the end of the sentence. A muscle in her chin spasmed and she had to press her lips together really hard. She moved away and stood behind the armchair I had just been sitting in. She had to turn away for a second, trying to stop her shoulders shaking.

'Take me seriously, Toril.' I felt that taking my clothes off had regained me the moral high ground. I could be quite stern, therefore.

'I can try,' she replied solemnly, perching on the back of the chair, able to look only at my knees.

'Don't look at my knees, I hate my knees,' I said peevishly. She pointedly looked at my cock. 'Look at me properly when I'm talking to you.'

'*Say* something then.'

'I don't know what to say.' My eloquence knew bounds. I opted to tell her why I maybe wasn't an ideal man. It proved much easier. 'If you need me to look *after you* then I can't do that all the time. I made that mistake before and I can't do it again. I need such a lot of looking after just to get through some days, it's frightening.'

'I know all that,' Toril said.

'Of course you do . . . and if you want a lifetime doing this dominatrix shit then that's not completely me either.'

'You quite like a little of it, by the looks of things.' She pointed at my widow's friend thickening out a bit in the warm draught from a radiator. It had enjoyed being out of the limelight and shrank again under inspection. She went on. 'But how did we manage to get taking about what *you* want, Chipolata Boy?'

'*Harsh*. The question was, why am I a good thing.'

'No,' Toril corrected. 'Why are you the man for me. Two separate things.'

'Oh, point taken. Well, firstly, this gets bigger . . .'

'*Even bigger?*' said Toril, wide-eyed with fear.

'Bless you for that . . . um . . . we've a *lot* in common, haven't we? We understand each other on a lot of things, it's why we've been friends for so long—'

We both forgot I was naked as Toril leaned over a little, pointing a warning finger at me, and whispered, 'You don't understand me *at all*. Got it?'

My balls retracted to somewhere level with my lungs in response. They travelled two feet in about half a second. I nodded my reply quickly. She had been quite frightening for a moment there.

'. . . Um . . .' I charmed. 'So, in conclusion, there seem

to be no reasons that spring immediately to mind why I am the man for you apart from that this gets bigger.'

'And you are not unique in that, are you?' Toril smiled at me, waiting, I thought, for me to say something. We had not yet addressed the big question, had we?

'Aren't you going to ask me about men?'

'I don't need your advice,' Toril said politely, still smiling.

'*No*, about me having been gay. You have to know that if you were you but male, I could still *happily* make love with you and be faithful to you. You must know that.'

She didn't even blink at this. It wasn't news.

'But that is the point, Simon,' Toril said. 'It's *about* fidelity.'

As she said this, I completely fell for Toril, utterly, *utterly*, head over heels. I *knew* that Toril and I could get to that last vital ten per cent of intimacy and honesty I never shared with Ruth. If I knew I could be faithful to Toril and still find men attractive and Toril knew all of that as well, then where was the big mind-bending, this-is-such-an-obstacle problem? Answer: it didn't exist. Life suddenly got simple and true.

Toril gave a Scandinavian equivalent of a Gallic shrug and said, 'It's got to be you as a person, me as a person. You haven't left, you danced, you've stripped for some strange reason. I know you well enough to know that you would not be here if you were not *serious*. Nobody is that cruel.'

'Not deliberately,' I said. I knew I had been cruel to her.

'Whatever. I don't care who you have slept with so long as we are right for each other. *And we are. I've* known that for years.' Toril took a deep breath, blinking back the shock of saying these innermost thoughts out loud. I knew just how she felt. I did understand her, better than she knew. She continued, 'Your being bisexual is a *given*. I can't have a lifetime with you wondering if you're sleeping with men. Or with other women for that matter. This will work only if we trust each other. If we are . . . *soulmates*.'

'*Love* each other.'

'Same thing – same word in Norwegian.'

'Really? That's incredible—'

'No, I lied,' Toril said. 'Or did I? You'll never know until you've learned Norwegian properly.'

Learned Norwegian? *Properly?* I was going to have to read the fine print of this contract. Not that I cared. I now knew with complete certainty that I wanted to spend the rest of my life with this wonderful person in dual-nationality heaven, as a best friend, soulmate, lover, husband. The full whack. Bring it on, let's get married today.

Toril stated, 'We will take this very *slowly*, so that you can *earn* me.'

'Good,' I said. Thank God one of us was still thinking clearly.

We looked at each other from across the room, little smiles playing around our mouths. Grown-ups looking forward to a life together. There was no cynicism. No irony. What a *relief*. Truth be told, there was a little irony bodding around since I had no clothes on, but even so, it was a good moment. Cut out and keep.

'Simon?' Toril spoke with a different tone now, all defences down. She looked younger or less sophisticated suddenly, the vulnerability she hid so well showing through. 'I hope you are thinking what I'm thinking.'

I love you.

'God, I hope so too,' I said.

Toril stuck out her hand, beckoning me over. I think she wanted me to go and sit with her but I shook her hand instead.

'I'm Simon, pleased to meet you.'

'Toril, likewise.'

'That's an unusual name,' I said cheesily. 'It's foreign, right?'

'Maybe we won't have to take things quite *that* slowly, Simon.'

Toril was still holding my trousers and she stooped to pick up my boxers. She looked at her watch and exclaimed in very badly acted surprise, '*Oh*, it's eight o'clock. The others are coming through from Patrick's at eight.'

'Who?'

'Everyone, the gang.' She moved away from me, nearer the hallway.

'You're joking? There *is* a surprise party?' *Fabulous.*

I was naked.

'Pass me my clothes.'

Toril shook her head, stepped into the hall, opened the front door and stood there, beaming at me, as twenty people I had known for years erupted into the room. People did surprise-party things, *cameras flashed*, party-popper streamers cascaded through the air, one landing in my pubes, garlanding my JT. In fact, what everybody screamed was '*Surpr*—' because they were more surprised than me. They all stared intently at my penis, which turned tail and tried to burrow into my body because it was scared.

Callum and Patrick started a chorus of 'Happy Birthday' and I stood there, pulling my T-shirt over myself. All my friends could barely see let alone sing for laughing. The top note, 'Happy *birth*-day, dear Si-mon', was *very* ragged.

'I think we're even *now*,' said Toril with a big smile and threw me my clothes.

My thirty-first birthday, the first day of the rest of my life.

Epilogue

It's two years on.

Have I got everything. Keys, where are my keys? There they are. Good. Wallet, chequebook (call me old-fashioned but I still like to use them). Bag by the door. What's the time? Quarter to seven. Jesus, I hate these early starts.

I'll just look in on her one last time, I've got five minutes. I'm staying up at Toril's at the moment and commuting to Brighton for work. It's a pain but I can't be away from her for any longer than I have to be.

We did it, everybody, we made it, Toril and me. We were best friends and then we were lovers. We did what we said we should: we took it slow, we got to know each other all over again. I earned her. She earned me too, dammit.

I creep up the stairs, avoiding the seventh one. It's got a creak like a pistol shot at this time of the morning. The house is a real tip from last night – Toril goes spare at the mess I create. Give me a Sunday paper and I can make a room look papier-mâchéd inside of an hour. I do my bit at tidying up. I haven't learned Norwegian yet.

I'm working my way along the landing slowly. I don't

want to wake her. She doesn't have to get up until half-past. Part-timer. I open the bedroom door slowly and look in. She's out cold. She managed to sleep last night but I couldn't. It was so muggy; having the window open was no good, it just made things worse. She's thrown off the covers. That's my girl that is, that one, the gorgeous one in the bed. In the morning light, you can really see the bump of her belly. There's still four months to go before D-Day. *I'm going to be a dad.*

My cup runneth over, folks. No wonder I can't sleep. I hardly dare mention how hunky-dory life is for fear some-one will creep up behind me and say, There's been a terrible misunderstanding, Mr Lyndon, would you step this way, we have a white jacket here with deceptively long sleeves . . . I'll dare mention it anyway: isn't it just wonderful how life keeps turning up surprises? *We're having a baby. We're having a baby.*

I've been faithful. Completely. Totally. No other women, no other men, though God knows, there have been moments after rows, or if business trips split us up for any length of time, when I have wanted to. A lot. I've wanted to with men mostly, a couple of times with women. BUT I HAVEN'T DONE ANYTHING. I don't hate myself enough to spoil what I have in this room. My Toril. Our baby. I want a girl, I think. A girl, then a boy.

I stand at the end of the bed and watch her sleeping. She stirs and turns over. She's telepathic or something, I swear it. She knows I'm watching her now. I love that bump so much. You should see me at antenatal classes. I'm a fucking *whizz*, honest to God. Eat my dust, all you other young dads.

Actually, there's one young dad at the class, quite good-looking. I tell you he *cruises* me during the breathing exercises. He gets off on it. We start the exercises, the women are lying back, I look up and sure enough there he is, checking me out and panting helpfully. I've been twinkled at by a lot of men in a lot of weird places but an *antenatal class*? There's a time and a place for everything. I told Truman about him and Truman nearly fell off his barstool. There's a lot of it about, as my grandad used to say. I see a guy in the street or in the queue at Tesco and we twinkle at each other and I know that something could happen if I followed it up. But I don't. I'm looking at beautiful men now like I look at great art: it's erotic, sensuous, a masterpiece, its dimensions are sometimes very impressive – but I don't necessarily want it in my bedroom. Sometimes I twinkle at women as well; it's not as if Toril and Ruth are the only women who have ever turned me on. Twinkling at people in the street is one of the great privileges of urban life. But I don't confuse it with reality.

I meet some people, people I know quite well but I haven't seen for a while and they assume Toril and I did nefarious things with a turkey-baster to get her pregnant. They seem genuinely shocked that the conception was an act of love rather than me in a cubicle with a racy edition of *Take A Break*, a plastic cup and Toril hovering outside with a syringe. At some point they sidle up and whisper, 'Simon, so exactly which side of the street are you peddling your wares these days?', or something similar. I always tell them I'm a gay straight or a straight gay. Some of them even nod, as if they completely understand. Bozos.

I think it's time those old words were consigned to the council skip of history. I'm so sick of them polarising and alienating instead of helping to liberate and unite like they used to. They paralysed me for a decade, pretty much. They're not useful any more: we don't need 'em, so dump 'em.

I DON'T BELIEVE IN 'GAY' AND 'STRAIGHT' ANY MORE. I'M SORRY.

A stately homo of England said we went wrong when we turned them into nouns: I am *a* straight, I am *a* gay. There's no room for manouevre, for choice, for development.

Fuck nouns, sexuality is about adjectives. Today I'm wearing a *blue* shirt, but I nearly wore a *white* one. Sexual orientation should be about as highly charged an issue as that.

Maybe it's too soon to say a lot of this. A few die-hards will huff and puff but now we have got rid of the twentieth century, we can jettison these stupid twentieth-century words as well. All the different 'teams' could meet in No Man's Land and play football. Or netball, whatever. We could have a great party, a Bring a New Word Party. I'll bring *individual*, *diversity*, *versatility*, *imagination*, *Mongolian Barbeque*.

Toril took me to one about a month ago – they're great. They are the perfect metaphor for post-millennial love and Genghis Khan will become an icon of enlightened sexuality, I predict it. At these places, you choose exactly the combinations of foods you want, you mix it all up, taking a bit of whatever pleases you and makes you happy. If you want to, you can follow the little recipe sheets they have pinned on the wall around the raw-ingredients counter, but the real fun of those places is that you make up your own recipe. You are the chef, the boss, so the dish you end up with is individually yours. Sometimes it tastes great, other times it's *awful*, but it's always yours.

The next time you choose something else and try a different combination. It's *allowed*. Nobody minds. It's not a U-turn or a failure. It's not a betrayal.

And you eventually end up with something that is perfect for you. Bespoke sexuality rather than off-the-peg ill-fitting definitions. It's all about what makes you happy. Ruth and I could never have worked because we somehow stuck to those twentieth-century antique notions. I fell in love with Ruth but then I consciously *became* straight and tried to *be* straight instead of just loving Ruth. I miss Ruth. I last saw her over a year ago and she seemed in great form. She was pleased for me that I'd got together with Toril. At least, I think she was. 'I knew she was trouble, that Danish one,' she said. We've written to each other a few times in the last year and we *are* friends but she's been busy with her final exams. When I last heard from her she had a guy on the books but I was pretty sure she was only using him for light relief and eye-candy during revision. Both the girls are fine; Sarah must be a teenager now. They're coming up to London in the autumn so perhaps we'll all get together. I think Ruth and me would still get on.

I think Toril's having a dream or something. She's got that REM thing going nineteen to the dozen. I move round and sit on the edge of the bed, not taking my eyes off her.

Is this me deluding myself that I'm not becoming just a dot in the crowd, that I haven't turned into a salaryman norming out with a girlfriend and a baby? In fact, just what I was planning to do with Ruth? The whole stereotype. But I've got to tell you, it doesn't feel like a bland 2.4 dreariness. It's the most extreme thing I've ever done. There's nothing 'normal' about it for me.

I could be rationalising myself into a dangerous situation where this will explode in my face somewhere down the line. If it does, it will be because I have screwed it up, thrown away this chance and taken an easy option. No one said the long haul, the lifetime commitment was easy. But it's not made any harder or easier by the fact I find both sexes attractive now. *That's irrelevant.* I've always wanted the long haul and I'm lucky enough that Toril wants the same thing. I've found out what makes me happy, I'm not hurting anyone, I love and am loved, I make my joy happen.

Toril opens a bleary eye at me. 'Still here?'

How could she think I wouldn't be? I crawl over the bed to her.

'*I'm still here. Of course I am.*'

'No, you melodramatic twat,' slurs Toril, 'I mean, you're late, it's nearly seven. You'll miss your train.' She mutters something foul in Norwegian and goes back to sleep for another thirty minutes.

I kiss her goodbye, run out of the house and race for the tube, my head full of tomorrows.

Friends Like These	Victoria Routledge	£5.99
Soft Touch	Maeve Haran	£5.99
An Ocean Apart	Robin Pilcher	£5.99
Unholy Trinity	Paul Adam	£5.99

WARNER BOOKS
Cash Sales Department, P.O. Box 11, Falmouth, Cornwall, TR10 9EN
Tel: +44 (0) 1326 372400, Fax: +44 (0) 1326 374888
Email: books@barni.avel.co.uk

POST AND PACKING:
Payments can be made as follows: cheque, postal order (payable to Warner Books) or by credit cards. Do not send cash or currency.

| All U.K. Orders | **FREE OF CHARGE** |
| E.E.C. & Overseas | 25% of order value |

Name (Block letters) ....

Address ....

....

Post/zip code: ....

☐ Please keep me in touch with future Warner publications

☐ I enclose my remittance £ ....

☐ I wish to pay by Visa/Access/Mastercard/Eurocard

Card Expiry Date

☐☐☐☐☐☐☐☐☐☐☐☐☐☐☐☐☐☐   ☐☐☐☐